Adam and Charles Black

London and its Environs

a practical guide to the metropolis and its vicinity, illustrated by maps, plans and

views

Adam and Charles Black

London and its Environs
a practical guide to the metropolis and its vicinity, illustrated by maps, plans and views

ISBN/EAN: 9783337293680

Printed in Europe, USA, Canada, Australia, Japan

Cover: Foto ©Andreas Hilbeck / pixelio.de

More available books at **www.hansebooks.com**

LONDON
AND ITS ENVIRONS

A PRACTICAL GUIDE

TO THE METROPOLIS AND ITS VICINITY

ILLUSTRATED BY MAPS, PLANS, AND VIEWS

TEMPLE BAR.

EDINBURGH: ADAM & CHARLES BLACK

1862

PREFACE.

"I hope to see London once ere I die," was the aspiration of Justice Shallow's Davy,* an aspiration that, in the year of grace 1862, is certainly being echoed by many a man and woman at home and abroad. To supply a guide book for visitors, which, in the plainest and fewest words, should point out and describe the salient features of this great metropolis, has been the aim of the writer. He has had in view simply to state what is most worthy of being seen, and what is the best way of seeing it, leaving those who would study manners and customs, or the works of art, constructive, architectural, or pictorial, or the minute details which compose the vast result called London, to consult the volumes specially devoted to these large subjects.

As any route proposed by the writer for visiting the various objects mentioned in the following pages would probably be as unreasonable to as many persons as it assisted, he will leave each reader to devise his own scheme for making the tour of London. It seems desirable, however, to mention here, for the benefit of total strangers, what would be generally considered the objects best worth seeing.

* Henry IV., Part II., Act v. 3.

In London.

The Thames from Chelsea to Greenwich.
The Tower.
The Mint.
The Custom House.
The London Docks.
Bank of England.
Royal Exchange.
Mansion House.
Guildhall.
The Monument.
The Post Office.
St. Paul's Cathedral.
The Temple Church.
Westminster Abbey.
The Houses of Parliament.
Westminster Hall.
National Gallery.
South Kensington Museum.
Soane Museum.
Lord Ellesmere's Picture Gallery.
Annual Picture Exhibitions.
British Museum.
Museum of College of Surgeons.
Museum of Practical Geology.
United Service Museum.
India Museum.
Lambeth Palace.
Buckingham Palace.
Whitehall Banqueting House.
St. James' Palace.
St. James' Park.
Hyde Park, and Kensington Gardens.
Pall Mall and its Club Houses.
Regent Street and its Shops.
Trafalgar Square.
Waterloo Bridge.
Westminster Bridge.
Thames Tunnel.
The Foundling Hospital.
Covent Garden, Market, and Floral Hall.
Metropolitan Cattle Market.
The Zoological Gardens, Regent's Park.
The Theatres.
Tussaud's Wax Work Exhibition.
The Soho or Pantheon Bazaar.

In the Environs.

Greenwich Hospital.
Woolwich Dockyard and Arsenal.
Crystal Palace.
Dulwich Picture Gallery.
Kew Gardens.
Richmond.
Hampton Court.
Windsor Castle.

Then there are various places where the English assemble in numbers and there see certain pageants, special musical performances, business proceedings, etc., which rank amongst the most interesting sights.   Such are—

The Opening or Closing of the Session of Parliament by the Sovereign in person.

A Debate in the House of Commons.

A Trial in a Court of Law.

The Lord Mayor's Show on the 9th of November.

The Anniversary Festival of the Sons of the Clergy at St. Paul's, about the middle of May.   Performance of Sacred Music.

The Anniversary Festival of the Charity Children under the dome of St. Paul's.   First Thursday in June.

An Oratorio at Exeter Hall or the Crystal Palace.

The Floral Fêtes at the Horticultural Gardens, South Kensington, and the Botanic Gardens, Regent's Park.

The Derby day at Epsom in June.

A Boat Race on the Thames.

The Game of Cricket at Lord's Ground, St. John's Wood Road, where this national pastime may be seen played in perfection.

We add a few hints to strangers who wish to make as much of their time as possible in London :— In the first place, study well the plan of the metropolis, so as to acquire a knowledge of the localities of the various objects and of the roads to them.   Then make up your mind as to what you consider best worth seeing.   Tastes differ ; whilst one person would wish to devote more time than is usually allotted to the inspection of scientific museums, another would prefer to study pictures, and another architectural works.   Before visiting any place, read our description of it, so that you may go prepared to look for the most interesting things.

If ever at a loss as to your road, make inquiry in a shop or of a policeman, not of casual passers by.

Kelly's Post Office Directory, which may be seen in every hotel and in many shops, contains the addresses of all persons in business as well as those of persons of independent means.   Webster's Red Book only gives the addresses of the latter when having houses of their own.   Kelly's Directory also contains a great mass of information as to persons in government offices, the conveyances and post offices throughout the kingdom, etc.   Bradshaw's Railway Guide, published monthly, gives every information about trains and fares.

J. Y. J.

CONTENTS.

CHAPTER I.

CHAPTER VII.

CHAPTER VIII.

CHAPTER IX.

CHAPTER X.

CHAPTER XI.

CHAPTER XII.

CHAPTER XIII.

CHAPTER XIV.

CHAPTER XV.

CHAPTER XVI.

CHAPTER XVII.

CHAPTER XVIII.

CHAPTER XIX.

LIST OF ILLUSTRATIONS,

CONSISTING OF

General Plan of London, Map of Environs,
Plans of Public Buildings, Museums and Gardens, Railway Stations, Views of Public Buildings, and Places of Resort.

Plan of London, engraved expressly for this work from the most recent and best authorities.

Map of the Environs, extending from Windsor to Greenwich, etc.

Index Map of London.

      Do.   Do.   Environs.

St Pauls Cathedral

CHAPTER THE FIRST.

INTRODUCTORY.

LONDON, the capital of the British Empire, lies upon both banks of the river Thames, some fifty miles from its mouth. Its latitude may be roughly taken at 51° 31′ N. It extends into four counties, but the largest portion is in Middlesex. It returns sixteen members to the Commons' House of Parliament, four elected by the City of London proper, two by the City of Westminster, and two each by the boroughs of Marylebone, Finsbury, Tower Hamlets, Southwark, and Lambeth, the two last of which are on the south side of the river.

POPULATION.—According to the census returns of 1861, the population of the metropolis amounted to 2,803,921 persons, living in 360,237 houses, spread over 78,029 acres of ground, or about 121 square miles.

The following table shews the population of the different districts of the metropolis :—

DISTRICTS OF LONDON.	Inhabited Houses.	Population in 1861.
MIDDLESEX.		
Kensington	25,854	186,463
Chelsea	8,318	63,423
St. George's, Hanover Square .	10,421	87,747
Westminster	6,880	67,676
St. Martin-in-the-Fields . .	2,283	22,636
St. James, Westminster . .	3,331	35,324
Marylebone	16,370	161,609
Hampstead	2,653	19,104
Pancras	21,928	198,882
Islington	20,676	155,291
Hackney	13,412	83,295
St. Giles	4,662	53,981
Strand	3,815	42,956
Holborn	4,125	44,861
Clerkenwell	7,686	65,632
St. Luke	6,368	56,997
East London	4,495	40,673
West London	2,616	27,144
London City	6,367	45,550
Shoreditch	17,231	129,339
Bethnal Green	14,812	104,905
Whitechapel	8,667	78,963
St. George-in-the-East . .	6,187	48,878
Stepney	7,465	56,567
Mile-end Old Town . . .	10,768	73,064
Poplar	11,163	79,182
SURREY.		
St. Saviour, Southwark . .	4,495	36,026
St. Olave, Southwark . .	2,214	19,053
Bermondsey . . .	8,211	58,355
St. George, Southwark . .	7,234	55,509
Newington	12,815	82,157
Lambeth	23,001	162,008
Wandsworth	11,136	70,381
Camberwell	12,122	71,489
Rotherhithe	3,529	24,500
KENT.		
Greenwich	17,826	127,662
Lewisham	9,701	67,752

With the local government of this vast body, 7000 persons are connected. During the ten years between 1851 and 1861, the population has annually increased at the rate of 1·722 per cent. From 1600 to 1700 children are born every week, and from 1000 to 1100 persons die during that time. The annual rate of mortality is about 2·2 per cent, that is, out of every 45 persons one dies in the course of the year—a rate lower than that of any other large city in Europe, and to be ascribed to our superior sanitary regulations, in which, however, there is still much room for improvement. It has been ascertained that one in six of those who leave the world dies in one of the public institutions, a poor-house, hospital, asylum, or prison. The relief of the poor during a severe winter costs about £40,000 a-week.

HISTORICAL SUMMARY.

LONDON was a British settlement before the Romans came to the island, and its etymology is thought to be LLYN DYN, the city of the lake, transformed by the Roman conquerors into LONDINIUM. Cæsar, not foreseeing its future importance, has not mentioned it, though he arrived at the valley of the Thames, which he crossed at Oatlands. The first mention of London in a Roman writer occurs in Tacitus, who speaks of it as a place of great resort by merchants, although it had not attained the dignity of a *colonia*, which it did at a later date under the name of *Augusta*. Suetonius, who commanded the foreign troops, was obliged to abandon the place when Boadicea raised the standard of revolt (A.D. 62). Colchester and Verulam were both made Roman stations before Londinium, which it is believed was not occupied until 105 years after Cæsar's invasion, and not walled round until A.D. 306. The ancient wall commenced near the spot where the Tower now stands, and was carried by the Minories to Cripplegate, Newgate, and Ludgate, inclosing an area of rather more than 3 miles in circumference. On the wall, which was 22 feet in height, there stood 15 towers 40 feet high. It is conjectured that the prætorium and its adjuncts were on the site of the Poultry and Cornhill, and LONDON STONE, now in Cannon Street, is supposed to have been the central stone or *milliarium* from which distances were measured. A hundred years ago some towers of the Roman wall still existed, but now it has all disappeared with the exception of two or three fragments. The curious may still, however, gaze on a little of the work of those stern conquerors in Cripplegate Churchyard and at Barber-Surgeons' Hall, which was partly formed out of a bastion by Inigo Jones. The name of "London

Wall," a city street, perpetuates the site of another portion. Roman remains have frequently been discovered in laying the foundation of modern houses, and in the British Museum, the City of London Museum, Guildhall, the museum of the Society of Antiquaries, Somerset House, and in some private museums, they may still be seen. A hypocaust well and other Roman structures were come upon when the Coal Exchange in Lower Thames Street was built. The depth at which these and other remains have been found from the surface, from 11 to 20 feet, shews on what a mass of ruin and rubbish modern London stands.

Of Anglo-Saxon London we know very little. It was made the capital of the so-called kingdom of Essex in the sixth century, and in the next it became a bishop's see.

In 851 those restless robbers, the Danes, while on a second visit to the island, sailed up the Thames with 300 vessels, and burned London, as well as ravaged Canterbury. Although rebuilt by Alfred in 886, it was totally destroyed by an accidental fire seven years later. The Danes continued their attacks, until at last Canute established himself as king of England and made London his residence, it having been again rebuilt. Some names still exist to keep us in mind of the dominion of those fierce northmen. They had a church and burial-place where St. Clement-Danes now stands ; St. Olaf was one of their saints, and St. Olave's church in Southwark occupies the spot where the original edifice stood (the name Tooley Street is but a corruption of that of the saint) ; there are two other churches dedicated to the same saint in the city ; again, St. Magnus was another of their saints, and his name still survives in connection with a church near London Bridge.

The time, however, came when the Danish power was put an end to by the Anglo-Saxons, whom in turn William the Conqueror subdued. Of him the great white Tower still speaks, and there are a few crypts of his time still existing, but buried under modern edifices.

It has been pointed out that three of the great landmarks of the present day stand on the sites where the original edifices were placed many hundred years since. St. Paul's minster, founded by the Cantian Ethelbert in 610 ; Westminster Abbey, commenced by Sebert on Thorny Island in 616 ; and the White Tower of the first William—the last in great part the very building of the Conqueror. These all testify that modern London has not shifted its position like some cities that could be named ; it has only grown larger.

There are traces of ancient Roman Catholic establishments left in the names of several places, although the buildings themselves have long since disappeared, viz., Black-Friars, White-Friars, Crutched-Friars, Austin-Friars, the Minories, the Chartreuse (now the Charter-House), with various priories and nunneries. With the exception of Westminster Abbey, the Temple Church, and the church of St. Saviour (or Mary Overy), Southwark, there is nothing of ancient ecclesiastical architecture on a large scale now to be seen ; still the chapel in the White Tower, the church of St. Bartholomew-the-great, Smithfield, and the crypt under St. Stephen's Chapel, Westminster, are well worth the notice of the man of taste. (See the chapter on churches.) *Westminster Hall, Lambeth Palace,* and *Crosly Hall,* Bishopsgate Street, lately restored, are examples of ancient royal, baronial, or domestic architecture.

Looking at an old map of London, prepared soon after Elizabeth began her reign, and at a time when there were about 145,000 inhabitants, we perceive the tower standing apart from the city on the east, Finsbury and Spitalfields on the north, with fields and trees ; on the west beyond Temple Bar, there are various scattered hamlets, including St. Giles' and Charing, whilst Westminster is far away as a separate city. The Strand, the road connecting London and Westminster, has between it and the river, the houses and gardens of bishops and noblemen.

Previous to the census of 1801, we are left to conjecture what the population of London was at any given period. By Graunt it was estimated in 1661 to be 384,000, which number would be probably brought up to 460,000, by adding the population of Westminster, Lambeth, Stepney, and other neighbouring places. Gregory King, a careful writer, thought that the population of the city and the out parishes amounted in 1696 to 527,560. Between 1740 and 1750 the population is known to have decreased, and at no time during the first seventy or eighty years of the last century did it increase rapidly. Dr. Price calculated that in 1777 it was 543,420, but there is reason for supposing that this estimate was too little by 100,000.

It is amusing to find Sir William Petty, a clever man in his day, calculating in 1683 that the metropolis could not possibly increase any more after the year 1800, at which time it would contain 5,359,000 persons (in point of fact, there were about 830,000 people in it) ; but that if we were to suppose for a moment that the population would still extend after that date, it would amount in 1840 to 10,718,880 persons.

LOCAL DIVISIONS.

NORTH OF THE RIVER.

The nucleus of London is the City, bounded on the north and east by the borough of Finsbury, on the west by the city of Westminster, to which Marylebone adjoins on the north.

In the west there are the districts of Pimlico, Brompton, Chelsea, Kensington, Bayswater, and Notting Hill.

In the north-west, St. John's Wood, Portland Town, St. Pancras, Somer's Town, Camden Town, Kentish Town, Islington, Holloway, and Highbury, with Hampstead and Highgate on the hill behind.

In the north-east, Kingsland, Stoke Newington, Dalston, Hackney, and Clapton.

In the east, Bethnal Green, Whitechapel, Stepney, Limehouse, Poplar, Oldford, Boro', and Bromley.

SOUTH OF THE RIVER.

In the east Southwark, known as " The Boro'," including Bermondsey and Rotherhithe ; population, 193,942.

In the west, Lambeth, with the adjacent districts of Kensington, Walworth, Newington, Wandsworth, and Camberwell ; population, 386,027.

Several of these divisions must have a few words of further description. THE CITY will have a chapter to itself.

WESTMINSTER derives its name from the abbey minster, and was made a city in the reign of Henry VIII. In Domesday book, it is styled a village with fifty holders of land, and " pannage for a hundred hogs." In 1174, the royal palace stood about two miles westward from the City of London, with gardens and orchards between. In 1560, an old plan shews that a double line of buildings connected London and Westminster, whilst a town had grown up around the hall and abbey. The present city with the adjacent districts, called the Liberties of Westminster, has a population of 213,383 persons. It is governed by a high steward and a high bailiff.

MARYLEBONE, now one of the most populous parishes in London, was at the beginning of the last century a small place, separated from London by a mile of open ground. A brook or bourne ran by the village, and the church being dedicated to St. Mary, it came to be called St. Mary-on-the-bourne, which has been corrupted into its present designation. The parish has a circumference of eight miles and a quarter, an area of 1700 acres, and a population of 161,609 persons. Two-thirds of its area were pasture fields until 1760.

PIMLICO, a name of uncertain origin, applied to the district between Hyde Park and the Thames. It is now covered with streets and houses, but so late as 1763, it is said that Buckingham House had an uninterrupted view south and west to the river, there being only a brewery and some scattered cottages between it and the Thames. It was a district of public gardens, much frequented on holidays, all of which have given way to buildings. Here are Belgrave, Lowndes, Eaton, Chester, Eccleston, and Warwick Squares, with many streets, and the new Victoria railway station.

CHELSEA, a large parish with 63,423 inhabitants, extending by the river side westward from Pimlico. The place is mentioned in Domesday book. Henry VIII. gave the manor to Katherine Parr on her marriage with him. It afterwards came into the possession of Sir Hans Sloane, from whom it went to an ancestor of the present Earl Cadogan. This will explain the names of some of the streets, etc. At the end of the seventeenth century, there was established a china manufactory, which existed for some time, the work having obtained celebrity, but it has now disappeared. Chelsea can boast of having been selected as a residence by many eminent persons, within the last two hundred years. It is connected by two bridges with the opposite bank of the river. Here are the Hospital for old soldiers, the Botanical Garden of the Apothecaries, and Cremorne Gardens, so well-known to pleasure-seekers.

KENSINGTON, including Brompton, lies north and north-west of Chelsea. In the interval between the last two censuses, it has made an immense stride in population. In 1861 it had 186,463 inhabitants, an increase of 66,459 since 1851. And yet this large town population is without a representative in Parliament. The palace is not in Kensington (lucus a non lucendo), but in the parish of St. Margaret's, Westminster. At one end of this district are the International Exhibition Buildings, the Royal Horticultural Society's Gardens, and the South Kensington Museum, and at the other end Holland House.

PANCRAS is the largest parish in Middlesex, having a circumference of 18 miles, and a population of 198,882 persons, according to the last census. It was anciently a lonely hamlet, one mile distant from Holborn Bars, and is still called Pancras-in-the-fields. Less than a hundred years ago, the population did not amount to 600. It is mentioned in Domesday book. Of its old church (recently enlarged), it has been said that it does not yield in antiquity to St. Paul's. Norden, quaintly speaks of it in 1592, as being "all alone, utterly forsaken, old, and wether-beten, yet about this structure have bin manie buildings, now decaied, leaving poore Pancras without companie or comfort ; yet it is visited by theeves who assemble there not to praye, but to wait for praye ; and manie fall into their handes clothed that are glad when they are escaped naked. Walke not there late." Camden Town, Agar Town, Somers' Town (so called from its being the freehold estate of Lord Somers), and Kentish Town, are all in Pancras. The termini of the London and North Western Railway (Euston Square), and the Great Northern Railway (Kings Cross), are in Pancras. It has a cemetery of 87 acres in the Finchley Road.

FINSBURY takes its name from the fenny ground that existed here. The manor is held by the Corporation of London under a lease originally granted so far back as 1315. This has been renewed from time to time, and the present lease will expire in 1867. It is said that the Mayor derives his title of lord from being lord of this manor. The tract once called Moorfields is in this district, the whole of which is now covered with buildings.

ISLINGTON, once a village two miles away from London, is now connected with it by a dense mass of houses. Its population of 155,291 persons has increased to the extent of 59,962 since 1851. Under the name of Iseldon it is mentioned in Domesday book, where it was stated to have 1000 acres of arable land. It includes Holloway, Highbury, and part of Kingsland.

The new Metropolitan Cattle Market and the Model Prison are in this district.

SOUTHWARK was an early settlement of the Romans, as the remains that have been from time to time discovered testify. The name, which appears to signify the southern fortification, has been spelled in no fewer than ninety-seven ways in old writings. Edward III. sold the place to the citizens of London, making certain reservations, but Edward VI. granted the full control of it to them. The affairs of the Borough, as it is now styled, are managed by a high bailiff and steward, appointed by the Corporations of London. It was constituted a ward of the city, under the name of Bridge-Without, and sends an alderman to the court. It has returned Members to Parliament ever since Edward the First's reign. Extensive manufactures are carried on here ; at Bermondsey the tanners and rope-makers abound ; at Rotherhithe, timber-merchants, sawyers, and boat-builders.

LAMBETH adjoins Southwark on the west. It was originally a Surrey village, with a name of uncertain derivation, but it has become a thickly populated district, covering much ground. Here are Lambeth Palace, Bethlehem Hospital, St. George's Roman Catholic Cathedral, the County Prison, and the Queen's prison. It is the seat of much manufacturing industry, including Price's Patent Candle Works, Pellatt's Glass Works, Beaufoy's Vinegar Works, Maudslay and Field's Engineering Works, and Clowes' Printing Office and Foundry, each of which is the largest of its class in the metropolis.

Let us now glance for a moment at this mighty world of London, with reference to the districts where certain classes of its inhabitants congregate.

The City is the great focus of commercial business, densely crowded with banks, counting-houses, and shops.

In Paternoster Row the publishers and booksellers meet in force ; in Spitalfields the silk-weavers ; in Clerkenwell the watch-makers ; whilst between Leadenhall Street and Houndsditch the Jews predominate.

The Temple, Chancery Lane, Lincoln's Inn, and Gray's Inn, are filled with the chambers of the lawyers.

Regent Street, Bond Street, Piccadilly, and part of Oxford Street, are stocked with the best and most expensive shops, where persons having a supply of the one thing needful may procure every luxury under the sun.

The nobility, and people of the first fashion, chiefly reside—1st, In the district included by Regent Street, and Hyde Park, Oxford Street, and Piccadilly, within which are Grosvenor and Berkeley Squares, Park Lane, and Mayfair, the last designation being applied to the streets between Park Lane and Berkeley Square, which cover some fields where a fair was held for many years under grant from James II., not finally discontinued until late in the reign of George III. 2d, The district (often styled Belgravia), lying between Grosvenor Place and Sloane Street, and including Belgrave Square. 3d, St. James Square, and the east side of the Green Park.

A district of very high respectability, staid, grave, and decorous, like the streets, is that which lies westward of Portland Place, between Oxford Street and Marylebone Road. (Portman and Cavendish Squares, included in this district, must be considered as an offshoot of that on the south side of Oxford Street, for several of the nobility reside in them.)

The new, handsome, and healthy district westward of the Edgware Road, and north of Hyde Park, is also highly respectable. It includes Westbourne Terrace, and many squares, inhabited by merchants, bankers, and lawyers.*

The terraces around the Regent's Park and the districts of St. John's Wood and Portland Town, west of that park, are tenanted by the same classes.

Lambeth, Southwark, and the eastern parts of London, are chiefly peopled by handicraftsmen and small shopkeepers. In these districts the manufactories of the metropolis are for the most part situate.

LOCAL MANAGEMENT.

By an Act of Parliament passed in 1855 (18th and 19th Victoria, chapter 120), a Board of forty-six persons, to be elected by

---

* This district has been styled by Thackeray, " The elegant, the prosperous, the polite Tyburnia, the most respectable district in the habitable globe ! Over that road which the hangman used to travel constantly, and the Oxford stage twice a week, go ten thousand carriages every day. Over yonder road by which Dick Turpin fled to Windsor, and Squire Western journeyed into town, what a rush of · civilisation and order flows now ! What armies of gentlemen with umbrellas march to banks and chambers, and counting houses ! What regiments of nursery maids and pretty infantry ; what peaceful processions of policemen ; what light broughams and what gay carriages ; what swarms of busy apprentices and artificers, riding on omnibus roofs, pass daily and hourly !"

the ratepayers, was constituted for the purpose of superseding a great number of local boards in the management of the streets, drains, and buildings of the metropolis. This board was authorized to construct a system of main intercepting drainage, to improve the streets and make new ones, to provide parks and places of recreation, to attend to the naming of the streets, and the numbering of the houses therein; and in the building of new houses to enforce compliance with the existing regulations. This board is known as the Metropolitan Board of Works, and it has lately built for its own use a handsome set of offices on the site of Berkeley House, Spring Gardens, at the cost of £15,000. A ground rent of £500 a-year is paid to the Crown.

In addition to the main drainage works, which will be described hereafter, the board has been forming new streets and widening others. The cost of improvements of this nature in London is extremely great, owing in great part to the enormous value of the land. The sums that have been paid for small patches of only a few square yards sound quite fabulous, and it becomes more valuable every day. Land has been sold in the city at the rate of £900,000 an acre! Such being the case, it is easy to conceive that the progress of improvements is slow in consequence of the very large sums required to carry them out. Improvements involving the outlay of sixteen and a half millions sterling have been pressed on the board, and of these they admit that a large proportion are urgently demanded for the accommodation of the traffic. Another measure involving a large expenditure has been prominently brought forward of late, viz., the embankment of the Thames; but as yet no scheme has been adopted, though it seems likely that the requirements of the public will be best provided for by establishing a spacious thoroughfare between Westminster Bridge, and Blackfriars' Bridge, by means of a simple embankment and roadway; and that the new thoroughfare thus created will be continued eastward from Blackfriars' Bridge, by a new street from the west end of Earl Street, across Cannon Street to the Mansion House. The line of embankment at Westminster would coincide with the terrace of the New Houses of Parliament, and the general level would be four feet above Trinity high-water mark. As far as the Temple Gardens it is proposed to make the road 100 feet in width, and solid throughout. From this point eastward, it would be reduced to the width of 70 feet, and carried on a viaduct supported on piers of masonry, leaving spaces between the piers available for barges to lie in. The cost of this scheme has been estimated at £1,500,000. If carried out, it is probable that an embankment would likewise be formed on the Surrey side of the river.

SUPPLY OF FOOD.

The quantity of food consumed by the people of London must be something enormous, but no exact information can be obtained on this head. Nevertheless, the results of some calculations may be interesting.

Of fresh fish, excluding shell-fish, upwards of 400 millions of pounds weight come to market in the course of a year. As to shell-fish proper, oysters may be taken as an example; about 500 millions of these are swallowed by the Londoners. Of lobsters, something like 1,200,000, and of crabs, about 600,000 are annually consumed. To supply the metropolis with flesh meat during the year, it is calculated that 400,000 oxen, 1,900,000 sheep, 130,000 calves, and 250,000 pigs, are sent hither, as well as about 40,000 tons of country killed meat. As to poultry, game, and wild birds, it is believed that 2,000,000 of domestic fowls, 350,000 ducks, 105,000 turkeys, the same number of geese, and 1,300,000 rabbits are devoured; and probably the total number of these things, from grouse, partridges, and pheasants, down to pigeons and larks, is not far short of six millions, weighing several thousand tons. Upwards of 20,000 cows are kept in and near London to supply part of the milk and cream required, the rest, amounting to perhaps four millions of quarts, coming from the country by railway. Around London there are probably not less than 12,500 acres under cultivation for the supply of vegetables, and 5000 acres stocked with fruit trees. Strawberry plants alone cover more than 200 acres. Vast quantities of vegetables and fruit are poured into the London markets both from the country and from abroad. Sixty millions of oranges and fifteen millions of lemons are imported to supply the wants of London alone. It is supposed that nearly 1,700,000 quarters of wheat are turned into flour for the bread and pastry of the metropolis; whilst nearly 800,000 quarters of malt are employed by the sixteen or seventeen great brewers of London in making 2,800,000 barrels of beer, to say nothing of the beer made by the thousands of smaller brewers, and that sent to the metropolis from Burton and other places.

An account of the methods by which all this vast quantity of comestibles is collected and distributed would fill a volume. All quarters of the world send their contributions, and there are labourers in every zone tilling the land, or searching the sea.

SUPPLY OF WATER.

It is supposed that the daily supply of water to the metropolis cannot be far short of a hundred millions of gallons, or about forty gallons per head per diem, the charge for which does not exceed five per cent on the rental of the houses supplied. This quantity is furnished by nine water companies, viz., 1, The New River Company ; 2, The East London Company ; 3, The Southwark and Vauxhall Company ; 4, The Lambeth Company ; 5, The West Middlesex Company ; 6, The Chelsea Company ; 7, The Grand Junction ; 8, The Kent Company ; and 9, The Woolwich and Plumstead Company. The capital embarked in these undertakings is about seven and a half millions sterling. In addition to the water supplied by these companies water is obtained in considerable quantities from wells sunk through the London clay. The great brewers obtain all their water from these so-called Artesian wells, several of which penetrate to a great depth. The Messrs. Barclay's well is 367 feet deep. The well at the Royal Mint, Tower Hill, is 400 feet deep, and one of the two wells that supply the Trafalgar Square fountains has the same depth. It is said that the water in these wells, which in no instance rises to the surface, is gradually sinking at the rate of a foot a year. Complaints having been made as to the quality of the water supplied by the London Companies, it has been proposed to obtain a supply abundantly sufficient for the requirements of the entire metropolis from some of the Welsh lakes. The cost of the scheme is estimated at from six to seven millions sterling. The quality of the London water has been much improved of late, but the organic impurities per hundred gallons still amount to from 167 to 200 grains.

Of the undertakings above mentioned, we will single out the New River as more deserving of notice for its history and extent than the others. The stream called the New River is well known to those who traverse the country to the north of London from its winding well-marked course. It commences between Hertford and Ware, at a distance of 21 miles from the Metropolis. It flows at the rate of two miles an hour, having a width of 18 feet, and a depth of 4, with a fall of 3 inches in the mile, sending a supply of water into London at the rate of 18 millions of gallons per day. The total length of its course is $38\frac{3}{4}$ miles, and the whole of it is open until it reaches Stoke Newington, where it is conducted by a subterranean channel of 300 yards under part of Islington. At Stoke Newington there are two reservoirs covering 38 acres. Here the water remains for a few days that the earthy particles in it may subside. The reservoir in Clerkenwell known as River Head has an extent of about 5 acres, and is placed at a height of 85 feet above the mid-tide level of the Thames. Iron pipes conduct the water thence to the houses of the lower district; that for the high services being derived from another reservoir close by in Claremont Square, 30 feet higher, into which the water is forced by steam pumps. At Highgate are two more reservoirs.

This useful undertaking was planned in the reign of James I. by Hugh Myddelton, "citizen and goldsmith," a native of Denbigh. He began the works in April 1608, having divided the undertaking into 36 shares. When stopped for want of funds, he applied for aid to the king, who consented to defray half the expense on being made a partner. In September 1613 the affair was brought to a successful termination, and on the 29th of that month the water was made to flow into the Clerkenwell basin amidst much ceremony and rejoicing. The total cost at that time had been about £500,000. No dividend was paid until 20 years had elapsed. More capital being required, Charles I., instead of advancing it, preferred to transfer the whole of his father's interest to Sir Hugh Myddelton (he had been made a baronet in 1622), receiving instead a fixed rent of £500 a year, which rent is still paid annually by the company into the Exchequer. That interest was then divided into 36 shares, which are known as "king's shares," whilst the others are called "adventurers' shares." From first to last about a million and a half sterling have been laid out on the New River works. A single share has been sold for £14,000, and the annual net profit is put down at from £50,000 to £60,000. Sir Hugh's family, we are sorry to say, came to poverty, and the baronetcy is extinct.

PUBLIC DRINKING FOUNTAINS.

Previous to the month of April 1859 there was not a drinking fountain for the use of the public in the Metropolis. In that month the first fountain of the kind was erected in the wall of St. Sepulchre's churchyard, City, and its utility to the poor being apparent, the movement was promoted by the Metropolitan Free Drinking Fountain Association, and has spread so rapidly that between 80 and 90 have been put up, several of them, like the first, at the expense of generous individuals. At that which stands in front of the Royal Exchange, upwards of 6000 callers have been counted in one day. It is to be regretted that so little taste has been displayed in the planning of these structures.

As to fountains of a purely ornamental character, London has little to boast of. It is generally agreed that those in Trafalgar Square are not worthy of their situation.

DRAINAGE.

The effectual drainage of any large city, so essential to the good health of the inhabitants, must always be attended with great expense, and not unfrequently with great difficulty. The extraordinarily rapid growth of the British metropolis has made the work of drainage one of continually increasing embarrassment and anxiety. Hitherto the plan adopted has been to cast the sewerage into the nearest part of the Thames, and the consequences have been most injurious to the river, and to those who dwell upon its banks. In hot and dry summers its condition has been so bad as to breed fevers amongst the neighbouring population ; and various temporary expedients have been had recourse to, at great cost, partially to remedy so lamentable a state of things. It has been calculated that about seven millions of cubic feet of sewerage were discharged daily into the river from the north bank, and about two millions and a half from the south side. This quantity is equal to a depth of 6 feet over an area of 36 acres ! Besides, the system of drainage thus attempted to be carried out was inadequate to the purpose, in consequence of the low level of the ground on the south bank, and the tidal rise of the river, which latter operated to stop for several hours a day the outflow of the sewerage. The subject of an improved system becoming at last of the first importance, was discussed at great length, and many schemes were put forward, as well as many conflicting opinions. When the Metropolitan Board of Works was constituted by Act of Parliament (18th and 19th Victoria, chapter 120), the main drainage of London was the first and chief object to engage their attention. After much consideration, and aided by another Act passed in 1858, the board decided upon adopting a scheme which was the result of the consultations of several engineers, the chief credit being, however, due to Mr. Bazalgette. This scheme is being rapidly carried into effect, and it is supposed that the works will be completed in the course of 1863-4. The cost is calculated at three millions sterling, which is to be raised by a rate of three pence in the pound on the annual value of the property, such rate to be leviable for forty years.

The scheme consists in constructing a system of intercepting sewers on both sides of the Thames, making a total length of 72 miles. On the north side of the river there are three independent arterial lines of sewers at different levels, which converge at the river Lea, and proceed thence side by side in one large embankment to Barking Creek, a part of the river below London. In this way the sewerage will be kept out of the Thames until a point 14 miles below London Bridge is reached. It will then be thrown into the river at high water, so that the ebb tide may remove it. On the south side of the river the sewerage will be similarly dealt with. The point of discharge of the south London sewage will be midway between Woolwich and Erith, a single tunnel passing under the town of Woolwich, and uniting with the high and low level sewers near Deptford Creek. The sewers have the form of tunnels made of bricks, and are for the most part concealed under ground, but those on the north of the Thames emerge from high ground on approaching the sea. Over that stream they are carried by an iron aqueduct, and across the West Ham and Barking marshes by an embankment. Each tunnel is made large, to carry off the greatest flow of sewage which a greatly increased population will occasion, as well as a fall of rain equal to a quarter of an inch in 24 hours on the area drained. Near the sea the tunnels are $9\frac{1}{2}$ feet in height internally, and 12 feet wide. There are to be reservoirs at the outlets, and at certain points pumping engines and machinery for lifting the sewage of the low lying districts. The works at the Deptford pumping station, where the sewage will be lifted out of the two arterial sewers into the single outfall sewer, will be on an extensive scale. The pumping engines will have a power of 500 horses.

Scientific persons who are desirous of inspecting these gigantic works, should apply for permission to the chief clerk of the Board of Works, at the offices in Spring Gardens, Charing Cross.

FIRES.

In a city like London the losses annually occasioned by fire must be expected to be enormous. Public building after public building falls a prey to the flames. Within the last thirty years the Houses of Parliament, the Royal Exchange, and the Tower, have been destroyed. The history of the theatres is a history of fires. To guard against such losses every parish possesses two fire-engines ; and nearly every public establishment of consequence is similarly provided. The insurances offices, of course, take care to have their own engines in readiness in case of emergencies. Besides these there is the fire brigade, which costs about £25,000 a year, and has rather more than a hundred men distributed amongst nineteen stations, which are supplied with nearly 40 fire-engines, a very insufficient establishment, as is generally admitted, notwithstanding the energy and skill of the men. It is the universal custom to insure houses and combustible property in some of the numerous insurance offices which do business in London, some of which have made very large gains. Some of these offices (such as the Commercial Union) combine the business of life and marine assurance with fire assurance, but most of them attend exclusively to the last. No night passes without there being at least one alarm. The engines rattle by at full speed, and a crowd flocks to the place to see a sight which, if the fire is a large one, is very striking. A very few hours suffice to destroy property of great value. Some years are known by connoisseurs of wine as " the comet years," from the fact of a good vintage having coincided with the appearance of a great tailed star ; the summer of 1861 will be known for some time as " the fire summer," from the number and magnitude of the fires that took place in London. One of them, which occurred during the month of June, ravaged a large piece of ground on which stood piles of warehouses, in the neighbourhood of London, and caused damage to the amount of a million and a half sterling. Mr. Braidwood, the able superintendent of the fire brigade, lost his life in assisting to extinguish this conflagration, which continued alight for some weeks. The total number of fires in London during 1861 was 1183, of which 53 ended in total destruction.

POLICE.

The police force of the Metropolis (exclusive of the city) consists of about 5800 men, who wear blue cloth dresses with the number and letter of the division of each man worked in *white* on the collar. The force was constituted under an act of Parliament passed in the tenth year of the reign of George IV., and is known as Peel's act. It has been of excellent service to the well-being of London. The stations are scattered over the metropolis, but the chief station is in Scotland Yard, Whitehall, where the Commissioners of Police, headed by Sir Richard Mayne, sit daily. The courts where police cases are heard are thirteen in number. They are presided over by Magistrates who are barristers, and these gentlemen are under the control of the Home Secretary. The courts of the Metropolitan police are in Bow Street; Clerkenwell; Great Marlborough Street; High Street, Marylebone; Vincent Square, Westminster; Bagnigge Wells Road, Clerkenwell; Worship Street, Shoreditch; Arbour Street, Stepney (Thames Police Office); Lower Kennington Lane, Lambeth; Blackman Street, Southwark; Blackheath Hill, for Greenwich and Woolwich; Brick Lane, Hammersmith; and Love Lane, Wandsworth. The vans sometimes seen about the streets, which in some respects resemble an omnibus, with policemen for drivers and conductors, are the vehicles employed to remove offenders from the police-offices to prison.

Between 60,000 and 70,000 cases are annually brought before the magistrates of the City and Metropolitan police courts.

The CITY POLICE, a distinct body from the Metropolitan police, are under the control of a Commissioner whose office is at 26 Old Jewry. They consist of a body of 627 men, who are distinguished from other policemen by the city arms on the collars of their coats, and by the *yellow* colour of their numbers. The only two police courts in the city are at the Mansion House, where the Lord Mayor presides, and at Guildhall, where an Alderman sits.

GAS LIGHTING.

London at night is everywhere illuminated with coal gas, which has done almost as much as an improved system of police in abating robberies and acts of violence. It was first introduced by an ingenious German, named Winsor, who lighted the Lyceum Theatre with it in 1803. It does not appear to have been used for street illumination until 1807, when the same person employed it to light one side of Pall Mall. Two years later he sought to obtain a charter, but the evidence of Accum the chemist in support of the invention appeared so supremely absurd to Mr. Brougham that he made it a topic of most effective ridicule, and stopped the project. Even at a later period the scheme of illumination by gas seemed highly preposterous, for Sir Humphrey Davy asked "if it were intended to take the dome of St. Paul's for a gasometer." The first gas company was established in 1810-12. In 1814 Westminster Bridge was lighted on the new method, and at the end of that year the general lighting of the Metropolis began. But such was the alarm occasioned by an explosion in a gas seasoning-house, that many persons asserted that gas was too dangerous to be used for the purpose, and the Royal Society appointed a committee to inquire how far this assertion was true. The stronghold of fashion, Grosvener Square, held out against the innovation until 1842. At the doors of mansions in the older streets, the iron extinguishers may still be seen in which the links or torches of past times were put out.

There are now eighteen gas companies in the Metropolis, producing about 5000 millions of cubic feet of gas in the year. More than 2000 miles of pipes have been laid down. The charge to the public is about 6s. per 1000 feet.

CEMETERIES.

The barbarous practice of interring human bodies within the precincts of the Metropolis has not yet been wholly abandoned, though of late years it has been much abated ; but not before several of the churchyards had become full to overflowing, and the neighbourhood had been rendered notoriously unhealthy, " the plague spots of the population." Vaults and catacombs underneath churches have been in many instances closed against the future deposit of coffins therein. The coffins previously there, if not removed by the relatives of the deceased, have been collected in one common vault, which has been closed and built up, never afterwards to be opened on any pretence whatever. Within the last few years numerous cemeteries have been formed in the environs of the Metropolis, of which the largest is at Woking in Surrey, 24 miles from London by the South Western Railway; but the most accessible, and the one the best worth visiting, is *Kensal Green Cemetery*, about two miles north-west of Paddington Green. Omnibuses from the Edgeware Road take passengers to the Cemetery gates. Between 50 and 60 acres were laid out in 1832, and a considerable part of it has been well adorned with monuments of all sizes and shapes. The cemetery is open to visitors on all week-days throughout the day and on Sunday afternoons. *Highgate Cemetery* comprises about 22 acres. Lying on the south slope of the hill, below the church, it commands a good view of London. *Nunhead Cemetery*, near Peckham Rye, and *Norwood Cemetery*, near the Lower Norwood Station of the West End and Crystal Palace Railway, are to the south of London, and each contains about 50 acres. Near Stoke Newington, on the north, is the *Abney Park Cemetery*. In the *West London Cemetery* at Brompton Lord Cremorne has erected a splendid family tomb which cost upwards of £2000. It is of granite, and the design is Egyptian.

METEOROLOGY.

A minute and very carefully-taken series of meteorological observations has been made for several years at Greenwich Observatory. Taking a series of 21 years, from 1840-1860, the mean temperature of the air is 49.2° Fahr.,[*] the highest annual mean during that period being 51.3° (1846), and the lowest 46.9° (1855). Taking the average of 89 years, the mean temperature of the four quarters of the year has been as follows :— Winter (Jan.-March), 38.4°; spring (April-June), 52.1°; summer (July-September), 59.5°; autumn (October-December), 43.6°. The mean daily range of the thermometer during 19 years was found to be—for the year, 15.9°; for autumn and winter, nearly 11.1°; for spring, 19.9°; and for summer, 19.7°.

[*] The annual mean temperature of Paris is 51.5° Fahr., and of Rome 60.7° Fahr.

The mean pressure of the air during 19 years was 29.778 inches.

The mean annual fall of rain in the above-mentioned series of 21 years was 23.95 inches, ranging from 17 inches in 1858 to 34.4 in 1852. The mean annual fall, however, taking a series of 45 years, was 25.3 inches. The weight of vapour in a cubic foot of air, taking the mean of 19 years, was calculated to be 3.4 grains.

CHAPTER THE SECOND.

GENERAL INFORMATION FOR STRANGERS.

Hotels — Lodgings — Restaurants — Dining-Rooms—Coffee Houses—
Hackney Carriages—Toll Gates—Omnibus Routes—Railway Stations—Electric Telegraph Companies—Messengers—Conveyance
of Parcels—Patents—Foreign Money.

HOTELS.

LARGE and well managed hotels, at which the charges are
regulated by printed tariff, have been erected by companies at
most of the railway stations; at the Paddington terminus of the
Great Western Railway ; at King's Cross, the terminus of the
Great Northern Railway ; at the terminus of the London and
North-Western Railway (the Euston and Victoria Hotels); at the
London Bridge Railway Station (an hotel containing 250 bed-
rooms) ; and at the Victoria Railway terminus, Pimlico, where a
very handsome hotel, known as the Grosvenor Hotel, has been
built. The Great Western Hotel cost, with its furniture, £86,000,
and it has been highly successful as a commercial speculation.
Besides these, two other large hotels have been lately erected by
public companies, viz., the Westminster Palace Hotel at the east
end of Victoria Street ; and the Palace Hotel, Buckingham
Gate, about 450 yards from the Victoria Railway terminus,
Pimlico. The former of these two, from its immense size, deserves a few words of description, as hotels of this class are much
wanted in other parts of London.

The WESTMINSTER HOTEL, at the bottom of Victoria Street,
Westminster, and in the immediate neighbourhood of the Houses
of Parliament and Courts of Law, is a new building erected by
a company in the Renaissance style at a cost of £60,000. It is a
large structure of eight storeys, with more than 400 rooms, but the
India Board has obtained possession of nearly one-half, for which
a rental of £6000 a year is paid. The coffee-room is 92 feet

in length, by 33 feet in width, and the dining-room is not much less. It is calculated that there are more than five acres of flooring in the hotel. Upon the site of this building stood the house and printing press of old Caxton ; and here also stood the ancient Bede-house of Westminster Abbey.

As to houses in the hands of individuals, visitors will do well to obtain the recommendation of some friend before fixing upon an hotel ; but the following may be safely mentioned as deserving of patronage :—

WEST END.—Claridge's, 42 Brook Street, Grosvenor Square ; the Clarendon, 169 New Bond Street ; Steven's, 181 New Bond Street ; Gullon's, 7 Albemarle Street ; Hawkin's, 29 Albemarle Street ; Brown's, 21 Dover Street, Piccadilly ; Balt's, 41 Dover Street, Piccadilly ; Ellis's, 59 St. James' Street ; Fenton's, 63 St. James' Street ; Farrance's, Belgrave Street, Belgrave Square ; Ford's, 127 Brook Street ; the Blenheim, Bond Street ; Long's, Bond Street ; the Gloucester, 76 Piccadilly ; Limmer's, Conduit Street ; Hatchett's, 67 Piccadilly ; the Burlington, Cork Street ; the Queen's, same street ; and many other hotels in Piccadilly, Jermyn Street, and the neighbourhood.

CENTRAL.—Union, Cockspur Street ; British, Cockspur Street ; Morley's, Trafalgar Square. In Covent Garden, chiefly used by bachelors, are the Bedford, New Hummums, Old Hummums, the Tavistock, and Richardson's. In or near Leicester Square, are several hotels frequented by the French, amongst which may be mentioned the Sablonière, Hotel de Provence, Hotel de Versailles, Hotel de l'Europe, Bertolini's, the Panton.

CITY.—Bridge House Hotel, London Bridge ; Keyser's Royal Hotel, Bridge Street, Blackfriars ; Radley's, same street ; the Queen's, St. Martin's le Grand ; the Castle and Falcon, same street ; Cathedral Hotel, 48 St. Paul's Churchyard ; the Albion, Aldersgate Street ; the Queen's, same street.

LODGINGS are to be obtained in every part of London, at prices varying according to the situation and accommodation afforded. In the north (Islington, Pentonville, etc.), a single man may procure a clean bedroom and sitting-room, from 12s. to 20s. a week. In the more fashionable quarters, well-furnished rooms will cost him from two to five guineas a-week ; and families must pay for a suite of handsomely furnished apartments, from ten to fifteen guineas. At the west end, the streets where lodgings are chiefly found are the streets leading out of Oxford

Street, Regent Street, and Piccadilly. If first-class accommodation is required, the best method of obtaining it is to apply to a house-agent in this neighbourhood, who will also supply a list of furnished houses with their rents. A lower class of lodgings, but still respectable, and very suitable for people who wish to be economical, and yet within easy reach of the principal sights, is to be obtained in the quiet streets leading from the Strand towards the river.

A very common arrangement in middle class boarding-houses is to charge a fixed sum per day or week for bed and breakfast, the boarder obtaining his other meals at dining-rooms or coffee-houses. In this case he has not the exclusive use of a sitting-room.

RESTAURANTS AND DINING-ROOMS.

These are scattered up and down London in great numbers, and are to be found of all degrees of goodness and badness.

GENERAL DINING-ROOMS.

WEST END.—Verrey's, Regent Street, corner of Hanover Street, has long been noted for the excellence of the fare, chiefly French, and proportionately high charges. Good general dining-rooms are the St. James' Restaurant, St. James Hall, Regent Street; and the Wellington, 160 Piccadilly; the Albany, 190 Piccadilly; Feetum's, Regent Street, corner of Burlington Street; and Campbell's, Beak Street, Regent Street; John-o'-Groat's, Rupert Street, Haymarket; Pye's, Church Place, Piccadilly.

CENTRAL.—At Simpson's, 103 Strand; the Albion, Great Russell Street, near Drury Lane Theatre; and the London, Fleet Street, corner of Chancery Lane—a good plain dinner with a glass of malt liquor, may be obtained at a minimum cost of 2s. 6d.

CITY.—Izant's, 21 Bucklersbury, and other places in the same Street; His Lordship's Larder, Cheapside; Commercial Dining-Rooms, Cheapside; Hill and Lake, 49 Cheapside, and 13 Gracechurch Street.

ORDINARIES.—Salutation, Newgate Street (5 o'clock). Three Tuns Tavern, Billingsgate Market (1 and 4 o'clock).

HOUSES FOR SPECIAL DISHES.

Turtle—at the Ship and Turtle, Leadenhall Street.

Chops and Steaks—Ned's, Finch Lane; Joe's, Finch Lane, Cornhill; the Cock, 201 Fleet Street; the Rainbow, 15 Fleet Street; the Cheshire Cheese, Wine Office Court, Fleet Street; Dolly's, Queen's Head Passage, Paternoster Row.

Boiled Beef—Williams', Old Bailey.

A-la-mode Beef—Jaquet's, Clare Court, Drury Lane.

White Bait.*—Season, June, July, August—Lovegrove's East India Dock Tavern, Blackwall; Quartermaine's Ship, and the Trafalgar, Greenwich.

SUPPER ROOMS.

The Albion, Great Russell Street; Evans' Covent Garden; Cider Cellars, Maiden Lane; the Coal Hole, Strand; the Cock, 201 Fleet Street; the Rainbow, 15 Fleet Street, etc.

COFFEE-HOUSES.

Except in the City, coffee-houses have no longer the importance for the middle classes they once possessed, having been superseded by our modern clubs. But in the neighbourhood of the bank, there are certain establishments of this description, which are the rendezvous of commercial men, and where files of newspapers connected with commercial matters are kept ready for consultation.

Deacon's Coffee and Dining House, 3 Wallbrook, has a file of the *Times*, extending back nearly seventy years, and files of many other newspapers.

Garraway's Coffee House, 3 Change Alley, Cornhill, much frequented for light luncheons; many sales by auction take place here.

Jamaica Coffee-House, 1 St. Michael's Alley, Cornhill, which persons connected with the West Indian trade frequent.

Jerusalem Coffee-House, 1 Cowper's Court, Cornhill, the haunt of merchants, captains, etc., connected with the trade of India, China, and Australia, and where files of papers published in these countries are to be seen.

---

* The white bait is a fish from two to three inches long, closely allied to the herring, pilchard, and sprat, known to zoologists under the name of *clupea alba*. "The fashion of enjoying the excellent course of fish, as served up at Greenwich or Blackwall, is sanctioned by the highest authorities, from the Court at St. James' Palace in the West, to the Lord Mayor and his Court in the East, including the Cabinet Ministers and the philosophers of the Royal Society."—Yarrell's History of British Fishes.

New England, and North and South American Coffee-House, 59 and 60 Threadneedle Street.

There are upwards of 800 coffee-houses distributed over the metropolis, chiefly frequented by the humbler classes, to whom they are of great use, in affording a temperate meal at a cheap rate. The fare supplied consists mainly of tea, coffee, and cocoa ; chops, steaks, ham and eggs. Under a recent regulation, wine may be sold at these houses. Newspapers, as well as the monthly and weekly literary periodicals, are to be seen in most of them. A cup of good coffee is to be had at Verrey's, 229 Regent Street ; Kilpack's, 42 King Street, Covent Garden; Ries's Divan, 102 Strand ; Groom's 16 Fleet Street ; and Pursell's, 78 Cornhill.

HACKNEY CARRIAGE FARES AND REGULATIONS.

Those who have occasion to make much use of cabs will find of great service a small red book, published under the authority of the Metropolitan Police Office, and to be obtained at any bookseller's, price 1s. It contains an authorized list of fares, and gives the distance in yards from numerous points in London to others.

There are many places in the public streets called cab stands, where cabs are in waiting to be hired, but vehicles may frequently be met with proceeding along the streets. Every hackney carriage in the street, with the Stamp Office plate upon it, is to be deemed as plying for hire, unless actually hired ; and the driver, in case of dispute, must produce evidence of his carriage being hired.

Fares by distance—Within four miles of Charing Cross, the fare for cabs is sixpence a mile (1760 yards), and sixpence for any fractional part of a mile. If taken beyond that distance the fare is one shilling a mile, back fare not being allowed in either case. For any stoppage or number of stoppages, amounting to fifteen minutes, the driver is entitled to sixpence, besides the distance-fare, and sixpence more for each additional fifteen minutes for which the carriage is detained. If the driver be not paid when the hirer alights, it will be considered that he is ordered to wait, and he must be paid accordingly.

Two persons are to be carried in a cab at a single fare ; for each additional person sixpence for the whole journey is to be paid. Two children under ten years of age are to be considered as one adult person. An infant in arms is to be considered a person, and must be paid for extra, if there be two other persons in the cab.

The driver must drive at a speed not less than six miles an hour, unless the hirer requests him to drive more slowly.

Fares by time.—If it is intended to pay by time, this must be stated to the driver at the time of hiring the cab. The fare by time is 2s. for an hour, and sixpence for every 15 minutes beyond. If taken out of the four-mile circle, and there discharged, the fare beyond the circle is to be charged by distance at the rate of 1s. a mile. A driver cannot be compelled to hire his conveyance by time before six in the morning, or later than eight in the evening. If more than two persons employ the cab, the extra person or persons must be paid for as before. If the driver be ordered to drive at a greater speed than four miles an hour, he will be entitled to an additional sixpence per mile above the four miles per hour. He is bound to drive to any place not exceeding six miles from the place of hiring, or for any time not exceeding an hour.

Luggage.—A reasonable quantity of luggage is to be conveyed, either inside or outside the carriage, without extra payment; but when more than two persons are being carried, and there is more luggage than can be taken inside, twopence must be paid for each package carried outside.

Tickets, etc.—The driver of a hackney carriage is bound, when hired, to deliver to the hirer a card, with the number of the Stamp Office plate affixed to his carriage. He is also bound to produce, when requested, a book of fares for inspection. The regulations as to the fares are to be distinctly painted inside and outside every hackney carriage.

Disputes.—If any dispute should occur between hirer and driver, the hirer may require the driver to take him to the nearest police office, where, if a magistrate be sitting, he will adjudicate on the case at once. If it should be after the closing of the police courts, then the driver is to drive to the nearest police station, where the complaint will be entered, and decided by the magistrate at his next sitting.

Property left in hackney carriages should be inquired for at the office of the Commissioners of Police in Great Scotland Yard, Charing Cross. A driver is bound to take property which has been left in his carriage to the nearest police station within 24 hours. The owner will receive it on proving his title to it, and on payment of the expenses incurred.

Turnpike or Toll Gates.—On most of the roads leading out of

London are stationed these vexatious barriers, which persons on horseback, or driving in a vehicle, cannot pass without payment, according to a settled rate of toll. After paying the collectors, the money is laid out on the repairs of the roads. The repairs now done, amount, it is said, to £40,000 a-year. Various attempts have been made to get rid of the nuisance, but as yet without having discovered any plan which is satisfactory to all concerned. A list of tolls leviable at every gate is conspicuously painted on a board, and should be referred to in case of doubt. Tolls are levied on several of the bridges, not only on vehicles, but on foot passengers.

OMNIBUSES AND THEIR ROUTES.

There are many lines of omnibuses from one part of London to another, the routes of which will not be understood by a stranger unless he consults a map. They are principally in the hands of a company, styled the London General Omnibus Company, established a few years back, in imitation of the Parisian system. Notwithstanding the promises to employ new roomy vehicles, the omnibuses continue to be very inconveniently small. The system of correspondence with which they started has been abandoned. The use made of these conveyances in London is very great, and in the principal thoroughfares, several omnibuses are in sight at one time. It has been ascertained that 1800 of these vehicles pass the Angel, Islington, daily. The highest fare is seldom more than sixpence for the whole distance, with a lower charge for shorter distance. The top of an omnibus affords a good means for seeing the streets of London, and the exteriors of the principal buildings. Before taking a seat, ascertain that the omnibus is going to the place you wish to be taken to. Inside the door there is a list of fares, which the stranger should consult before paying. In case of overcharge take the conductor's number from his badge, and apply to the nearest police office. The number of passengers to be carried in and upon an omnibus is to be conspicuously painted inside; and no more than the proper number of passengers is to be carried under a penalty of £5 each against driver and conductor.

BAYSWATER—BANK AND LONDON BRIDGE STATION. Route:—Notting Hill Gate, St. John's Church, Royal Oak, Regent Circus, Oxford Street, Cheapside, Bank, London Bridge. Fares, 3d., 4d.; all the way, 6d.

BLACKWALL—REGENT CIRCUS (PICCADILLY)—Every twelve minutes. Route:—
West India Docks, Poplar, Limehouse, Stepney, Commercial Road, Leadenhall
Street, Cornhill, Bank, Cheapside, St. Paul's, Ludgate Hill, Fleet Street, Strand,
Charing Cross. Fares, 6d., 4d., and 3d.

BOW AND STRATFORD—OXFORD STREET—Every ten minutes. Route:—Bow, Whitechapel, Aldgate, Leadenhall Street, Cornhill, Bank, Cheapside, Ludgate Hill,
Fleet Street, Strand, Charing Cross, Pall Mall, Waterloo Place. Fares, 6d., 4d.,
and 3d.

BRENTFORD—ST. PAUL's—Every hour. Route:—Kewbridge, Chiswick, Turnham
Green, Hammersmith, thence by the same route as the Hammersmith. Fares,
Hammersmith, 6d. ; Brentford, Isleworth, or Hounslow, 1s.

BRIXTON—CALEDONIAN ROAD—NORTH LONDON (RAILWAY STATION)—Every twenty
minutes. Route:—Caledonian Road, King's Cross, Gray's Inn Lane, Chancery
Lane, Temple Bar, Strand, Charing Cross, Parliament Street, Westminster
Bridge, Lambeth, Kennington, Brixton Church. Fares, 9d., 6d., and 4d.

BRIXTON—GRACECHURCH STREET—CITY—"PARAGON"—Every ten minutes. Route:
—Brixton Hill, Tulse Hill, Kennington, Newington Causeway, London Bridge.
Fares, 9d., 6d., 4d., and 3d.

BROMPTON—ISLINGTON—Every twelve minutes. Route:—Queen's Elm, Brompton;
Knightsbridge, Hyde Park Corner, Piccadilly, Regent Street, Mortimer Street,
Great Portland Street, New Road, Euston Square, King's Cross, Islington.
Fares, 2d., 3d. ; all the way, 6d.

BROMPTON—LONDON BRIDGE RAILWAY—Every seven minutes. Route:—Knights-
bridge, Piccadilly, Waterloo Place, Pall Mall, Charing Cross, Strand, Fleet
Street, Ludgate Hill, St. Paul's, Cheapside, Bank, King William Street, London
Bridge. Fares, 4d. and 3d. Sunday after 8 P.M., 6d.

CALEDONIAN ROAD (NORTH LONDON RAILWAY STATION) TO PIMLICO (VAUXHALL
ROAD)—"CALEDONIAN"—Every twenty minutes. Route:—Caledonian Road,
King's Cross, Gray's Inn Lane, Chancery Lane, Strand, Westminster Abbey,
Victoria Street, Vauxhall Road. Fares, 3d. and 4d.

CAMBERWELL—GRACECHURCH STREET—CITY—Every ten minutes. Route:—Walworth Road, Elephant and Castle, Newington Causeway, Borough, London
Bridge, Gracechurch Street. Fares, 2d. and 3d. ; all the way, 6d.

CAMDEN TOWN—CAMBERWELL GATE—"WATERLOO"—Every six minutes. Route:—
York and Albany, near Gloucester Gate, Regent's Park, through Albany Street,
Great Portland Street, Regent Circus, Regent Street, Charing Cross, Strand,
Waterloo Bridge, Waterloo Road, London Road, Old Kent Road or Walworth
Road, to Camberwell Gate. Fares, 4d., 2d. ; all the way, 6d.

CAMDEN TOWN—HUNGERFORD MARKET—Every five minutes. Route:—Red Cap
(top of High Street, Camden Town), through Hampstead Road, Tottenham
Court Road, St. Giles', Seven Dials, St. Martin's Lane, Trafalgar Square. Fares,
to Oxford Street (outside), 2d. ; all the way, 3d.

CAMDEN TOWN (NORTH LONDON RAILWAY STATION)—KENNINGTON GATE—KING'S
CROSS—Every eight minutes. Route:—Camden Town Railway Station, through
College Street, Charrington Street, near the North-Western Railway Terminus,
Euston Square, King's Cross Railway Terminus, Gray's Inn Lane, Chancery
Lane, Fleet Street, Temple, Farringdon Street, New Bridge Street, Blackfriars
Bridge, London Road, Elephant and Castle, High Street, Kennington Road,
Kennington Gate. Fares, 6d., 4d., and 3d.

CHELSEA (NEAR CREMORNE GARDENS)—BETHNAL GREEN (CAMBRIDGE HEATH GATE)

—Every twelve minutes. Route :—Battersea Bridge, King's Road, Sloane Square, Knightsbridge, Piccadilly, Regent Street, Strand, Bank, Cornhill, Bishopsgate Street, Shoreditch (Eastern Counties Railway Station) Bethnal Green Road, to Cambridge Heath Gate. Fares, 3d., 4d. ; all the way, 6d. Sundays after 8 P.M., 6d.

CHELSEA (NEAR CREMORNE GARDENS)—HOXTON—Every twelve minutes. Route :— Battersea Bridge and Cremorne Gardens, King's Road, Sloane Square, Sloane Street, Knightsbridge, Piccadilly, Regent Street, Pall Mall, Strand, Cheapside, Bank, Moorgate Street, Finsbury Square, Pitfield Street, New North Road, Hoxton. Fares, 4d., Charing Cross, 3d. ; all the way, 6d. Sundays after 8 P.M., 6d.

CHELSEA—CADOGAN PIER—Up Oakley Street to International Exhibition building.

CHELSEA (SLOANE SQUARE)—ISLINGTON (ANGEL)—Every twelve minutes. Route :— Sloane Square, through Sloane Street, Knightsbridge, Hyde Park Corner, Piccadilly, Regent Street, Mortimer Street, Great Portland Street, New Road, Euston Square, King's Cross, Islington. Fares, 3d., 2d. ; all the way, 6d.

CLAPHAM—GRACECHURCH STREET—CITY—Every ten minutes. Route :—Stockwell, Kennington, Newington Causeway, Boro', London Bridge, Gracechurch Street. Fares, 4d., 6d.

CLAPHAM—OXFORD STREET (REGENT'S CIRCUS)—Every fifteen minutes. Route :— Stockwell, Kennington Green, York Place, Westminster Bridge, Whitehall, Charing Cross, Regent Street, Regent Circus (Oxford Street). Fares, 6d., 4d. ; all the way, 9d.

CLAPTON AND HACKNEY—BANK—Every twelve minutes. Route :—Hackney Road, Shoreditch, Bishopsgate Street, to Bank. Fares, 6d., 4d., 3d., and 2d.

CRYSTAL PALACE AND NORWOOD—GRACECHURCH STREET—CITY. Fares, Kennington or Camberwell Gate, 4d. ; Brixton Church, 6d. ; Brixton Hill, 9d. ; Upper or Lower Norwood, 1s.

CRYSTAL PALACE AND NORWOOD—OXFORD STREET (REGENT CIRCUS). Fares, 1s., 9d., 6d.

EDGWARE ROAD (END OF PRAED STREET)—LONDON BRIDGE RAILWAY—"CITIZEN" —Every twelve minutes. Route :—Edgware Road, Oxford Street, Holborn, Newgate Street, Cheapside, London Bridge. Fares, 2d. and 3d. ; all the way, 4d.

EDMONTON—BANK AND ROYAL EXCHANGE—Every twenty minutes. Route :—Tottenham, Stamford Hill, Stoke Newington, Kingsland, Kingsland Road, Shoreditch, Bishopsgate Street, Bank. Return from end of Threadneedle Street in Bishopsgate Street. Fares, 9d., 8d., 6d., and 3d.

GREAT WESTERN RAILWAY STATION—LONDON BRIDGE AND BLACKWALL RAILWAY, by New Road—Every ten minutes. Route :—Royal Oak, Westbourne Grove, Bishop's Road, Edgware Road, New Road, Euston Square, King's Cross, Angel, City Road, Finsbury Square, Moorgate Street, Threadneedle Street, Leadenhall Street. Fares, 3d. and 4d. ; all the way, 6d.

HACKNEY ROAD—ELEPHANT AND CASTLE, NEWINGTON—Kingsland and Old Kent Road—Every ten minutes. Route :—Shoreditch Church, Bishopsgate Street Gracechurch Street, King William Street, London Bridge, Borough, Newington Causeway, Elephant and Castle. Fares, 3d. and 2d.

HACKNEY (UPPER CLAPTON)—OXFORD STREET (REGENT CIRCUS)—Every half hour. Route :—Dalston Lane, Kingsland, Ball's Pond Road, Islington, City Road, New Road, Great Portland Street, Regent Circus, Oxford Street. Fares, 4d., 6d. ; all the way, 9d.

HAMMERSMITH—BANK AND LONDON BRIDGE. Route :—Kensington, Knightsbridge,

Piccadilly, Haymarket, Charing Cross, Strand, Fleet Street, Cheapside, Bank King William Street, London Bridge. Fares, 6d., 4d., and 3d.

HAMPSTEAD—BANK—Hampstead Conveyance—Every twelve minutes. Route :— Haverstock Hill, Camden Town, Hampstead Road—Tottenham Court Road, Oxford Street, Holborn, Newgate Street, Cheapside, Bank. Fares, 3d., 4d., 6d. all the way, 9d.

HIGHGATE AND KENTISH TOWN—BANK—Conveyance Society—Every twelve minutes. Route :—Camden Town, cross New Road, Tottenham Court Road, Holborn, Newgate Street, Cheapside, Cornhill, Leadenhall Street, Aldgate, Whitechapel Fares, 3d., 4d. ; all the way, 6d.

HIGHBURY AND ISLINGTON—BLACKFRIARS—"Favorite"—Every twenty minutes. Route :—Holloway Road, Highbury, Islington, High Street, Goswell Street, Post Office, St. Paul's, Ludgate Hill, Blackfriars Bridge. Fares, 4d.

HIGHGATE HILL—WESTMINSTER—"Favorite"—Every ten minutes. Route :— Holloway Road, Highbury, Islington, High Street, John's Street Road, Exmouth Street, Gray's Inn Lane, Chancery Lane, Fleet Street, Strand, Parliament Street to Westminster. Fares, 3d. ; all the way, 6d.

HOLBORN HILL—MARBLE ARCH—Every five minutes. Farringdon Street, Holborn Oxford Street, Marble Arch. Fares, 2d.

HORNSEY ROAD, HIGHBURY, AND ISLINGTON—LONDON BRIDGE RAILWAY—"Favorite"—Every eight minutes. Route :—Seven Sisters' Road, Holloway Road, Highbury, Islington, High Street, City Road, Finsbury Circus, Moorgate Street Bank, King William Street, London Bridge. Fares, 4d. ; all the way, 6d.

HOXTON TO CHELSEA—(See Chelsea to Hoxton).

ISLINGTON (BARNSBURY PARK)—KENSINGTON GATE—Every seven minutes. Route —Barnsbury Road, Islington, Goswell Road, Goswell Street, Aldersgate Street, Post Office, St. Paul's, Ludgate Hill, Blackfriars Bridge, London Road, Elephant and Castle, High Street, Kennington. Fares, 4d. ; all the way, 6d.

ISLINGTON (LOWER ROAD) TO KENT ROAD (SOUTHWARK) — Every ten minutes. Route :—Lower Road, New North Road, Hoxton, Old Street, City Road, Moorgate Street, London Bridge, Borough, Old Kent Road. Fares, 2d., 3d., and 4d.

ISLINGTON TO CHELSEA—(See Chelsea to Islington).

KENSINGTON NEW TOWN TO LONDON BRIDGE RAILWAY—"Brompton." Route :— Gloucester Road, Old Brompton, Knightsbridge, Piccadilly, Regent Street Bank. Fares, 3d. ; all the way, 4d.

KENSINGTON—BANK—Every five minutes. (Same as Hammersmith to Bank.)

KEW TO BANK—Every Hour. "Kew Bridge." Fares, Kew, 9d. ; Hammersmith or Kensington. 6d. ; Charing Cross to Bank, 4d.

KILBURN GATE OR ROYAL OAK—WHITECHAPEL—Every fifteen minutes. Route :— Maida Hill, Edgware Road, Oxford Street, Holborn, Cheapside, Leadenhall Street. Fares, 4d. and 6d. Same to London Bridge and Blackwall Railway.

KINGSLAND GATE TO BANK.—Every five minutes. Route :—Kingsland Road (Dalston), Shoreditch, Bishopsgate Street, Bank. Return from end of Threadneedle Street. Fare, all the way, 2d.

MARBLE ARCH (REGENT'S PARK) — FARRINGDON STREET. — Every five minutes. Route :—Oxford Street, Holborn. Fare, 2d.

NOTTING HILL AND BAYSWATER TO WHITECHAPEL ROAD.—Every six minutes. Route :—Notting Hill, Uxbridge Road, Oxford Street, Holborn, Cheapside, Bank, Cornhill, Leadenhall Street, Aldgate, Whitechapel.

NOTTING HILL AND BAYSWATER—MILE-END GATE—Every six minutes. Route :—
Shepherd's Bush, Notting Hill, Bayswater, Uxbridge Road, Hyde Park, Oxford
Street, Regent Street, Piccadilly, Charing Cross, Strand, Fleet Street, Ludgate
Hill, St. Paul's, Cheapside, Bank, Cornhill, Leadenhall Street, Aldgate, White-
chapel, Mile End. Fares, 6d., 4d., and 3d.

NOTTING HILL AND BAYSWATER—LONDON BRIDGE—Route :—Notting Hill Gate, St.
John's Church, Royal Oak, Regent Circus, Oxford Street, Cheapside, Bank,
London Bridge. Fares, 3d. and 4d. ; all the way, 6d.

PADDINGTON (GREAT WESTERN RAILWAY STATION), HUNGERFORD MARKET (STRAND)
—Every eight minutes. Route :—Edgware Road, Oxford Street, Regent Street,
Piccadilly, Waterloo Place, Pall Mall, Cockspur Street, Charing Cross. Fares,
3d. and 4d.

PLIMLICO (GROSVENOR ROAD)—BLACKWALL RAILWAY—"Royal Blue"—Every eight
minutes. Route :—Victoria Road, Grosvenor Place, Piccadilly, Charing Cross,
Strand, Bank, Cornhill, Leadenhall Street, Blackwall Railway. Fares, 2d. ; all
the way, 4d.

PUTNEY AND BROMPTON — LONDON BRIDGE—Route : — Putney Bridge, Fulham,
Brompton, Knightsbridge, Piccadilly, Waterloo Place, Pall Mall, Charing Cross,
Strand, Fleet Street, Ludgate Hill, St. Paul's, Cheapside, Bank, King William
Street, London Bridge. Fares, 4d., 3d., 2d.

ROYAL OAK, BAYSWATER—BANK, AND LONDON BRIDGE STATION—(See Great Western
Railway).

RICHMOND, HAMPTON COURT, KINGSTON, KEW, AND CHERTSEY, TO BANK—Every half
hour. Route :—Chertsey, Sunbury, Hampton Court, Richmond, Kingston,
Twickenham, Kew, Turnham Green, Hammersmith, Strand, Bank. Fares,
Chertsey, 2s. 6d. ; Sunbury, 2s. ; Hampton Court, 2s. 6d. ; Richmond, 1s. ; intermediate, 6d.

ST. JOHN'S WOOD—CAMBERWELL GATE, AND OLD KENT ROAD—Atlas—Every five
minutes. Route :—Baker Street, Portman Square, Orchard Street, Oxford
Street, Regent Street, Charing Cross, Westminster Bridge, Lambeth, London
Road, Newington, Walworth Road. Fares, 3d., 4d., and 6d.

ST. JOHN'S WOOD—LONDON BRIDGE RAILWAY—"City Atlas"—Every seven minutes.
Route :—Swiss Cottage, Marlborough Road, Wellington Road, Alpha Road,
Baker Street, Portman Square, Orchard Street, Oxford Street (Tottenham Court
Road), Holborn, Newgate Street, Cheapside, Bank, King William Street, London
Bridge. Fares, 6d., 4d., and 3d.

STOKE NEWINGTON—BANK—Every ten minutes. Route :—West Hackney Church,
Kingsland Road, Shoreditch. Fares, 3d. and 4d. ; all the way, 6d.

WESTMINSTER—BANK—Every six minutes. Route :—Strand, Parliament Street,
Westminster, to Vauxhall Bridge. Fare, all the way, 3d.

WESTMINSTER—HIGHBURY—"Favourite"—Every ten minutes. Route :—Parliament Street, Charing Cross, Strand, cross Holborn, Gray's Inn Lane, St. John
Street Road, Angel, High Street, Islington, Highbury. Fares, 3d., 4d., and 6d.

RAILWAYS AND RAILWAY STATIONS.

For fuller particulars as to the stations on the several lines,
the times of departure and arrival of trains, and the fares, the
reader is referred to the official time-tables or to "Bradshaw,"

which latter publication contains a map, shewing the courses of all the railways in the kingdom.

BLACKWALL, Fenchurch Street, City. This line, 3¾ miles long, is supported for nearly its whole length on brick arches. At the terminus, Brunswick Wharf, steamers to convey passengers to the Victoria Docks, to Woolwich, and various places on the river.

EASTERN COUNTIES, Shoreditch. This line is carried on brick arches through the unsightly districts of Spitalfields and Bethnal Green to a great depot and station at Stratford, where many lines diverge, the two principal of which, the Cambridge line and the Ipswich line, connect London with the eastern parts of the island.

EUSTON SQUARE, the terminus of the London and North-Western Railway, the most gigantic concern of the kind in the kingdom, which connects London with the northern and north-western parts of England, covers 12 acres of ground, and cost, with the great depot at Camden Town, covering 30 acres, £800,000. At the Euston Square terminus is a huge gateway in Grecian Doric, 72 feet high, the supporting columns being 44 feet in height. The hall, 125½ feet by 61½ feet, and 60 feet high, contains a colossal marble statue by Baily, of George Stephenson the engineer, erected by subscription. The bas-reliefs of figures representing the principal cities and towns connected by the line, are by John Thomas. Just outside the station are the Victoria and Euston Hotels, both under the same management.

GREAT WESTERN STATION, Paddington, with a great hotel fronting Praed Street. This line connects London with the west of England. The late Mr. Brunel was the engineer, and he insisted on laying down the broad guage, but a narrow guage line is now being made. It has been a very expensive line, and a great number of branches have been made from time to time. The middle roof of the station has a span of 90 feet, and the lateral roofs have spans of 70 feet. There are four platforms 700 feet long, and their total width is 240 feet.

KING'S CROSS.—Here is the terminus of the Great Northern Railway, which communicates with the midland and northern parts of England. It covers 45 acres. The passenger station has platforms 800 feet long. Each roof has a span of 105 feet, and is 71 feet high. The goods shed is 600 feet long by 80 feet

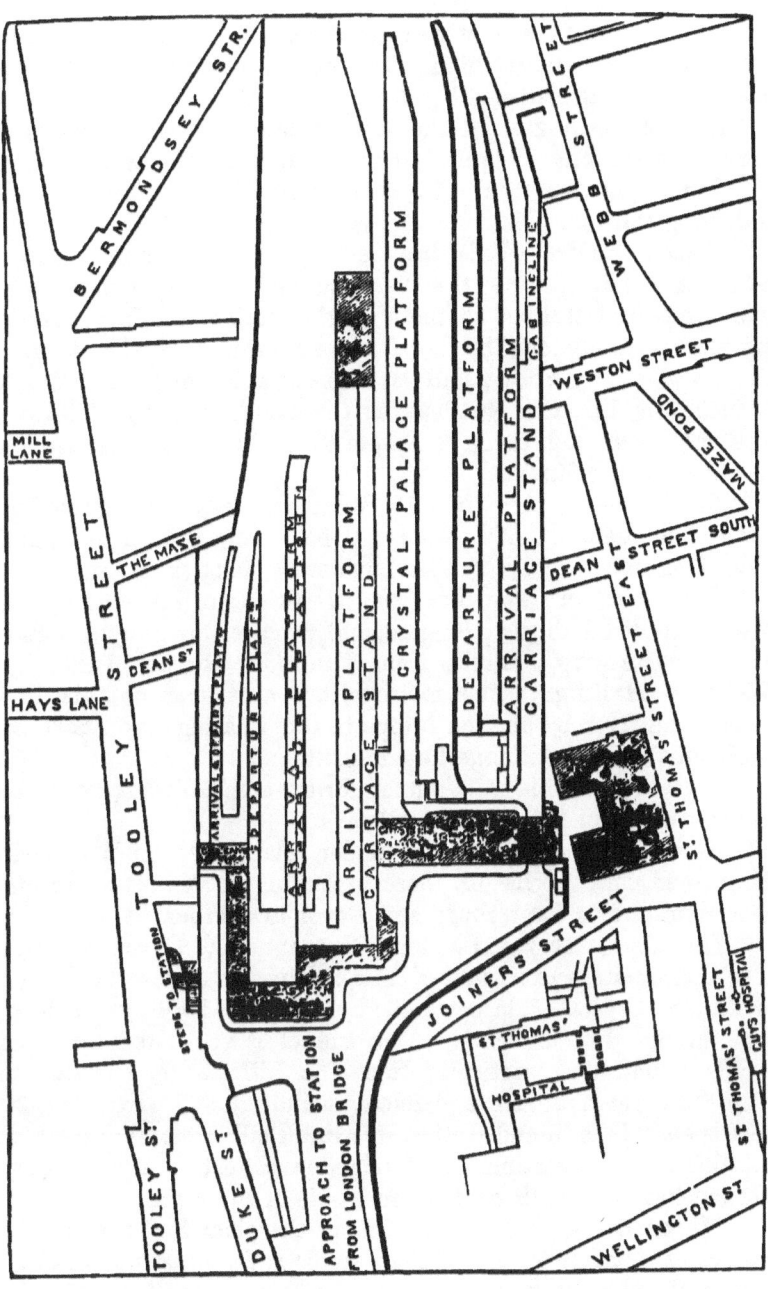

wide. The clock tower, which separates the two arches in the street front, is 120 feet high. In connection with the station is a large and well managed hotel.

LONDON BRIDGE.—On the south side of London Bridge is a cluster of stations, irregularly combined, and without any unity of plan or architectural beauty, forming the terminus of the following railways :—

Crystal Palace.—This line is carried by a tunnel under Sydenham Hill to join the West-end and Crystal Palace line, which has its terminus at the Victoria Station, Pimlico. Many trains run throughout the day from one terminus to the other.

Croydon ; by Forest Hill, Sydenham, and Norwood ; with a branch line through Nutcham to the South-Western Railway ; and another branch through Epsom to Guildford on the London and Portsmouth line.

Brighton.—By this line, 55 miles in length, Brighton has been made a suburb of London. It has many branch lines, and from Brighton railways run east and west along the coast.

South Eastern ; branches from the Brighton line at the great station of Red Hill near Reigate, and reaches Dover by a round-about course with a branch from Tunbridge through Tunbridge Wells to Hastings. The metropolitan extension of this line crosses the river by an iron bridge to the Charing Cross Station, built on the site of Hungerford market.

Greenwich. This line is upon brick arches throughout, and is the earliest of the London railways.

North Kent ; by a tunnel under Blackheath to Woolwich, Gravesend, and Rochester, there branching to Maidstone in one direction, and to Canterbury and Dover in another.

Mid-Kent ; or the London, Chatham, and Dover Railway. The metropolitan extension of this line passes under the hill on which the Crystal Palace stands, by a tunnel 2000 yards long, cut through London clay. This tunnel is ventilated by seven shafts, penetrating vertically from the hill above. There are also 6200 yards of brick viaducts, including 600 arches, of 30 feet span. It is intended that this line shall cross the river at Blackfriars to a station at Farringdon Street. A temporary station has been built on the south side of the river.

METROPOLITAN RAILWAY.—One of the plans for relieving the streets of London of part of their traffic is the construction of an underground railway, which commences by a junction with the

Great Western Railway at Paddington, and passes under Praed
Street and the New Road to King's Cross, in an archway 28½ feet
wide, and from 16½ to 18½ feet high. The minimum thickness of
the brickwork in the side walls and arches is 2 feet 5 inches. At
King's Cross a junction is effected with the Great Northern Railway, and the Metropolitan Railway then proceeds in open cut-
ting to Victoria Street, Holborn Bridge, and thence to Smithfield
Market, the entire basement of which will be filled up as a railway depot. There will be six intermediate stations in addition
to those at the termini. By means of an extension half a mile in
length, it is purposed to continue the line from Smithfield to
Finsbury Pavement, within 400 yards of the Bank. The principal stations will be covered with roofs of glass, extending across
the line and platforms, and all the stations will be well lighted.
A large sum has been expended upon this novel and difficult
undertaking, which it is hoped will be completed in the course
of 1862.

THE NORTH LONDON RAILWAY is a line which connects the
Blackwall Railway with the London and North-Western Railway,
passing through the northern suburbs of the metropolis, and having stations at Stepney (at its east end), Bow, Victoria Park,
Hackney, Kingsland, Newington Road, Islington, Caledonian Road,
and Camden Town. Here the *Hampstead and City Junction Railway* commences, by means of which, and the *North and South-
Western Junction Railway*, which passes near Acton, the loop
line of the Richmond Railway may be reached at Kew.

VICTORIA STATION, PIMLICO.—At the end of Victoria Street,
Pimlico, a quarter of a mile from Buckingham Palace, a large station has been erected on what was formerly the basin of the
Grosvenor Canal, for the use of the London, Brighton, and South
Coast Railway Company, the London, Chatham, and Dover Railway Company, the West End and Crystal Palace Railway Company, and the Great Western Railway Company. Ten acres and
a quarter of ground have been covered by the station. The line
on the north of the river follows the course of the old Grosvenor
Canal, and is enclosed by high walls, supporting a roof of iron
and glass half a mile long. It is then carried across the Thames
by an iron bridge, which is in close proximity to the new Battersea Park Bridge. South of the river the line joins the West End
and Crystal Palace Railway on the one hand, and the West London Extension Railway on the other. The iron bridge is 920

feet long, 32 feet broad, and it is supported by two stone abutments at each end, and by three piers in the river, carrying four arched spans of 175 feet each.

A large and very handsome hotel, to be called the Grosvenor Hotel, is now building, contiguous to the station with which it is connected. It has a frontage of 300 feet, and a depth of 80 feet. It will be nine storeys in height, including the basement, and contain upwards of 500 rooms.

WATERLOO STATION, Waterloo Bridge Road.—Here is the terminus of the South-Western (Southampton) Railway, and the Richmond, Windsor, and Reading Railway, the latter having a loop line through Kew and Hounslow. The station is spacious, but makes no pretence to architectural effect. The extension of the line from Nine Elms, Vauxhall, to this station, only two miles and fifty yards, cost £800,000.

ELECTRIC TELEGRAPH COMPANIES.

The LONDON DISTRICT TELEGRAPH COMPANY have offices in all parts of London, from which messages can be sent to any other part of London, at the rate of sixpence for fifteen words, and ninepence for twenty words, with free porterage within certain limits; and to all parts of the United Kingdom and the Continent, by arrangement with other offices. The chief office is at 90 Cannon Street, City, E. C.

The ELECTRIC AND INTERNATIONAL TELEGRAPH COMPANY. Chief office, Lothbury, near the Bank of England. Branch offices at Charing Cross, Regent's Circus, and other parts of London. Messages at a settled rate of charge according to length, can be sent to any part of the British Islands, or to the Continent.

BRITISH AND IRISH MAGNETIC TELEGRAPH COMPANY have their chief office in a new and handsome building in Threadneedle Street, near the Bank of England, erected on the site of the Baltic Coffee-house. The wires of this Company extend throughout the United Kingdom. Messages are received for transmission in a lofty hall forty feet square.

The SUBMARINE TELEGRAPH COMPANY have also offices here. The cables of this Company bring London into direct communication with all parts of Europe. The clock in the turret indicates true Greenwich time.

MESSENGERS.—A charitable society, in order to give employ-

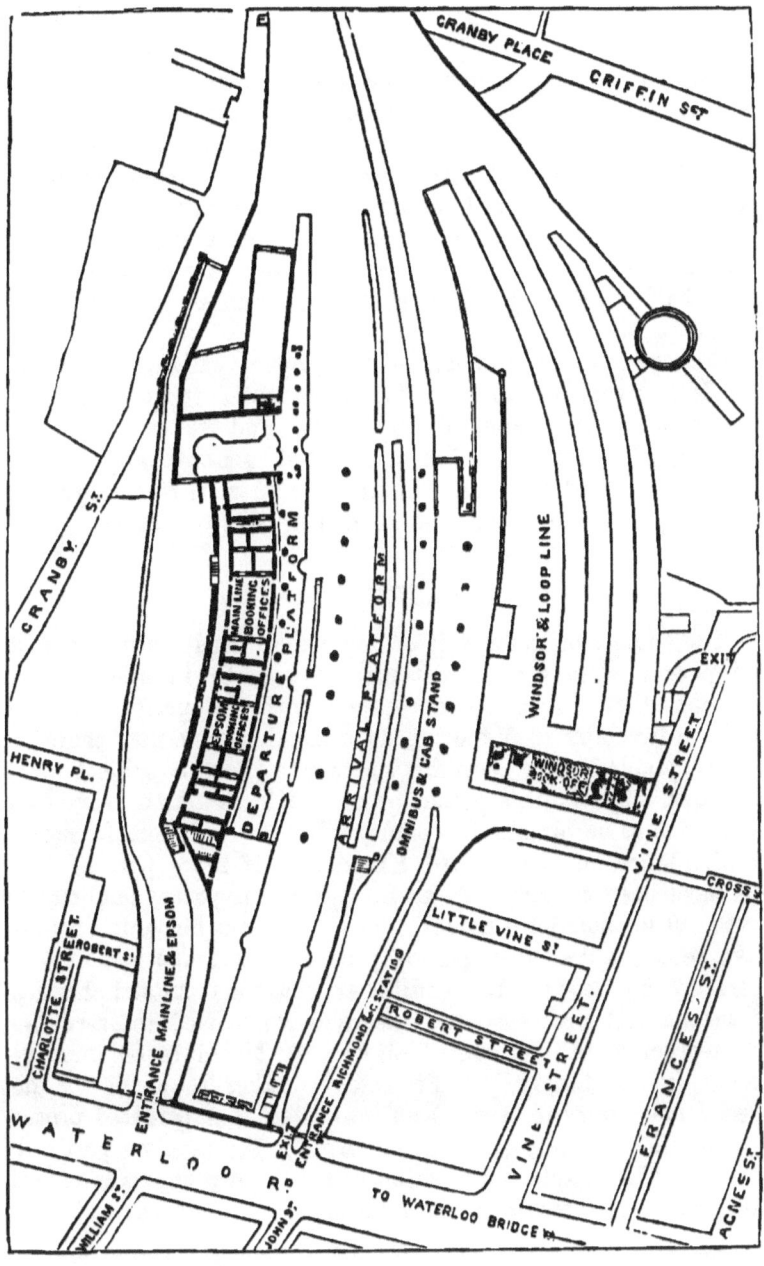

ment to soldiers who have been disabled by losing a limb in the service of the country, has undertaken to form a corps of trust-worthy messengers (sometimes styled *commissionaires*). They are dressed in a dark green uniform, and wear badges; and are stationed about the principal streets of the east and west ends of the town. The authorized tariff of charges is—by distance, two-pence for half a mile or under; three-pence for a distance from half a mile to a mile. By time, sixpence an hour, or two-pence a quarter of an hour, walking at the rate of $2\frac{1}{2}$ miles an hour; half a crown for a day of eight hours. For calling a carriage, a penny.

CONVEYANCE OF PARCELS.—A Company called the London Parcels Delivery Company, with their chief station in Roll's Buildings, Fetter Lane, Fleet Street, undertakes to deliver parcels in all parts of London at a settled rate of charge, according to weight and distance. There are numerous receiving offices in every part of the town, and at all the railway stations.

PATENTS.*

The subject of patents is of more than usual importance, at this period when foreign nations are pouring in upon us the results of their invention to compete with the performances of our own inventors. A few words upon this topic may therefore be acceptable. Any person, whether a British subject or a foreigner, may obtain a patent protecting for fourteen years, such inventions as he himself has made, or has derived from foreigners not domiciled in the United Kingdom. If more persons than one have been concerned in an invention, the patent ought to be taken out in their joint names. The inventions for which patents have been granted, may generally be classed under some one of the following heads. 1. Vendible articles, the results of chemical or mechanical processes, such as dyes, vulcanized india-rubber, water-proof cloth, and useful alloys. 2. Machines or improvements in machinery. 3. Processes whether requiring or not special machinery to carry them into effect. A patented process is sometimes entirely new, but much more commonly a part only is new. The simple combination of two known things is patentable, when the result is advantageous; and, indeed, a process

* Communicated by Messrs. J. Henry Johnson, and Co., Patent Agents, 47 Lincoln's Inn Fields.

which differed from one previously known in nothing but the omission of a step, has been decided by a court of law to be patentable. The fact that an invention has been patented abroad does not prevent an inventor from obtaining a patent in the United Kingdom, provided that the particulars of the invention have not been made known here. The business relating to patents is conducted at the office of the Commissioners of Patents in Southampton Buildings, Chancery Lane, where there is a collection of books connected with all departments of invention, to which the public have free access. Prints of specifications (*i.e.*, descriptions of inventions that have been patented) are sold at the same office at a cheap rate; as well as some useful abridgments of specifications grouped under the different heads of invention. The Commissioners have a museum of models and patented machines at South Kensington, which is free to the public. The number of patents annually granted is about 2000.

FOREIGN MONEY.

The following table may be of use to strangers from abroad :—

AMERICA, UNITED STATES OF.

Gold.					£	s.	D.	£	s.	D.
Eagle	10	dollars	.	. from	2	1	0	to 2	1	3
Half Eagle,	5	,,	.	.	1	0	6	to 1	0	7½
Quarter Eagle,	2½	,,	.	.	0	10	3	to 0	10	3½
Silver.										
Dollar	100	cents	.	.	0	4	2	to 0	4	3

AUSTRIA.

Gold.					£	s.	D.	£	s.	D.
Sovereign .	.	.	.	.	0	13	6	to 0	13	10
Ducat	.	.	.	.	0	9	2	to 0	9	4
Silver.										
Crown	2	florins	.	.	0	3	11	to 0	4	0
Florin	60	kreuzers	.	.	0	1	11	to 0	2	0
Zwanziger	20	,,	.		0	0	7½	to 0	0	8

FRANCE.

Gold.				£	s.	D.	£	s.	D.
Napoleon	20	francs	.	0	15	10	to 0	16	0
Silver.									
5 franc piece,	100	sous	.	.	0	3	11	to 0	4	0
1 franc	20	,,	.	.	0	0	9¼	to 0	0	9½

GERMAN STATES.

Gold.	£	s.	D.	£	s.	D.
Louis d'or	0	16	2	to 0	16	4
10 Gulden piece	0	16	7	to 0	16	10
Ducat	0	9	3	to 0	9	4
Silver.						
Crown dollar	0	4	4	to 0	4	6
Convention dollar . . .	0	3	11	to 0	4	0
Florin 60 kreuzers . .	0	1	7¼	to 0	1	8

PORTUGAL.

Gold.				£	s.	D.
Moeda, moidore, 4800 reis . .			...	1	1	0½
Silver.						
Milrei or dollar, 1000 reis . .			...	0	4	4½
Crusado novo, dollar, 480 reis .			...	0	2	1¼
Testao, 100 reis			...	0	0	5¼

PRUSSIA.

Gold.				£	s.	D.
Frederic d'or	0	16	7	to 0	17	3
Silver.						
Thaler, 30 silber groschen . .	0	2	11	to 0	3	0
1 silber groschen . . .	0	0	1	to 0	0	1¼

RUSSIA.

Gold.				£	s.	D.
Half Imperial	0	16	2	to 0	16	3
Ducat	0	9	2	to 0	9	3
Silver.						
Rouble, 100 kopecks . . .	0	3	0	to 0	3	1

SPAIN.

Gold.				£	s.	D.
Doubloon, 16 dollars . . .	3	7	0	to 3	7	6
Pistole, 4 „ . .	0	16	6	to 0	16	9
Silver.						
Dollar or piastre, 20 reals . .	0	4	2	to 0	4	3
Peseta			..	0	0	10½

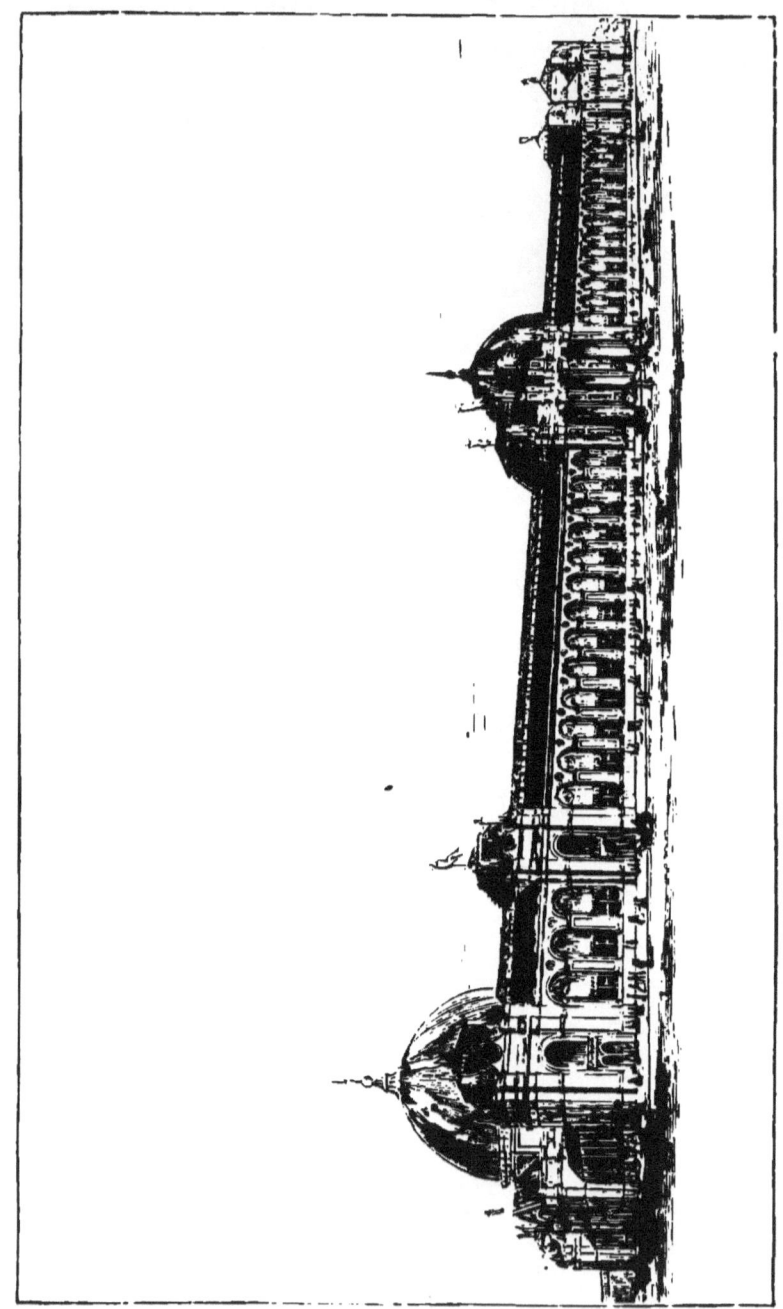

INTERNATIONAL EXHIBITION BUILDING.

CHAPTER THE THIRD.

THE INTERNATIONAL EXHIBITION BUILDINGS OF 1862.

THE International Exhibition Buildings of 1862 are situate at South Kensington in immediate proximity to the Royal Horticultural Gardens, and at a distance of 4 miles and 50 yards from the General Post Office. The principal front is in Cromwell Road, and here, in the centre of the south side, is the grand entrance. The buildings extend from Exhibition Road on the east to Prince Albert's Road on the west, from each of which there is an entrance. They cover 24 acres of ground, and have been designed not only for the International Exhibition of 1862, but with the view of serving for future exhibitions, if the funds for their purchase should be forthcoming. In the first instance they will be made simply to serve the main object of utility; their architectural decoration will be left to the future, as the funds required shall be supplied. It has been calculated that the cubical contents of the entire structure are equal to 73 millions of feet. The arcades of the south front of the building are to be decorated with pictures in mosaic, the tints employed being mainly dull reds, pale buffs, browns, and grays. All the colours will be quiet, avoiding much chromatic display. The figures will be on a large scale, representing the employments of those engaged in commerce, manufactures, trade, and labour. Maclise will exemplify masonry; Mulready, the fine arts; Hook, the labours of fishermen; Millais, navigation; and so on. The site belongs to the Commissioners for the Exhibition of 1851, who purchased a large piece of ground with the surplus funds of that exhibition.

The Commissioners have issued the following regulations as to admission :—

1. The Exhibition will open on Thursday the 1st of May, and will be open daily (Sundays excepted) during such hours as the Commissioners shall, from time to time, appoint.

2. The Royal Horticultural Society having arranged a new entrance to their gardens from Kensington Road, the Commissioners have agreed with the council

of the society to establish an entrance to the Exhibition from the gardens, and to issue a joint ticket giving the owner the privilege of admission both to the gardens and to the Exhibition on all occasions when they are open to visitors, including the flower shows and fêtes held in the gardens, up to the 18th of October 1862.

3. There will be four principal entrances for visitors :—1. From the Horticultural gardens, for the owners of the joint tickets, fellows of the society, and other visitors to the gardens.—2. In Cromwell Road.—3. In Prince Albert's Road.—4. In Exhibition Road.

4. The regulations necessary for preventing obstructions and danger at the several entrances will be issued prior to the opening.

5. Admittance to the Exhibition will be given only to the owners of season tickets and to visitors paying at the doors.

SEASON TICKETS.

6. There will be two classes of season tickets. The first, £3, 3s., will entitle the owner to admission to the opening and all other ceremonials, as well as at all times when the building is open to the public. The second, price £5, 5s., will confer the same privileges of admission to the Exhibition, and will further entitle the owner to admission to the gardens of the Royal Horticultural Society at South Kensington and Chiswick (including the flower shows and fêtes at these gardens) during the continuance of the Exhibition.

PRICES OF ADMISSION.

7. On the 1st of May, on the occasion of the opening ceremonial, the admissions will be restricted to the owners of season tickets.

8. On the 2d and 3d of May the price of admission will be £1 for each person ; and the Commissioners reserve the power of appointing three other days, when the same charge will be made.

9. From the 5th to the 17th of May, 5s.

10. From the 19th to the 31st of May, 2s. 6d., except on one day in each week, when the charge will be 5s.

11. After the 31st of May the price of admission on four days in each week will be 1s.

SALE OF SEASON TICKETS.

12. Season tickets are now for sale between the hours of 10 and 5 daily, at the offices of her Majesty's Commissioners, 454 West Strand, London, W.C.

13. Applications through the post (stating Christian name and surname) must be addressed to the secretary, and must be accompanied by post-office orders, payable to Mr J. J. Mayo, at the Post-office, Charing Cross.

14. No checks or country notes will be received.

15. Cases for preserving the season tickets may be obtained at the office for 1s. each.   F. R. SANDFORD, Secretary.

THE BUILDINGS.

The buildings may be considered, with reference to the chief objects which have been kept in view in planning them, viz :—

I. Galleries for Pictures.

II. Courts and Galleries for the exhibition of Works of Industry.

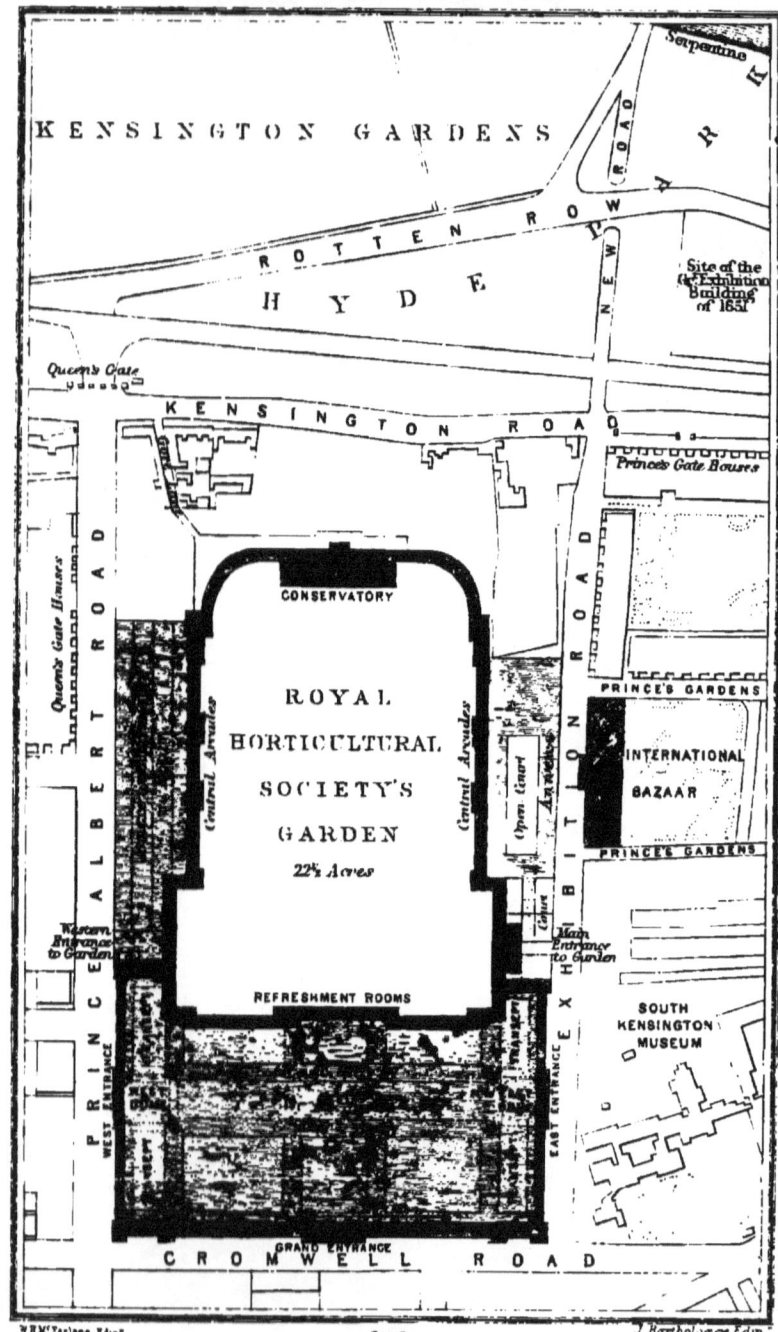

INTERNATIONAL EXHIBITION BUILDINGS
& ROYAL HORTICULTURAL SOCIETY'S GARDEN.

III. Platforms and wide passages for Ceremonials and Processions.

IV. Galleries for Refreshments.

V. The two Annexes of woodwork.

I. *The Picture Galleries*, stored with modern works of art, contributed by all nations.—This part of the building is of brickwork, three feet thick, and its upper storey forms the principal gallery, extending uninterruptedly along the Cromwell Road for the whole length of the edifice. It is 1150 feet long, 50 feet wide, and 50 feet above the ground floor. The lighting is on the principle adopted with so much success for the picture galleries at the South Kensington Museum, complete ventilation, so important in galleries of this kind, being provided for. At each end there is another picture gallery, at right angles to the grand gallery. Each of these is 600 feet long, 25 feet wide, and 30 feet high. The walls are covered with coloured paper, and they will afford about 72,000 square feet of hanging space, one half of which will be retained for our own pictures, the other half handed over to foreign artists. The grand effect of the principal gallery, so long, so spacious, filled with works of art, the choicest of our own and other nations, must be seen to be appreciated. For particulars as to the contents we must refer to the authorized catalogue.

II. *Exhibition of Works of Industry.*—Entering the Industrial part of the building from the Cromwell Road, the visitor passes under the centre of the principal picture gallery. The piers at the entrance are 14 feet wide and 7 feet thick. Crossing a vestibule and hall 150 feet long and 110 feet wide, he is conducted at once to the main body of the building. This portion is divided longitudinally by a nave 800 feet long, 85 feet wide, and 100 feet high, terminated at each end by a great dome. It is formed of pairs of columns, one circular, the other square, each 12 inches across, coupled together. These pairs of columns are placed 25 feet apart, the circular shafts carrying the roof girders, the square shafts those of the galleries, and the latter serve as pipes for the conveyance of water from the roof. Right and left of the nave are two side aisles, formed of iron columns, 25 feet apart. On the side next the Horticultural Society's grounds, and beyond the 25-feet side aisles, there are two other aisles, formed of a fourth row of columns and the garden party wall. On the opposite side of the building, and beyond the two side aisles, there is a third aisle, which fills up the space up to the walls of the picture gallery. At each end of the nave there is a transept, equalling it in width and height, but having a length of only about 630 feet. Both nave and transepts are lighted on both sides by clerestory windows upwards of 25 feet long. On the north side of the nave are two courts, each 250 feet by 86 feet ; and a central court, 150 feet by 86 feet. On the south of the nave there are also three courts, but of larger dimensions, the central court being 150 feet square, and the two others 250 feet by 200. All these courts are 50 feet high, and are lighted by glass roofs. The upper galleries, of which there is more than a mile and a half in length, inclose the courts, and extend along the sides of the nave and picture galleries. They are supported on cast-iron columns and girders, are 25 feet above the ground-floor, and are 50 feet wide, with the exception of those that run along the sides of the picture galleries, these being 25 feet wide. As to the chromatic decoration of the interior, it may be stated that many experiments were tried before it was decided to apply the colours we now see. The angular columns have been painted a bronze green, with a hue of buff along each angle. The round columns are also bronze green, and their capitals are alternately red and blue, with gilt mouldings. The bands at the middle of these columns are likewise red and blue alternately. Bronze green has been applied to the ornamental iron work along the front of the galleries. The roof of the nave is gray. The arching girders or spanners are alternately red and blue, with a buff line on the edges. Upon each of these spanners has been painted the name of some country.

And now as to the most striking feature of the whole structure—the great domes. We have already stated that there is one at each end of the nave. Each has a diameter of 160 feet, and a height of 250 feet. They exceed the height of the monument by 48 feet, and are the largest that have ever been erected, either in ancient or modern times. The dome of St. Paul's is only 112 feet in diameter, and 215 feet high, whilst the great dome of St. Peter's at Rome has a diameter two feet less than these, with a height of 263 feet. Each dome springs from the intersection of the nave and a transept, and is supported by eight hollow cylindrical columns, two feet in diameter, cast in five pieces, and bolted one piece on another by internal flanges. This work was done by a boy who was sent down the inside of each piece, as it was mounted in its place. On the outside, the domes are surmounted by a finial, composed of a gilt ball, seven feet in diameter, and a gilt spike. The columns are held in their places by an iron collar encircling their tops, from which spring the ribs of the dome, which is of glass, and provided with an outer and an inner gallery. To judge of the immense size of the domes, they must be surveyed from a distance.

The level of the floor of the main building is about five feet below the level of the road; but the visitor, instead of descending at once into the building from the side entrances, has to ascend two steps to a platform under each dome, from which the descent into the building is effected by three flights of steps, 80 feet wide. By this arrangement, a striking view of the entire nave is obtained on entering from either end.

So much more space was demanded by exhibitors than had been anticipated, that after the planning and partial execution of the brick and iron buildings, it was decided to erect an additional wooden structure or annex on the east side, along Exhibition Road, for the reception of mining products and minerals, agricultural machinery, chemicals, animal and vegetable products, etc.

III. From the general sketch of the arrangement of the interior already given, it will have been seen that the nave, transepts, and raised platforms beneath the domes, afford ample space, and splendid vistas for ceremonials and processions.

IV. The space allotted for the distribution of refreshments, viz., about 120,000 square feet, must be considered ample. Refreshments are to be obtained on the ground floor of the building, on the north side, next the gardens of the Horticultural Society; also on the first floor in two spacious galleries, each 160 feet long, besides other smaller apartments. The grand central dining saloon will be on the second floor. Both these floors command views of the gardens, and facing the north they will be cool. The façade will be of a highly ornamental character. Provisions are also supplied in the annex, and light refreshments in various parts of the building. As to the existing arrangements in regard to refreshments, and the prices to be charged, the visitor will examine the notices in various languages distributed about the building.

V. *The Western Annex or Machinery Department* is of a temporary character. It is placed alongside Prince Albert's road, and is 915 feet long, divided partly into three, and partly into four avenues of 50 feet wide, with an arched roof of 25 feet radius. The ribs of the roof spring from a height of 10 feet from the ground, from the lateral columns. It is entirely made of framed timber-work, without any joining. Looking at its highly effective appearance, the simplicity of its construction, and the small quantity of material employed, it does very great credit to the designer, Captain Fowke, who has furnished the designs for the whole of the buildings, wood, brick, and iron. The roof, which is on the ridge and furrow plan, is of wood-work and glass, in about equal proportions, the whole of the light coming from above. The wooden part of the roof is covered with felt, the roofs of the nave and transepts being covered with zinc upon felt. At the north end of the annex is placed the steam-engine, which drives the machinery in motion. It has six furnaces, with a chimney 100 feet high and 12 feet in diameter, and is capable of working up to 300 horse-power, at a pressure of 30 pounds per square inch.

The Cellars.—The contractors for the refreshment department pressed so strongly upon the commissioners the desirableness of cellars for storing beer and other articles, that it was determined, when the rest of the edifice was nearly finished, to excavate a capacious depository for this purpose. Accordingly, three cellars have been constructed at a cost of nearly £5000; one under the eastern portion of the refreshment arcade, the others under the eastern and western annexes.

The rapidity with which the works were executed is not the least of the wonders connected with this wonderful edifice. A commencement was not made until the middle of April 1860. To those who paid visits to the place after that date, the progress seemed marvellous. The first of the dome columns was put up on the 26th of August; and shortly after that time, the huge mass of brickwork forming the picture galleries had been completed. From 800 to 900 men were at first employed upon the works, but afterwards the force was increased to 2600 men. That so much should have been accomplished, and in so short a time, certainly exhibits the mechanical contrivances of the age in a striking light. The contractors were Mr. Kelk, and Messrs. Charles and Thomas Lucas, brothers, distinct firms, who became partners for these works. The contract was in this form: a sum of £200,000 is to be paid absolutely to the contractors for the use and waste of the buildings, the whole of which, in case of their receiving no further payment, will revert to them; in the event of the receipts exceeding £400,000, they are to be entitled to the further receipts until they have obtained an additional sum of £100,000; in case this sum shall be received by them, then a portion of the central picture gallery becomes the property of the Society of Arts. Lastly, the contractors are bound to sell all their remaining rights over the buildings for a further sum of £130,000, which sum it is hoped may be obtained from the receipts of the Exhibition. The sum and substance of the contract is that for a sum of £430,000, the buildings of brick and iron can be obtained for future Exhibitions, and it is to be hoped that the pecuniary success of the Exhibition will be such as to allow of this being done. If the worst should ensue, £200,000 will be paid to the contractors for the use of the buildings, which, at the termination of the Exhibition, they will demolish, and make what use they can of the materials. Those materials consist of about 5200 tons of iron, out of which have been formed nearly 1000 columns, and more than 1100 girders; besides pipes, railings, brackets, etc.; of about 17,000 loads of timber, the greater part cut up into 630 miles of planking; and of more than ten millions of bricks. Amongst the other materials may be mentioned 22,000 tons of mortar, 600 tons of paint, 500 tons of glass, 50 tons of putty, and 600,000 square feet of felt for the roofs. The iron castings were executed at the Stavely Iron Works, Derbyshire; the wrought-iron work was supplied by the Thames Iron Company, the builders of the " Warrior" iron-plated frigate; the timber-work was executed at the yards of the contractors; and the bricks were supplied by Messrs. Smeed of Sittingbourne, Kent. The painting of the interior was executed by Mr. Crace.

In the construction of this immense edifice, every ingenious contrivance that could be thought of was adopted. A steam-engine was placed in the middle of the works, from which ropes, coiling on and off a barrel, were conducted to all parts of the building. By its aid, iron columns which would have taken fifteen men a quarter of an hour to elevate through fifty feet, were lifted by means of a hoist in two minutes, two men only attending to the engine. In this way, 75 columns and girders were hoisted and fixed in one day. Heavy loads could, by the same contrivance, be drawn along the tramways which intersected

E

the ground, in all directions to the extent of two miles. These tramways were also of great use in enabling smaller loads to be carried along them by human labour. A couple of men could move a truck with a load of four or five tons, faster than six or eight horses could transport it in a waggon. Then there was a great travelling scaffold mounted on twelve wheels, and running on rails the whole length of the central nave. This could be easily moved by four men with levers.

As to the arrangement of the contents of the Exhibition, we may state generally that in the north-eastern transept are placed the products of our colonies, in the galleries above, the fabrics, jewels, etc., of India. Hardware and steel are exhibited in the south-eastern court, with separate courts for Sheffield, Birmingham, and Wolverhampton. Pottery, porcelain, glass, precious metals, musical instruments, articles connected with engineering, and naval architecture, are also in this locality. The north-eastern court is chiefly occupied by furniture. Carriages stand on the gallery under the eastern picture gallery. In the southern galleries, textile fabrics are shewn. In the northern galleries will be seen philosophical and surgical instruments, watches, stationery, and fancy goods.

Many people will come again and again to examine this marvellous accumulation of objects and the vast building in which they are lodged; but to those who can only afford time for one visit we should recommend the following route :—Enter under one of the domes and walk up the nave, at each side of which are placed the most interesting articles. Upon arriving at the opposite end turn into the transept and thence ascend to the picture gallery, the finest in Europe ; then descend into the two chief courts, French and English, whence go to the second transept and the remaining courts. Ascend to the refreshment rooms and complete the day's work with an examination of the two annexes.

The management of the present Exhibition has been intrusted to five persons, viz., Earl Granville, the Duke of Buckingham, Thomas Baring, Esq., Sir C. W. Dilke, Bart., and Thomas Fairbairn, Esq., who are styled " The Commissioners for the Exhibition of 1862," and who, as such, have been incorporated by Royal Charter. In order to protect these commissioners from possible loss, about a thousand persons have voluntarily come forward and bound themselves to produce a sum not far short of

£450,000 in case it should be needed. It is not at all likely, however, that one penny will be called for, as we shall all be grievously disappointed if a large surplus beyond the expenses is not paid over to the commissioners. The articles exhibited have been divided into four sections, each with a number of classes ; and gentlemen specially acquainted with the subject-matter of these classes have been appointed committees for the purpose of examining the articles and reporting upon the most meritorious. Foreign nations have come to measure their strength with others, and to shew us articles that we are unable to produce. Foreign powers have named commissioners of their own to co-operate with our authorities, and to look after the interests of their exhibitors. Our own colonies have hastened to send us specimens of their products, and have named their own commissioners.

THE INTERNATIONAL BAZAAR.

Close by the International Exhibition is a large temporary building, which will not be without its attractions for visitors. Its object is to afford those who were not fortunate enough to obtain space in the larger building an opportunity of exhibiting and selling articles for the most part of a portable character, the selling of articles in the larger Exhibition not being permitted. The bazaar is in the Exhibition-road, almost directly opposite the entrance to the Horticultural Gardens. The building was designed by M. Eugene Delessert, the eminent decorator to the Emperor of the French. It is 400 feet in length, 100 feet wide, and 56 feet in height. The ground plan consists of a large central hall and two smaller ones. There are galleries running round the building 24 feet wide, and beneath them are courts 24 feet in width, well lighted from all sides. This building having been commenced only on the 5th of March, shews a rapidity of construction almost incredible, were not the facts there to speak for themselves. There is no charge for admission ; and among the other attractions provided are Strauss's, and other bands of music, which perform daily. The building has been constructed entirely at the expense of Mr.

Freater, the owner of the estate upon which it is situated. The supplementary exhibition, from designs of Sir Joseph Paxton, has been abandoned. It was to have been erected on some land on the west side of the Exhibition building, whereas the present bazaar is at the east side.

BUCKINGHAM PALACE.

CHAPTER THE FOURTH.

Buckingham Palace—St. James' Palace—Marlborough House—Whitehall—Kensington Palace.

THE palaces belonging to the Crown in London are—Buckingham Palace, where the Queen resides ; St. James', where Court drawing-rooms, levees, etc., take place ; Kensington Palace, which has been for some time unoccupied ; a fragment of the large palace which formerly stood at Whitehall, namely, the Chapel Royal, built for a banquetting house ; and Marlborough House, Pall Mall, the residence of the Prince of Wales.

BUCKINGHAM PALACE, St James' Park.—On this site stood a house, built in 1703 in the Dutch style by Sheffield Duke of Buckingham. George III. purchased it in 1761 for £21,000, and shortly afterwards removed there from St. James'. All their children, except the Prince of Wales, were born in that plain brick mansion, where the splendid library was formed which is now at the British Museum. George III. passed away, but the house, " dull, dowdy, and decent," stood on until 1825, when, by direction of his successor, Nash undertook to reconstruct it, but adhering to the old site and dimensions. It is much to be regretted that an entirely new palace was not built by some architect of skill and taste. Neither George IV. nor his brother William IV. lived in it, but it was open to the visits of the public in 1831. Mr. Blore had previously raised the building a storey. In July 1837, Queen Victoria took possession of the palace, and has continued to reside there when in London ever since. The private apartments extend along the north front. The palace having become too small for the Queen's increasing family, and affording no accommodation for the reception of foreign sovereigns when visiting Her Majesty, a large addition, in the shape of an east wing, was commenced in 1846 from Mr. Blore's designs. This wing is 360 feet long and 77 feet high, and stands 70 feet in advance of the other wings. It cost £150,000. In 1851 the marble arch which stood on the east side of the palace, and formed its entrance gate, was removed to Hyde Park, and a state ball-room was afterwards erected on the south side. This ball-room is 111 feet long by 60 wide. Here are hung Vandyck's portraits of Charles I. and his queen, and portraits of Queen Victoria and her husband. The adjoining supper room is 76 feet by 60. In the sculpture gallery are busts of the royal family and eminent statesmen. The library contains a valuable collection of books made by the present sovereign, for George III.'s valuable collection is now in the British Museum. The grand staircase is of marble, the ceiling ornamented with frescoes by Townsend. Tickets of admission to this hall to see the Queen pass in state on her way to open, prorogue, or dissolve Parliament, are issued by the Lord Chamberlain. The Green Drawing Room is in the middle of the east front, and opens on the upper portico. The Throne Room, 64 feet long, is gorgeously decorated with crimson satin, and gilding. The marble frieze, representing the wars of the Roses, was designed by Stothard—his last great design—and sculptured by Baily. In a recess is placed the royal throne, and here the Queen receives addresses, surrounded by her ministers and officers of state. Privy Councils are also held in this room.

The Picture Gallery, 180 feet long by 26 wide, is in the centre of the palace, and runs from north to south, forming a corridor, opening at each side into suites of apartments. The lighting is said not to be well contrived, and to be insufficient. Here are placed about 200 pictures, principally collected by George IV., whose taste led him to the selection of Dutch and Flemish paintings. He began to collect in 1802, and was assisted by Sir Charles Long, afterwards Lord Farnborough. Sir Francis Baring's very select gallery was purchased for £24,000, although it is said to have been valued at £80,000. " On the whole (says Mrs. Jameson), this is certainly the finest gallery of this class of works in England." Of Berghem there are six examples :— Cuyp 9, G. Douw 8, Karel du Jardin 5, de Hooghe 2, G. Metzu 6, Franz Mieris 4, Wilhelm Mieris 3, Adrian Ostade 9, Isaac Ostade 2, Paul Potter 4, Rembrandt 7, Rubens 7, Jan Steen 6, David Teniers 14, Terburg 2, Vandyck 4, Adrian van der Velde

7, W. van der Velde 4, Philip Wouvermans 9, Watteau 5. Here is also Wilkie's Blind Man's Buff. To see the pictures, an order must be obtained from the Lord Chamberlain when the Queen is not at the palace.

In the gardens, which are about 40 acres in extent, is a pavilion, the centre room of which is adorned with eight frescoes by eight painters, the subjects taken from Milton's Comus. Other rooms are beautifully embellished with paintings. The chapel where the court attends divine service is in the garden ; it was formerly a conservatory.

The Queen's stables or mews are in Queen's Row, at the rear of the palace, from which they are concealed by a high mound. Here are the State Coach (designed by Sir. W. Chambers in 1762, painted by Cipriani, and built at a cost of £7600), and the ordinary carriages, of which there are houses for forty ; a room for state harness ; a riding house ; and stables for the royal stud. To see the mews an order must be obtained from the Master of the Horse. There are other royal mews in Princes Street, Westminster, where the Speaker's state carriage, and the carriages and horses of other official persons are kept. The term " mews," now generally applied to a stable-yard in London, arose from the fact of some royal stables having been built upon the place where the king's hawks had been kept.

St. James' Palace, Pall Mall, at the foot of St. James' Street, stands on the site of a lepers' hospital, dedicated to that saint. Henry VIII. obtained the hospital in exchange for some land, and having pulled it down, he erected a " faire mansion," and made a park out of the meadows round about. Holbein is thought to have designed the house. The gate-house and turrets facing St. James' Street belong to the original structure. Here Mary died ; here Charles II., his nephew the old Pretender, and George IV. were born. Queen Anne, the four Georges, and William IV. resided in the palace, which has had many additions made to it since Henry VIII.'s time. In 1814 the Emperor of Russia, King of Prussia, and Marshal Blücher, were lodged in the palace. Queen Victoria only holds drawing-rooms and levees here, having always used Buckingham Palace as her residence. Some members of the royal family have apartments here ; and part of the palace is used for the transaction of the business of the great officers of state.

Passing through the gate-way we enter the quadrangle, called the Colour Court, from the colours of the household regiment on duty being placed in it. The band plays for a short time at eleven o'clock daily. The Ambassadors' Court is to the west, and beyond it is Stable Yard, where stands Stafford House, the Duke of Sutherland's residence. The State Rooms are in the south front, looking across the gardens into the park. They contain a few pictures, chiefly portraits. In the Chapel Royal divine service is performed at eight A.M. and twelve on Sundays by the gentlemen of the choir, and ten boy choristers. An admission fee of two shillings is charged. Several of the nobility have seats ; the late Duke of Wellington regularly attended the early service. The Queen no longer comes here. Charles I. attended service in this chapel on the morning of his execution, and walked hence through the park to Whitehall guarded by soldiers. Many royal marriages have been celebrated in this chapel, including that of the Queen and Prince Albert.

With regard to presentations at Court, information may be obtained at the offices of the Lord Chamberlain in St. James' Palace, or of the Lord Steward at Buckingham Palace. The carriages freighted with beautiful and richly dressed women going to a drawing room, form one of the sights of London. On such occasions the Yeomen of the Guard, a body first instituted by Henry VII., line the Guard Chamber, carrying partisans, and dressed as they were in the time of Charles II. The Gentlemen-at-Arms, another body that comes out on these days, wear a uniform of scarlet and gold, and carry small battle-axes, covered with crimson velvet. This body was first instituted by Henry VIII. A nobleman, with the title of captain, is at the head of each body, and these officers are usually changed when the ministry is changed.

MARLBOROUGH HOUSE, the town residence of the Prince of Wales, stands at the west end of Pall Mall, next to St. James' Palace. The garden front is cheerful, that towards Pall Mall is gloomy, and much concealed from public view by a wall. The house was built in 1710 for the first Duke of Marlborough, from Wren's designs. The duke and his duchess both died here. It was bought in 1817 for the Princess Charlotte and her husband, Prince Leopold. The latter lived in it for some years. After the death of William IV. his widow resided here. A new portico has been added, and other improvements have been made, to make it a fit residence for the young Prince, on whom the eyes of the nation have been anxiously directed since the untimely death of his lamented father.

WHITEHALL PALACE has altogether disappeared, saving the Banqueting-House, to be described presently. This locality had been previously called York Place, from the residence of the Archbishops of York, which stood here. Cardinal Wolsey lived here in splendour until his fall, when the palace was taken from him by Henry VIII., and its name altered, as Shakspere tells us—

> You must no more call it York Place—that is past;
> For since the Cardinal fell, that title's lost,
> Tis now the King's, and called WHITEHALL.

Henry VIII. and Anne Boleyn were married and crowned here. The King made large additions, and in fact built a large palace. Holbein, when under the King's patronage, resided here, and designed a great gate-house. Henry died, and his eight successors resided at this palace. In the King's bed-chamber Guy Fawkes was examined, and when James was in Scotland Lord Bacon lived in the palace. It was during this reign that several masques, composed by Inigo Jones and Ben Jonson, were acted at Whitehall. Milton has alluded to the "quaint emblems and devices from the old pageantry of some Twelfth-night's entertainment at Whitehall." The architect designed a magnificent palace to cover 24 acres, which, if completed, would have been the glory of the metropolis; but only the existing banquetting-house was erected, and, fragment as it is, this building is a master-piece in the Palladian style. Rubens was commissioned by Charles I. to paint pictures representing the apotheosis of his father for the ceiling. Here was brought together that splendid collection of 460 pictures, which, after the King's death, was so lamentably dispersed. Charles' execution took place in front of the banquetting-house, and he was led to the scaffold out of one of the windows. Cromwell lived and died at Whitehall, where Milton served him as Latin secretary. Here Charles II. revelled, and James II. confessed. Then came the Revolution, and the King left the palace, first secretly, and then in his state barge. In 1691 a fire consumed the greater part of the palace, and six years afterwards the rest (except the banquetting-house) was destroyed by a like cause. Various grants were made of portions of the site, which thenceforth became private property.

The Banquetting-House, 111 feet long by 55½ feet deep and 55½ feet high, was completed in 1622. It is of Portland stone, and cost £14,940. Rubens' paintings on canvas, for which he was paid £3000, are still on the ceiling, although the room was converted into a royal chapel by George I., and again altered in George IV.'s reign by Sir R. Smirke. Here one of the Queen's chaplains preaches every Sunday. The paintings commemorate events in the reign of James I., and in the centre-piece the King is seen on the clouds, with several allegorical figures. A bronze bust of James I., by Le Sueur, is over the door inside. The annual distribution of alms in the Queen's name takes place here on the day before Good Friday, Maunday Thursday. Behind the banquetting-house is a bronze statue of James II., the work of Grinling Gibbons, and executed at the cost of one Tobias Rustat. It was not disturbed at the Revolution, the peaceable character of which was thus indicated.

KENSINGTON PALACE is a plain irregular structure of red brick, standing on the west side of Kensington Gardens. After William III. had purchased the house from the grandson of Finch, Lord Chancellor Nottingham, whose residence it had been, Wren was employed to enlarge it, and the whole upper story was designed by him. William and Mary, Anne and Prince George, all died here. George II. made additions to it, and also died here. Queen Victoria was born here, and here she held her first council. The collection of old German pictures which the late Prince Consort placed in this palace has been removed altogether, or in great part, so that there is nothing to repay the trouble of visiting the interior. On the old Kitchen Garden have been erected some spacious dwelling-houses, known as Palace Gardens. These are amongst the best private residences in London.

THE TOWER.

CHAPTER THE FIFTH.

THE TOWER OF LONDON.

THE collection of buildings, various in aspect, age, and application, which bears the designation of the Tower of London, has a somewhat elevated position on the northern bank of the Thames, a little beyond the old city walls. The shape of the ground, which measures twelve acres and five roods, is an irregular square. It is encircled by a moat, now drained of its water, and then a battlemented wall, the outer ballium, is seen, with towers at intervals. Within this is a similar line of circumvallation, the inner ballium, with towers, and various buildings interspersed. In the middle of the enclosed space rises high above everything else the great square White Tower, the keep of the old fortress ; and scattered about this, the inner ward, are the chapel, the jewel-house, barracks, ordnance stores-houses, etc. Such of these as are shewn to the public we will proceed to describe ; but there are many interesting objects from which they are excluded, although we are not aware of any good reason why this should be so.

To this famous fortress tradition has assigned a very early date, but written records do not go further back than the time of William the Conqueror, who employed Bishop Gundulph to erect what is now known as the Keep or White Tower about 1078. Succeeding sovereigns enlarged or strengthened the place, and Stephen kept his court here in 1140 ; King John also at a later period. The moat was made about 1190 by Bishop Longchamp the regent. Edward II.'s eldest daughter was born here, and was known as Joan of the Tower. David king of Scotland, John king of France, and Philip his son, were imprisoned in this for-

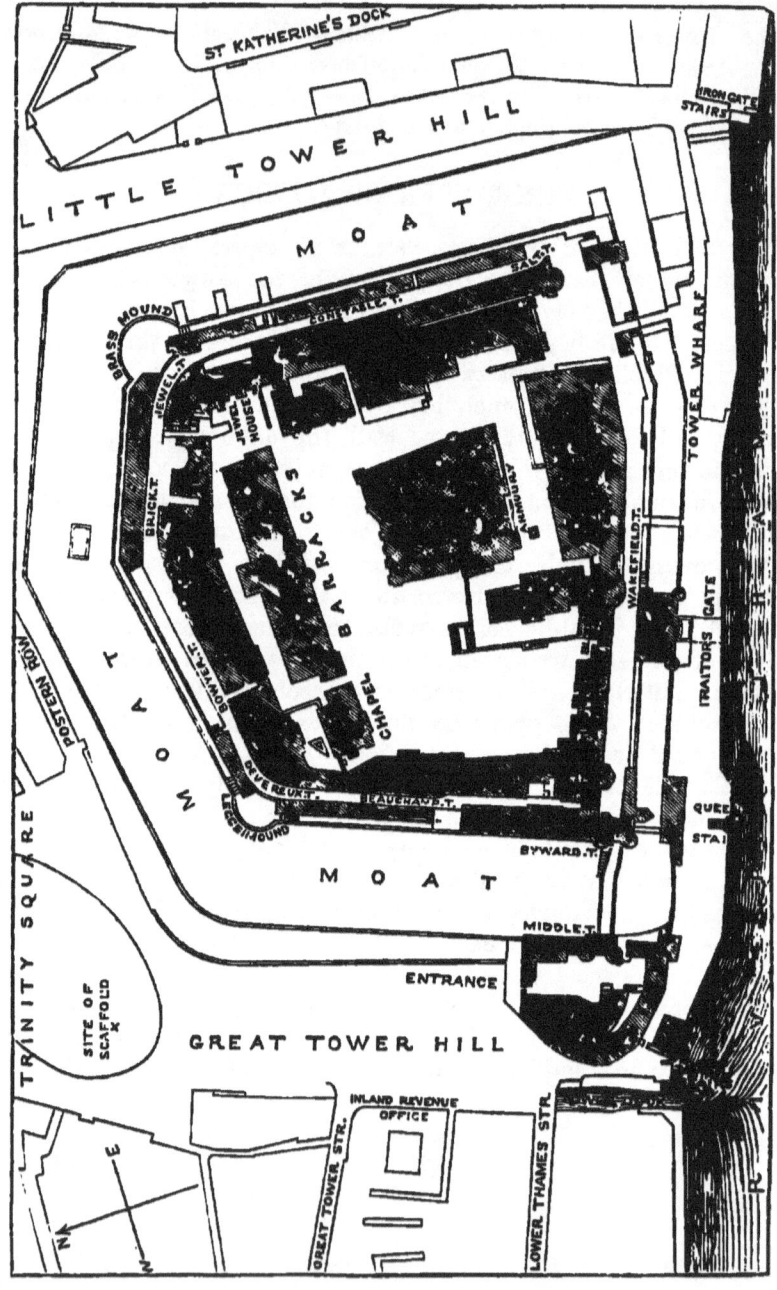

tress by Edward III. Richard II. took refuge here with his court and nobles to the number of 600 persons at the time of Wat Tyler's insurrection. In 1399 whilst being imprisoned here he was deposed. Edward IV. kept splendid court in the Tower. Henry VI., twice a prisoner here, died in the fortress in 1471. The tradition that George Duke of Clarence was drowned in the Tower in a butt of malmsey is well known ; and equally well known is the story of the two princes, Edward V. and his brother, murdered here at the wish of the usurper Richard, whose deposer and successor, Henry VII. often made the Tower his residence, and here held a great tournament in 1501, two years before the death of his queen, who expired here. His son received here in state all his wives before his marriages, and two of them, Anne Boleyn and Catharine Howard, were beheaded where they had seen so much splendour. The youthful Edward VI. held his court here before he was crowned. The Protector Somerset was imprisoned here before he was beheaded on Tower Hill. Lady Jane Grey and her husband suffered the same punishment within the precincts of the Tower. The princess (afterwards queen) Elizabeth having been suspected of abetting Sir Thomas Wyatt's schemes was sent to the Tower, and as she entered traitor's gate she exclaimed, " Here landeth as true a subject, being a prisoner, as ever landed at these stairs ; and before thee, O God, I speak it." The pedant James frequently amused himself with witnessing the combats of the wild beasts then kept in the Tower. He was the last of our sovereigns who resided here, and the palace itself having become ruinous, was pulled down 150 years ago. It occupied the south-eastern portion of the inner ward.

It may be interesting to recount the names of the more distinguished persons who have been confined in this fortress :—Griffin, Prince of Wales, killed in attempting to escape, 1240 ; Baliol, king of Scotland, and some of his nobility, 1296 ; William Wallace, 1305 ; the Knights Templar, 1307 ; Lord Mortimer, Queen Isabella's paramour, 1324 and 1330 ; David Bruce, king of Scotland, and his chieftains, taken prisoners at Neville's Cross, 1347 ; the Governor and twelve citizens of Calais, 1347 ; John, king of France, captured at Poictiers, 1357 ; Duke of Orleans, father of Louis XII., 1415 ; John Fisher, bishop of Rochester, 1534 ; Sir Thomas More, 1534 ; Cromwell, Earl of Essex, 1540 ; Latimer, 1541 ; Duke of Norfolk and his son, the poet, Earl of Surrey, 1547 ; Cranmer, Latimer, and Ridley, 1553 ; Sir Thomas Wyatt, 1554 ; Earl of Southampton, Shakspere's patron, 1562 ; Guy Fawkes and the other conspirators, 1606 ; Sir Thomas Overbury, 1613 ; Countess of Somerset, 1616 ; Sir Walter Raleigh on three occasions ; Lord Bacon, 1622 ; Sir Edward Coke, 1622 ; Felton, Buckingham's assassin, 1628 ; John Seldon, 1628 ; Earl of Strafford, Archbishop Laud, and Bishop Hall, 1641 ; Jeremy Taylor, 1648 ; Sir Wm. Davenant, 1651 ; Villiers, second Duke of Buckingham, 1651 ; Harrington, the author of Oceana, 1661 ; Viscount Stafford (afterwards beheaded), 1678 ; Samuel Pepys, 1679 ; Earl of Shaftesbury, 1681 ; Lord William Russell and Algernon Sidney, 1683 ; James, Duke of Monmouth, 1685 ; Lord Jeffreys, William, the seven bishops, the first Duke of Marlborough, 1692 ; Sir Robert Walpole, 1712 ; Harley, Earl of Oxford, Earl of Derwentwater, and Earl of Nithsdale, 1715 ; Bishop Atterbury, and Lord Orrery, 1722 ; Lords Kilmarnock, Balmerino, and Lovat, 1746 ; Earl Ferrers, 1760 ; John Wilkes, 1762 ; Lord George Gordon, 1780 ; John Horne Tooke, and others, 1794 ; Sir Francis Burdett, 1810 ; Thistlewood, 1820.

It may also be mentioned that Chaucer was appointed clerk of the works in the Tower in Richard II.'s reign, and that he composed his poem, "The Testament of Love," here. Sir Walter Raleigh wrote his "History of the World" in the fortress, and here his son Carew was born. Mrs. Lucy Hutchinson, and the Countess of Bedford, mother of Lord William Russell, were born here. The latter was the daughter of the infamous Countess of Somerset, who was implicated in Sir Thomas Overbury's murder.

Visitors, on entering the gates near the east end of Lower Thames Street, must obtain tickets at the office on the right. For an armoury ticket admitting one person sixpence is charged, and for a ticket to see the Regalia the same sum. A warder takes charge of visitors every half hour, or as soon as a party of 12 has assembled, from half-past ten to four, for six days in the week. The warders, who form a body of 48 men, are usually meritorious soldiers who have seen service, and they are dressed on state occasions in the attire of yeomen of the guard of Henry VIII.'s time. At ordinary times they wear black velvet hats and dark blue tunics. Refreshments are to be obtained in the waitingroom of the ticket-office. This was the site of the building where the lions were kept formerly, one of the attractions of the Tower (hence the phrase " to see the lions "). The last animals were sent to the Zoological Gardens in 1834.

Crossing the moat-bridge, and passing under the Middle Tower, we arrive at *Traitors' Gate*, a square building erected over the moat. Here persons charged with high treason were brought into the Tower, and through it " went Sidney, Russell, Raleigh, Cranmer, More." It now contains a steam-engine employed in the raising of water. Opposite this is the *Bloody Tower*, where it is said the princes were smothered. Raleigh was confined in the room over the Bloody Tower, and this was the scene of his lite- rary labours, of Ben Jonson's visits to him, and of Prince Henry's lessons. Adjoining the Bloody Tower is the *Wakefield Tower*, so called from some of the Yorkists having been imprisoned in it after the battle of Wakefield (1460). After the White Tower, it is the largest Tower. The walls are 13 feet thick. Until lately it was used as a depository for records. Passing through Bloody Tower gateway, we arrive at the base of the White Tower and the entrance to the Horse Armoury, outside of which are several pieces of ancient cannon. Amongst those may be noticed a brass gun of Henry VII.'s time, the earliest brass gun in the collec- tion ; a brass gun and an iron gun obtained from the wreck of the " Royal George ;" two brass guns taken from the Spaniards at Vigo in 1702 by Sir George Rooke ; an iron gun which lay at the bottom of the sea for 300 years in the wreck of the " Mary Rose," Henry VIII.'s ship ; a gun taken from the Chinese in 1842. The pile of building on the south of the space where these cannons are placed belongs to the ordnance office, the head- quarters of which are in Pall Mall.

The *Horse Armoury* is at the south foot of the White Tower, and was completed in 1826. It is 150 feet long and 34 wide, and is filled with specimens of ancient armour, arranged by the late Sir Samuel Meyrick, well known for his researches into the subject, and the author of a critical work on ancient armour. Trophies and emblematic devices composed of weapons are taste- fully arranged on the walls and ceiling. There are many curi- ous pieces of armour and weapons in the vestibules at each end of the gallery ; and in glass cases beneath the windows are de- posited many objects worth notice. Down the centre of the gal- lery is stationed a series of mounted figures in armour, to which various distinguished names have been assigned, although there is no evidence that the armour really belonged to them except in

a few instances.   The series begins with Edward 1. (1272), and
the armour worn by the effigy of this monarch (undoubtedly
dating from his reign) consists of chain mail, the spurs being
prick-spurs.   Henry VI. (1422-61), the back and breastplates of
flexible armour, composed of overlapping plates and moving on
pivots; the sleeves and skirt of chain mail.   Edward IV. (1461-83),
in tournament armour ; the lance is modern, but its guard is ancient
and highly curious.   Richard III.'s time (1483-85), ribbed armour ;
this suit was worn by the late Marquis of Waterford at the Eglin-
ton tournament.   This kind of armour was worn in the wars of the
Roses, and at the battle of Bosworth field.   The helmet is a salade
with ear-guards.   Henry VII. (1485-1509), fluted armour with
globular breastplate, the helmet a burgonet.   The horse armour
is also fluted, and is a complete suit except the flank pieces.   Of
the same period is another suit of fluted globose armour, worn by a
standing figure.   Henry VIII. (1509-46).   This suit was actually
worn by that king.   It is inlaid with gold.   Notice the large
square-toed stirrup shoes.   Next to this is a specimen of an Italian splinted cuirass such as was worn by the banditti at the end
of the 15th century ; and next to this, two figures named Charles
Brandon, Duke of Suffolk, and Edward Clinton, Earl of Lincoln,
with suits resembling that of Henry VIII. Of the same period, is
that of a foot soldier, which has raised figures of polished steel
on a dark ground.   In the middle recess of the southern wall is
another equestrian figure of Henry VIII. wearing a suit of very
curious armour of German make, which is supposed to have been
presented to that monarch, on his marriage with Katherine of
Arragon, by the Emperor Maximilian.   The rose and pomegranate badges of the king and queen appear as ornaments.   The
king's badges, the Portcullis, the Fleur-de-lys, and St. George and
the Dragon, are also seen, as well as the initials of the royal pair
united by a lover's knot. Edward VI. (1552), russet armour inlaid
with gold, and ornamented with arabesque designs ; the helmet
a burgonet.   Notice the badges of Burgundy and Granada, which
have led to the conjecture that the armour belonged to the young
Duke of Burgundy, afterwards king of Spain, and father of the
Emperor Charles V.   Francis Hastings, Earl of Hastings, time of
Queen Mary (1555) ; the armour very heavy.   Robert Dudley,
Earl of Leicester, Queen Elizabeth's courtier (1560).   On the
chanfron of the horse's head is the family badge of the Dudleys,
the bear and ragged staff, and the initials R. D. are engraved on

the knee-guard, so that no doubt can be entertained that this suit was actually worn by the Earl. Sir Henry Lee, Queen Elizabeth's master of the ceremonies (1570), formerly shewn as the armour of William the Conqueror! Robert Devereux, Earl of Essex, same period, richly inlaid and gilt. This was worn by the royal champion at the coronation of George II. James I. (1605), tilting armour. Of the same period are the suits assigned to Sir Horace Vere and Thomas Earl of Arundel, both figures armed with a mace. Henry Prince of Wales (1612), son of James I., a suit made for the prince, gilt, and engraved with battle designs. Prince Charles, afterwards Charles I., on foot. This gilt and chased suit was made for the prince; it was laid on the coffin of the first Duke of Marlborough on the occasion of his interment in Westminster Abbey. George Villiers, Duke of Buckingham; plate armour, with the wheel lock petronel. Wentworth, Earl of Strafford (1640). George Monk, Duke of Albemarle (1660), the helmet a burgonet. James II. (1685), said to be his own armour. In this gallery is to be seen a suit of ancient Greek armour in good preservation found in a tomb at Cumæ, a bronze Etruscan helmet, suit of Asiatic armour thought to be of the time of the crusades—and therefore the oldest armour here; Chinese military dresses; an ivory warder's horn of German workmanship; some small cannon presented by the brassfounders of London to Charles II. when a boy; these are placed under the military trophy at the east end of the gallery.

Ascending a flight of stairs, we enter a room recently added to that called Queen Elizabeth's Armoury. In the eastern compartment of this room notice the military trophy composed of cannon taken at Waterloo, two kettle-drums taken at Blenheim, and a collection of arms, comprising an example of every kind of weapon in the tower. Notice also very fine suits of armour, a knight in fluted armour of Henry VII.'s time, a suit of German black armour, a fluted and engraved suit of Henry VIII.'s time, a complete suit of the early part of Queen Elizabeth's reign. In a glass case is the cloak upon which General Wolfe was laid when mortally wounded at the seige of Quebec, and on which he died. Here also are two brass guns taken at Quebec, and a Maltese cannon, removed by the French, and taken by an English frigate. The western compartment of the room is principally occupied by Oriental arms and armour, amongst which are many interesting objects—group of Saracenic armour; collection of Kaffre weapons; swords, saddle, and other articles taken from Tippoo Sahib's armoury at Seringapatam; the King of Oude's executioner's sword, like a huge bread knife; Indian armour; Chinese armour, amongst which is a curiously combined sword and pistol; hempen armour from the South Sea Islands; New Zealand spears, clubs, etc.; two suits of Japanese armour. Ascending again the stairs, shewing the thickness of the wall (14 feet), of the White Tower, we enter *Queen Elizabeth's armoury*, with a vaulted roof, formerly used as a prison, the smallest room on the first storey of the Tower. Here are brought together various ancient forms of spears and lances, glaives, pole-axes, bills, pikes, halberds, etc.; bucklers of various structure, amongst which notice the brazen shield embossed with the labours of Hercules, and a shield of the sixteenth century inlaid and embossed, the subject of the middle portion being the death of Charles the Bold of Burgundy; ancient shot, chain, bar, link, etc.; curious specimens of ancient fire-arms, match-locks, wheel-locks, etc.; two yew bows which lay under water in the wreck of the "Mary Rose" for 300 years, and they look quite fresh notwithstanding; ancient instruments of torture and punishment, an iron collar of torture taken from the Spaniards in 1588, the "cravat," thumb screws, etc. In the centre of this room is the heading block, on which Lords Balmerino, Kilmarnock, and Lovat, suffered decapitation on Tower Hill in 1746, and a beheading axe, said to have been used when the Earl of Essex was executed in Queen Elizabeth's reign. On the north side of this room there is a low door-way leading to a dark cell in which it is said Sir Walter Raleigh was confined. There are inscriptions in the stone, near the entrance, made by Rudston, Fane, and Culpeper, who were implicated in Sir Thomas Wyatt's rebellion in 1553. Wyatt himself was beheaded. Descending into the Horse Armoury once more, and passing along its north side, we see in a glass case some pieces of armour that belonged to Henry IV. of France, a silvered suit made for Charles I. when a child, Venetian armour, and some pieces of the curious puffed armour made in the time of Henry VIII., to imitate the slashed dresses. A very fine suit of Italian armour, worn by Count Oddi of Padua, 1620; it is of russet, gilt and engraved with the imperial eagle. In a recess, an equestrian figure of Charles I. in a suit of gilt armour given him by the city of London. Examples of plate armour, chain armour, and mixtures of the two. Brigandine jackets, made of flat pieces of steel, quilted between two pieces of canvas. A series of helmets, some of them of great antiquarian interest. A glass case containing match-locks, wheel-locks, muskets, and swords. A specimen of "penny plate" horse armour. In a cabinet in the western vestibule of this gallery is an ancient saddle inlaid with ivory (1450), and the burlesque burgonet of Will Somers, Henry VIII.'s jester, having ram's horns and spectacles.

On quitting the armoury we shall have an opportunity of examining the exterior of the *White Tower*, which, as already mentioned, was originally built in the time of the Conqueror, but it has been much repaired at various times since. It measures externally 116 feet from north to south, and 96 feet from east to west, and its height is 92 feet. There are turrets at the angles. The north-eastern is circular, and was used by the king's astronomer as an observatory before the building at Greenwich was erected, contains within it a stair-case communicating with all the floors. The external walls are from ten to twelve feet thick. The original grand entrance was on the north side, where the remains of an archway may be traced. Internally each floor is divided into three rooms, by walls seven feet thick. On the first floor is Queen Elizabeth's armoury, previously described ; and on the second floor is the chapel of St. John the Evangelist, but from this excellent specimen of Norman architecture the public are excluded. Here is an apsis and twelve massive round columns with arches supporting a gallery. Records were, until lately, deposited here. At the foot of the stair-case leading to the chapel some bones were found, which were supposed to be those of the hundred princes, and by Charles the Second's order they were removed to Westminster Abbey. The council chamber of our early kings is on the third floor ; it has a dark massive timber roof. Here Richard II. resigned his crown to Bolingbroke in September 1399, saying, as Froissart reports, " I have been King of England, Duke of Aquitaine, and Lord of Ireland, about twenty-one years, which signory, royalty, sceptre, crown, and heritage, I clearly resign here to my cousin Henry of Lancaster, and I desire him here, in this open presence, in entering of the same possession, to take this sceptre." In the White Tower John King of France was lodged. Amongst the inscriptions in the vaults is one cut by Fisher, Bishop of Rochester.

The *Salt Tower*, formerly used as a prison, is at the south-east angle of the inner ward. On the inner wall is an astrological carving, a sphere with the zodiacal signs, etc., made by Hugh Draper in 1561. He was imprisoned here on the charge of having practised the art of sorcery to the injury of Sir William St. Lowe and his wife.

Visitors are next conducted to

The Jewel-House, where the Crown Regalia are kept within a glass case protected by an iron cage. The Tower was first employed as a depository for the crown jewels by Henry III. The place in which they are now kept was built in 1842. The chief object of attraction is Queen Victoria's state crown, which Professor Tennant has thus described :—" It was made by Messrs. Rundell and Bridge in the year 1838, with jewels taken from old crowns and others furnished by the command of her Majesty. It consists of diamonds, pearls, rubies, sapphires, and emeralds, set in silver and gold ; it has a crimson velvet cap, with ermine border, and is lined with white silk. Its gross weight is 39 oz. 5 pennyweights troy. The lower part of the band, above the ermine border, consists of a row of 129 pearls, and the upper part of the band a row of 112 pearls, between which, in front of the crown, is a large sapphire (partly drilled), purchased for the crown of King George IV. At the back is a sapphire of smaller size, and six other sapphires (three on each side), between which are eight emeralds. Above and below the seven sapphires are fourteen diamonds, and around the eight emeralds 128 diamonds. Between the emeralds and sapphires are sixteen trefoil ornaments, containing 160 diamonds. Above the band are eight sapphires surmounted by eight diamonds, between which are eight festoons, consisting of 248 diamonds. In the front of the crown, and in the centre of a diamond Maltese cross, is the famous ruby said to have been given to Edward Prince of Wales, son of Richard III., called the Black Prince, by Don Pedro, King of Castile, after the battle of Najera, near Vittoria, A.D. 1367. This ruby was worn in the helmet of Henry V. at the battle of Agincourt, A.D. 1415. It is pierced quite through, after the eastern custom, the upper part of the piercing being filled up by a small ruby. Around this ruby, to form the cross, are seventy-five brilliant diamonds. Three other Maltese crosses, forming the two sides and back of the crown, have emerald centres, and contain respectively 132, 124, and 130 brilliant diamonds. Between the four Maltese crosses are four ornaments in the form of the French fleur-de-lis, with four rubies in the centres, and surrounded by rose diamonds, containing respectively 85, 86, 86, and 87 rose diamonds. From the Maltese crosses issue four imperial arches composed of oak leaves and acorns, the leaves containing 728 rose, table, and brilliant diamonds, 32 pearls forming the acorns, set in cups containing 54 rose diamonds and one table diamond. The total number of diamonds in the arches and acorns is 108 brilliants, 116 table, and 559 rose diamonds. From the upper part of the arches are suspended four large pendant pear-shaped pearls, with rose diamond caps, containing twelve rose diamonds, and stems containing twenty-four very small rose diamonds. Above the arch stands the mound, containing in the lower hemisphere 304 brilliants, and in the upper 244 brilliants; the zone and arc being composed of 33 rose diamonds. The cross on the summit has a rose-cut sapphire in the centre, surrounded by four large brilliants, and 108 smaller brilliants. Summary of jewels comprised in the crown :—1 large ruby irregularly polished, 1 large broad-spread sapphire, 16 sapphires, 11 emeralds, 4 rubies, 1363 brilliant diamonds, 1273 rose diamonds, 147 table diamonds, 4 drop-shaped pearls, 273 pearls."

The other objects to be noticed are—*St. Edward's Crown* of gold, embellished with diamonds and other precious stones, made for the coronation of Charles II., and used at all subsequent coronations. It is placed, by the Archbishop of Canterbury, on the sovereign's head at the altar. Blood stole this crown from the Tower in May 1761. *The Prince of Wales' Crown*, of pure gold, without jewels. *The Queen Consort's Crown*, of gold, set with diamonds and other jewels. *The Queen's Diadem*, made for Maria d' Este, queen of James II.; adorned with diamonds and pearls. *St. Edward's Staff*, of beaten gold, 4 feet 7 inches long, surmounted by an orb containing, it is said, a part of the true cross. It is carried before the sovereign at a coronation. *The Royal Sceptre*, or Sceptre with the cross, of gold, 2 feet 9 inches long, the pommel adorned with rubies, emeralds, and diamonds; the cross with various jewels, and having a large table diamond in the centre. The Archbishop of Canterbury places this sceptre in the sovereign's right hand at a coronation. *The Rod of Equity*, or Sceptre with the Dove, of gold, adorned with diamonds. It is placed in the sovereign's left hand at a coronation. *The Queen Consort's Sceptre*, gold, adorned with precious stones. *The Ivory Sceptre*, made for Maria d' Este, queen of James II., bears a dove of white onyx. *A Sceptre*, supposed to have been made

for Mary, queen of William III. It was found behind the wainscotting of the old Jewel Office. *The Curtana,* or pointless Sword
of Mercy, steel, ornamented with gold. *Two Swords of Justice,*
temporal and ecclesiastical. They are borne before the Sovereign
at a coronation. *Armillæ,* or Bracelets; Spurs; the *ampulla* or
anointing vessel, and spoon for receiving the sacred oil from the
ampulla, all used at a coronation. The spoon is thought to be
the last relic of the ancient regalia. *The Golden Salt Cellar,* the
model of a castle. *The Baptismal Font* used at the christening
of the royal children, and service of sacramental plate. The
Koh-i-noor diamond, taken at Lahore in the Punjaub; it was
formerly the property of Runjeet Singh, and has a long history
attached to it; it is set in a bracelet, of Indian fashion, between
two large diamonds.

Near the Jewel House stands the ancient *Martin* or *Jewel
Tower,* where Anne Boleyn was imprisoned, as the inscriptions
in it testify.

THE NEW BARRACKS, on the north side of the Tower, were
erected on the site of the Grand Storehouse and Small Armoury,
destroyed by fire in 1841, when 150,000 stand of arms were in
it. The first stone was laid by the late Duke of Wellington,
then constable of the Tower. Behind, that is to the north of
these barracks, are two ancient towers, in the eastern of which,
the Brick Tower, it is said, Lady Jane Grey was imprisoned; and
in the western one, the Bowyer Tower, tradition asserts that
the Duke of Clarence was murdered. Only the basements of
these towers are old. *The Tower Chapel,* St. Peters ad Vincula,
was built in the reign of Edward I. on the site of an older chapel.
It consists of a chancel, nave, and north aisle, with a small bell
tower; but little of the original building remains, so many have
been the alterations. Here have been interred a great number
of distinguished persons who have fallen before the executioner's axe. " There is no sadder spot on earth (said Macaulay)
than this little cemetery. Death is there associated with whatever is darkest in human nature and in human destiny, with
the savage triumph of implacable enemies, with the incon-
stancy, the ingratitude, and the cowardice of friends, with all
the miseries of fallen greatness and of blighted fame." This
is the burial-place of Queen Anne Boleyn, Queen Katharine
Howard, Sir Thomas More; Cromwell, Earl of Essex; Margaret,
Countess of Shrewsbury; Thomas, Lord Seymour; his brother,

the Protector Somerset ; Dudley, Duke of Northumberland ; Lady Jane Grey and her husband ; Devereux, Earl of Essex ; James, Duke of Monmouth ; Lords Kilmarnock, Balmerino, and Lovat. All of these persons were beheaded. Sir Thomas Overbury, poisoned in the Tower, was also buried here.

Notice in the chancel a marble monument to Sir Richard Blount, and his son Sir Michael, lieutenants of the Tower in the sixteenth century; the tomb of Sir Allan Apsley, another lieutenant of the Tower (d. 1630); he was Mrs. Lucy Hutchinson's father ; and in the north aisle, the altar tomb of Sir R. Cholmondeley, lieutenant of the Tower in Henry the Eighth's time, and his wife. The place of execution on Tower Green, in front of the chapel, is marked by an oval of dark flints. Here perished Anne Boleyn, Katharine Howard, and Lady Jane Grey.

THE BEAUCHAMP TOWER, restored by Mr. Salvin in 1854, stands about the middle of the west side of the fortress. It was erected in the thirteenth century, and derives its name from the circumstance of Beauchamp, Earl of Warwick, having been confined in it in 1397. It consists of two storeys, access to which is gained by a winding staircase. The public are admitted only to the lower storey. On the walls are numerous inscriptions and devices, said to have been carved by the persons who have been imprisoned. Amongst these carvings, notice a large piece of sculpture by Dudley, Earl of Warwick, brother of Guildford, Lord Dudley, who married Lady Jane Grey, consisting of a shield, bearing the lion, bear, and ragged staff, the family cognizance, surrounded by a wreath of oak leaves, acorns, and roses, and four imperfect lines, telling us that the device referred to his four brothers, all of whom were imprisoned here in 1553. Near the north-western recess is the word IANE, supposed to refer to Lady Jane Grey, and to have been cut by her husband. No other trace of that unfortunate lady has been found in the fortress.

In the BELL TOWER, which stands in the south-west angle of the inner ward, Fisher, Bishop of Rochester, was confined ; and there is a tradition that the Princess Elizabeth was imprisoned here by her sister Mary. On leaving the inner ward of the fortress by the gate of the Bloody Tower, we pass near the *Lieutenant's Lodgings*, which are chiefly of timber of Henry the Eighth's time. In what is called the Council Chamber, Guy Fawkes and his accomplices were examined, as is mentioned in an inscription couched in Hebrew and Latin on a marble monument. An inscription carved on an old mantelpiece in another part of the building, related to the Countess of Lennox, who had been committed " to this logynge," for the marriage of her son Lord Darnley to Mary Queen of Scots. Here Sir Francis Burdett was confined in 1810, when committed for impugning the right of the House of Commons to imprison a man for commenting on their proceedings !

The government of the Tower is lodged on the Constable, a sinecure office with a salary of £1000 a-year, now held by Viscount Combermere, who succeeded the Duke of Wellington. Under him are a lieutenant and a deputy-lieutenant, but the duties are performed by the Major.

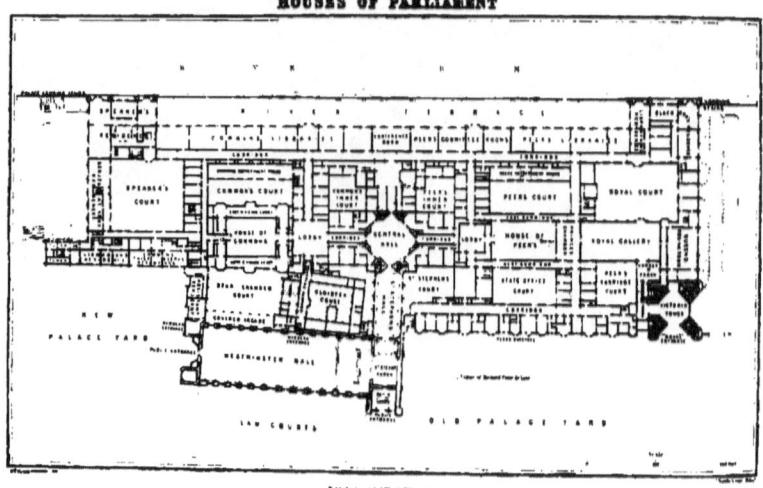

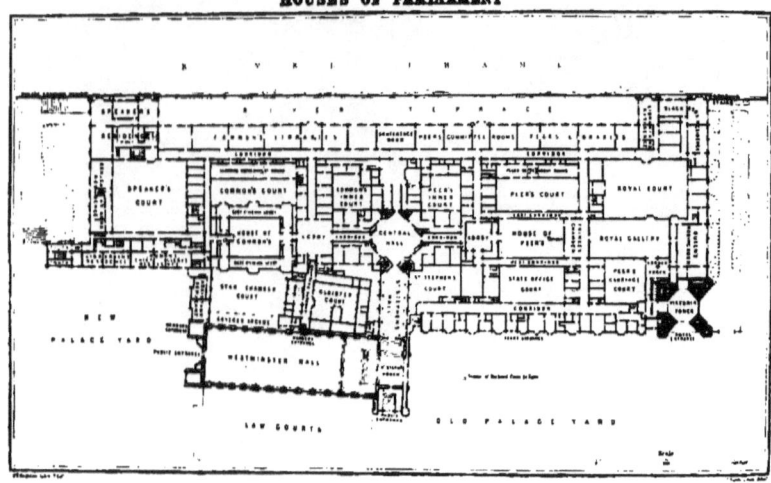

CHAPTER THE SIXTH.

The Houses of Parliament and Westminster Hall.

The House of Lords may be seen, free, when appeal cases are being heard. The sitting terminates at 4 p.m. To obtain admission to the stranger's gallery to hear debates, a peer's order is necessary. To hear debates in the *House of Commons*, a member's order must be procured. Ladies are only allowed to enter a gallery above the reporter's gallery, where they obtain an imperfect view of the House through a grating. The Speaker takes the chair at five o'clock. On Wednesday the House sits at noon and rises at six p.m.

The old Houses of Parliament, an unsightly pile of various dates, originally a royal palace, were destroyed by fire on the 16th of October 1834. As the best means of obtaining an edifice worthy of the age and nation, architects were invited to send in designs. From the designs then produced, that of Mr. (afterwards Sir) Charles Barry was unanimously admitted to be the most striking, and it was accordingly selected. The first stone of the present magnificent structure was laid on the 27th April 1840, and the builders have been adding stone to stone ever since. Strange and lamentable to say, that although great expense was incurred professedly in ascertaining what was the best stone to employ, the stone actually used is already in a state of decay ; and the authorities have been called on to consider whether some method of arresting the decay cannot be adopted, hitherto we believe without success.

The present Houses of Parliament cover nearly 8 acres of ground, an area twice as great as that occupied by the old buildings. They include 11 courts, 100 stair-cases, and 1100 rooms, connected by 2 miles of lobby. Their cost, up to the 31st of December 1859, had been £2,198,099, a sum which did not include the fresco paintings and statuary, nor the cost of maintaining and repairing the buildings and furniture. These items, up to the last day of March 1860, amounted to £107,000. The style adopted is that of Henry the Eighth's time'; and all must admit that a very noble, if a very costly, Tudor palace now graces our metropolis, which we may point out to foreigners with satisfaction and pride. The finest façade is the river front, which rises from a simple terrace 940 feet in length, and 33 feet wide. It is richly decorated with statues of kings and queens and panelled sculpture, representing coats of arms and royal devices, with shafted windows, with two pinnacled towers at each end, and two in the centre. At the end next Westminster Bridge rises the tall *Clock Tower*, 40 feet square and 320 feet high, which carries an eight-day clock made under the direction of the Astronomer Royal. Each dial is about 30 feet in diameter. The hour is struck on a bell weighing upwards of 8 tons, and the quarters are chimed upon eight small bells. This tower has been in a great measure copied from the celebrated clock tower at Bruges. From the middle of the palace a spire, crowning an open stone lantern which surmounts the dome over the central hall, reaches the height of 300 feet. The grandest feature of all is the Victoria Tower at the south-west angle, 80 feet square and 340 feet high. The Sovereign's entrance is here, with a grand and richly-decorated archway 65 feet high. Inside the porch, in niches, are statues of St. George, St. Andrew, and St. Patrick. the patron saints of the three kingdoms ; as well as a statue of Queen Victoria, between figures representing Justice and Mercy.

A bed of concrete twelve feet thick underlies the whole foundation. The stone of the river terrace is Aberdeen granite ; that of the exterior of the palace is magnesian limestone from Anston, Yorkshire ; that of the interior, Caen stone. The internal walls are of brick ; the bearers of the floors cast-iron. All the roofs are of wrought iron covered with zinced cast-iron plates. As little wood as possible has been employed, with a view to lessen the chance of destruction by fire. It was part of the plan that Westminster Hall should be retained, and it has accordingly been incorporated with the new palace, to which it forms a grand entrance for the public. The courts of law, which now stand on its west side facing St. Margaret's Church, will doubtless be removed, as their style of architecture is entirely different from the adjacent buildings, not to say anything of other reasons.

Whether we enter the palace by way of Westminster Hall, or by the Old Palace Yard entrance, we pass through *St. Stephen's Porch*,—a square-vaulted vestibule, containing the great south window removed from the south end of the old hall,—into *St. Stephen's Hall*, 95 feet by 30 wide, and 56 feet high, where statues of Hampden, Falkland, Clarendon, Selden, Sir Robert Walpole, Lord Somers, Lord Mansfield, Lord Chatham, Fox, Pitt, Burke, and Grattan have been placed. This hall is over the ancient crypt, to be mentioned presently. Thence we proceed into the Grand Central Hall, an octagon 70 feet across, and 75 feet high. In the sides, doorways and corridors alternate, the latter being filled with stained glass. The stone roof is groined, and contains more than 250 carved bosses, each four feet across, overhanging the encaustic-tile pavement. North and south from this hall corridors, adorned with fresco paintings, lead to the House of Peers and the House of Commons.

HOUSE OF PEERS.

Turning south we cross a vestibule styled *the Peers' Lobby*, pass between its gates of massive brass, of rich floriated design, and then reach that gorgeous room where the Peers of England meet to deliberate. It is a double cube 91 feet long by 45 feet wide, with a height of 45 feet. At each side are six lofty windows containing stained glass, with portraitures of sovereigns. At night these windows are lighted from the outside. At each end are three archways with frescoes by different artists, viz., behind the throne, Edward III. conferring the order of the garter on the Black Prince, by C. W. Cope ; the Baptism of St. Ethelbert, the founder of St. Paul's Cathedral, by W. Dyce ; and Prince Henry, afterwards Henry VI., submitting to the authority of Judge Gascoigne, by C. W. Cope. At the opposite end, over the Strangers' Gallery,— The Spirit of Justice, by D. Maclise ; The Spirit of Religion, by J. C. Horsley ; and the Spirit of Chivalry, by D. Maclise. The niches in the walls hold statues of the barons who compelled John to sign Magna Charta. Under the windows is a light gallery of brass, and the cornice beneath carries arms of sovereigns, lords chancellor, and bishops. The ceiling is divided into compartments containing symbols, devices, and monograms, amongst which, as historically interesting, may be noticed the white hart of Richard II., the sun of the house of York, the crown on a bush of Henry VII., the pomegranate of Castille, the portcullis of Beaufort, the lily of France, the lions of England and Scotland. The throne stands at the middle of the southern end of the room, with a door at each side leading into the Prince's chamber. At the right hand is a state chair for the Prince of Wales. The woolsack, where the Lord Chancellor sits, is a seat covered with crimson cloth placed about the middle of the room. The reporters have been provided with a gallery at the north end, and behind it is the strangers' gallery. Underneath, on the floor of the house, is the bar at which counsel in law appeal cases plead, and where deputations from the Commons make their appearance. Beyond this bar strangers cannot pass.

House of Commons.

Making our way back to the central hall, the corridor at the opposite side, and in a line with the one we have just traversed, leads to the *House of Commons*, a room 62 feet long, 45 feet wide, and 41 feet high, lighted by six windows at each side filled with stained glass, in which the arms of boroughs are represented. The walls are panelled with carved oak. At the north end is the Speaker's chair, over which is the reporters' gallery. Above the latter is a gallery for ladies, but the brass screen prevents their being seen from the house. Seats in the area, and in the side galleries, over the bar, are for the accommodation of 476 members out of the 656 composing the lower house of legislature ; the rest must manage as they can. The gallery to which strangers are admitted is at the south end of the hall, immediately opposite that for the reporters, and immediately below it are the seats reserved for the Peers who choose to visit the house, and for the sons of members attending schools. The ceiling is rich, but the other parts of the house are comparatively plain, as befits a place of business. The Ministerial side of the house is that on the Speaker's right, Ministers occupying the front bench, facing the leaders of the opposition, seated in the front bench on the other side. Outside the house are the lobbies into which members go on a division. In front of the Speaker's chair is the table where the clerks sit, and upon which is the Speaker's mace, which does not date earlier than the Restoration. The Serjeant-at-Arms, whose duty it is to take unruly members into custody, sits near the bar at the northern end. The floor is of cast-iron, perforated for the admission of fresh and warm air. The entrance into the house for members is by a doorway on the east side of Westminster Hall, and through the cloisters.

The entrance for the sovereign, who only attends the palace on state occasions, is at the Victoria Tower. In the *Norman Porch*, to which a flight of steps ascends, are statues of sovereigns of the Norman line, and frescoes commemorating events of their time. On the right hand of this porch are doorways into the Guard Chamber and into the Queen's Robing Room, which is adorned with frescoes by Dyce, representing the legends of King Arthur, and is otherwise splendidly decorated. When the ceremony of robing has been gone through, the Queen proceeds to the House of Peers through the longest room in the building, the *Victoria Gallery*, which has a length of 110 feet, with a width and height of 45 feet. Frescoes, the subjects taken from English history, adorn the walls; and the ceiling is panelled and richly gilded. To this gallery the public are admitted, by means of tickets issued at the Lord Chamberlain's office, to see the Queen pass on state occasions, such as the opening and prorogation of Parliament. Ladies are provided with seats, as far as practicable, in a gallery in the House, but as this is usually filled with peeresses or their kin, strangers must be content with a place in the grand gallery, where gentlemen are seated apart from the ladies. The room beyond is the *Prince's Chamber*, also splendidly fitted up; and containing a marble group by Gibson, representing the Queen between Justice and Mercy, bas-reliefs in oak of events connected with Tudor history, and a series of por-

traits of the same period.   Two doorways lead from this room
into the House of Peers.

The principal storey of the river front is occupied by the
libraries of the Lords and Commons, their committee-rooms, and
by a conference-room, where, in case of a difference between the
two houses, deputations from each meet to discuss the matter.
The Speaker's residence is at the clock-tower end of the palace ;
the Usher of the Black Rod and the Lords' Librarian have residences at the other end.   To each chamber is attached a re-
freshment-room.

The number of statues in and about the building is between
400 and 500 ; those which are part of the architectural design
have been executed by Mr. Thomas.

St. Stephen's Cloisters, built by Henry VIII., adjoin the east
side of Westminster Hall, from which there is a door leading to
them, but its use is limited to members of the House of Commons.   They are only on a small scale, 63 feet by $49\frac{1}{2}$, but are
beautifully ornamented with groining and tracery.   They were
restored by Sir C. Barry, and an upper storey added, to replace
one that had been destroyed.   A small chapel or oratory projects
from the middle of the western arcade, between two of the buttresses of the hall, and terminates in an apsis.   Although these
cloisters are not symmetrical with the modern buildings, as will
be perceived from the plan, their destruction could not be
thought of for a moment, and the architect received instructions
to incorporate them as best he could with the new structure.
Another interesting relic which escaped the fire is *St. Stephen's
Crypt*, under the modern St. Stephen's Hall.   It was called St.
Mary-in-the Vaults, or St. Mary-undercroft.   The exact date of
its erection does not seem to be known, but it appears that
Henry III. here married his sister, Eleanor, to Simon de Mont-
fort, his favourite.   An old picture represents Caxton presenting
his first printed book to Edward IV. in this place.   The Commonwealth soldiers grossly ill-treated what had always been used
up to that time as a chapel, destroying the altars and mutilating
the crosses.   It has lately undergone a complete restoration.
Polished columns of Purbeck marble have replaced those which
had been defaced, and the edifice is now used as a place of worship by the residents of the palace.

WESTMINSTER HALL was a part of the ancient royal palace
of Westminster, and was originally built by William Rufus.   It

was rebuilt, some say only repaired, but raised two feet, by Richard II. between 1395 and 1399 ; but all the exterior as we now see it, saving the north porch and window, is modern work. The interior, or the greater part of it, is ancient. Little of the exterior can be seen, for one side is concealed by the modern courts of law ; the other, the south end, by Barry's new Houses of Parliament. It is in the perpendicular style, and is striking for its size and its rich roof of oak (not of chestnut as usually stated). It is the largest room in Europe without pillars, with one exception, the great hall at Padua. The English hall measures internally 239 feet by 68 feet, the Italian hall 240 feet by 80. It is to be noticed that the upper half consists of timber, the walls being only about 21 feet high. Observe on the string course which passes round the hall below the windows, Richard the Second's device of the couchant hart, and the hammer beams of the roof carved with angels bearing shields. The dormer windows were added in 1820, previous to the coronation of George IV., at which time the roof was thoroughly repaired, and forty loads of oak from old ships were consumed on renewing parts that had decayed, and furnishing a portion of the north end, which had been left incomplete. The lead had been stripped from the roof in order to lighten the pressure, and slates substituted. The hall forms a grand entrance to the Houses of Parliament and the courts of law. The great south window was removed by Barry, and placed in an enlarged form in St. Stephen's porch, facing the steps at the south end of the hall.

This noble edifice has been the scene of many royal banquets and ceremonies. Richard II. gave a great feast on its completion, and not long afterwards he was here formally deposed, and sentenced to perpetual banishment. Cromwell, seated on the ancient coronation chair, " under a prince-like canopy of state,' was here inaugurated Lord Protector ; a few years passed and then his head, along with those of Ireton and Bradshaw, was placed upon the south gable, and there Cromwell's remained twenty years. In the roof were hung banners and ensigns taken on the fields of Naseby, Worcester, Preston, Dunbar, and Blenheim. In the hall great trials have taken place. Wallace was tried in the old hall. In this Sir Thomas More, the Protector Somerset, Devereux, Earl of Essex, Guy Fawkes and his fellow-conspirators, the infamous Earl and Countess of Somerset, and the Earl of Stafford, were tried and condemned. A grander occasion was that when Charles I. faced his judges. At a later period, the seven bishops, Dr. Sacheverel, the Earl of Derwentwater, and the rebel lords of Scotland, Kilmarnock, Balmerino, and Lovat, were tried here. The rafters have rung with the wonderful eloquence of Burke, Fox, and Sheridan, before a crowd of noble and beautiful auditors, when the deeds of Warren Hastings in India were laid before the world. The last trial that took place was Lord Melville's, when he was impeached by the Commons in 1806. George IV. gave his coronation banquet here to 334 guests, when Dymock, the King's champion, clad in armour, rode into the hall, and throwing down his gauntlet, challenged the world to gainsay the King's title, a ceremony which a Dymock had gone through at the coronation of Richard II., claiming the privilege as successor of the Marmions in the ownership of the manor of Scrivelsby in Lincolnshire.

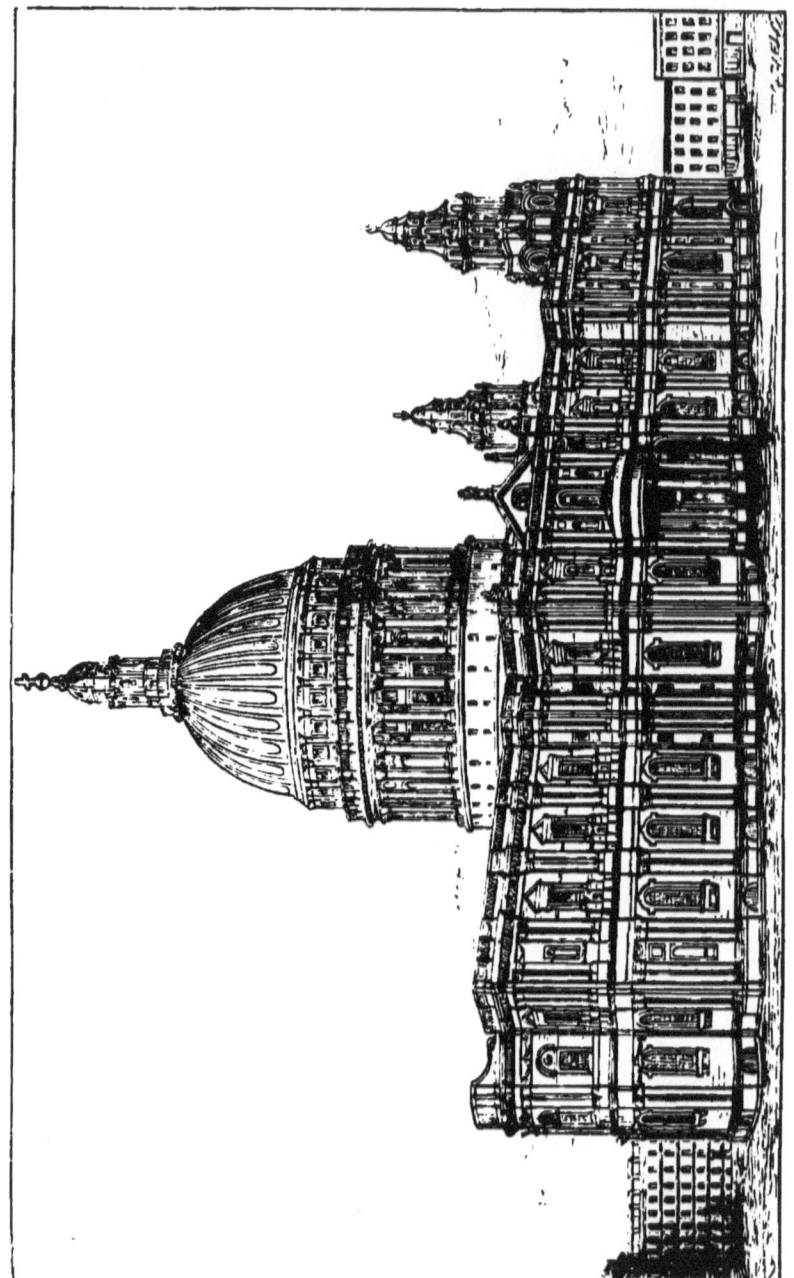

ST. PAULS CATHEDRAL—North Side.

CHAPTER THE SEVENTH.

THE cathedral church of the Bishops of London is not only
by far the finest building in the Italian style in London, but
the finest in Britain. The public are admitted free by the north
door from eleven to three daily, and during summer from the
conclusion of afternoon service until dusk. No person is allowed
to remain in the nave after service has commenced. Divine service is celebrated daily at eight A.M. in the morning chapel; at a
quarter before ten A.M., and at a quarter before three P.M., in the
choir. On Sundays, during the winter half year, there is an
evening service at seven, under the dome, where 3000 persons
can be accommodated. To see certain parts of the building, the
following charges are made:—

To the Whispering, Stone, and Golden Galleries, 6d.; to the
Library, Great Bell, Geometrical Staircase, and Model Room,
6d.; to the Crypt, where are the tombs of Nelson and Wellington, 6d.; to the Clock, 2d.; and to the Ball, 1s. 6d.

It is much to be regretted that no complete general view of
St. Paul's is obtainable, in consequence of the nearness of the
surrounding houses; but no view is more striking than that
from Blackfriars' Bridge, although the whole of the lower part
of the cathedral is concealed.

HISTORY OF THE SITE.—Ethelbert, King of Kent, built the
first church at this place in 610. This was destroyed by fire
in 1087, but another edifice, " Old St. Paul's," was shortly afterwards commenced. This was much damaged by a fire in 1137;
it was greatly injured by lightning in 1444; in 1561 it was
again damaged by fire; it became much dilapidated, and a considerable sum had been expended in repairing it, when the great

G

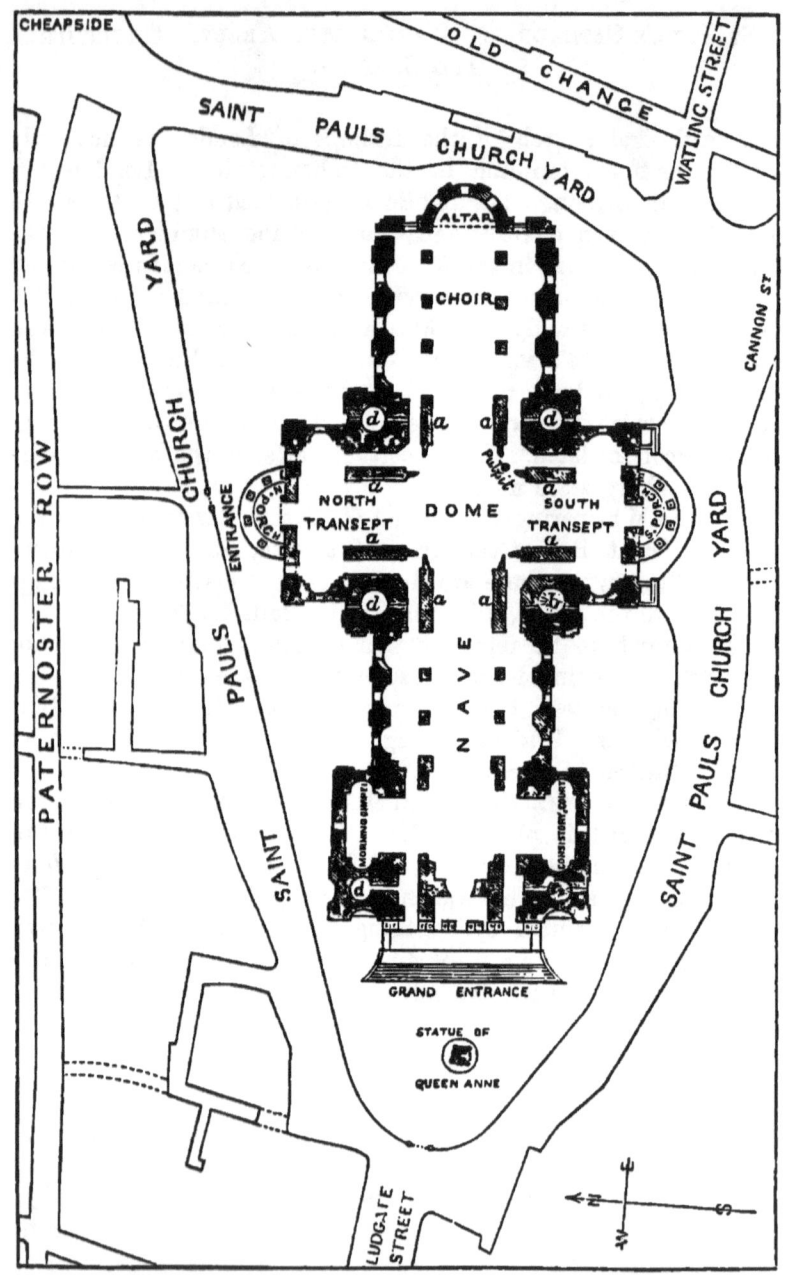

fire of 1666 utterly destroyed it. The structure was in the Gothic style, and its plan was a Latin cross. It was 690 feet long, 130 feet broad, and the spire, springing from a tower, rose to the height of 520 feet. Near the north-east end stood Powles' Cross, so often referred to in our early literature, and a pulpit where sermons were preached, and the pope's mandates—whether blessing or cursing—read aloud to the people. The middle aisle was termed Paul's Walk, from its being much frequented by idlers as well as by money-lenders and dealers in commodities. A scene in one of Ben Jonson's plays is laid " in the middle aisle of Paul's." One old writer compared the noise made by talkers and the walkers to " a kind of still roar or loud whisper." Desecrated within, it was no better treated without. A carpenter and a wine-dealer took possession of part of the vaults, trunkmakers of the cloisters ; buildings were planted against the outer walls, one being used as a play-house, and in another the owner made a hole in a buttress and baked his bread therein.

THE PRESENT CATHEDRAL.—The great fire of 1666, which has been referred to many times in this volume, destroyed 13,000 houses and 87 parish churches, reducing St. Paul's to a heap of ruins. These ruins remained pretty much as they had been left by the fire for nearly eight years. Charles II.'s Government having taken the matter in hand, intrusted the work of rebuilding to Sir Christopher Wren, whose first design was rejected. The second was approved of, and the first stone was laid on the 21st June 1675 by the architect, assisted by the freemasons of his lodge, which lodge still preserves the trowel and mallet used on the occasion. In 1697 the choir was opened, and in 1710 the architect's son placed the last stone on the top of the lantern, so that the building occupied 35 years. What rarely happens, in the case of a large edifice like this, it was completed in the architect's lifetime ; and, what is still more singular, the same persons held the offices of Bishop and Master Mason at the commencement and at the completion of the edifice. During the progress of the works, Wren received £200 a year, and for this (said the Duchess of Marlborough) he was content to be dragged up in a basket three or four times a week. The sum expended, £747,954, was made up by a grant of £10,000 by the crown, £5000 a year raised by a duty on coals, and by subscriptions. The stone was brought from the Portland quarries.

EXTERIOR.—Commonly classed, says a critic, as the second of Christian temples, this cathedral is really the *first* in completeness, unity of design, and solidity of construction ; only the *fifth* in extent or capacity (being excelled by St. Peter's, Florence, Milan, and Amiens) ; and about the *last* in richness and variety of ornaments. The ground-plan shews that the general form is that of a Latin cross. Its length is 500 feet, the width of the nave and choir 125 feet, the length of the transept 250 feet, the height of the north and south sides 100 feet. From the intersection of the transept with the main building springs a majestic dome, the glory of the edifice, upon which is a lantern carrying a gilt copper ball and cross, the top of which is 356 feet above the floor of the church, or 365 feet above the ground. The grand front is on the west, facing Ludgate Hill. It is approached by a double flight of steps from an area enclosed by iron palisading, within which is a statue of Queen Anne, erected in 1712. The portico is in two divisions ; the lower one consists of twelve Corinthian columns, coupled ; the upper one of eight. On the pediment is a basso-relievo of the Conversion of St. Paul. At the apex of the pediment is placed a statue of St. Paul, and at the sides statues of St. Peter, each fifteen feet high. At each side of the portico is a bell tower, with a pyramidal summit, and these, with their open lanterns covered by domes, rise to the height of 220 feet. At the angles are statues of the Evangelists. The south tower contains the clock and the great bell, ten feet in diameter, which is only tolled at the death of one of the royal family, or of the Bishop, Dean, or a Lord Mayor, dying during his year of office. Its weight is about 12,000 lbs.; its clapper weighs 180 lbs. The west front, including the towers, is 180 feet wide. Above the doors is a marble group of Paul preaching to the Bereans.

The "elevation" is composed of two orders ; the lower, Corinthian, has windows with semicircular headings ; the upper, Composite, has niches corresponding to the windows below. In each storey the entablature is supported by coupled pilasters. The balustrade, nine feet high, on the top of the north and south walls, was not designed by Wren, and was strongly objected to by him. Each arm of the transept is entered by an external semicircular Corinthian portico, reached by a lofty flight of steps. At the east end of the choir there is a circular projection or apse. The cypher W. and M., between palm branches.

and surmounted by a crown, indicates that this part was completed in the reign of William and Mary. The heavy iron railing which encloses a plot of 2 acres and 16 perches, weighs upwards of 200 tons. It was made at Lamberhurst in .Kent, and cost £11,200.

INTERIOR.—Entering the north arm of the transept we may make our way at once to the space under the cupola, whence the four unequal arms of the Latin cross radiate. The keystones of the arches were carved by Cibber. It will be noticed that the usual four piers at the crossing have been omitted, and that the weight of the dome is supported by eight surrounding piers, exactly as in Ely Cathedral. The cupola has an internal diameter of 108 feet. The cornice above the arches, and the rails of the Whispering Gallery, have been gilded. Above are seen Thornhill's paintings. Its height may perhaps disappoint the visitor, but he will be surprised to learn that it is the innermost of three shells. Like the outermost, it is merely ornamental, the weight of the lantern, ball, and cross, being borne by the intermediate conical shell. It rises to the height of 228 feet above the pavement, which is composed of pieces of light and dark marbles, radiating somewhat like a mariner's compass. In the middle a brass plate shews where Nelson's remains lie in the crypt beneath. In three of the angles are vestries, used by the Deans, the Canons, and the Lord Mayor ; and in the fourth is a circular staircase, which leads up to the Whispering Gallery. In the south arm of the transept will be seen an organ which was built by Mr. Hill for the Panopticon or Alhambra Palace in Leicester Square, and having been purchased for St. Paul's, has been lately placed here. The choir has three arches on each side, with a clerestory above. The old organ in the case, designed by Sir Christopher Wren, has been placed under the middle arch on the north side. The arch next the apse on each side has been left open to the aisle behind ; the other two have the stalls before them. Here is much of Grinling Gibbons' fine carving in wood ; the Archbishop's throne on the south side, near the altar, marked by the figures of a mitre and pelican ; the Bishop of London's throne ; the Lord Mayor's seat on the north, distinguished by the city arms ; the Dean's stall, indicated by an open Bible ; the stalls of the four canons and prebendaries. The seats in front of the stalls are for the twelve minor canons, the six vicars choral, and the choristers. The communion table is in the apsidal chancel. Wren's design for the decoration of this part of the building was never carried out. The nave has likewise three arches on each side which rest on piers that form aisles, and above is a clerestory. In the north-west angle, separated from the nave by a carved screen of wood, is the Morning Chapel ; and over against it is the Consistory Court. In the south aisle is the marble Font.

Ascending the staircase already mentioned, we reach the *Whispering Gallery*, which passes round the inside of the dome upon the cornice over the arches. The circular sides of the dome convey faint sounds very distinctly from one point in the gallery to the opposite point, so that a whisper, which in the open air would be inaudible at the distance of a few feet, is brought distinctly to the ear at the distance of 100 feet. By the same staircase we gain access to the *Library* by passing along the gallery over the south aisle of the nave. Here the books number about 7000. Notice the portrait of Bishop Compton, the donor of many books ; the specimens of wood carving by G. Gibbons ; and the floor inlaid with small pieces of oak. In the *Model Room* over the northern aisle is preserved a model of Wren's original design for the cathedral, which is without aisles, but these appendages, to his great sorrow, he was obliged to add by the heir presumptive to the throne, afterwards James II. This was with a view to the introduction of the Roman Catholic ceremonials. A staircase leads from the south gallery to the *Clock Room*, in the south-west tower. The clock was made in 1708 ; it has two dial plates facing west and south, each is nearly 19 feet in diameter. The minute hand is $9\frac{2}{3}$ feet long ; the pendulum 16 feet long, and the weights would balance 180 lbs. It has a beat of two seconds. This is an eight days' clock, and the hour is struck on the *Great Bell*, 10 feet in diameter, by a hammer weighing 145 lbs. placed outside the bell. The quarters are struck on two smaller bells. The bell tolled for prayers is in the northern tower. A curious geometrical stone staircase of 112 steps in the south-west tower affords another mode of reaching the library from the floor of the cathedral.

Returning to the dome, a series, or, as architects term it, a peri-style, of 32 pilasters will be seen above the Whispering Gallery, and above them on the carved surface which Wren had intended to cover with mosaics, are some paintings on scriptural themes by Sir James Thornhill, who was paid at the rate of 40s. per square yard. These pictures, having been much injured by damp, were lately restored by Mr. Parris. They represent the principal events in St. Paul's life, viz.—1, His Conversion ; 2, The Punishment of Elymas the Sorcerer ; 3, Cure of the Cripple at Lystra ; 4, Conversion of the Gaoler ; 5, Paul Preaching at Athens ; 6, Burning of the Magical Books at Ephesus ; 7, Paul before Agrippa ; 8, Shipwreck at Melita. This inner painted dome is of brickwork, two bricks thick ; and there is a circular opening at its apex. Ascending from the Whispering Gallery, we next reach the *Stone Gallery*, above the colonnade at the external base of the dome, whence there is an extensive view over London, highly interesting if the atmosphere be clear, which, however, it very seldom is. From this gallery we ascend by a steep, narrow, and obscure staircase, to the *Golden Galleries*. The inner Golden Gallery is at the base of the Lantern, the outer one at the summit of the dome, whence the country around London is seen stretching into the distance on all sides, the buildings of London being singularly dwarfed by the height at which we stand above them. An artist, a Mr. Hornor, once lived up here for several weeks for the purpose of sketching the panoramic prospect, and he saw the surrounding scene under all circumstances of light and shade, of quietness and bustle. The dome is of timber covered with lead, and during high winds the wood work creaks like a vessel in a storm at sea. The *Lantern* at the top of the dome is supported by the brick cone which is placed between the inner cupola and the outer dome. Above the Lantern is a globe 6 feet 2 inches in diameter, weighing 5600 lbs., and this is surmounted by a cross weighing 3360 lbs. The present globe and cross were substituted in 1826 for those originally erected, of which they are exact copies as regards shape and size. Eight persons may creep into the globe. There are 616 steps between the floor of the cathedral and this spot, which the great majority of visitors to the building will think too many for any advantage to be gained by the ascent.

We will now proceed to examine

The Monuments in St. Paul's.

Westminster Abbey has been made the mausoleum chiefly of those who have gained renown in the civil walks of life ; here the monuments for the most part relate to those who have done the state service in arms on land or sea. It is much to be lamented that so many of the monuments display a taste that is anything but agreeable to cultivated minds. Allegorical groups, and figures either naked or clothed in an attire like nothing the originals ever wore in life, disturb the thoughts by their artificial appearance. However, we must take things as we find them, and, with the intention of pointing out those best worth looking at, we will commence at the north entrance, and first notice, left of the door, Sir Charles Napier's monument, lately erected by public subscription. The General is represented in a standing position, supported by a burst cannon. He is in the ordinary undress costume of an officer, with a military cloak falling from the shoulders. The right hand rests on the hilt of a sword, the left, holding a scroll of paper, rests on the haunch. The figure is in Carrara marble, 8 feet 6 inches high, and was the work of G. C. Adams. The pedestal is inscribed, " Charles James Napier, a prescient General ; a beneficent Governor ; a just Man." —General Sir William Ponsonby, who fell at Waterloo : Fame crowning an almost naked figure near a fallen charger.— Captains Mosse and Riou (Campbell's " gallant good Riou ;" a sarcophagus with winged figures holding medallion portraits ; erected by the nation at the cost of £4200.—Admiral Lord Duncan, a standing figure holding a sword—R. Westmacott, sculptor—cost £2100.

In the North-East Ambulatory is a tabular monument to Major-General Bowes, who is represented as falling mortally wounded at the storming of Salamanca—Chantrey, sculptor.

In the North Aisle is Dr. Johnson's monument, by John Bacon ; cost 1100 guineas.

In the Nave, the monument of the Marquis Cornwallis, Governor-General of Bengal ; the Marquis on a pedestal, at the base of which are three figures—Rossi, sculptor—cost £6300.—Admiral Lord Nelson, by Flaxman, cost £6300. Nelson, in naval dress, stands on a pedestal, at the foot of which are Britannia and other figures, with a lion.—Sir Christopher Wren ; a marble slab with the inscription " Reader, do you ask his monument ? Look around."

In the South Aisle : John Howard the philanthropist, in Roman costume, by John Bacon ; cost £1365 ; the first monument erected in St. Paul's.—Bishop Heber, by Chantrey ; one of the best as a work of art in the Cathedral.

On the south-east side of the space under the Dome, a handsome marble pulpit has been lately erected " In memory of Captain Robert Fitzgerald, 12th Regiment Bombay Native Infantry," by his friends. The pulpit is 10 feet 3 inches high, and many kinds of marble have been employed in its construction, from Rome, the Grecian archipelago, Ireland, etc.

In the South Transept : Admiral Earl Howe ; another of Flaxman's groups, with Britannia, Victory, History, and a Lion ; cost £6300.—Admiral Collingwood ; his body represented as lying on the deck of a man-of-war with the allegorical figures—Sir. R. Westmacott—cost £4200.—General Lord Heathfield in full uniform, by C. Rossi ; cost £2100.—Generals Pakenham and Gibbs, who fell at New Orleans in 1815—Sir R. Westmacott—cost £2100.—General Gillespie, by Sir F. Chantrey ; cost £1575. Sir Astley Cooper, the eminent surgeon, by E. H. Baily, erected by his friends.—Sir John Moore, the dying General, and allegorical figures, by John Bacon, jun. ; cost £4200.—Wolfe's ode is a far better monument than this.—General Abercrombie, by Sir R. Westmacott. The General is represented as falling wounded from his horse.—The Egyptian sphynxes indicate the country where he received his death wound.—Sir William Hoste, in naval uniform, by Campbell.

In the South-West Ambulatory : Dr. William Babington, by W. Behnes.—Sir William Jones, the scholar and Indian judge, by John Bacon, jun.

In the South-West Aisle : Bishop Middleton in the act of confirming two Hindoos, by Lough.—Monument to the officers of the Coldstream Guards who fell at Inkermann. Eight names are inscribed on the tablet, over which are two guardsmen in mourning attitude ; by Baron Marochetti.

In the Nave : Sir Joshua Reynolds, in the gown of a doctor of Laws, by Flaxman.

In the North-West Ambulatory : Sir Pulteney Malcolm, a statue, by E. H. Baily.

In the North Transept : Lord Rodney, by Rossi ; cost £6300. —General Picton, who fell at Waterloo—a bust with a group of allegorical figures ; cost £3150.—Earl St. Vincent—a statue, by E. H. Baily, cost £2100.

In the *Crypt* below the church, the entrance is by a door near Howard's monument, are the remains of various distinguished persons. These vaults, dimly lighted by grated windows, are divided into three avenues by pillars of great strength.

In the South Aisle have been interred Sir Christopher Wren; John Rennie, the engineer; Sir Joshua Reynolds, and his brother artists, Opie, Barry, West, Fuseli, Dawe, Lawrence, and Turner. Here are preserved some monuments which were in old St. Paul's—the effigies of Dr. Donne, Sir Nicholas Bacon (Lord Bacon's father), and Lord Chancellor Hatton, and the mutilated bust of Dr. Colet founder of St. Paul's school.

In the Middle Aisle lie Lord Chancellor Wedderburn, Dr. Boyce, the musical composer, with others. A large porphyry sarcophagus contains the body of the Duke of Wellington, and close by is an altar tomb holding the remains of Sir Thomas Picton. The Wellington Chapel is lighted by gas issuing from granite candelabra. The state funeral when the great Duke was brought to rest in the vaults of St. Paul's will be well remembered.

Under the Dome is a sarcophagus of black marble, in which are laid the remains of our naval hero Nelson. His coffin was made out of the mainmast of the *L'Orient*, and was given to him by one of his captains, that he might be buried in one of his own trophies. Close by, lie Nelson's brother; "that gallant fellow Collingwood;" and Admiral the Earl of Northesk.

The cathedral establishment consists of a dean, a precentor, and sub-precentor, chancellor, treasurer, several prebends, and minor canons, six vicars choral, and several choristers. Dr. Milman, well-known for his historical works, is the present dean. Sydney Smith and Mr. R. H. Barham, the author of the "Ingoldsby Legends," were prebends at the same time.

In May, the anniversary festival of the sons of the clergy takes place in the cathedral, when there is a grand performance of sacred music. The anniversary of the charity schools is usually held in June, when the singing of many thousand children under the cupola produces a very impressive effect.

WESTMINSTER ABBEY.—The nave and transept are open free to the public between nine and three daily; and also in summer from four to six P.M. To see the rest of the abbey a fee of sixpence is paid, and parties are accompanied by a guide. Enter at "Poet's Corner," in the south transept. On Sundays there is choral service in the choir at ten A.M. and three P.M.,

WESTMINSTER ABBEY — North Side.

and in the nave at seven P.M.; and on week days service is performed at 7.45 A.M., ten A.M., and three P.M. During the time of service persons are not allowed to inspect the monuments.

This noble building, one of the few architectural boasts of London, stands on the site of a church commenced by Sebert, King of Essex, about the year 610, on what was then an island in the Thames, called Thorney Island. When King Edgar, 360 years afterwards, completed it, it was named from being the minster west of St. Paul's. That structure was laid waste by the Danes. Edward the Confessor (1050) erected another edifice, which was probably nearly as large as the present one. This has been thought the earliest church in what is called the Norman style erected in Britain. Portions of that building still exist in the "Dark cloister," the sub-structure or undercroft of the dormitory (the present Westminster school-room), the lower storey of the refectory which forms the south side of the cloister, and two massive piers in the chapel of the Pyx. Edward was buried here, and his successors did much in the next century and a half towards adorning and enriching the building. Trifling remains of late Norman are found in the fragment of a chapel seen to the east of the Little Cloister. Henry III. began in 1220 to rebuild the church, which was soon afterwards greatly damaged by fire. The choir chevets and transept of the church, and the chapter-house, belong to that period when the style in vogue was what we call pointed. Edward I. repaired the damage, and added the eastern half of the nave and the adjoining part of the cloisters. The west end of the nave, the remaining part of the cloisters, the abbot's house (the present deanery), and the Jerusalem chamber, were added in the reigns of Edward II. and Edward III. Henry VII. removed the Lady Chapel, and built the rich edifice at the east end, which is called after him. At the Dissolution, the government of the establishment was committed to a dean and prebendaries. Mary gave it to an abbot and monks; but Elizabeth abolished their rule, and appointed a dean with twelve canons. The completion of the church went on slowly, and in the meantime the stone of the exterior had become so much decayed, that Sir Christopher Wren was called upon to replace it. This he did, but having no liking for "carving full of fret and lamentable imagery," as John Evelyn

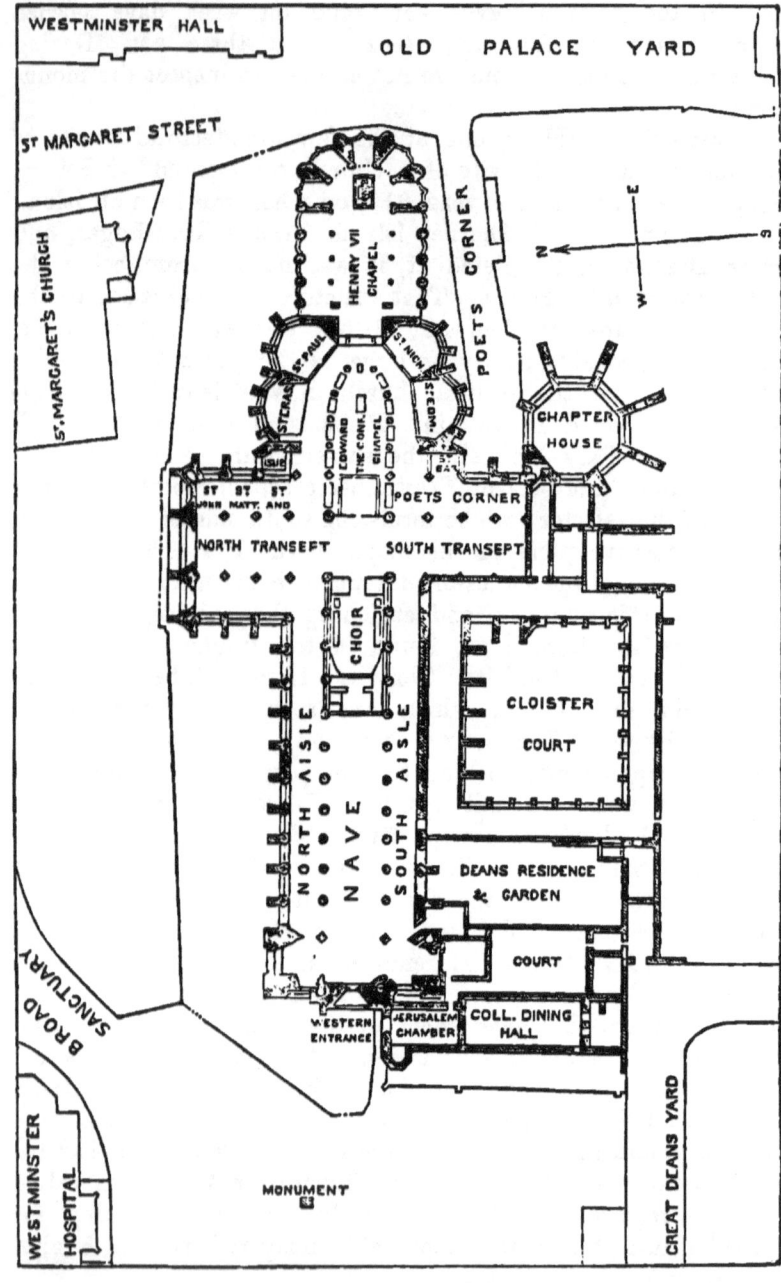

expressed it, he ruthlessly altered the details, and his successors were just as merciless. It is asserted that scarcely a trace of any original detail of the eastern portion of the exterior is left. In 1714 Wren removed the unfinished western towers, and put up what we now see, in a style wholly disagreeing with the rest of the building.

This church has been the place where our sovereigns, from Harold down to Queen Victoria, have been crowned. The ceremony was usually followed by a banquet in the great hall of the palace, known to us as Westminster Hall. The last occasion when this banquet was given was at the coronation of George IV., on which £268,000 of public money were wasted to gratify that sovereign's taste for extravagant display. The actual imposition of the crown has taken place of late years within the Sacrarium in front of the altar, before St. Edward's Chapel. When Queen Victoria was crowned, the nave, choir, and transept were fitted up with seats for spectators, and at the intersection of the choir and transept a temporary erection, covered with cloth of gold, was placed, enclosing the chair in which her Majesty was seated when she received the homage of her officers and the nobility after being crowned— enclosing also the pulpit where the coronation sermon was preached. The crown and coronation jewels are kept at the Tower, and are described elsewhere in this volume ; the ancient coronation chair in which the act of crowning is performed is in the Abbey.

In ancient times a character of sacredness was attached to all persons within the precincts of the Abbey, and hither many have fled from the persecutions of their enemies. Edward IV.'s queen fled to this sanctuary when her husband was imprisoned by the king-maker Warwick in 1470, and here she gave birth, " in great penury, forsaken of all her friends," to Edward V. On her husband's death, in 1483, she took shelter here again with the young Duke of York and her five daughters, when the Duke of Gloucester was laying his plans for seizing the crown. " She sate low on the rushes, desolate and dismayed," wrote Sir Thomas More.

The precincts of the " Collegiate Church of St. Peter's, Westminster," as this edifice is formally styled, was constituted a parish, called the Close of St. Peter's, under a recent Act of Parliament. It has been licensed for the celebration of marriages, and this ceremony is occasionally performed in it.

EXTERIOR.—Of the existing church, Mr. G. G. Scott, an architect well known for his acquaintance with the Gothic styles, has said that it claims attention for its merit as "a work of art of the highest and noblest order; for though it is by no means pre-eminent in general scale, in height, or in richness of sculpture, there are few churches in this or in any other country having the same exquisite charms of proportion and artistic beauty which this church possesses—a beauty which never tires, and which impresses itself afresh upon the eye and the mind, however frequently you view it."* The plan of the Abbey is that of a Latin cross—nave, transept, and chancel—which is apsidal, and has around it radiating chapels, which recall the *chevets* of the great French churches. Henry VII.'s Chapel, which has taken the place of the Lady Chapel, prolongs the edifice eastward from the transept almost as much as the nave extends westward. The cloisters are in the angle between the south side of the nave and the transept, part of which has been abstracted by them, so that the floor of the south arm is less wide than the northern. Examination shews that the eastern wall of the cloister is beneath the triforium of the west side of the south arm of the transept. Wren's western towers are 225 feet high. The great west window below was built in 1498. It was probably intended to erect a light tower where the transept and nave intersect, but this was never carried out; and even the intention to build one has been doubted, though Wren distinctly stated that the base of it existed in his day. The extreme length of the building, including Henry VII.'s Chapel, is 530 feet; exclusive of that chapel, 416 feet. The best view of the exterior is from the end of King Street. From this station we look upon the north side of the edifice, with its transept, containing a great rose window, 30 feet across, and a fine portico below, the beautiful gate of the temple.

INTERIOR.—The usual entrance is in the south arm of the transept, between the chapter-house and the chancel. This leads into what is called Poet's Corner, from the number of tombs of

* Gleanings from Westminster Abbey, by George Gilbert Scott, R.A., with appendices supplying farther particulars, and completing the History of the Abbey Buildings. 1861.

the poets it contains. Here vergers are in waiting, one of whom will take a party round the chapel as soon as a sufficient number of persons has collected. Visitors may walk round the transept and the nave unattended. The following are the principal admeasurements of the building :—Nave, exclusive of part used as a choir, 166 feet; width, including aisles, 71 feet 9 inches; height, 101 feet 8 inches; width of each aisle, 16 feet 7 inches. Choir, length from iron gate to altar screen, 155½ feet. Transept, 203 feet; width, including aisles, 84 feet 8 inches; height of south arm of transept, 165 feet 5 inches. Extreme length of church from west end to Henry VII.'s Chapel, 383 feet; including that chapel, 511 feet 6 inches.

On entering the church, the great height of the roof will strike the eye as remarkable. Most persons of taste will regret that the glorious architecture should have been so marred by monuments, many of which are in the worst taste, and the best out of place.

It will be seen that the choir has been constructed out of part of the nave, and that it extends across the transept. The wood work of the choir was designed by Mr. Blore, and executed in 1848. The ornamentation of the dean's stall is very elaborate. The canons' stalls have groined canopies, with pediments. There is much carving and tracery, representing foliage, etc., which were executed by hand. The organ formerly occupied a position that entirely obstructed a general view of the interior, but in 1848 it was rebuilt, and placed on the north, south, and east sides of the screen. It has thirty-seven stops and three cases, of which those under the north and south arches contain the "grand" and "swell" organs; whilst that on the east side of the screen contains the "choir" organ. The altar is modern, having been erected from B. Wyatt's designs at the coronation of George IV. The Mosaic pavement is very curious. It was laid down by Richard de Ware, abbot of Westminster, in 1260, in the form of a square, the stones and workmen being brought from Rome. All the brass letters of the inscriptions, and many of its marble tesseræ are gone. The circles contained some Latin verses, the meaning of which was thought to refer to the Ptolemaic system. Only one line can now be made out.

A good deal of stained glass has been placed in the windows within the last few years, and this adds considerably to the effect of the interior views. Memorials in the shape of stained glass have been inserted in the seven lancet windows of the north transept, and its west aisle, to the memory of officers who fell in the Indian mutiny. The rose window in the south transept contains the word " Jehovah" in the centre, which is surrounded by thirty-two subjects taken from the life of Christ, and exterior to these are various symbols interspersed amongst Mosaic ornaments.

Before setting out on our perambulation of inspection, let us quote Addison's words, always impressive, but never more so than when in presence of the objects on which he comments :— " When I look upon the tombs of the great, every emotion of envy dies within me ; when I read the epitaphs of the beautiful, every inordinate desire goes out; when I meet with the grief of parents on a tombstone, my heart melts with compassion ; when I see the tombs of the parents themselves, I consider the vanity of grieving for those we must quickly follow. When I see kings lying by those who deposed them ; when I consider rival wits placed side by side, or the holy men that divided the world with their contests and disputes, I reflect with sorrow and astonishment on the little competitions, factions, and debates of mankind. And when I read the several dates on the tombs, of some that died yesterday, and some six hundred years ago, I consider that great day when we shall all of us be contemporaries and make our appearance together." To this we will add some lines of the poet Wordsworth, taken from one of his sonnets :—

> " Be mine in hours of fear
> Or grovelling thought, to find a refuge here,
> Or through the aisles of Westminster to roam ;
> Where bubbles burst, and folly's dancing foam
> Melts if it cross the threshold ; where the wreath
> Of awe-struck wisdom droops."

THE CHAPELS—The first chapel we are taken to is that of *St. Benedict*, a square compartment next Poet's Corner, where may be seen some fragments of the decoration which originally extended round the church. In the middle is the tomb of Lord Treasurer Cranfield, Earl of Middlesex (temp. James I.) and his countess. On an ancient Gothic tomb lies the effigy of Archbishop Langham, 1376, who was monk, prior, and abbot of the Abbey. Marble tomb to Frances, Countess of Hertford, d.

1598. Mural recess, with kneeling figure of Dean Goodman, d. 1601; another dean's tomb, Dr. Bill, with engraved brass, 1561.

Left of the entrance-gate to the chapels is an ancient monument, date unknown, to the Saxon King Sebert and Athelgoda his queen. Over it is a curious piece of work inclosed in a glass case. It has apparently formed part of an altar decoration of the fourteenth century. Between St. Benedict's and the next chapel is a monument of Mosaic work, much defaced, to the children of Henry III. and Edward I.

CHAPEL OF ST. EDMUND.—This is of polygonal shape, like the three next chapels, and contains an alabaster statue of John of Eltham, second son of Edward II., d. 1334, at the age of nineteen ; a small table monument to William and Blanch, son and daughter of Edward III.; monument to the Earl of Stafford, d. 1762 ; statue by N. Stone of Francis Holles, son of Lord Clare, d. 1622, in Grecian armour, with an epitaph in English verse ; the sleeping figure, in alabaster, of Lady Elizabeth Russell, who died from pricking her finger with a needle ; a recumbent statue of Lord John Russell, d. 1584, erected by his wife, a learned lady, who wrote the epitaphs inscribed on the tomb, one in Greek, three in Latin, and some English verses, which do not give a high idea of her ladyship's poetical talent ; a canopied tomb and recumbent effigy to Sir Bernard Brocas, chamberlain to Richard II.'s first queen ; he was beheaded on Tower Hill, 1399 ; low altar tomb (the engraved brass is gone) to Humphrey Bourgchier, a knight slain on Barnet Field fighting for Edward IV., 1471 ; on the pavement two engraved brasses, one to Archbishop Waldeby, 1397 ; the other, thought the finest in London, to the Duchess of Gloucester, 1399 ; an elaborate tomb to the eighth Earl of Shrewsbury, d. 1617, and his countess ; their effigies on a table of black marble ; ancient monument, one of the oldest in the building, to William de Valence, Earl of Pembroke, slain at Bayonne, 1296 ; the wooden effigy was originally covered with copper, and was surrounded by thirty-three figures of the Earl's relations. This monument is supposed to be a French work, probably executed by an enameller from Limoges.

CHAPEL OF ST. NICHOLAS.—The screen is of the time of Henry IV. Here is the immense tomb of Ann, Duchess of Somerset, d. 1587, wife of the Lord Protector, who was beheaded on Tower Hill, 1551 ; another one as large (according to the guide book

" one of the most magnificent in the Abbey") to the wife and daughter of Queen Elizabeth's Lord Burghley. Her epitaph states that Lady Burghley was well versed in the Greek sacred writers ; a large monument in the middle, by Stone, to Sir George Villiers and his wife, the father and mother of James I.'s favourite, the first Duke of Buckingham ; monument, with a long inscription, to the Lady Elizabeth Percy, sole heiress of Algernon, Duke of Somerset, who brought the Percy estates to the Smithson's by her marriage with Sir Hugh Smithson, afterwards Duke of Northumberland. Amongst the old monuments are—against the screen a recumbent figure of Philippa, Duchess of York, d. 1431 ; under the middle window the tomb of Bishop Sutton (d. 1483) ; the brass figure has disappeared ; in the floor a brass of Sir Humphrey Stanley, knighted on Bosworth field, d. 1505. Sir Henry Spelman, the learned antiquary, was interred at the door of this chapel. The remains of Katharine Valois, Henry V.'s queen, d. 1437, originally interred in the Lady Chapel, were brought here and deposited under Sir George Villiers' tomb in 1776.

HENRY VII.'s CHAPEL.—We have now arrived at the foot of the marble steps that lead up to this splendid piece of Gothic architecture. Notice the curiously wrought brass gates, exhibiting numerous devices of the founder. It is usual to conduct visitors first into the *South Aisle* (for the chapel consists of a nave and two aisles) where will be seen a number of monuments that greatly injure the effect of the architecture. Monument to Lady Mary Douglas (d. 1577), whose relationship to fourteen kings and queens is fully chronicled thereon ; the sumptuous monument to Mary, Queen of Scots (d. 1587), erected by her son, James I., after her execution at Fotheringay ; her body was brought privately hither and interred in a vault under the monument ; monument by Torrigiano to Margaret, Countess of Richmond, mother of Henry VII. ; monument to the first wife of Sir Robert Walpole the minister ; monument to George Monck, first Duke of Albemarle, the chief instrument in the restoration of Charles II. (d. 1670), and his son and his wife. The royal vault is below, and contains the remains of Charles II., William III. and his Queen, Queen Anne and her husband, Prince George of Denmark.

We now quit the aisle for the NAVE. " Entering the middle aisle of this wonderful mausoleum the visitor knows not what to admire first or most. The fretted vault work overhead ' pendent by subtle magic ;' the close array of saints ranged beneath the upper windows, now nearly concealed by the banners of the Knights of the Bath ;* the elaborate wood-work of the canopies and stalls, wrought, as for more than mortal eye, alike in what is seen and what is unseen, carved even to the very undersides of the *misereres* or turning seats, whose unstable support, when turned up, was to ensure the wakefulness of the religious in their long night services ; how noble and real is all here !" The dimensions of this chapel within are—Nave, length, 103 feet 9 inches ; width, 35 feet 9 inches ; height, 60 feet 7 inches. The aisles are each 62 feet 5 inches long, and 17 feet wide. The entire breadth of the chapel is 70 feet. The ceiling is of stone, and persons have room to walk between it and the roof. " The plan of the chapel is neither complex nor unusual, a simple central avenue, terminating eastward in five sides of an octagon, and flanked by lower aisles, which would continue round this octagon apses did not six solid wedge-shaped masses divide this curved portion of the aisle into five square recesses or chapels as they are called, open to the central apses, but not to each other or the side aisles." At the east end is the black marble tomb of Henry VII. and his queen, executed by Torrigiano, an Italian sculptor. It is enclosed by a chantry of brass. Edward VI., the boy king, was interred at the head of the tomb. In a vault under the chapel lie the remains of George II. and his queen, his son the Prince of Wales, and the Duke of Cumberland, the hero of Culloden. In the recesses surrounding Henry VII.'s tomb are some modern monuments, which all must consider an intrusion ; one of brass to the Duke (d. 1623) and Duchess of Richmond ; a recumbent statue of white marble (by Westmacott) of the Duke of Montpensier (d. 1807), erected by his brother Louis Philippe, Duke of Orleans, the late King of France ; the effigy (by Scheemakers) of Sheffield Duke of Buckingham (d. 1720), who, according to his epitaph, lived doubtful, and died unresolved. On the north side of the King's tomb is that of George Villiers, Duke of Buckingham, who was assassinated by Felton in 1628. The effigies of the Duke and his Duchess are recumbent on a table supported by eight emblematical figures in gilt brass. The great west window of the chapel is 45 feet high by 31 feet wide.

* These are the banners of the Knights in 1812 ; none have been hung here since that date.

Leaving the nave for the *North Aisle,* the monuments of two Lords Halifax, of different families, are conspicuous. Near one of them was interred Joseph Addison (d. 1719), an honoured name in our literature. The late Earl of Ellesmere caused the spot to be marked by a white marble slab, which bears the lines written by Addison's friend Tickell—

> "Ne'er to these chambers, where the mighty rest,
> Since their foundation came a nobler guest ;
> Nor e'er was to the bowers of bliss conveyed,
> A fairer spirit or more welcome shade :
> Oh, gone for ever ! take this long adieu,
> And sleep in peace, next thy loved Mountague."

Close by is the sumptuous monument erected by James I. to his predecessor Elizabeth. When some bones, believed to be those of the princes Edward and Richard were found in the tower, they were brought here by command of Charles II., as an inscription on the tomb records. Underneath this aisle is a vault in which the remains of James I. and his queen, Anne, were deposited.

At the beginning of this century, £42,000 were laid out in restoring the exquisite workmanship of this chapel, but we are sorry to say that the stone employed, being soft, is already decaying.

On leaving King Henry's Chapel, we arrive at St. Paul's Chapel. The two oldest monuments here are those to Robsart, Lord Bourchier, Henry V.'s standard-bearer at Agincourt; and Sir Giles Daubeney, d. 1507. There is a curious monument of black marble to Lord Cottington (d. 1652), at the top of which is a circular frame of gilt brass, with the bust of that nobleman's wife. The epitaph of Sir James Fullerton has a sentence full of puns. The most interesting object here is the white marble statue of James Watt, executed by Chantrey. The pedestal bears this inscription, from the pen of Lord Brougham :—"Not to perpetuate a name which must endure while the peaceful arts flourish, but to shew that mankind have learned to honour those who best deserve their gratitude, the king, his ministers, and many of the nobles and commoners of the realm, raised this monument to James Watt, who, directing the force of an original genius, early exercised in philosophical research, to the improvement of the steam-engine, enlarged the resources of his country, increased the power of man, and rose to an eminent place among the most illustrious followers of science, and the real benefactors of the world."

Outside the Chapel, near the monument of Admiral Holmes, John Pym the Parliamentarian, was interred. Ascending a short narrow flight of steps, we find ourselves in

THE CHAPEL OF ST. EDWARD, which has a raised floor inside the columns of the apse, and is separated by a screen from the transept. Against this screen is placed the Coronation Chair, in which all our sovereigns have been crowned since Edward I., who brought from Scotland the black stone of Scone, which will be seen under the seat, as to which the superstition ran that it was part of Jacob's pillow. It had been previously preserved as a sacred object by the Scottish Kings. The second chair was made for William III.'s queen, and is used when a queen consort is crowned. Above the chairs on the screen, are some legendary sculptures relating to Edward the Confessor (d. 1065), whose shrine, erected by Henry III. in 1269, is in the middle of the floor. It was richly decorated with gold and jewels, but is now a sad wreck. Editha, his queen, lies interred on the south side, and somewhere near, Matilda, queen of Henry I., but there is no record of the exact place. On the north side is the tomb of Henry III. (d. 1272), composed of porphyry and mosaic, and supporting an effigy in gilt brass. At his feet is the tomb of Eleanor, Edward I.'s queen, d. 1290. At the east end of this chapel is the chantry of Henry III., and beneath is the tomb of Henry V., where lies an oaken effigy without the head, which, being made of silver, was stolen many years ago. The saddle, helmet, and shield, in the chantry, are said to have been used by the king at Agincourt. The next tomb is that of Philippa, queen of Edward III.,* adjoining which is the tomb of Edward himself, his effigy reposing on a slab of grey marble. Only six out of many statues remain around the tomb, and these represent six of his children. Observe the shield and sword, seven feet long, carried before the king in France. Next to the stone covering Thomas of Woodstock, brother of the Black Prince, is the tomb of Richard II. and his queen, covered by a canopy of wood, on which are the remains of an ancient painting of the

---

* We are sorry to say that some unprincipled person lately stole from Queen Philippa's tomb two ancient statuettes, which the conservating architect of the church had only recently replaced there. It is believed that the thief knew the artistic value of his spoil.

Virgin. The body of Edward I. (d. 1307), lies under a large rude tomb composed of five marble slabs. The inscription calls him "Scotorum malleus," and on the north side, facing Scotland, is the command "pactum serva" (observe the treaty). When this tomb was opened in 1774, the king's body, measuring six feet two inches, was found well preserved, wrapped in two robes, with a crown on the head, and a sceptre in each hand.

Descending from this chapel of the kings, we next enter the CHAPEL OF ST. ERASMUS where, besides some older tombs, is an Elizabethan monument to Lord Hunsdon, d. 1596 ; and the tomb of Cecil, Earl of Exeter, d. 1622 ; the marble effigy of his first wife lies beside his, and a space was reserved on the left side for his second wife, but she refused to occupy an inferior position. Nevertheless, she was buried in the vault below. ST. JOHN THE BAPTIST'S CHAPEL.—A square compartment formerly contained the tomb of Abbot Islip, who was employed by Henry VII. in decorating his new chapel. In various places will be seen the abbot's punning device—an eye, and the branch or *slip* of a tree, making together Islip. Tomb of Sir Christopher Hatton (d. 1619) and his wife, with their recumbent effigies. Near this chapel are two monuments of Knights Templar, one of Edmund Crouchback, son of Henry III., and the other of Aymer de Valence, "Proud Pembroke's earl was he," son of the William de Valence whose tomb is in St. Edmund's Chapel. The tomb of Aveline, Countess of Lancaster, wife of Crouchback, is the oldest in the Gothic style here. Close by is the monument of General Wolfe, killed at Quebec in 1759. There is a monument to him in St. Paul's also.

THE CHAPELS OF ST. JOHN THE EVANGELIST, ST. ANDREW, AND ST. MICHAEL, once separate, but now thrown together, occupy the east aisle of the north transept, and are almost filled up with monuments.—Sir Francis Vere (d. 1608), four kneeling knights, of excellent sculpture, support a slab on which loose armour is laid.—Admiral Kempenfeldt who went down in the *Royal George* at Spithead, 1782. Cowper's lines on the occurrence are well known.—Telford, the engineer, has a white marble statue of colossal size by Baily. As his epitaph declares, "his noblest monuments are to be found amongst the great public works of this country."—Quite at the end is a simple tablet to Dr. Thomas Young, the first promulgator of the undulatory theory of light, a man of eminent and very various ability, d. 1829.—White marble statue of Mrs. Siddons as Lady Macbeth in the night scene, by Thomas Campbell.—Sarah, Duchess of Somerset, d. 1692, a monument with weeping charity boys.—Next to this is a monument by Roubiliac to husband and wife named Nightingale, which has been much admired for the vivid reality of the sculpture. It represents the young lady supported by her husband, who is endeavouring to ward off the dart aimed at her by the figure of death issuing from a tomb below.—Near the entrance to the chapel is a tablet to Sir Humphrey Davy, the eminent chemist, d. 1829.—On leaving the chapel, Lord Ligonier's monument is seen, bearing his likeness in profile. He was one of Marlborough's lieutenants.

We are now in the north transept, where the guide takes his leave of visitors. Notice from this point the rose window on the south transept. The tracery and stained glass are modern.

NORTH TRANSEPT.—Statue, by Gibson of Rome, of Sir Robert Peel (d. 1850), represented as addressing the House of Commons in *Roman costume.*—Roubiliac's monument to Admiral Warren (d. 1752), with Hercules, the figure of Navigation, etc.—Tablet to Mrs. Grace Scott (d. 1645), with a punning verse.—Chantrey's monument to Sir John Malcolm (d. 1833), who served in India —the figure is in uniform.—Large monument to William Cavendish, Duke of Newcastle (d. 1676), and Margaret, his Duchess, "a wise, witty, and learned lady," which her many books do well testify." "Of all the riders of Pegasus," says Horace Walpole, "there have not been a more fantastic couple than his Grace and his faithful Duchess, who was never off her pillion." Large monument to another Duke of Newcastle, John Holles, who married the grand-daughter of the preceding (d. 1711). His only child, a daughter, married the eldest son of Queen Anne's minister, Harley; to effect which marriage was said to be the sole object of Harley's tenure of office.—Statue, by Chantrey, of the statesman Canning.—Rysbrack's monument to Admiral Vernon.— Scheemakers' monument to Admiral Sir Charles Wager.—Bacon's statue of the first Earl of Chatham (d. 1778) in Parliamentary robes, "erected by the King and Parliament" at a cost of £6000 —"gives Chatham's eloquence to marble lips" (*Cowper*).—Nollekens' monument to three captains who were killed under Admiral Rodney in April 1782.—Statue of the Marquis of Londonderry, better known as the minister Lord Castlereagh.—Hereabouts are interred—William Pitt, Lord Castlereagh, George Canning, C. J.

Fox, Grattan, and Wilberforce. Flaxman's fine monument to the great judge Lord Mansfield (d. 1793), the friend of Pope, who has dedicated one of his poems to him.

"Here Murray, long enough his country's pride,
Is now no more than Tully or than Hyde."

This was erected at the expense of a private gentleman.—Flaxman's statue of John Kemble in the character of Cato ; Behne's statue of Sir W. W. Follett, Attorney-General, d. 1845 ; Sir R. Westmacott's monument to Mrs. Warren, with the beautiful sculpture of a woman and child ; Bacon's bust of Warren Hastings, the Indian governor, d. 1818 ; Chantrey's statue of Francis Horner, d. 1817 ; monument to Jonas Hanway, the philanthropist, d. 1786 ; large monument, by Scheemakers, to Admiral Watson, d. 1757, " where you see in the centre of a range of palm trees an elegant figure of the Admiral in a Roman toga ;" Scheemaker's monument to Admiral Balchen (d. 1774), who was lost in the " Victory," with nearly a thousand other persons, the vessel being overtaken by a violent storm in the English Channel ; " from which sad circumstance we may learn that neither the greatest skill, judgment, or experience, joined to the most firm, unshaken resolution, can resist the fury of the winds and waves ;" Scheemaker's monument to Lord Aubrey Beauclerk, killed in action at Carthagena, 1740.

NORTH AISLE.—Pursuing our way down this aisle towards the west entrance, we shall first see the monument by Thrupp to Sir T. F. Buxton (d. 1845), well known for his labours against slavery and the slave trade ; an old monument to Sir Thomas Heskett (d. 1605), with his recumbent effigy on a tufted gown ; a tablet to Dr. Charles Burney (d. 1814), the epitaph written by his daughter, the authoress of Evelina ; tablets to three other older musicians, Dr. Blow, Dr. Croft, and Purcell (d. 1695), the composer of some delightful melodies. The inscription says, he " is gone to that blessed place where only his harmony can be exceeded." Brass to Bishop Monk, the Greek scholar, d. 1859 ; Chantrey's seated figure of Sir T. S. Raffles, Governor of Java, d. 1826 ; monument to Lord Kinsale (d. 1719), descended from that de Courcy, who, by reason of his great valour, obtained for himself and his heirs the extraordinary privilege of standing covered in the presence of the sovereign ! a privilege claimed by the present Lord Kinsale ; Joseph's statue of William Wilberforce (died 1833), who was honoured by a public funeral ; Chantrey's monuments to the Rev. E. L. Sutton and Sir G. L. Staunton ; Bacon's monument to Archbishop Agar, who, during the tenure of his archiepiscopal office, was made an earl.

On arriving at Admiral Baker's monument, turn to the left and inspect the new screen behind the organ. Figures of Edward the Confessor, Edward III. and his queen Eleanor, and Eleanor, queen of Edward I., will be seen on pedestals.—Notice Rysbrack's monuments to Sir Isaac Newton (d. 1726), and the Earl of Stanhope, d. 1720. Returning to the aisle, Scheemakers' monument to Dr. Mead, d. 1754 ; Westmacott's monument, in the window, to Spencer Percival, the minister assassinated, 1812, by Bellingham, who took him for another person ; erected at the public expense.—Opposite Mrs. Beaufoy's monument lie the remains of Telford, the engineer, Robert Stephenson, and Sir Charles Barry. —In front of General Killigrew's monument, Ben Jonson was interred in a standing position ; near whom are the remains of John Hunter, lately removed from the vaults of St. Martin's-in-the-Field. The College of Surgeons, who now possess Hunter's museum, have placed over him an inscribed brass, let into red granite in the pavement. Near this is another brass, to the memory of General Sir Robert Wilson and his wife.—Scheemakers' monument to Dr. Woodward, d. 1728 ; the head and lady's figure have been much admired.

At the *West end of the Nave*, Sir R. Westmacott's monument to C. J. Fox, d. 1806 ; Theed's bust of Sir James Mackintosh, d. 1832 ; the younger Westmacott's bust of Tierney the statesman ; Baily's monument to Lord Holland (d. 1840), the host of the literary and political celebrities whom he assembled at Holland House ; Weekes' bust of Zachary Macaulay, father of the historian. Over the west door, Sir R. Westmacott's monument to William Pitt, d. 1806, erected by Parliament. An immense monument, 36 feet high, to Captain James Cornewall, killed at the sea-fight off Toulon, 1743, erected by Parliament.

Do not omit to notice the grand view to be had from the western doorway. Looking up the nave, the eye sweeps the whole body of the church up to the semicircular termination enclosing the chapel of Edward the Confessor. Notice also the gallery above the aisles, or, as it is usually called, the triforium, which is very spacious, and capable of containing thousands of persons. It was no doubt intended by the architect for spectators of ceremonials and processions. The arcade, towards the nave below the clerestory, is very beautiful, perhaps the most beautiful example in existence. It is conjectured that Caxton, our first printer, first set up his printing press somewhere in this gallery.

SOUTH AISLE.—Monument to Secretary Craggs, d. 1720, the friend of Pope, who wrote his epitaph.—Thrupp's statue of Wordsworth the poet (d. 1850), placed in the baptistry. The inscribed lines, one of his own sonnets, refer to the *place*, and to the *man*. Half-length marble portrait of William Congreve the dramatist (d. 1728), erected by Sarah, Duchess of Marlborough, to whom he bequeathed his money. Opposite Bishop Sprat's monument, Atterbury, the intriguing bishop, was interred, in a vault of his own construction when Dean of this church; monument to Dean Buckland the geologist, d. 1856; Roubiliac's monument to Field-Marshal Wade (d. 1748), over the door into the cloisters (his services to the roads in Scotland, where he was governor of Fort-William, are commemorated in a popular rhyme); monument to Carola Harsnet, with inscriptions in Hebrew and Greek; another to Ann Filding, the inscriptions in Hebrew and Ethiopic; these ladies were the wives of Sir Samuel Morland, and the epitaphs are alluded to in the Spectator as being so modest, that they conceal their praises in language understood by few; monument to Sir William Temple and his family, Sir William was Swift's early patron; Roubiliac's monuments to General Fleming and General Hargrave; Bird's bust of Earl Godolphin, Lord Treasurer in Queen Anne's reign; monument to Sir John Chardin the traveller; monument to Sir Palmer Fairholme, killed 1680, when Tangier, of which place he was governor, was besieged by the Moors, the epitaph was written by Dryden; Van Gelder's monument to Major André, executed as a spy by Washington during the American war, the figures of the bas-relief have been repeatedly stolen and repeatedly renewed; monument to Thomas Thynne, Esq., who was murdered in his coach, 1682, by assassins hired by Count Konigsmarck (who himself afterwards came to a violent end), to prevent him marrying the heiress of the Northumberland Percies, the Count wishing to gain her for himself; she, however, married the Duke of Somerset; notice the bas-relief representing the murder: Flaxman's bust of General Paoli, the Corsican patriot, d. 1807; Banks' monument to Dr. Isaac Watts, d. 1748; Bird's monument to Sir Cloudesly Shovell, who perished by shipwreck on the rocks of Scilly;

monument to Sir Godfrey Kneller the painter (d. 1723), designed by Kneller himself, the bust by Rysbrack, the epitaph by Pope ; Kneller, on his deathbed, desired he might not be buried in Wesminster Abbey, for " they do bury fools there," and he was interred elsewhere.

SOUTH TRANSEPT AND POET'S CORNER.—Monuments to Garrick, d. 1779 ; to Camden the historian, d. 1623 ; to Dr. Isaac Barrow. In front of the east, Sir William Davenant's remains are interred ; he succeeded Ben Jonson as poet laureate, and d. 1668. Statue of Joseph Addison, d. 1720. Near this, and in front of Dr. Outram's monument, lies Lord Macaulay. Roubiliac's monument to Handel, d. 1759, the last executed by this sculptor. Roubiliac's monument (admired by Canova) to the Duke of Argyle, d. 1743 ; over a doorway, the monument by Nollekens of Oliver Goldsmith, d. 1774 ; monument to Gay the poet, d. 1732, the epitaph by Pope, except the two lines, " Life is a jest," etc., which were his own composition ; Rysbrack's monument to Nicholas Rowe, poet laureate ; monument to James Thomson, " the sweet-souled poet of the seasons ;" monument to William Shakspere, the glory and boast of our nation, designed by Kent, executed by Scheemakers in 1742. The heads on the pedestal represent Henry V., Richard III., and Queen Elizabeth, three personages who appear in his plays. Dr. Johnson, Garrick, R. B. Sheridan, and Thomas Campbell, the poet, lie buried in front of Shakspere's monument ; statue of Campbell, lines from his poems are inscribed on the monument ; tablet to Anstey (d. 1805), author of the " Bath Guide," a witty satire, once very popular ; Chantrey's medallion of Dr. Granville Sharp, d. 1813 ; bust of the French wit, St. Evremond, d. 1703 ; Rysbrack's monument to Matthew Prior (d. 1721), executed by order of Louis XIV. ; Bacon's medallion of William Mason, the friend of Gray, d. 1797 ; monument to Thomas Shadwell, poet laureate (d. 1692), bitterly satirised by Dryden, and not forgotten by Pope ; Rysbrack's monument to John Milton (d. 1674) ; Bacon's monument to Gray the poet (d. 1771), a medallion held by the lyric muse, who points up to Milton's bust ; monument with bust of Samuel Butler, author of Hudibras, d. 1680, erected by Barber, Lord Mayor of London, " that he who was destitute of all things when alive, might not want a monument when dead ;" monument to Edmund Spencer, the prince of poets in his time, d. 1598, of marble—replacing an older one of Purbeck stone which had become decayed ; medallion with the inscription "O Rare Ben Jonson" (d. 1637) ; the emblematical figures are supposed to refer to the alleged envy and malice of his contemporaries ; monument to Michael Drayton, author of the Polyolbion and other poems, d. 1631 ; the inscribed lines have been variously ascribed to Ben Jonson and Quarles. It is more in Jonson's manner, says Southey. Anne Clifford, Countess of Dorset, is said to have erected the monuments of Spencer and Drayton ; bust of John Phillips, d. 1708 ; the Latin motto from Virgil was that prefixed to his poem "Cider." This monument was erected by Lord Chancellor Harcourt, the epitaph was written by Atterbury ; monument, much defaced, to Geoffrey Chaucer (d. 1400), erected 1556 ; monument to Cowley, d. 1667, a clever poet, but not exactly the Pindar, Horace, and Virgil of England, as his epitaph asserts ; erected by George, first Duke of Buckingham of the Grenvilles ; Scheemaker's monument to Dryden (d. 1700), erected by John Sheffield, Duke of Buckingham. Near this monument the remains of Francis Beaumont the dramatist were buried. Against the screen of the choir is a monument to Dr. Robert South, the able and virulent royalist divine, d. 1716. Between this monument and Dr. Busby's, a fragment of that of Anne of Cleves, the fourth wife of Henry VIII., may be seen ; and near her lies, without any record, Anne, the poisoned queen of Richard III. Monument to Dr. Busby, master of Westminster College, d. 1695. In the middle of the transept, a white stone covers the remains of "Old Parr" (d. 1635), who is reputed to have reached the age of 152 years, and to have lived in the reigns of ten sovereigns.

From this sketch of the monuments, it will be seen that the abbey serves the purpose of a Valhalla or a Pantheon, and that it is—

"Filled with mementos, satiate with its part
Of grateful England's overflowing dead."

Behind the wall at the back of Milton's monument, in the south transept, is the CHAPEL OF ST. BLAISE, or the old Revestry, occupying the space between this transept and the vestibule leading from the cloister to the chapter-house. Few visitors to the abbey are aware of the existence of this interesting apartment.

CLOISTERS.—To reach the beautiful *Cloisters*, when the door out of the abbey is not open, go through Great Dean's Yard, passing the Jerusalem chamber in which Henry IV. expired.   Recall the passage in Shakspere's play—

> " It hath been prophesied to me many years
>   I should not die but in Jerusalem,
>   Which vainly I supposed the Holy Land ;—
>   But bear me to that chamber ; there I'll lie ;
>   In that Jerusalem shall Harry die."

The Dean's residence is on the left after passing through the arch, but before arriving at the cloisters.   Other dignitaries have residences close by, with entrances from the cloisters.   The north and east arcades are of the reign of Edward I. ; the south and west are of later date, and have vaultings of a highly-finished geometrical character.   It will be seen by an observer standing in the south walk, that the northern arcade has been brought so closely up to the wall of the nave, that it was necessary to throw the arched buttresses over the arcade, a curious and perhaps unparalleled feature.   As to the east arcade, it will be seen from the plan that it actually enters the church, half its length being enclosed in the south transept.   As to the monuments, the oldest ones are in the south walk, where the foot-worn effigies of some early abbots will be seen.   One slab of black marble, covering the remains of a natural son of King Stephen, is known as Long Meg, from its great size.   In the east walk is a monument to General Withers, with lines by Pope ; near the first pillar, under a piece of blue marble, lies Mrs. Aphra Behn, the writer of some unreadable plays.   In this ambulatory lie also the actors Betterton, Foote, and Mrs. Bracegirdle.   Tom Brown, the wit, and Milton's friend, Henry Lawes, the composer of airs which have been praised in verse by the poet.   In the north walk is a monument to one John Lawrence, inscribed with some curious lines—

> " Short-hand he wrote, his flower in prime did fade,
>   And hasty death short-hand of him hath made."

Also a monument to Ephraim Chambers, "nec eruditus, nec Idiota," the compiler of the first encyclopædia in the English language.   In the west arcade is a tablet to Dr. Buchan, the author of a well-known work on Domestic Medicine ; and a monument to Woollett the engraver.   Scattered about are monuments to various historical names, Pulteneys, Montagues, and Godolphins, usually inscribed with long pompous epitaphs.

CHAPTER HOUSE.—A rich doorway in the east arcade leads to the *Chapter House* of Henry III.'s time. The Commons sat here before they met at St. Stephen's Chapel. At the Reformation, when taken possession of by the Crown, it was made a repository for records, which have been lately removed to the new Record Office, Chancery Lane. On the east side there is a mural decoration, dating, it is supposed, from the fourteenth century, and representing Christ surrounded by the Christian virtues. The building is octagonal in plan, has a Norman crypt, and is supported by massive buttresses. There are eight large windows, and the vaulting of the roof springs from a central clustered pillar. A very large sum would be required to renovate this beautiful edifice, which is in a disgracefully dilapidated state.

A little to the south-east of the chapter-house are the remains of the *Jewel House*, built by Richard II. The walls, parapets, and original doorways are said to be perfect ; but the interior has been changed to make it a place of deposit of the records of the House of Lords. In the basement are the original groined vaults, with their moulded ribs and carved bosses.

In the *Chapel of the Pyx*, not easily accessible, are two massive early Norman piers of Edward the Confessor's time. This chapel was used as a royal treasury. In the reign of Edward I. it was the scene of a singular robbery, when the sum of £100,000, nearly equal to two millions of our money, was abstracted. The money was intended by Edward to defray the expense of his wars against Scotland. Under the hinges of a door in this building was found not long ago some pieces of white leather, which a skilful microscopist declared to be human skin. There could be little doubt that some thief had been flayed, and that his skin had been attached to the portal as a warning to future depredators, as a farmer nails a kite to his barn-door.

CHURCHES.

The noble Cathedral of London and the ancient Abbey of Westminster having been described at length, there still remain for notice the parish and district churches, of which upwards of 460 exist in connection with the establishment. Of these it will not be expected that we can do more than select a few of the more important for mention. It is to be regretted that the remains of Gothic edifices are so scanty, there being left only a few fragments here and there to tell of structures which were doubtless glorious in their day. There is the Norman chapel in the White Tower, which the public are not admitted to see ; the Norman choir, and some arches of later date in St. Bartholomew's, Smithfield ; the transition Norman of the round church in the Temple ; the early English choir and transept of St. Saviour's ; the cloisters of St. Stephen's, Westminster, and these are absolutely all. The Gothic style is now generally thought to be the most suitable for ecclesiastical purposes. But Wren was of another opinion ; his predilections were for the Italian style, and when he was called upon to add the towers to Westminster Abbey, he abjured all "cut work and crinkle-crankle," and made the things we see. The architects who followed Wren adopted his views for several generations. The time however came again when the Gothic style was once more in fashion ; but so difficult is it to shake off the trammels of authority, that it is only quite of late years that our architects have displayed any real feeling for its beauties.

Some of the city churches bear very strange names, and we cite a few without attempting to explain them : St. Bennet-Sherehog, St. Peter-le-poor, St. Margaret-Pattens, St. Michael-le-quern, St. Mary's-Matfelon, St. Mary's Woolnoth, St. Dionis-Back-church, St. Catherine-Cree. And some of the names of the saints to which they are dedicated are not of every-day occurrence, for example, St. Vedast, St. Alphage, St. Sepulchre, St. Pancras, St. Magnus.

ALL HALLOWS BARKING, east end of Tower Street, contains an ancient communion-table, font-cover, and screen, with some early funeral brasses. In the churchyard the Earl of Surrey, Bishop Fisher, and Archbishop Laud were interred after their execution on Tower Hill, but their headless bodies were afterwards removed.

ST. ANDREW'S UNDERSHAFT, Leadenhall Street, built 1520-32, on the site of an older church, contains much stained glass, and many brasses, tablets, and monuments, including the terra cotta monument to John Stow, the chronicler (d. 1605), representing him seated at a table with his pen and a book. Stow was by trade a tailor, who neglected his business for literary pursuits.

From James I. he received—a license to beg. His industry was great, and deserved something better than this from a literary king. In the British museum there are sixty quarto volumes of old Stow's manuscript.

ALL SAINTS' CHURCH, Margaret Street, Regent Street, was consecrated in 1859, having been nine years in building. It has cost, with organ, bells, and furniture, about £65,000, of which £30,000 were contributed by a wealthy banker, and £10,000 by another individual. Mr. Butterfield was the architect. It is of variegated brick externally, the interior being resplendent with marbles, alabaster, gilding, and stained glass. Dyce painted the frescos, including forty-eight figures on the east end wall. The Marquis of Sligo presented the marble font and baptistry. The pulpit is of marble, ornamented with inlaid patterns, and supported by polished pillars of red granite. The nave is 63½ feet long, the chancel 33½ feet, the banded spire 220 feet high. The service is intoned and chanted daily in this, one of the leading show churches of the metropolis, which has been sarcastically spoken of as " a sort of casket tabernacle where no poor person dare enter, and where the beadled pew-opener would be sure to turn away the twelve apostles if they presented themselves with anything so vulgar as nets on their shoulders."

ST. BARNABAS, Pimlico.—A church and college built from the designs of T. Cundy in 1846–1849 at a cost of £20,000. The Rev. W. J. E. Bennett was the officiating minister here for some years. All the seats are free. This is one of the principal places of worship of the High Church party.

ST. BARTHOLOMEW THE GREAT, West Smithfield, is a fragment of the Priory Church of St. Bartholomew, founded in the time of Henry I., and the interior well deserves a visit from the archæologist. Specially notice the Norman choir, with its immensely strong columns, the lofty triforium with its slender pillars, and the four noble arches that once upheld the central lantern of the cruciform building. Two of these present very early examples of the pointed arch. The north and south arms of the transept have disappeared, and only part of the first bay of the nave remains. A straight wall has replaced the apsis with which the choir terminated. The surrounding ambulatory should be inspected, the style being similar to that of the Norman chapel in the White Tower. An oriel contains the rebus, a crossbow, arrow, or *bolt*, and a *tun* of Bolton, prior from 1506 to 1532.

The brick tower is dated 1628. The roof is of timber with compartments. The entrance archway, now some distance from the church, is early English, with dog-tooth ornament. Notice amongst the monuments in the church that of Rahere, the founder and first prior, but much later than his time. It is a canopied tomb, with the prior's effigy on the north of the altar. On the opposite side is Sir Walter Mildmay's monument. He was founder of Emmanuel College, Cambridge, and died 1589. Hogarth the painter was baptised in this church. Under what was the refectory of the priory there is a crypt of considerable length, with a double row of aisles, having early pointed arches.

St. Bride's, Fleet Street, one of Wren's churches, on the site of one destroyed by the great fire. This church cost £11,430. It is remarkable for its beautiful steeple, which Wren made 234 feet high, but having been struck by lightning in 1764, much of it was rebuilt, and the height was lowered by 8 feet. In 1843 it was again struck by lightning, and much damaged. The interior of the church deserves examination. The east window contains a copy on stained glass of Rubens' Descent from the Cross. In the old church were interred Wynkin de Worde, one of our early printers; Sackville, the poetical Earl of Dorset; and Lovelace, the cavalier poet; in the present church, Richardson the novelist. The opening of a short avenue from Fleet Street, after a destructive fire, cost £10,000.

St. Etheldreda's Chapel, Ely Place, Holborn, is the only part remaining of the palace of the bishops of Ely for some centuries. In Ely House John o' Gaunt died (1399). Shakspere has made the Duke of Gloucester thus address the Bishop—

> " My lord of Ely, when I was last in Holborn
> I saw good strawberries in your garden there."

Queen Elizabeth compelled the then Bishop to dispose of the property to Sir Christopher Hatton, who lived at the mansion in great state. During the time of the Parliamentary war the property went to ruin, and streets were built upon the garden. Ely Place was not erected until 1775. The chapel is now used for services in the Welsh language.

St. Giles', Cripplegate, is remarkable for its noble tower and musical chimes. It was built soon after 1545, when an older church was destroyed by fire, the tower being raised to the present height in 1682. John Fox, the martyrologist, described in

I

the register as " householder and preacher," was interred here in 1587 ; as also Sir Martin Frobisher, an early arctic voyager ; and in 1615, the famous author of Paradise Lost. The bust of this glory of our literature, and the commemorative tablet, were set up by Samuel Whitbread in 1793. Oliver Cromwell was married in this church to Elizabeth Bowchier, on the 20th August 1620. In the churchyard is a bastion of old London Wall.

St. Giles'-in-the-Fields, High Street, Holborn, is the third church erected on this site, and was completed in 1734. This church gives a name to a parish of poor people, which comes to be often contrasted with St. James'. Over the entrance gateway is a bas-relief of the Last Judgment, preserved from the Lich gate (i.e., the gate under which the corpse rested for a while at a funeral) of the old church. Chapman, the translator of Homer, Lord Herbert of Cherbury, Shirley, the dramatist, Sir Roger l'Estrange, the political writer, and Andrew Marvell, the incorruptible patriot, were buried here. Chapman's monument, erected at the expense of Inigo Jones, is placed against the exterior south wall of the church. In the cemetery in the Lower St. Pancras Road are the remains of Flaxman, the sculptor, and Sir John Soane, the architect. Not far distant from the church, to the south-west, was a place of public execution, where, in the reign of Henry V., Lord Cobham was roasted in chains.

St. George's, Hanover Square, the most fashionable church for marriages in London, was opened in 1724, having been erected from the designs of John Jones. It has an ambitious portico ; the altar picture of the Last Supper is attributed to Sir James Thornhill, Hogarth's father-in-law. Three painted windows are of Belgian work, dating from the early part of the sixteenth century. Emma Harte, who fascinated Nelson, and whom Romney painted so often, was married in this church to Sir William Hamilton.

St. George's, Hart Street, Bloomsbury, designed by Hawksmoor, consecrated 1731, is remarkable for a fine portico of eight Corinthian columns, but still more for having a statue, in Roman costume, of George I., on the top of the steeple, which is composed of a series of steps—a masterpiece of absurdity said Walpole.

> " When Harry the Eighth left the Pope in the lurch,
> The people of England made him head of the church ;
> But George's good subjects, the Bloomsbury people,
> Instead of the church, made him head of the steeple."

St. Helen's, Bishopgate, City, was the church of the priory of St. Helen, founded 1216, by Basing, Dean of St. Paul's. A series of the nun's seats is to be seen against the north wall. The interior is rich with old brasses and monuments. Amongst the latter, observe the freestone altar-tomb, with effigies, of Sir John Crosby of Crosby Hall, and his wife ; the knight has an alderman's gown over plate armour. Sir William Pickering, in dress-armour, reclining under a canopy ; Sir Andrew Judd, founder of Tunbridge School, in armour, with several kneeling figures, painted and gilt ; Sir Thomas Gresham, the founder of the Royal Exchange, a large altar tomb ; Martin Bond, a captain of train bands at the time of the Spanish Armada, represented as seated in a tent with sentinels ; Francis Baneroft, the founder of alms-houses at Mile End—it was built in his lifetime ; Sir Julius Cæsar, Master of the Rolls in the time of James I.; a deed with a pendant seal is represented, and the Latin words purport that he had given his bond to Heaven to yield up his life willingly when God should appoint—this was carved by N. Stone; Sir John Spencer, ancestor of the marqueses of Northampton, and Lord Mayor in 1594.

St. James', Piccadilly, was designed by Wren for Jermyn, Earl of St. Albans, and was consecrated in 1684. The exterior is very plain ; the interior is thought a masterpiece of the architect. The stained glass in the east window was inserted in 1846. The organ was built for James II.'s oratory at Whitehall, and was given by his daughter to this parish in 1691. The white marble font is the work of Gibbons. The cover was stolen about sixty years ago. The flowers and garlands in wood over the altar was also by Gibbons. The list of the celebrated dead interred here includes Tom d'Urfey, the play writer; Charles Cotton, Walton's friend ; Dr. Sydenham ; the two marine painters, the Vander-veldes ; Dr. Arbuthnot, Pope's friend ; Dr. Akenside ; Gillray, the caricaturist ; and Sir John Malcolm. Lord Chesterfield, the letter writer, and the first Lord Chatham, were baptised here. In the vestry is a collection of the portraits of the rectors, three of whom became Archbishops of Canterbury—Tenison, Wake, and Secker.

St. Margaret's, Westminster, on the east side of the Abbey, the church of the House of Commons, stands on the site of a church built by Edward the Confessor, about 1064. The crucifixion is represented on the painted glass of the great east window. This was executed at Gonda, in Holland, for the purpose of being presented, it is said, by the magistrates of Dort to Henry VII. It was given by the king to Waltham Abbey. At the Dissolution it was sent for safety to the abbot's private chapel at New Hall, which came into the possession of General Monk, who, to preserve the window from the Puritans, caused it to be buried in the earth ; but it was replaced at the Restoration. When the chapel was pulled down, the window was preserved in a case. In 1758 it was purchased by the churchwardens of St. Margaret's for 400 guineas, and placed in its present position. The Dean and Chapter of Westminster, however, were not willing that it should remain there, for they commenced a suit in the ecclesiastical courts against the parishioners for setting up "a superstitious image or picture." The suit lasted seven years, and was then decided in favour of the parishioners. Notice the richly-carved pulpit and recording-desk put up in 1802 ; the Speaker's chair of state in front of the west gallery ; and the painted glass of the north-east window. On certain occasions the chaplain of the House of Commons preaches here, and the Speaker with his officers, and a few members, represent the House. The walls have echoed the voices of some eminent Puritan divines, such as Calamy, Baxter, and Lightfoot. Case had the boldness to censure Cromwell, one of his auditors ; and the same preacher, when General Monk was present, said, " There are some who will betray three kingdoms for filthy lucre's sake," and then, that there might be no mistake, he cast his handkerchief into the pew where Monk sat. Amongst the persons buried here, were Skelton, Henry VIII.'s poet laureate ; Sir Walter Raleigh ; Sir William Waller, the general of the Parliament ; Hollar, the engraver ; and Blood, who stole the regalia. After Charles II. had returned, several bodies which had been previously buried in Westminster Abbey, were dug up and thrown into a pit in St. Margaret's churchyard. Amongst them were the bodies of Cromwell's mother, Sir W. Constable, one of the judges of Charles I., Admiral Blake, Pym, and May the poet. One ancient brass alone remains in the church, the others having been sold in 1644, at fourpence a pound. Amongst the monuments, notice—the Roxburgh Club's tablet to Caxton put up in 1820 ; the alabaster figures at the tomb of Marie Lady Dudley (d. 1600) ; a brass to the memory of Sir W. Raleigh, who was interred in the chancel the day he was beheaded in Old Palace yard ; Mrs. Corbet's monument, the epitaph written by Pope ; Sir Peter Parker's monument with Byron's lines ; Cornelius Van Dun's bust, in the uniform of a yeoman of the guard (d. 1577). The removal of this church has often been proposed on account of its interfering with the view, and not harmonising with the surrounding buildings.

St. Martins-in-the-Fields, Trafalgar Square, was erected by Gibbs, 1721-26, at a cost of nearly £37,000. Its length is 161 feet, and the width 80½ feet. The portico is much admired, but the position of the steeple does much to spoil its effect. This is the church of the parish in which Buckingham Palace stands, and the births of some of the Queen's children are entered in its register books. The register of 1561 records the baptism of Lord Bacon. Amongst the persons interred here may be mentioned Nell Gwynn ; the painters Vansomer, Laguerre, and Dobson ; the sculptors Stone and Roubiliac ; Robert Boyle, the chemist ; Farquhar, the play writer ; Jack Shepherd, and John Hunter. In the vaults is the tomb of Sir Theodore Mayerne, physician to James I. and Charles I., and the coffins of Miss Reay, and her murderer Hackman, connected by a chain.

St. Mary-le-bone New Church, Marylebone Road, was completed in 1817, from the designs of Thomas Hardwicke, at a cost of £60,000. The name of the district signifies St. Mary on the bourne or brook, viz., Tyburn stream.

St. Mary-le-Bow (Bow Church), Cheapside, City, is one of the most admired of Wren's churches, especially the steeple, 225 feet high, which, however, wants the grace of St. Bride's. The dragon upon it is nearly nine feet long. To have been born within the sound of Bow bell is the criterion of a cockney. A church stood on this site in very early times. It is said to derive its name, *de arcubus*, from having been built upon arches. The Ecclesiastical Court of Arches, the Supreme Court of Appeal in the Archbishopric of Canterbury, derives its name from having formerly been held in this church. There is an ancient Norman crypt here, consisting of columns and simple groinings, used by Wren to support his church. The crypt is full of coffins.

St. Mary-le-Savoy, a church standing south of the Strand, near Waterloo Bridge, which derives its name from having been built on the site of the chapel of the hospital of St. John the Baptist in a palace called the Savoy, erected by Peter, Earl of Savoy, uncle of Eleanor, queen of Henry III. The present church was built in 1505. Henry VII. endowed the chapel, and the incumbent still receives a stipend from the Crown. The ceiling, a curious relic of the old palace, was much damaged by fire in 1860, but has been restored. Notice the altar screen which has been restored of late years ; also the remaining niche of tabernacle work. George Wither, the poet, was interred here (1667). Here is a recumbent figure, doubtfully called the monument of the dowager Countess of Nottingham, who died 1681 ; a tablet to Mrs. Anne Killigrew, celebrated by the poets ; a brass on the floor near the stove indicating the resting-place of Gawin Douglas, Bishop of Dunkeld, known in literature as the translator of Virgil (d. 1522) ; a tablet to Richard Lander, the African traveller. It was here that the "Savoy Conference" between the bishops and Presbyterian clergymen took place in the reign of Charles II., with a view to a compromise. Here the Book of Common Prayer was settled. Fuller, the quaint author of "The Worthies of England," was lecturer here. A German Lutheran church is in the Savoy, as the neighbourhood is called.

St. Michael's, Cornhill, one of Wren's churches, is remarkable for having a Gothic tower (130 feet high), whilst the body is Italian. A Gothic porch has been recently added by Mr. G. C. Scott, under whose superintendence the interior has been renovated in good taste.

St. Pancras, Euston Square, one of the handsomest of the modern churches, was commenced in 1819 from Messrs. Jerwood's designs, and cost £76,679. The body was designed from the Erectheum at Athens ; the steeple, 168 feet high, from the Tower of the Winds also at Athens. The grand portico is supported by six columns with ornate capitals ; and the three doorways are copied from the Erectheum. The lateral porticoes at the east end are apparently supported by caryatides in *terra cotta*, but really by iron pillars inside the figures. The wood for the pulpit and reading-desk was furnished by the once celebrated Fairlop oak in Henhault Forest. Beneath the church are catacombs sufficient for the reception of 2000 coffins.

St. Paul's, Covent Garden, was built 1631-38, from the designs of Inigo Jones, at a cost of £4500, defrayed by the Earl of Bedford. In 1795 a fire destroyed everything but the walls, but the church was restored soon afterwards. Butler, the author of "Hudibras" ; Sir Peter Lely, who expressed a wish not to be laid in Westminster Abbey, because they buried fools there ; Wycherley, the dramatist ; Mrs. Centlivre ; Grinling Gibbons ;

Dr. Arne, the composer ; and Dr. Armstrong, the author of a poem on the " Art of Preserving Health," now almost forgotten, were interred here : Strange, the engraver, also, in the church-yard.

St. Saviour's, Southwark, near London Bridge, one of the most interesting of the metropolitan churches, was originally the church of an Augustine priory dedicated to St. Mary Overie. It was cruciform in plan, but many alterations and restorations have been made, so that at present we have but the noble choir, Lady Chapel, and transept of the ancient church, which dated from the reign of Henry III. The nave was removed in 1840, and a paltry substitute put up in its stead. The altar-screen is attributed to Fox, Bishop of Winchester about the begin-ning of the sixteenth century. The pelican, Fox's device, is seen upon it. The Lady Chapel, restored in 1832, is re-markable from the fact of its lying north and south with three aisles of equal height. The arches supporting the central tower, and the view along the transept, are striking. In this church a commission sat in 1555 for the trial of heretics, and Bishop Hooper was one of the first condemned. The ancient monuments are numerous. Notice that to the poet Gower, who died in 1402, a recumbent effigy under a canopy. It was restored in 1832 by the first Duke of Sutherland, whose family name is the same as the poet's ; John Bingham, saddler to Queen Elizabeth and her successor ; Dr. Lockyer, a quack in the reign of Charles II. ; John Trehearne, James I.'s gentleman porter, with busts of the man and his wife ; Alderman Humble and his two wives, with figures of their children, time of James I. ; cross-legged effigy, in oak, of a knight; an emaciated figure wrapped in a shroud. In the Lady Chapel a marble monument to Andrews, Bishop of Winchester (died 1626), with a recumbent effigy. In the church-yard were interred, the places unmarked, Shakspere's brother, Edmond ; John Fletcher, the dramatist ; his brother-dramatist Philip Massinger, called on the register " a stranger."

St. Stephen's, Walbrook, near the Mansion House, City, is concealed by houses, but the interior is a celebrated work of Wren, the chief feature being a dome supported on Corinthian columns. The Grocers' Company is patron of the living, and was at the cost of the wainscoting and the stained glass of the east window. Notice the rich pulpit ; and West's painting of the Martyrdom of St. Stephen. Pendleton, the vicar of Bray, whose happy facility of agreeing with the dominant party has passed into a proverb, was rector here. Dr. Croly, the author of several poems and romances, was the last rector. Sir John Vanbrugh, the play-writer, and architect of Blenheim (the subject of the epigram

> " Lie heavy on him, earth, for he
> Laid many a heavy load on thee.")

was interred in the family vault under this church.

St. Stephen's, Westminster, stands in Rochester Row, Tothill Fields. It was built in 1847 by Miss Burdett Coutts, from the designs of B. Ferrey, and is a good example of modern Gothic. The late Duke of Wellington gave the altar-cloth.

CHAPELS.

As to the places of meeting of religious bodies not connected with the Established Church, we have only space to give a very summary account. The Independents possess about 120 chapels, the Baptists 100, the Wesleyans 80, the Roman Catholics 30, the Calvinists 10, the English Presbyterians 10, the Quakers 7, the Jews 10, and other sects have from 1 to 5 each.

INDEPENDENTS' CHURCHES.

The principal Independent chapels are Weigh House Chapel, King William Street, City (Rev. Dr. Binney's) ; James Street, Westminster (Rev. Samuel Martin's); Surrey Chapel (Rev. Newman Hall).

SCOTTISH CHURCHES.

NATIONAL SCOTCH CHURCH, Crown Court, Covent Garden (Rev. Dr. Cumming's).

CROSS STREET, Hatton Garden.

SWALLOW STREET, Piccadilly.

SCOTTISH FREE CHURCH, Regent Square, where (before it became the property of the present congregation) Irving preached and the unknown tongues were heard (Rev. Dr. James Hamilton's).

WESLEYAN CHAPELS.

THE CHAPEL IN THE CITY ROAD, opposite the Burnhill Fields burial-ground. The first stone was laid by Wesley in 1777. On his death in 1791, his body " lay in a kind of state becoming the person" in this chapel, and he was interred in a vault which he had prepared for himself.

WESLEYAN MODEL CHAPEL, East India Road, Poplar, built in 1848 on an improved plan ; style decorated, with traceried windows. The Wesleyans have many other chapels in London. In 1839 this body erected a centenary hall and mission-house in Bishopsgate Street, to celebrate the 100th anniversary of its foundation.

CALVINISTIC METHODISTS.

WHITFIELD'S TABERNACLE, Tottenham Court Road, was begun in 1756 from the designs of George Whitfield, the founder of Methodism. He preached the opening sermon, and when he died in New England, Wesley preached his funeral sermon here. The chapel is 126 feet long by 76 feet, and it will hold 7000 persons. It contains monuments to Whitfield, Toplady, and Bacon the sculptor. The Tabernacle, Finsbury, and the Surrey Chapel, Blackfriars' Road, where Rowland Hill preached for fifty years, are also places of meeting for members of this persuasion.

BAPTISTS.

METROPOLITAN TABERNACLE (Spurgeon's), Newington Butts, near the Elephant and Castle, a large building erected for the Rev. C. H. Spurgeon, and chiefly by his exertions. It is built of Kentish rag, with a handsome sextile portico, and cost upwards of £31,000, which sum was subscribed by the Baptists, one individual contributing £5000. The total external length is 208 feet, and its width is 106 feet. The internal height from the basement floor to the lantern light of the roof is 89 feet. There are two tiers of galleries within the chapel, which will hold about 7000 persons. Such is the preacher's popularity that it is always filled. Admission to the seats is obtained by tickets, which are sold at the booksellers, or at the vestry, the charge being 5s. a quarter each sitting.

BLOOMSBURY CHAPEL, Bloomsbury Street, New Oxford Street (Rev. Mr. Brock's), opened in 1848. The principal front has a gable pediment, and large wheel window flanked by two tall spires.

FRIENDS' MEETING HOUSES.

The Friends or Quakers have several places of meeting in

London. The principal one is Devonshire House, Houndsditch, in the City, where the yearly meeting takes place in May.

IRVINGITE.

The followers of Edward Irving, the preacher in unknown tongues, have erected a handsome church, which they call the Catholic Apostolic Church, in Gordon Square. Brandon designed it in the early Gothic style. It is 180 feet long, and the plan is cruciform.

UNITARIAN.

The chief place of meeting for the Unitarians is at Essex Street Chapel, Strand, which was built on part of the site of Essex House. There are other chapels in Stamford Street, Blackfriars ; and Carter Lane, Doctors Commons.

SWEDENBORGIAN.

The followers of Emmanuel Swedenborg have a church in Argyle Square, King's Cross, opened in 1844. It is a neat edifice, in the Anglo-Norman style, with towers and spires 70 feet high.

FOREIGN PROTESTANT CHURCHES.

FRENCH.—Bloomsbury Street, New Oxford Street, a Gothic edifice built in 1845.

FRENCH.—St. Martin's-le-Grand, opposite the General Post-Office, opened in 1842. It was founded by King Edward VI.

FRENCH.—Dutch Church, Austin Friars', City, founded by Edward VI.

GERMAN LUTHERAN.—St. James' Palace.

GERMAN LUTHERAN.—Savoy, Strand, near the church of St. Mary-le-Savoy belonging to the establishment.

SWEDISH.—Prince's Square, Ratcliffe Highway. Emmanuel Swedenborg was interred here in 1772.

SWISS.—Moor Street, Soho.

ROMAN CATHOLIC CHURCHES AND CHAPELS.

The Roman Catholic population of London is very large. It probably amounts to 250,000, for whom there are about sixty churches and chapels, as well as several religious houses. In the principal churches the service is performed with the music of the great masters, in the execution of which the first singers in

London are engaged. High mass usually takes place at eleven on Sundays. Cardinal Wiseman, Archbishop of Westminster, is the Pope's representative in this country. His residence is at 35 Golden Square, where he is "at home" on certain days each week.

ST. GEORGE'S CATHEDRAL, St. George's Road, Southwark, is the largest building for Roman Catholic worship erected in this country since the Reformation. It is of yellow brick and Caen stone, in the decorated style of the time of Edward III., and was designed by the late celebrated architect Augustus Welby Pugin to hold about 3000 persons. The cost so far has been about £38,000, and it is still unfinished, though opened for service in July 1848. It is 235 feet long, and the spire, when completed, is intended to be 320 feet high. The stained glass of the chancel window was given by John Earl of Shrewsbury. Notice the high altar with its bas-reliefs and superb furniture, the elaborately carved stone reredos behind the altar, the pulpit, Cardinal Wiseman's throne, the font in the baptistry, and the perpendicular chantry outside the church, erected to the memory of the late Hon. E. Peter, where mass is daily performed for the repose of his soul. Adjoining the cathedral are a convent, priests' houses, and schools.

ST. MARY'S CHAPEL, Bloomfield Street, Finsbury Circus.— Pope Pius VII. presented the sacramental plate. Here lay the remains of Weber the composer until they were removed to Dresden.

CHURCH OF THE IMMACULATE CONCEPTION, Farm Street, Berkeley Square, was designed by Scoles, and opened in 1849. It was built by the Jesuits, and was the first church possessed by the order in London. The high altar was designed by Pugin for the donor, Miss Monicia Preston, and the cost was nearly £1000.

BAVARIAN CHAPEL, Warwick Street, Golden Square, stands on the site of a chapel destroyed in Lord George Gordon's riots of 1780.

FRENCH CHAPEL, Little George Street, King Street, Portman Square. French preachers of celebrity are sometimes heard here.

SARDINIAN CHAPEL, Duke Street, Lincoln's Inn Fields, the oldest of the existing Roman Catholic places of worship. It was built in 1648, and for many years the only entrance to it was through the Sardinian ambassador's house. It was partly demolished in the riots of 1780, but was afterwards restored and enlarged.   The late King of Sardinia presented the altar furniture, which cost 1000 guineas. Victor Emmanuel attended service here when visiting this country.

SPANISH CHAPEL, Spanish Place, Manchester Square, is attended by the Spanish embassy.

GREEK CHURCH.

A striking edifice, the first in London appropriated to the Greek form of worship, was opened in 1850 in London Wall, City. The style is Byzantine, the plan a Greek cross, and the cost is said to have been nearly £10,000. The service partakes of the magnificence of the Roman Catholic ritual, but no instruments are employed to assist the singing. Mass is celebrated at the richly-adorned altar with lights, etc. The priest preaches with his hat on. During the performance of service the whole congregation is standing. The Greeks in London probably do not much exceed 300.

JEWISH SYNAGOGUES.

There are several Synagogues in London. The chief one is in Great St. Helen's, Bishopgate, City. The West London Synagogue, Margaret Street, Cavendish Square, was completed in 1850. The New Synagogue, Upper Bryanston Street, Bryanston Square. The Jewish Sabbath commences at sunset on Friday, and terminates at sunset on Saturday, during which time all the shops kept by members of the Hebrew persuasion are closed. The service, with its peculiar style of singing, is highly interesting. The men worship with their hats on, and the women sit apart.

CHAPTER THE EIGHTH.

GOVERNMENT BUILDINGS AND PUBLIC OFFICES.

General Post Office—Mint—Somerset House—Treasury Buildings—
Horse Guards—Admiralty—Burlington House—Trinity House—
Herald's College.

THE GENERAL POST OFFICE, St. MARTIN'S-LE-GRAND, CITY,
was erected in 1825-9, from the designs of Sir R. Smirke. The
locality derives its name from a church and collegiate buildings,
dedicated to St. Martin, and founded so far back as the year
700 by Withred, king of Kent. Receiving large privileges from
subsequent kings, who now and then came to reside here, it had
the addition of le-grand made to its name. William of Wykeham
was one of the deans and rebuilt the church. On clearing the
site for the erection of the Post Office very numerous remains of
the Romans were discovered. The west façade of the present
Post Office is 400 feet long, in a plain Grecian style, with three
porticos, the central one of which has six columns, and leads to a
great hall, 80 feet long and 60 wide. This hall extends to the
entire width and height of the building. The receiving offices
are on the north side of this hall, and here, at the evening post
time may be witnessed a lively scene of bustle. It is said that
about 130 houses, and nearly 1000 people, were displaced when
this huge edifice was erected, and it is now too small for the
transaction of business. The nominal chief of this Government
establishment is styled the Postmaster-General, who is a member
of the ministry, and usually a peer. The actual working head
is the secretary, Sir Rowland Hill, K.C.B., who, in the face
of strenuous opposition from the authorities, succeeded in bringing about the system of a universal penny rate, in January
1840, a system which has had the most beneficial result for the
entire community, assisting commerce, and furthering the work of
education. The Government derives a large income from this insti-

tution, which is admirably managed throughout, and continually receiving improvement.

The number of letters delivered through the post-office in England in 1860 was 462 millions, which is at the rate of 22 letters for every unit of the population. In London, the average number of letters for each person was 43 for the year. Then nearly 71 millions of newspapers were delivered in that year, and about 11,700,000 book-packets. To convey this immense mass of correspondence the mails travelled daily over 144,000 miles, and the persons employed throughout the British isles were 25,200. The gross revenue for 1860 was £3,267,662 from postages, and £121,693 from money orders. The amount disbursed in salaries and pensions was £1,066,920, and for carriage, etc., £1,184,397, leaving as the net revenue of the year £1,102,479.

Small sums of money can be remitted from one place to another by means of *money-orders*, which are obtained and paid at money-order offices. A money-order can be obtained for any sum up to £10; and the charges are, for a sum under £2, threepence; above £2, and not exceeding £5, sixpence; not exceeding £7, ninepence; not exceeding £10, a shilling. The total amount remitted during 1860 by money-orders was upwards of thirteen millions sterling. The chief money-order office in London is a distinct building near the General Post Office, but on the opposite side of St. Martin's-le-Grand.

The number of misdirected and nondirected letters in the course of twelve months is something quite extraordinary. The property in such letters amounts to £200,000 a year. If the person to whom a letter is addressed cannot be found, the letter is retained for a month, and is then turned over to the Dead Letter Office.

The post-offices in London are now very numerous. To facilitate the posting of letters, iron pillar boxes have been erected at the corners of the streets, from which the letters are collected several times a-day. The postage-label stamps, which have now been imitated by all civilized nations, came into use in 1841, and the system of dividing them by perforations, the invention of Mr. Archer, was first employed in 1854. They are to be purchased at all post-offices. The cost of their production and gumming is fivepence per thousand.

When letters are addressed, " Post Office, London," or " Poste Restante," they can only be obtained between 10 and 4 at the

General Post Office (St. Martin's-le-Grand), and foreigners must produce their passports.

London and the neighbourhood have been recently divided into ten postal districts, and there is a list of streets published by the Post Office indicating the district of each.   By placing the initials of these districts on the backs of letters their early delivery will be accomplished.   The districts are—East Central (E.C.), West Central (W.C.), North (N.), North-East (N.E.), East (E.), South-East (S.E.), South (S.), South-West (S.W.), West (W.), and North-West (N.W.)

THE ROYAL MINT, TOWER HILL.

This is the place where the current coins of the United Kingdom, and of several of the colonies, are struck.   The mint was originally within the walls of the Tower.   The present buildings were commenced in 1806, and upon them and the machinery £250,000 have been expended.   At the head of the establishment is a master, who was formerly a man of mark in political affairs; but of late years the office was the award of high scientific attainments.   Sir Isaac Newton held the appointment.   Sir John Herschel was the last master; the present one is Thomas Graham, Esq., the eminent chemist.   The machines employed are of highly ingenious construction; and it is said that such is its efficiency, that if £50,000 worth of gold bullion be sent to the mint one day, the coins will be ready for delivery the next day.   Of late years such has been the influx of gold from Australia and elsewhere, and such the extension of our commerce, that the work executed here has been astonishingly great, as will be perceived from the following statement of the numbers of gold and silver coins that have been struck at the mint during the ten years ending with 1860 :—

Sovereigns	48,911,848
Half sovereigns	14,416,569
Crowns	466
Half crowns	1,493
Florins	15,633,372
Shillings	23,025,506
Sixpences	21,735,183
Groats	1,880,874
Fourpences	41,580

Threepences	.	.	.	.	.	13,605,101
Twopences .	.	.	.	.	.	47,520
Pence	.	.	.	.	.	78,408

The precious metal to be coined is first alloyed, and then cast into small bars, which are passed through rollers in order to be reduced to the exact thickness required. The sheets are then subjected to the action of the punching machines, which cut out circular disks. The blanks, as these are called, are separately tested for weight and soundness. After the rim has been raised they are taken to the coining presses, which nick the edges and stamp both sides at the same stroke, all the time feeding itself with blanks. A single press will coin from 4000 to 5000 pieces in the hour. The dies that impress the figures on the coin are made in this way. A matrix is cut by the mint engraver in soft steel, and after this has been hardened it will strike many dies.

It may perhaps interest our readers to learn the approximate number of the coins in circulation at the present time, all of which have been issued from the Royal Mint. Of gold coins (sovereigns and half sovereigns), about one hundred millions. Of silver coins, as follows :—Crowns, 2,320,000 ; half-crowns, 37,500,000 ; florins, 10,000,000 ; shillings, 112,554,000 ; six-pences, 76,132,000 ; fourpences, 30,142,000 ; threepences, 7,572,000 ; making a total of 276,220,000 pieces of silver money. Of copper money there are about 500 millions in circu-lation, which would weigh 6000 tons.

We will now give a short account of the mode of converting bar gold into coins. The gold goes to the mint from the Bank of England in the shape of ingots 8 inches long, 3 inches wide, and 1 thick, each of which is worth £800. On receipt it is assayed, and is then transferred to the melting-house, which is at the back of the edifice that fronts the Tower. Here a certain quantity is placed in a crucible along with the copper, which appears to be necessary from the assayer's report, to reduce the gold to the standard, and the crucible is subjected to the heat of a furnace. When melted, the mass is poured off into cast iron moulds, from which, when cold, the solid gold is ex-tracted in the shape of bars from 21 to 24 inches long, and 1 inch thick. These bars are assayed in order to make sure that the standard has been obtained, that is, that there are exactly two parts of copper to every 22 parts of gold. This being ascer-tained, the bars are handed over to the coiners, who transmit them to the rolling-room, an apartment 70 feet long and about 50 wide, in which there are six pairs of laminating rollers acting in frames that are firmly bolted to the granite pavement, and propelled by steam power. Each bar is passed singly between a pair of rollers, adjusted so as to be kept a certain distance apart. The result of this operation is to compress the bar and make it thinner. The operation is again and again repeated with the rollers nearer together, until the requisite thinness has been obtained. This repeated compression having had the effect of hardening the metal, this is counteracted by subjecting it for a short time to a moderate temperature, in what is called an annealing oven. The slips of gold go next to the adjusting room, which has machinery driven by steam, and where they are finally brought to the precise thickness required. In the cutting-out presses round pieces of gold are punched out of the slips at the rate of 60 a minute. The disks thus made are weighed in automatic machines costing £200 each. The action of each of these delicate machines is such, that if a disk is too light by a quarter of a grain, or too heavy by half a grain, it is separated from those of just weight, which alone are passed on to the next operation. This, technically called " marking," consists of raising a rim round the edge of the disk, and is effected by special machines in a separate room. The gold pieces, or " blanks," then go into the annealing furnace in order to be softened previous to their being stamped. Before they are taken to the coining press they are immersed in dilute sulphuric acid, made boiling hot with a view to render them bright. In the coining room, 70 feet long by 35 broad, there is a series of presses worked by atmospheric pressure, each provided with a pair of dies, one for each face of the coin. A *rouleau* of blanks being placed in a feeding tube, one of them is mechanically placed upon the lower die ; upon it descends the upper die, whilst a steel collar milled on its inner side surrounds the piece of gold. The blow is struck, and the gold, now a perfect coin, is ejected to make room for another blank about to be similarly treated. Sixty coins a minute are struck by a single press, and are turned out by it in all respects ready for circulation ; made up into collections of 701 pieces, they are then returned to the bank for issue to the public.

Applications to view the mint should be made in writing to the master, giving the writer's name and full address, and stating the number of the proposed party. If there be no objection, an order will be sent to the applicant, which is not transferable, and is only available for the day specified.

SOMERSET HOUSE, Strand, occupies the site of and derives its name from a palace commenced about 1547 by the Protector Somerset, who, however, did not live to see its completion, for he was beheaded in 1552. After having been the residence of several royal personages, it was ordered to be demolished, in order that public offices might be erected on the spot. The present building was begun in 1776 from the designs of Sir William Chambers. It is one of the few really handsome edifices that London has to boast of, and it ought to be handsome, for it cost half a million of money. The Strand front is 155 feet long; its centre is pierced by three arcades, leading into a quadrangle 319 feet by 224. The river front* about 800 feet in length, is very noble. Since Chambers' time the east wing, forming King's College, has been erected by Sir R. Smirke, and the west wing, facing Wellington Street, only recently built by Pennethorne at a cost of £81,000. The river terrace is 50 feet wide and elevated 50 feet above the bed of the stream. The central water-gate is surmounted by a colossal mask emblematic of the Thames. It is said that there are 3600 windows in Somerset House. There are about 900 persons employed here, who derive £275,000 a year from the country. On the right hand, in the entrance arcade, are the offices of the Registrar-General of Births, Deaths, and Marriages for England, the door of which is surmounted by a bust of Michael Angelo; and on the left hand is the entrance, surmounted by a bust of Sir Isaac Newton, to the rooms of the *Society of Antiquaries.* Entering the quadrangle, and turning eastward towards the gateway leading to King's College, we pass the apartments of the *Astronomical* and *Geological* Societies. Conspicuous in the quadrangle is a bronze group of George III. with a rudder, lion, and a figure of the Thames. This was the work of John Bacon and cost £2000. A large portion of Somerset House is taken up by offices connected with the affairs of the royal navy for which there is no accommodation at the Admiralty. In this department is a *Naval Museum* or model room, which may be seen on application to the surveyor general. Besides models and sections of large British ships, there are models of various foreign craft—Chinese junk, Burmese war-boat, etc.

* " My other fair and more majestic face."—COWLEY.

The *Audit Office* (where the public accounts of the realm and its colonies are audited) is here ; also the *Inland Revenue Office*, occupying the new west wing, where the sums arising from the public taxes, and the stamp, legacy, and excise duties, are dealt with.   The chairman of the commissioners of this department receives £2500 a year, the largest salary in Somerset House. In the basement stamps are impressed on deeds, etc., by machinery, postage stamps and newspaper stamps printed, etc. Several other public offices are contained in this huge building besides those we have mentioned.

TREASURY BUILDINGS, Whitehall.   Here are the offices of the *Privy Council*, the *Treasury*, the *Home Office*, the *Board of Trade*, and the official residence of the first Lord of the Treasury. The façade has a length of 296 feet.   The shell is old.   The present handsome front was designed by Sir Charles Barry (1846-7), to replace Soane's insipid exterior, and with a view to extensive changes and improvements in the neighbourhood, which were afterwards abandoned.   The front towards the Parade Ground, St. James' Park, was built by Kent in 1733.   There has been no Lord High Treasurer for many years.   The office is put in commission, and the first lord is usually chief of the cabinet or prime minister.   The other commissioners are styled lords, though commoners without titles.   Since the accession of George III. the Sovereign has never sat at the Treasury table, but the throne still remains at its head.   At the *Privy Council Office* the Judicial Committee sits to hear appeals, and other cases in which Acts of Parliament have given it jurisdiction.   Here are preserved the minutes of the proceedings of the privy council since 1540.   A privy councillor is styled " Right Honourable" although a commoner.   The official designation of the *Board of Trade* is, the Committee of the Privy Council for Trade, and it has a distinct president, who has a seat in the cabinet.   The *Home Office* is the place where the Secretary of State for the Home Department transacts business.

The *Colonial Office* and the *Foreign Office* are in the mean cul-de-sac called Downing Street.   Each is presided over by a principal secretary of state and cabinet minister. At the first, the business connected with our numerous colonies is transacted ; at the second, the business arising out of our relations to foreign powers.   Here foreign office passports are issued to British subjects, on the recommendation of a banker, at a charge of 2s.

The *Chancellor of the Exchequer's Office* is also in Downing Street. He is a cabinet minister and frequently the leader of the House of Commons. This is the office into which the vast income of Great Britain passes, whilst all payments are made through the medium of the Treasury and other offices. The Chancellor's duties are now purely ministerial, he no longer having judicial functions in the Court of Exchequer. The *Office of the Secretary of State for War* (a post first established during the Crimean war), is in the old Ordnance Office, 86 Pall Mall, with the addition of Buckingham House. The Office of the *Secretary of State for India in Council* (a newly created post) is at present in the Westminster Hotel, Victoria Street.

It has been for some time past in contemplation to erect a large pile of buildings, to contain the offices of several departments of the government, and premiums were awarded, on competition, for designs sent in. Great differences of opinion exist as to the style of architecture, and nothing further has been done.

THE HORSE GUARDS, Whitehall, in front of which two mounted cavalry soldiers stand on guard during the day. The building was erected in 1753, from whose design is not certainly known, though Kent has usually the credit of it. The central turret bears a clock, facing two ways, which has a high character for accuracy, and is consequently the standard public time-keeper for the west end of London. The offices of the Commander-in-Chief, the Adjutant-General, and the Quarter-Master-General are at the Horse Guards. In the audience-room, where the Commander-in-Chief and his military secretary hold their levees, are portraits by Gainsborough of George III. and his Queen, and a marble bust of their son, the late Duke of York. Through the centre of the building is a carriage-way into St. James' Park, which only the royal family and certain privileged persons are allowed to use. Foot passengers are permitted to pass through the side arch-ways. At the rear is the parade-ground, where inspections of the troops are made.

THE ADMIRALTY, Whitehall, a building which cannot be praised for its architectural beauty, is the place where the business connected with the management of the Royal Navy is transacted. The present front was put up about 1726 by Ripley, satirized by Pope in the Dunciad. The screen, with its characteristic ornaments, was designed by the brothers Adam in 1776.

The remains of Lord Nelson lay in state here in 1806, and hence the procession moved with the body to the place of its interment, St. Paul's. The office of Lord High Admiral has been put in commission for nearly 200 years, with the exception of a few short periods, and many of our naval worthies have been first lords. It is now usual to make a civilian first lord, and the others are chiefly naval men. Adjoining the Admiralty is a house for the first lord, and some of the junior lords have residences in the northern wing. There is here a portrait of Lord Nelson, painted at Palermo in 1799 by Guzzardi, wearing the Sultan's diamond plume, and in the secretary's house are portraits of the persons who have filled that office, from Pepys down to the present. The Admiralty has direct telegraphic communication with Portsmouth.

BURLINGTON HOUSE, 49 Piccadilly, is divided from the street by a high wall. It was built by Boyle, Earl of Burlington, the amateur architect, the friend of the poets. "Who builds like Boyle?" asked Pope; and Gay declared that "Burlington's beloved by every muse." Inside the wall there is a colonnade, which has been the subject of much exaggerated praise. Kent, the architect, and Handel were patronized by the Earl, and lived in this mansion. The Duke of Portland, George III.'s minister, resided and died here. The Burlington Arcade, which is said to produce a rental of £4000 a year, was built in 1819 on a slip of the ground. A few years ago Government purchased the house and garden, about 8 acres altogether, for £140,000. The Royal Society, Linnæan Society, and Chemical Society are now established here, and the examinations of the University of London are conducted in the mansion. The whole of the National Gallery, Trafalgar Square, being required for the National collection of pictures, it has been proposed that the Royal Academy should build a series of saloons in the gardens of Burlington House, where their profitable annual exhibitions may take place.

TRINITY HOUSE, north side of Tower Hill, built from the designs of Samuel Wyatt, 1793. This is the seat of an ancient guild, founded by Sir Thomas Spert, Captain of the Henri Grace de Dieu, and Comptroller of the navy in the time of Henry VIII. It was incorporated 1529, and now consists of a master, a deputy-master, about thirty elder brethren, who are for the most part either naval men, or persons connected with the civil administration of the navy, and a large number of younger brethren.

Prince Albert, who was master before his death, succeeded the Duke of Wellington. This corporation is intrusted with the charge of lighthouses, sea-marks, the licensing of pilots, etc. Its revenue amounts to about £300,000 a year, of which about one fourth remains after meeting the expenses, and this surplus is chiefly expended in pensioning disabled seamen, or the widows and orphans of seamen. They have hospitals at Deptford, which are annually visited in a state yacht on Trinity Monday. At the Trinity House are busts of many naval heroes, a picture 20 feet long by Gainsborough, representing the elder brethren of the time. In the museum are models of lighthouses, life-boats, etc., a fine model of the Royal William, made 160 years ago, a flag taken by Drake from the Spaniards in 1588, and other curiosities. To see them, apply for the secretary's order.

HERALDS' COLLEGE (College of Arms), Benet's Hill, Doctors Commons, a relic of the feudalism of the Middle Ages, presided over by an Earl Marshal, a post made hereditary in the family of the Duke of Norfolk by Charles II. We are told that the duties of this college (which was first incorporated by Richard III.) consists in marshalling and ordering coronations, marriages, christenings, funerals, interviews, and feasts of kings and princes; also cavalcades, shows, jousts, tournaments, and combats before the constable and marshal; also in taking care of the coats of arms and genealogies of the nobility and gentry. If any one wishes to assume armorial bearings, he must apply to Heralds' College. The usual cost is about seventy-five guineas. The present building was erected by Wren, in 1683, on the site of an older one destroyed by the great fire. The hall in which the court of chivalry was formerly held, with the judicial seat of the earl marshal, is on the north side of the yard. Here is an old library, and a fire-proof record room. In the college are preserved several curiosities; the Warwick roll, with figures of all the Earls of Warwick from the Conquest to Richard III.; a tournament roll of the time of Henry VIII.; a pedigree of Saxon Kings from Adam, with pen and ink illustrations of Henry VIII.'s time; a portrait of Talbot, Earl of Shrewsbury from his tomb in old St. Paul's; a sword, dagger, and turquoise ring, said to have been the property of James IV. of Scotland, who was killed at the battle of Flodden Field; a volume in the handwriting of Cambden the historian; MS. collections of heralds' visitations, records of grants of armorial bearings, etc. There are also some old portraits of officers of the college. Since 1622 the college has consisted of thirteen officers, viz., three kings-at-arms, Garter, principal ; Clarencieux ; Norroy—six heralds, Lancaster, Somerset, Richmond, Windsor, York, Chester—and four pursuivants, Rouge Croix, Blue Mantle, Portcullis, and Blue Dragon. In old time these mock kings were crowned with pompous ceremonies in the presence of the sovereign. Amongst the officers of this college, the following have rendered themselves of note as historians or antiquarians : William Cambden, Sir William Dugdale, Elias Ashmole, and Francis Grose.

CHAPTER THE NINTH.

COMMERCIAL BUILDINGS.

Bank of England—Royal Exchange—Stock Exchange—Custom House—Coal Exchange.

THE BANK OF ENGLAND covers a quadrangular space of about four acres, with a street on every side. The buildings are of one storey, and have no windows towards any of the thoroughfares. There is little in the external architecture to attract attention except the north-west corner, which was copied from the temple of the Sybil at Tivoli. The interior, which is well arranged for business, contains nine courts in addition to the offices. Several architects have been successively employed to make the bank what it now is. Sir Robert Taylor from 1766 to 1786, followed by Sir John Soane and C. R. Cockerell. The principal part of the exterior is Soane's work.

This wonderful establishment, which makes itself felt in every money market in the world, and at home occupies such a conspicuous position in commercial and financial affairs, was planned by a Scotchman, named Paterson, in 1691, and three years afterwards received a charter of incorporation under the style of the Governor and Company of the Bank of England, from William III. The subscribed capital of £1,200,000 was advanced to the government. Business was carried on at several places before the company removed in 1734 to premises on the site of part of the present bank, the other part being covered by a church, some taverns, and private houses. The first charter was only for fourteen years; it has been renewed eight times since then, for various terms, the longest of which was thirty-three years. During its lengthened existence it has had to pass through some dangerous crises, such as the rebellion of 1745, when its payments were made in sixpences to gain time; the trouble occasioned by the wars with France, at the end of the last century, when cash payments were suspended under the authority of an Act of Parliament, and not resumed until 1823 ; and during the time of the commercial difficulties in 1825, when its treasure was reduced to a very low ebb, but luckily the tide turned before it was exhausted. The bank has met with some heavy losses through forgeries ; by Astlett it lost £320,000, and by Fauntleroy £360,000.

The management of the affairs of the bank are intrusted to a governor, deputy-governor, and twenty-four directors, eight of whom go out of office every year, but are usually re-elected. The proprietors of stock to the value of £500 are entitled to vote for directors. The governor must be a proprietor to the extent of at least £4000, the deputy-governor £3000, and a director £2000. The directors and governors meet in the " Bank Parlour," where the dividends are declared and the rate of discount announced, a point of great importance in the money market. The dividend on £100 stock is 7 per cent, and the market price of that amount is about £228.

The number of persons employed in the bank is about 900. The salary of a clerk entering at seventeen is £50, and that of the head of a department £1200. The sum paid in salaries is about £210,000. Some of the clerks have amassed large fortunes. There was Daniel Race, whose portrait is in the parlour lobby, who was fifty years in the service, and died worth £200,000 ; and Abraham Newland, a cashier, whose name formed the burden of a once popular song, left behind him a very considerable sum. There is a library in the bank for the use of the clerks.

The profits of the Bank arise from various sources. They issue notes and carry on the business of an ordinary bank, receiving deposits, discounting bills, making loans, etc. A large cash balance belonging to the nation is always in its hands, and of this a profit is made. The remuneration allowed to the Bank for its services in managing the National Debt (which now amounts to £775,000,000), keeping the books, attending to transfers, receiving the taxes, paying dividends, etc., is about £200,000 a-year.

A very large amount of bullion is kept in its vaults, usually from 14 to 17 millions, as a reserve to meet any run that may be made upon it. The Bullion Office is a special department with its own staff of clerks. The gold is in bars, each weighing 16 lbs., and being worth £800 ; the silver is in pigs and bars, or else in bags of dollars. Here is some delicate apparatus for weighing large quantities of gold and silver. In the Weighing Office, in another part of the bank, Mr. W. Cotton's ingenious machine is employed to detect light gold coin. The light pieces are separated in the process of weighing from those of full weight, and so quick is the operation, that 35,000 may be weighed in a day by one machine. When the gold coin has been weighed it is put into bags of £1000, which are deposited in the iron presses of the Treasury, a well-secured apartment.

The operation of printing bank notes is well worth seeing. The paper is of peculiar make, the texture and water marking almost beyond imitation. The printing machinery is of most ingenious construction, the invention of a father and son named Oldham. Each half of a note is numbered alike, and as the printing proceeds, the machine alters the number in readiness for the next note. When a note that has been issued is returned to the bank, it is immediately cancelled, and consequently new notes are continually issuing to replace those that come in. Notes representing from 18 to 19 millions sterling are usually in circulation.

The principal offices are the Pay Hall, 79 feet by 40 ; the Rotunda or Dividend Pay Office, with a dome 57 feet in diameter ; Transfer Offices ; the £5 note Office ; the Private Drawing Office ; and the Post Bill Office. A small military force is stationed in the bank at night to protect it from attack, and some of the clerks remain up through the night keeping watch.

The public may walk through the principal offices during business hours. Admission to the other parts can only be obtained by an order from a director, the governor, or deputy-governor, and a special order is required for the Bullion Office.

THE ROYAL EXCHANGE,

the head-quarters of London commerce, occupies a conspicuous position near the Bank of England, between Cornhill and Threadneedle Street, on the site of the first Exchange, built by Sir Thomas Gresham, and presented by him to his fellow merchants in the reign of Elizabeth. That edifice had shops like the present Exchange, and we read in the old plays of "the gaudy shops of Gresham's burse." This structure was destroyed by the great fire of London in 1666. Three years afterwards the second Exchange was opened. This building was also destroyed by fire, an event which occurred in January 1838.

The present Exchange, which cost £180,000, designed by Mr. W. Tite, was opened by Queen Victoria in October 1844. Its total length is 308 feet. The west front has a fine portico, 96 feet wide, supported by 12 columns 41 feet high, and having the pediment ornamented by numerous allegorical figures by R. Westmacott. On the south side of the building, over the three centre arches, are the arms of Gresham, of the City, and of the Mercers' Company; and these arms are again given on the entablature at the east end. On the north side, over the three central arches, are some mottoes; that in the middle is Sir Thomas Gresham's *Fortun à my;* that on the east side is the City's *Domine dirige nos;* and on the other side is the Mercers' Company's *Honor Deo.* Passing through the great portico we reach an open area, surrounded by a spacious arcade or ambulatory, the roof and walls of which have been painted in fresco by F. Sang. Coats of arms, with arabesque designs are here given in rich and lively colours. In the middle of the area stands a marble statue of the Queen by Lough; and in the eastern corners of the arcade are statues of Elizabeth and Charles II. The chief days on 'Change are Tuesday and Friday, and the busy time is from half-past three to half-past four. A tall tower on the east side carries a clock, and is surmounted by a great gilt grasshopper, the device of Sir Thomas Gresham. Shops and offices occupy the ground floor on three sides, which greatly spoil the effect as a piece of architecture. The principal floor is occupied by rooms appropriated to two of the great insurance offices and to the underwriters' establishment of Lloyds. To the latter, access is gained by a flight of steps at the east end of the building. The great room, where the business of underwriting (*i.e.* insuring ships) is transacted, is 98 feet long and 40 feet wide. In the vestibule is a statue of the statesman Huskisson by Gibson, and a mural tablet with an inscription recording the extraordinary exertions of the *Times* newspaper in the exposure of a remarkable fraud on the mercantile public. In the various rooms meet merchants, ship-owners, insurance-brokers, and other persons interested in foreign commerce. To this place the agents of the establishment, who are scattered all over the world, forward the earliest news of the departure, the arrival, the loss, or the damage of ships. The subscribers are about 1900 in number; members pay an entrance fee of 25 guineas, and an annual subscription of four guineas, but if underwriters and insurance-brokers the annual subscription is 10 guineas. To aid the calculations of insurers, there in here a self-registering anemometer with a set of meteorological instruments. Two other rooms are called the *Merchants' Room* (annual subscription four guineas) and the *Captains' Room.* In the latter refreshments can be obtained. This great and useful establishment is managed by a committee of nine members whose chairman is elected annually. Six subscribers must recommend a candidate for admission, who is then balloted for by the committee.

The name Lloyds originated in the fact that a man so called kept a coffee-house in Abchurch Lane, where mercantile men were in the habit of meeting.

At No. 2 White Lion Court, Cornhill, is a distinct Society called *Lloyd's Register of British and Foreign Shipping,* whose affairs are managed by a committee of twenty-four members. The object of this society is to ascertain by the survey of competent persons, the character and condition of ships. It is here that the classification A 1, etc., applied to ships, originates.

In front of the great portico of the Royal Exchange is a bronze equestrian statue on a granite pedestal, bearing the simple inscription—

WELLINGTON.

Erected June 18, 1844.

Close by is a neat fountain; a female figure in bronze pours water from a vase into a granite basin.

THE STOCK EXCHANGE,

Capel Court, near the Bank of England, was built in 1801, on the site of a house belonging to Sir William Capel, Lord Mayor in 1504. Here the stock-jobbers and brokers meet, to buy and sell stocks and shares. Jobbers are persons who buy and sell on their own account; brokers, those who act only on account of others. The annual subscription is £10, and none but subscribers are admitted. They are from 800 to 900 in number, and are chosen by ballot by the committee, a body of 30 elected annually by the whole body of members. Every member must be re-elected at the end of the year. The hubbub during business hours is great, from the brokers calling out their terms aloud. The regular commission of a broker, on buying or selling, is 2s. 6d. per cent. Stocks and funds are the barometers of states; they are in continual fluctuation under the influence of a variety of circumstances, which are looked upon as favourable or adverse to the will or ability of those states to pay their debts. False reports have often been circulated with a view of acting upon the funds, and our criminal courts have been sometimes called upon to investigate charges of conspiracy connected with attempts to raise or lower prices. The late Earl of Dundonald, then Lord Cochrane, was convicted of being implicated in a conspiracy of this nature, although it is now generally believed that he was entirely innocent. The quantity of spare money in the country has also much to do with the prices. Several slang terms are in use here. A *bull* is a person who contracts to buy on speculation, in the hope of a rise, when he will clear a profit. A *bear* is one who contracts to sell without holding stock at the time, in the expectation that a fall will ensue; the contracts being made for a distant date, or "for the account," as it is termed. *Lame duck* is a name given to defaulters.

THE CUSTOM HOUSE,

Lower Thames Street, presents a conspicuous front to the river, half-way between the Tower and London Bridge. It is the fifth Custom House built on the site. The front, 488 feet long, was designed by Sir Robert Smirke, the architect of the Post Office and the British Museum, when the centre of the building, built by David Laing in 1814-17, was taken down on account of the foundation giving way. The total cost was enormous, viz., £435,000. Between the building and the river is a broad esplanade. Upwards of 2200 persons are employed in the custom house, or are connected with it; for a very large proportion of the total sum raised by the customs duties (not far short of one-half) is collected at the port of London. The management of the business is intrusted to a board of commissioners appointed by Government. There are about 170 rooms in the building, in addition to warehouses and cellars. The Board Room contains portraits of George III. and George IV., the latter by Lawrence. The business is chiefly transacted in the "Long Room," which has a length of 190 feet, and a width of 66, and where about 80 officers and clerks sit. In the queen's warehouse and the fire-proof cellars are kept the articles which have been seized. These are sold at quarterly sales, but the amount realized by them is not more than £5000 a year. Office hours from 10 to 4.

THE COAL EXCHANGE,

Lower Thames Street, City, was opened by the late Prince Consort in 1849, having been erected by the corporation from the designs of J. B. Bunning. It is in the Italian style, and has two principal fronts. The tower is 106 feet high. The hall where the merchants meet is a rotunda, 60 feet in diameter, with three tiers of galleries round it, covered by a dome of glass, which is 74 feet above the floor. The floor of this rotunda is beautifully inlaid with wood, of which there are 40,000 pieces, representing a mariner's compass, with the arms of the city in the middle. The blade of the dagger on this shield is a piece of the mulberry tree, planted by Peter the Great, when working as a shipwright at Deptford. The walls of the vestibule and rotunda have been richly decorated by F. Sang, with representations of the plants found in the coal-beds, of coal-mines, and mouths of shafts, of coal-digging implements, and with emblematic figures of rivers. In digging the foundations of this building a Roman bath was discovered, which was preserved, and access to it can still be obtained. The consumption of coal in the metropolis is enormously great, as strangers would be led to guess from its soot-laden atmosphere; and the number of persons engaged in the carriage alone is large. On all sea-borne coal the corporation levies a duty, which realizes about £170,000 a year, but a considerable portion of the quantity introduced (between three and four millions of tons) is now brought by railway.

CHAPTER THE TENTH.

MUSEUMS.

British Museum—Museum of College of Surgeons—Museum of Practical Geology—United Service Museum—India Museum—Missionary Museum.

THE BRITISH MUSEUM,

Great Russell Street, Bloomsbury.

The chief collections of this great national establishment are open, free to the public, on Mondays, Wednesdays from 10 to 4, and on Saturdays from 12 to 4 during November, December, January, and February ; from 10 to 5 during March, April, September, and October ; and from 10 to 6 during May, June, July, and August. It is closed on Ash-Wednesday, Good-Friday, Christmas-day, and any public fast or thanksgiving-day, also between the 1st and the 7th of January, the 1st and the 7th of May, and the 1st and 7th of September inclusive. Artists are allowed to study in the Sculpture galleries between 9 and 4 every day except Saturday.

Sir Hans Sloane, who had collected a considerable number of curious and valuable objects at an outlay of £50,000, directed by his will that they should be offered to Government for the sum of £20,000, and in 1753 an Act of Parliament was passed to authorize the acceptance of the offer, and to vest that collection, as well as the Cottonian and Harleian collections of MSS., in certain persons, to be styled the Trustees of the British Museum ; in this way our great national establishment originated. In the year following the trustees purchased Montague House from Lord Halifax for the reception of these collections, and on the 15th January 1759 the Museum was opened to the public. George III. having presented a collection of Egyptian antiquities, and the Hamilton and Townley antiquities having been purchased, it became necessary to build in order to obtain accommodation for these successive additions. In 1816 the Elgin marbles were

L

acquired, and the utter inadequacy of the existing buildings was manifest. In 1823 George III.'s library was handed over to the nation, and it was then determined to provide an entirely new edifice to contain the whole of the collections. The eastern side of the present structure was thereupon designed by Sir R. Smirke, and the Royal library placed in it in 1828. The northern, southern, and western sides of the Museum were subsequently added, old Montague House meanwhile disappearing piece-meal, the last portion being removed in 1845. In 1827 the department of Botany was created, in consequence of Sir Joseph Banks having bequeathed his botanical collections to the Museum.

The contents of the Museum are now divided into eight departments, viz. :—

Printed Books.	Botany.
Manuscripts.	Zoology.
Antiquities and Art.	Palæontology.
Prints and Drawings.	Mineralogy.

Each department is under the immediate care of an under-librarian as keeper, over whom is the principal librarian, an office now held by Signor Antonio Panizzi. There is also a superintendent of the Natural History departments, a situation now held by Mr. Richard Owen, the English Cuvier. The appointment of officers, and the management of the affairs, are in the hands of the trustees, a rather numerous body, some of whom are appointed by Government and others by certain families, to whose ancestors the nation is indebted for important gifts.

Seven acres of ground are occupied by the Museum buildings and their court-yards. Their cost, including that of the new reading-room, has been nearly a million sterling. Extensive as they are, more room is urgently required, and many plans have been brought forward, but nothing has been definitely determined on. At one time the separation of the collections of antiquities and art, and their removal to South Kensington, was a plan that found favour.

The grand entrance is from Great Russell Street, from which the principal court-yard is separated by a massive iron railing. Entering at the great gates, we pass buildings occupied as residences by the chief officers, and approach a splendid portico, supported by columns 45 feet high, and having at their bases a diameter of 5 feet. The entire front is 370 feet in length, and is

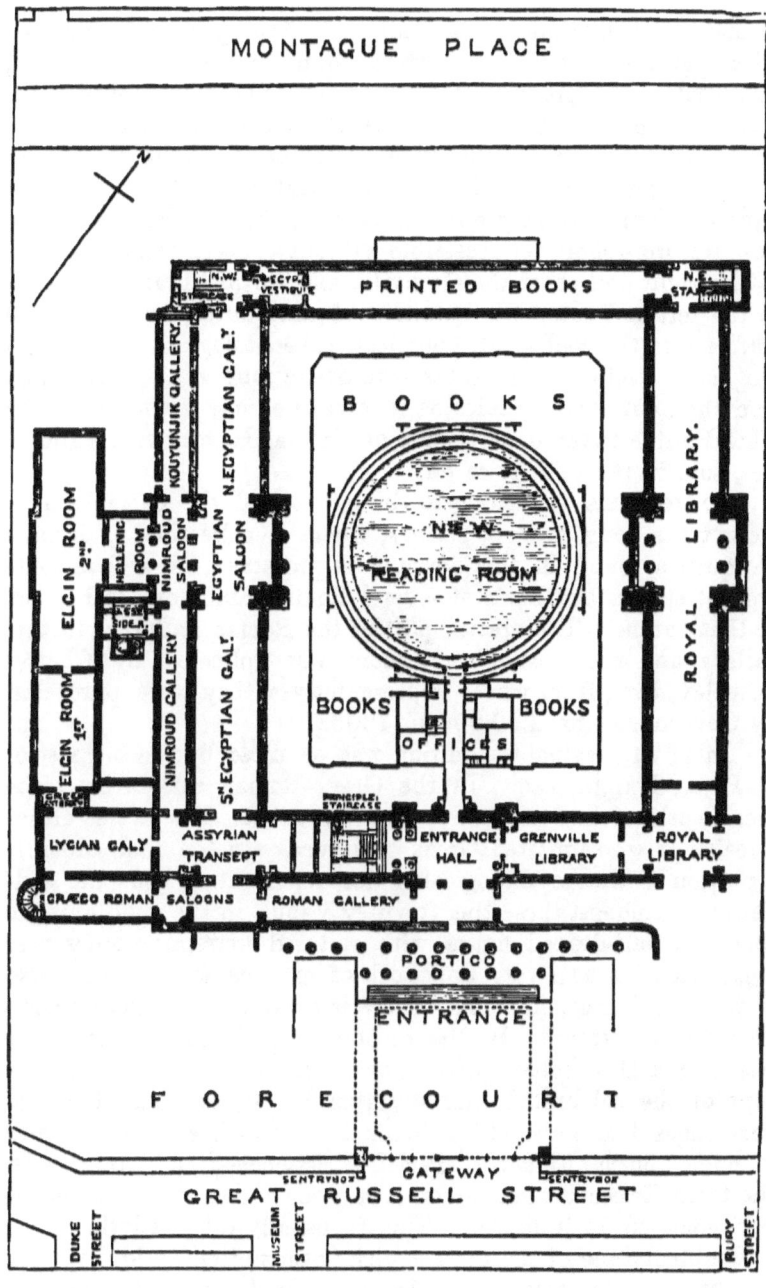

of elegant proportions. The pediment of the portico is enriched
with a group of figures in Portland stone by Sir R. Westmacott,
representing the progress of civilization. The whole of the exterior of the buildings is in the Grecian-Ionic style. If the
visitor will take the trouble to consult the plans, he will more
easily understand our directions. Entering the great hall
(Grecian-Doric), we may either cross it to the door leading to the
new reading-room (not accessible without a special ticket), or turn
to the right and enter the Grenville and Royal libraries, or turn
to the left and enter the galleries of antiquities, or ascend the
staircase to the zoological, botanical, palæontological, and mineralogical collections. To those who desire more detailed information than our space enables us to give, we may recommend the
official guide to the departments of Natural History and Antiquities, sold in the hall, price 6d.

ANTIQUITIES.—Turning to the left, out of the entrance hall,
we enter a long narrow gallery, where a collection of Roman
antiquities found in this country is preserved, as well as some
ancient statues and busts of several Roman Emperors, and others
of that nation. The greater part of the Roman sculpture in this
gallery and the succeeding saloons was collected by Charles
Townley, Esq., from whose representatives they were purchased
by Government for £20,000 in 1805.

In 1824 a valuable addition was acquired by the bequest of
R. Payne Knight, Esq. In the Græco-Roman saloons are to be
seen works found in Italy, but by artists who were either
Greeks, or who imitated Greek sculpture. In the first saloon is
a portion of the mythological series, representing gods and god-
desses. Amongst these the Townley Venus, in the middle of the
room—a half-draped figure with restored extremities, deserves
close attention as a very fine work of art ; as well as the torso
of another Venus, stooping. Here is a head of Apollo, remarkable for its beauty. In the second Græco-Roman saloon is a
statue of a Discobolus (quoit-thrower), life size, supposed to be a
copy of the celebrated bronze statue by Myron ; and busts of
personages distinguished in Greek history or literature—Homer
(a noble bust), Epicurus, Pericles, Sophocles, and others. In
the third Græco-Roman saloon is a female bust with the lower
part enclosed in a flower. This is usually called Clytie ; it is
undoubtedly one of the most exquisite heads of all antiquity. At
the end of this saloon a staircase leads down to the Græco-

Roman basement room, where will be seen miscellaneous objects of subordinate rank to those in the saloons, such as vases, candelabra, animals, etc. Ascending again, we may next enter the Lycean Gallery, of which the principal contents are architectural and sculptural remains obtained from ancient cities (chiefly from Xanthus), in Lycia, Asia Minor. They were discovered by Sir C. Fellows, and removed by two expeditions sent out by the Government in 1842-46. They range in date from the subjugation of the country by the Persians, B.C. 545, to the period of the Byzantine empire. Notice the bas-reliefs from the Harpy tomb, executed not later than 500 B.C.

Passing through a small ante-room, we reach the first of the two rooms containing sculptures and inscriptions from Athens and Attica, known as the Elgin marbles, in consequence of their having been obtained by Lord Elgin when ambassador at Constantinople (1801-1803). The earl's collection was purchased from him for £35,000. The most important part of this collection consists of the two groups arranged one on each side, which originally adorned the eastern and western pediments of the Parthenon at Athens. [See a model of the Parthenon in the Phigalian saloon.] These sculptures are world-renowned. They were executed under the superintendence of Phidias, and they are universally acknowledged to be the most valuable examples of Greek art which modern times possess. The group on the western side of the room belonged to the eastern pediment. The central figures have perished, but when entire, the miraculous birth of Minerva from the head of Jupiter was represented. Beginning at the south end, we have the upper part of the figure of Hyperion driving his chariot, of which the heads of two of the horses are seen ; Theseus or Hercules reclining, Ceres and Proserpine seated ; Iris, the messenger of the deities. At the north end is a torso of Victory ; then a group of the three Fates, two seated, one lying down ; head of a horse from the Mon's chariot. The remains of the western pediment are on the opposite side of the room. It was intended to represent the contest of Minerva with Neptune for the guardianship of Athens. Some of the statues of this group remain at Athens, and casts of them appear here. Beginning at the north end, we have the river god Ilissus ; cast of two figures called Heracles and Hebe ; torso of Cecrops, first king of Attica ; part of Minerva's head ; part of torso of Neptune ; torso of Amphitrite ; part of Latona's figure, seated ; cast of the torso of the river god Cephissus ; part of the recumbent figure of a nymph. In other parts of the room are casts from parts of figures believed to have formed portions of these pediments. The sculptures from the temple of Wingless Victory at Athens, from marble slabs belonging to the upper frieze of the building, should also be inspected as being very finely executed ; and there is here an undraped statue of Cupid of remarkable workmanship.

In the second Elgin room are further specimens of the Parthenon sculptures, viz., some of the metopes and portions of the frieze that surrounded the temple within the colonnade. This frieze represented in bas-relief the Panathenaic procession which took place at the quadrennial festival in honour of Minerva at Athens. The metopes were detached pieces of sculpture in high relief, that surmounted the colonnade, and represented combats between Greeks and Centaurs. There are here also some remains of the sculptures of the Erectheum, another Athenian temple, of the Propylæa, and other celebrated buildings at Athens.

In the Hellenic room are deposited marbles that have been conveyed at various times from Greece (excepting Attica) and its colonies ; as well as casts from a temple in the Island of Ægina, erected in the fifth or sixth century B.C. The originals, which our government foolishly neglected to purchase when it had the opportunity, are at Munich. Here are 23 sculptured slabs, part of a frieze from the temple of Apollo Epicurius near Phigalia in Arcadia, which was erected by Ictinus, the architect of the Parthenon, to commemorate the delivery of the Phigalians from the plague, B.C. 430. One series of the slabs represents the contest of Greeks and Centaurs ; another series the invasion of Greece by the Amazons. The Phigalian marbles cost £19,000.

In the Assyrian galleries, low narrow apartments more than 300 feet long, is a collection of sculptures obtained chiefly by Mr. Layard, 1847-50, at ancient Nineveh. Commencing our examination of these remains in the *Northern Gallery* (to reach which from the Greek collection we must pass through the Nimroud central saloon), we shall find here a collection of bas-reliefs obtained from the ruins of a great edifice at Kouyunjik, which is thought to have been the palace of Sennacherib, who began to reign about B.C. 721. The slabs were very much broken by the action of fire, as if the palace had been burned.

For the most part, the sculptures refer to the battles of Sennacherib and his grandson Ashurbanipal. One series represents the building of an edifice, it may be the very palace from which the slabs were taken. In the middle of the room is an obelisk of white stone, brought from Kouyunjik, but originally executed for Sardanapalus the Great, who reigned about two centuries before Sennacherib. In the table cases will be seen clay statuettes, seals, fragments of glass vases, bronze weapons, etc. The arrow-headed characters will be observed. in numerous places. The interpretation of them has been undertaken by Sir H. Rawlinson and others, who have displayed much ingenuity in prosecuting their difficult task.

Returning to the *Central Saloon*, we find here sculptures obtained from different parts of the great mound at Nimroud, including colossal lions and bulls—some human-headed. Some of these date from the time of Sardanapalus the Great. There is a colossal head of a human-headed bull, which is on a larger scale than any yet brought to Europe. Bas-reliefs represent battles and sieges. An obelisk of black marble in the middle of the room is one of the most important historical monuments yet obtained. The bas-reliefs are in five tiers, representing the offering of tributary presents to the king Silima Rish, son of Sardanapalus. The names of Jehu and Hazael have been decyphered in the cuneiform inscriptions, which are supposed to give a complete history of the Assyrian king's reign. The adjoining gallery contains a continuation of the same Nimroud series. Battles and sieges are again prominent amongst the objects represented in the bas-reliefs. A series of six slabs represent Sardanapalus amongst his attendants, supernatural and human, sumptuously attired. He seems to have returned from battle or from the chase. These are considered to rank amongst the best examples of Assyrian sculpture. Certain parts of them are coloured black and red. In the table cases are deposited various articles of ivory and bronze. One fragment of a glass vase bears the name of the founder of Khorsabad, and is to be looked on as the oldest known specimen of glass manufacture. Some of the ivory carvings bear Egyptian hieroglyphics, and afford proof of the connection between Egypt and Assyria at an early period.

Out of the Assyrian side-room a staircase descends into the basement, where are placed bas-reliefs from the latest period of Assyrian art, viz., the time of Ashurbanipal. They were brought from Kouyunjik, and chiefly represent hunting scenes and martial subjects. In an adjoining room are some remains, chiefly mosaics, with a few seals bearing Phœnician characters, brought from Carthage. Ascending the staircase and passing through the Nimroud Gallery into the *Assyrian Transept,* we shall find more monuments of Sardanapalus, including two colossal human-headed lions winged and three-horned. On the opposite side are two colossal human-headed bulls and two colossal figures of mythological character. These were obtained at Khorsabad by Sir H. Rawlinson.

We may now turn our attention to the *Egyptian Galleries,* where are placed a very fine collection of remains from that land of wonders, Egypt. The antiquities obtained at the capitulation of Alexandria are here, as well as objects purchased from or presented by various individuals. Memphis, opposite Cairo, has contributed early sepulchral monuments, but the main portion of the collection was obtained from Thebes, the capital of Egypt, under the kings of the eighteenth, nineteenth, and twentieth dynasties. Hieroglyphics are seen on many of the stones, and have afforded scholars a most difficult subject for investigation. The characters are meant to represent visible objects, and they were employed partly as *symbols* to indicate the objects represented or their leading qualities, and partly *alphabetically*, to express the first letter of the name of the object. Where a ring is employed, it was to indicate that the characters inside represented a royal name. Perhaps the most interesting object in the *Southern Gallery* is the celebrated Rosetta stone, with three inscriptions having the same purport ; two of them Egyptian, viz., hieroglyphical and enchorial, and the third in Greek. The subject is a decree of Ptolemy V., of about B.C. 196. It was these inscriptions which afforded Dr. Young a key to the interpretation of Egyptian characters. It was one of the objects collected by the French when they invaded Egypt, but surrendered to the English at the capitulation of Alexandria. Here also are—a large stone beetle, the symbol of the Creator ; the sarcophagus of King Nectanebo I., with representations on the outside of the sun passing through the heavens in his boat ; a finely cut group in sandstone of a male and female figure seated ; and a statue of a king on his throne, with a ram's head on his knees, from Karnak.

In the *Central Saloon* mark a colossal granite fist from Memphis, and colossal head and shoulders in granite from the

Memnonium at Thebes ; also a granite statue of Rameses II., the Sesostris of the Greeks, from Karnak. In the *Northern Gallery* observe two statues in black granite of King Horus ; two red granite lions from Nubia ; the head of a colossal ram from an avenue of ram-headed sphynxes that lead to a gateway built by King Horus at Karnak ; two seated statues of Amenophis III. from Thebes ; two colossal heads of the same monarch ; several statues of the cat-headed goddess Pasht (Bubastis), with the same monarch's name inscribed ; a colossal head of Thothmes IV. found by Belzoni at Karnak ; and in the central recess of the east side of the gallery, the Tablet of Abydos, with an inscription of great importance in making out the regal history. Near this are specimens of painting, representing banqueting scenes, fowling, etc. In the *Northern Vestibule*, at the foot of the great staircase, are placed the most ancient sculptures preserved in the museum. Some of the carving stones of the pyramids are here. On the staircase itself are placed Egyptian papyri, formed of slices of the pith of the papyrus or water plant of the Nile, and shewing the three forms of Egyptian writing, viz., the hieroglyphic already mentioned, the hieratic, which has the same characters, breaking down into a running hand ; and the demotic or enchorial, a still greater debasement of the original hieroglyphics. The language of the common people was written in this hand. The papyri consist principally of portions of the Ritual of the Dead. At the top of the staircase is the *Egyptian Anteroom*, where are kept casts from bas-reliefs painted in imitation of the originals. In the two *Egyptian Rooms* that follow are deposited a great number of the smaller antiquities. Most of them have been discovered in tombs, and they are in an excellent state of preservation. The objects are chiefly kept in cases, and may be classed as relating, 1st, to the religion, 2d, to the civil and domestic life, and 3d, to the death and burial of the Egyptians. Notice the figures of deities, of animals sacred to them, household furniture, articles of dress, vases, armour, weapons, carvings in ivory and wood, musical instruments, etc., etc. Amongst the mummies and coffins observe part of the mummy-shaped coffin of King Men-ka-re, builder of the third pyramid, one of the earliest inscribed monuments of Egypt. The body near it is supposed to be that of the king.

In the second Egyptian Room is placed a collection of Italian antiquities made by the late Sir William Temple, the British Minister at Naples, and bequeathed by him to the museum.

They embrace specimens of the arts of the Etruscans, Italian-Greeks and Romans, and consist of mosaics, sculptures, terra-cottas, vases, lamps, glass, personal ornaments, and a great number of other things. Here may be seen specimens of fresco painting from the walls of houses at Pompeii.

We may now proceed to the *Vase Rooms*, where we shall find a large number of ancient painted fictile vases, usually called Etruscan. In the first room there are two series—1st, those found in Etruria and Magna Græcia, Italy; and 2d, those from Greece and the adjacent islands. In the second room, the vases are in a later style (about 350—150 B.C.), and have been chiefly brought from the south of Italy.

In the *Bronze Room* is kept a collection of Greek, Etruscan, and Roman bronzes—representations of a great variety of objects, mythological personages, animals, arms, candelabra, lamps, mirrors, personal ornaments, etc. The collection bequeathed by Mr. Payne Knight embraced 800 articles. Observe in case F, two inscribed helmets found at Olympia in Greece. They were dedicated to Jupiter, one by Hiero, tyrant of Syracuse, having been taken from the Etruscans at the naval engagement off Cumæ, B.C. 472; the other by the people of Argos from the spoils of Corinth.

The next room contains two collections—1st, Antiquities found in Great Britain and Ireland, dating from the earliest times to the Norman Conquest; 2d, Remains, both British and foreign, of the middle ages. The first collection is arranged under the heads of British antiquities before the Romans, Roman antiquities found in Britain, and Anglo-Saxon antiquities. The British antiquities begin with stone implements, then bronze articles are seen, and then specimens of pottery. Amongst the Roman objects will be seen a case containing articles discovered in London. The Anglo-Saxon remains have been chiefly found in barrows and ancient places of sepulture. The mediæval collection embraces metal work, paintings, ivory carvings, enamels, jewelry (notice the signet ring of Mary Queen of Scots), pottery, Venetian glass and Majolica ware (so called from the early examples having, it is supposed, been taken from the Island of Majorca into Italy, where the art was cultivated in several towns). Observe Wedgwood's copy of the Portland vase, the original of which is preserved in the Medal Room, and refer to that head.

In the *Ethnographical Room* are placed articles made by

extra-European nations, arranged so as to complete a geographical cycle, beginning with China and proceeding westward until the eastern Archipelago is reached. There are many interesting objects here, but our limited space prevents detail.

The Medal Room can only be seen by special permission. The collection of coins is very extensive and valuable. Sir Hans Sloane's coins formed the nucleus, and large additions have been subsequently made to it, until it ranks amongst the first in Europe. In this room is kept the Barberini or Portland vase, belonging to the Duke of Portland. It has been deposited in the Museum since 1810, and formerly was placed in one of the public rooms until a madman in one of his lunes broke it into fragments. It has been so well repaired that the fractures are scarcely visible. This beautiful vase is of glass, $9\frac{3}{4}$ inches high, and $21\frac{3}{4}$ inches in circumference. It was found in the early part of the seventeenth century in a sepulchral chamber a few miles from Rome. It went into the hands of the Barberini family, and then into Sir William Hamilton's, who sold it to the Duchess of Portland for 1800 guineas. When her effects were disposed of in 1786 the family bought it for £1029. The opaque white figures are relieved on a dark amethystine blue ground, which is semi-transparent. It is supposed that the whole vase was originally covered with white enamel, and that the figures were cut out in the manner of a cameo. The meaning of these figures has given rise to much difference of opinion. Mr. Wedgwood made copies of this vase and sold them at 50 guineas each. In this room is also preserved a gold snuff-box, bearing on the lid, set with diamonds, a portrait of Napoleon, who presented it to Mrs. Damer, and by her it was bequeathed to the Museum. Another gold snuff-box, with a cameo lid; this was presented by Pope Pius VI. to Napoleon, who bequeathed it to Lady Holland.

In a shed under the grand portico are concealed certain interesting sculptures from Queen Artemisia's grand edifice to the memory of her husband Mausolus, erected about 353 B.C. These were obtained by Mr. C. T. Newton, at Halicarnassus, the modern Budrum, in Asia Minor. Here also are some ancient sculptures from Cnidus.

NATURAL SCIENCE.

ZOOLOGY.—Ascending the great staircase out of the entrance hall, we enter a saloon, on the floor of which are placed stuffed specimens of large mammalia, and in the wall cases are exhibited specimens of antelopes, goats, sheep, and bats. In the adjoining gallery are seen on the floor more specimens of large mammalia

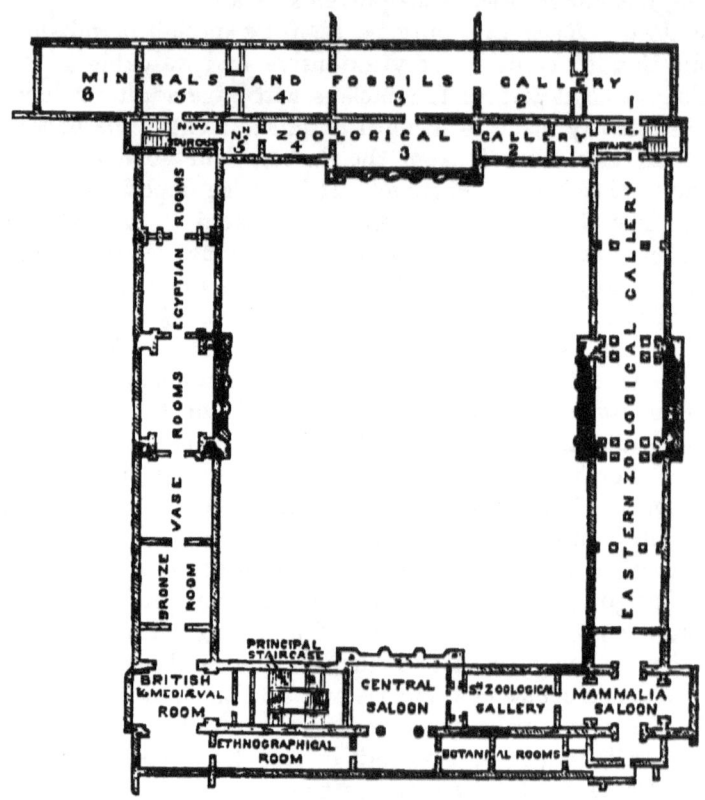

GROUND PLAN OF GALLERY—BRITISH MUSEUM.

(rhinoceros, elephant, hippopotamus, etc.), and in the wall cases are llamas, camels, oxen (notice the white wild bull from Chillingham Park), antelopes, armadilloes and other shielded beasts, sloths, deer, zebras, and others of the horse tribe. In the third saloon the cases in the centre are occupied by corals in great variety, and the wall cases are filled with carnivorous quadrupeds, pouched animals such as kangaroos, gnawing animals such as porcupines, beavers, marmots, etc., monkeys, apes, and baboons. Notice the chimpanzee, the orang outang, and the gorillas brought by Du Chaillu from the Gaboon country of West Africa, also the entellus or sacred monkey of the Hindoos ; the Barbary ape, the only quadrumanous animal which has obtained a footing in Europe, viz., on the rock of Gibraltar. Suspended on the walls are specimens of seals, dolphins, and other marine mammalia.

The door at the south side of this saloon leads to the botanical department, to be noticed hereafter : At present we proceed northwards into the Eastern Zoological Gallery, where the table cases will be found crowded with shells, and the wall cases with birds, above which is a series of horns of deer and rhinoceros. On the walls hang 116 portraits, which, it is to be hoped, will be transferred to the national portrait gallery, unless they can be better placed than they are at present. Amongst the raptorial birds notice the condor of the Andes, which soars to a greater altitude than any other bird. The gorgeously-plumaged humming-birds, birds of paradise, macaws, parakeets, peacocks, pheasants, etc., will attract attention. Notice the apteryx, the wingless bird of New Zealand, that sleeps during the day and feeds at night ; the foot of the dodo, that singular bird which formerly inhabited the Mauritius, but is now extinct. The painting was made, it is said, from a living bird. Many of the specimens of shells will attract attention from their beautiful shape or colour, but we cannot stop to enter into particulars. There are models of the *animals* which inhabit shells that deserve the inspection of naturalists.

In the first room of the *Northern Zoological Gallery* nests of birds and insects are exhibited in the wall cases (observe the gelatinous nests of the esculent swallow, a Chinese luxury), whilst the table cases contain objects connected with insects. On the walls are hung specimens of the larger reptiles. In the second room there are stuffed exotic reptiles, and batrachia such as frogs and toads in the wall cases, and radiated animals (sea-urchins, star-fish, etc.) in the table cases. Observe the green turtle, the alderman's friend, the imbricated turtle, which yields the tortoise-shell of commerce, the lepidosiren, or eel-shaped mudfish of the Gambia river, which, on the approach of the dry season buries itself in the mud, and becomes torpid until the river is swollen with rains. Naturalists differ as to whether it ought to be classed with fishes or reptiles. This specimen was kept alive for some months at the Crystal Palace.

The Third Room contains illustrations of the zoology of Great Britain, in all its divisions. There are specimens of two birds which have become extinct in these islands—the caper

cailzie or wood grouse, and the great auk. In the next room is
a collection of stuffed fishes, placed in the wall cases, whilst the
table cases contain select specimens of annulose animals, amongst
which notice the sacred scarabæus of the Egyptians, the diamond
beetles of Brazil, and other beetles of large size or singular shape ;
the walking-stick insect, the leaf-insect, and some enormous
butterflies, moths, and spiders. The tsetse of South Africa, a fly
which destroys cattle with its sting, is also here. Amongst the
crustaceans many strange forms may be seen. In the fifth small
room, which brings us to the staircase, the wall cases contain
exotic fish belonging to tribes in whose structure cartilage takes
the place of bone, such as the sharks, rays, and sturgeons. Sponges
and other objects of low organization occupy the table cases.

There are large collections of fishes, crustaceans, and insects
in cabinets, not exhibited in the public rooms, but they may be
seen by naturalists on application to the keeper of the Zoological
Collection every Tuesday and Thursday. It is desirable to give
two days' previous notice of an intended visit. The fishes, a large
number of which are kept in spirit, are now in course of arrangement by Dr. A. Günther, who is preparing an elaborate catalogue
of them, of which three volumes have been published.

PALÆONTOLOGY AND MINERALOGY.—The collections relating to
these sciences are placed in the North Gallery, a series of six
saloons, numbered over the doors from I. to VI., beginning at the
east end. The table cases, in Rooms from I. to IV., are filled
with minerals ; in Rooms V. and VI. with fossil shells. The
wall-cases in all the rooms contain fossils. Amongst the minerals
will be found specimens of meteoric stones, of native gold in the
form of grains, nuggets, etc. ; of native silver ; of diamonds, with
glass models of the most celebrated examples ; of rubies, emeralds, amethysts, opals, and other gems. In Room I. is a piece of
jade carved into the form of a tortoise, found in India. The
fossils in Room I. are chiefly vegetable remains, including a large
series from the coal. Fish remains occupy the cases in the
Second Room, and reptilian remains chiefly those of the Third
Room. Here notice the bones of the great Iguanodon and Megalosaurus (land reptiles), those of the Plesiosaurus and Ichthyosaurus (sea reptiles), and those of the Pterodactyle or flying
lizards. In one of the cases is a collection of bird remains from

New Zealand. One species of *Dinornis* is thought to have been from 10 to 11 feet in height. In Room V. are the remains of mammalia, amongst which will be seen the bones of two rhinoceroses, an elephant, and a hippopotamus, found in England. The table-cases contain fossil sea-urchins, crabs, corals, and shells in great variety. Those from the chalk are particularly beautiful. In Room VI. are the bones of large Pachydermata, including elephants, mastodons, and the dinotherium, a great beast having large tusks in the lower jaw, directed downwards. Here also are the bones of the megatherium, a huge extinct animal allied to the sloth. It is supposed to have fed upon the leaves and tender branches of trees which it uprooted. In this room is the fossil human skeleton brought from Guadaloupe in the West Indies, where it was found in a calcareous stratum of very late date. Arrow heads, fragments of pottery, and other articles of human workmanship, are found in the same bed.

BOTANY.—In the guardianship of the under-keeper in this department are placed the Herbaria of Sir Hans Sloane and Sir Joseph Banks, the latter including the plants collected by him during his voyage with Captain Cook. Other herbaria have swollen the number of dried plants (all mounted on paper and placed in cases according to a natural arrangement) to a considerable total. Still, the collection is much inferior to Sir W. Hooker's at Kew. These specimens are only interesting to botanists, and can only be seen by the special permission of the under-keeper. This situation was held for many years by the late Dr. Robert Brown, the " summus Brownius" of continental botanists. Two rooms, however, are occupied by specimens of wood and other vegetable structures, and to these the public are admitted. They are adjacent to the Southern Zoological Gallery. Here will be seen a great variety of interesting contributions from the vegetable kingdom, arranged according to the natural orders. Woods, fibres, fruits, resins, etc., come in for illustration. As we could not here mention a tithe of the objects which deserve inspection, and as they are all named, we shall leave the visitor to act as his own guide.

NEW READING ROOM—LITERATURE AND ENGRAVINGS.

The Print Room can only be seen by special permission, and it is closed on Saturdays. Large sums have been expended in the purchase of rare prints and brilliant impressions. The collection is very rich, and its money value is considerably more than £100,000. Some choice specimens of drawings and engravings have been framed and glazed, and are exhibited to the public in the King's Library. Amongst the remarkable things in this room may be mentioned a series of etchings by Claude ; prints and etchings after or by Rembrandt, the finest existing collection—one, the portrait of a Dutch writing master, is worth 500 guineas ; and a fine series after Albert Dürer. Single prints after Ostade and Backhuysen have cost 200 guineas each. The following curiosities are here :—A carving on stone by Albert Dürer, dated 1510, and representing the birth of John the Baptist, cost 500 guineas ; a richly chased silver cup, attributed to Benvenuto Cellini.

The New Reading Room is approached by a long corridor, the entrance to which is on the north side of the great hall. Admission to read here is only granted on special application to the principal librarian, supported by the recommendation of some person of known respectability. When admission is granted to the applicant he receives a ticket, which must be renewed at the end of six months. A ticket is not transferable and must be produced whenever required by an officer of the museum. The room is open daily from 9 to 4 during the four winter months ; from 9 to 5 during September, October, March, and April; and from 9 to 6 during the four summer months. It is closed on Sundays, and on the special days, and during the special weeks, when the museum collections are closed. Persons under eighteen years of age are not admissible.

The new reading room, the finest room for the purpose in the world, was built in 1855-56 in the inner quadrangle of the museum, where it occupies an area of 48,000 superficial feet. It is circular in plan, and is covered with a dome 140 feet in diameter, and 106 feet high. In point of diameter it is larger than any existing dome, except the Pantheon at Rome which exceeds it by only two feet. The cubic contents of the room are a million and a quarter of feet. It is constructed principally of iron, of which more than 2000 tons were used. The total weight of the materials employed in the dome was about 4200 tons. The quantity of glass was about 60,000 superficial feet. Effectual means for warming and ventilating the interior have been employed ; and all the skylights, lanterns, and windows have been made double. Light colours and gilding have been employed in decorating the interior. The entire cost was about £150,000, which includes the cost of new libraries exterior to the reading room. Here comfortable accommodation is afforded to 300 readers, each of whom has a space of 4 feet 3 inches allotted to him, with an inkstand, a hinged desk, and a folding shelf. Through the top of the screen, which divides the seats of one row from those of another, warm, or simply fresh air, can be forced into the room. There are 35 reading tables, two of which are set apart for the exclusive use of ladies. The material called kamptulicon has been laid on the floor in order to deaden the sound ; and a great many ingenious contrivances have been adopted for the purpose of rendering this a comfortable place of quiet study. Near the centre of the room are placed on shelves the catalogues of books and manuscripts contained in the library, and which readers must consult for the "press-mark" before they can send for a volume. Around the dome-room are shelves for the reception of 80,000 volumes. Those under the gallery are filled with books of reference (about 20,000 in number), which readers may remove to their desks without any formal application. All other books must be applied for through the medium of signed tickets, and handed to attendants, who pass them to others by whom the books are fetched from their shelves in the library. The great catalogue, which has been so many years in hand, is not yet completed.

The Library is supposed to exceed in extent all libraries in the world except, perhaps, the Imperial Library of Paris. It contains upwards of 600,000 volumes, and the rate of increase is not less than 20,000 volumes a year. They are deposited in the east and north sides of the ground floor of the museum buildings, and in the new reading room with its contiguous buildings. The public is only admitted into that part occupied by the Grenville and the Royal Libraries which will be noticed presently, and there will be seen several of the rarities of the collection. Books of divinity have blue bindings, history red, poetry yellow, and biography olive. Into this vast accumulation of books have been swept many collections, each large, or having a special interest. Four years after the foundation of the museum, George II. presented to it the library of the English kings, from the time of Henry VII., which contained many curiosities, and this is known at the museum as the " old royal collection."

There are about 1700 copies of the Bible in various languages and editions ; Garrick's collection of old plays ; the musical libraries of Sir John Hawkins and Dr. Burney ; a very valuable collection of tracts relating to the contest between Charles I. and the Parliament ; a large collection of works and tracts relating to the French Revolution ; an extensive collection of English and foreign newspapers (the oldest of which is a Venetian Gazette of 1570). The manuscripts are very numerous and valuable, and have been accumulated from some large collections—the Cottonian, Harleian (cost £10,000), Lansdowne (cost £4925), Sloane, Burney (cost £13,500), Arundel (cost £3559), etc.

Turning to the right hand out of the entrance, between Roubiliac's statue of Shakespere bequeathed by Garrick, and Chantrey's statue of Sir Joseph Banks, we enter the room in which is deposited a valuable library of 20,240 volumes, collected at a cost of £54,000 by the Right Honourable Thomas Grenville, the holder for many years of a sinecure office, and bequeathed by him, " as a debt and a duty, to the British museum, for the use of the public." In this room are placed some cases containing *Block Books*, that is, books printed from engraved wooden blocks before the invention of type printing. In the next room a selection of autographs and original documents is seen arranged on both sides in glazed frames. Here will be found specimens of the handwriting of many eminent persons. The most interesting of these is undoubtedly the signature of Shakespere to the mortgage of a house in Blackfriars, conveyed to him and others by a deed, the original of which is in the City Library, Guildhall. The handwriting of many royal, historical, and literary persons may be inspected here. Queen Elizabeth's prayer-book, entirely in her own writing when princess ; the original draft of the will of Mary Queen of Scots ; Sir Walter Scott's autograph manuscript of the novel of Kenilworth ; part of the manuscript of Sterne's Sentimental Journey ; the original draft of Pope's translation of the Iliad and Odyssey, for the most part written on the backs of letters ; a masque by Ben Jonson ; a MS. work of Tasso ; the original agreement between Milton and Symons the printer for the sale of the copyright of Paradise Lost ; Nelson's unfinished letter, written on the eve of the battle of Trafalgar ; and part of Macaulay's manuscript of the fifth volume of his history, are exhibited. Here also may be inspected the famous Magna Charta of King John, dated at Runnymede, with a fragment of the Great Seal attached. We next enter a long gallery, built expressly to hold George III.'s library, which was handed over to the nation in 1823. It comprised upwards of 80,000 volumes, and cost about £130,000. This collection is said to be remarkable, not only for the judicious selection of the works, and the discriminating choice of the editions, but for the bibliographical peculiarities and rarity of the copies. In cases kept in the King's Library, are exposed to public view specimens of the earliest productions of the printing-press in Germany, the Low Countries, Italy, France, and England ; specimens of fine and sumptuous printing ; illuminations, illustrations on wood and copperplate, typographical and literary curiosities, oriental manuscripts, specimens of bookbinding, and a series of impressions of the Great Seals of the English Sovereigns from Edward the Confessor to Queen Victoria. Notice a volume of the Arabic Koran written in gold about 860 years ago ; the original Bull of Pope Innocent III. granting the kingdoms of England and Ireland in fee to King John and his successors ; and the original Bull of Pope Leo X., conferring on Henry VIII. the title of Defender of the Faith, a title still retained by our Sovereigns. In this library are some screens appropriated to a highly interesting display of original drawings by the great masters. From a series of fine engravings the development of design may be traced during the fifteenth, sixteenth, and seventeenth centuries. In glazed cases are also shewn some fine examples by the Italian workers in niello. Notice an engraved silver plate (a Pax) by Maso Finiguerra cost 300 guineas ; an impression on sulphur of a similar plate, by the same engraver, cost 250 guineas ; and an impression on paper of a similar plate, thought to be the earliest known exemplar, cost 300 guineas.

The visitor will find a useful companion in the Official Guide (price 3d.) to the printed books, autograph letters, and drawings and prints exhibited in these libraries.

The ROYAL COLLEGE OF SURGEONS, on the south side of Lincoln's Inn Fields, was erected from the designs of Sir Charles Barry, 1835-7, at a cost of £40,000. It contains a very fine museum, a library, and theatre for lectures. In the library is a portrait of Sir Cæsar Hawkins, by Hogarth, and in the Council-Room, Reynolds' often engraved portrait of John Hunter, Flaxman's posthumous bust of Hunter, and some busts by Chantrey.

The museum is open on the first four days of the week (except in the month of September), from 12 to 4 o'clock, to fellows and members of the college, and to strangers introduced by them personally, or by written orders which are not transferable. It originated in the purchase by Parliament of John Hunter's museum, for which £15,000 were paid. In addition to the preparations illustrating the normal and abnormal structures of the human frame, which embrace subjects of the highest interest to the professional man, there are illustrations of vegetable and animal structures and forms, the whole arranged and kept in very beautiful order, and described in printed catalogues, which are distributed about the museum for the use of visitors. Amongst the numerous curiosities we shall only mention the skeletons of giants (the tallest 8 feet high) and dwarfs; the diseased intestines of Napoleon; some Egyptian and other mummies; the embalmed body of the first wife of Martin van Butchell, prepared by injecting the vascular system with oil of turpentine and camphorated spirits of wine; and the skeleton of the gigantic elephant Chunee, formerly exhibited in London. The base of one of the tusks became inflamed, and this produced paroxysms of ungovernable rage, so that it became necessary to kill him; but he did not die until he had received more than a hundred bullets.

MUSEUM OF PRACTICAL GEOLOGY has fronts both in Jermyn Street and Piccadilly, the entrance being in the former. It is in the Italian Palazzo style, erected from Mr. Pennethorne's designs at a cost of £30,000. Open free of charge every week day, except Friday, from ten to four.

This museum has Sir R. I. Murchison for its director. It was established in 1835, with the view of exhibiting the rocks, minerals, and organic remains obtained during the geological survey of the United Kingdom, and in illustration of the maps and sections made by the surveyors; and also to exemplify the applications of the mineral productions of these islands to useful or ornamental purposes. Here may be studied—1. The *Natural Materials* yielded by the earth as to their lithological character, their geological order, or their mineralogical constitution; and 2. *Artificial Productions* formed out of those natural materials by the art of man. In addition to these principal groups there may also be seen—3. The *Implements* and *Machinery* employed in working up the raw materials; 4. *Specimens* of *Ancient* artificial productions placed alongside *Modern* specimens, with a view of shewing the progress or retrogression of the arts ; and 5. *Foreign* and *Colonial Minerals.* To this establishment is attached the Government School of Mines, in which such branches of science are taught as have reference to mining and metallurgical industry. Lectures are delivered in the theatre (large enough to contain 500 persons seated) by men eminent in their several sciences ; and there is a library attached to the institution. Another branch of the establishment is the Mining Record Office, in which plans and sections of mines, and important statistical details, are preserved with a view to the prevention of loss of life and property. From this office annually issues a publication setting forth the mineral statistics of the United Kingdom. The importance of an establishment of this kind may be gathered from the fact that the annual value of the mineral produce of the British Isles, exclusive of building stone and clay, is upwards of thirty millions sterling.

The contents of the museum (says the official prospectus) may be classed under the following heads :—1. Fossil organic remains, arranged in their order of superposition or age, so as to illustrate the geological maps and sections. 2. The geological maps of England and Wales united in one general map, to exhibit the progress of the survey (see the large map hanging on the western wall of the hall), with illustrative sections, the remainder of these documents being kept in the map office. 3. Specimens of British sedimentary rocks, arranged partly in order of superposition, and partly with reference to their mode of accumulation and their subsequent modifications ; also specimens of igneous rocks arranged lithologically. 4. Specimens illustrative of the ores of the useful metals, of their mode of occurrence, and of the methods used in preparing them for smelting. 5. The various arts, such as pottery enamelling, glass-making, founding, etc., connected with the mineral and metallurgical resources of the country, as illustrated by specimens shewing varieties or peculiarities of manufacture. 6. Models of mines, mining tools, and working models of mining machinery, with a view of exhibiting the various modes of mining in different districts.

In the Vestibule and Hall are deposited specimens of building and ornamental stones, marbles, granites, etc. Ascending a flight of stairs we find ourselves on the principal floor, where many objects of interest are preserved. Worthy of notice are cases illustrating the manufacture of swords and gun barrels, the manufacture of glass, the art of painting on enamel, the art of printing and painting pottery, and the art of working in mosaic. Here also will be found cases containing cut agates of great beauty, models of gold nuggets, models of celebrated gems, models of coal and lead mines ; also the model of an Australian gold digging, with quartz - crushing machinery ; and Captain Ibbetson's model of the Isle of Wight. In the Model Room at the north end of the museum are many models of mining machinery and tools. In the two galleries which surround the upper part of the principal room are deposited fossils illustrating the geology of the British Isles.

UNITED SERVICE MUSEUM, WHITEHALL YARD.—Free to persons with members' orders, which are easily procurable, from eleven to five in summer, and from eleven to four in winter. This museum was founded in 1830, and is supported by the subscription of members belonging to the two services. In the theatre, lectures are occasionally delivered on subjects connected with the profession of arms ; and there is a good collection of books relating to military and naval affairs. Here are preserved autograph letters of Nelson, Wellington, and other heroes. On the ground floor of the museum is a large collection of the armour, weapons, and accoutrements of many nations. There are also the swords of several distinguished persons, Cromwell's, Wolfe's, and Nelson's being amongst them. Notice the dress worn by Tippoo Sahib when he was killed at Seringapatam, and his pistols. One room is filled with models of steam-engines from the earliest times; another with models illustrating naval construction. In an adjoining room is an intensely interesting assemblage of articles belonging to Sir John Franklin and his unfortunate comrades, brought from the Arctic Regions by Captain M'Clintock. Close by are more relics of Nelson ; and Captain Cook's chronometer. Ascending the stairs we find a room containing models illustrating various systems of fortification, methods of attack and defence, etc. Here is a model of a New Zealand War-Pah. In an adjoining room are specimens of military accoutrements, with models of guns and mortars. The manufacture of the Enfield rifle is likewise illustrated by specimens of the different parts in various stages. Up a second flight of stairs is Captain Siborne's vast model of the battle of Waterloo, with 190,000 metal figures ; also Colonel Hamilton's model of Sevastopol and the surrounding country. In this room are Russian relics from the Crimea, French relics from Waterloo, the skeleton of Marengo, Napoleon's charger at Waterloo, and some relics of Wellington.

INDIA MUSEUM, *Fife House, Whitehall Yard.* Open free to the public on Monday, Tuesday, Wednesday, and Saturday, from 10 to 4. On Thursday, persons who have obtained special orders from members of the Indian Council, or from Heads of Departments, can alone be admitted. The expenses are paid out of the revenue of India. This collection of objects from our Indian Empire was removed from the India House, in Leadenhall Street, previous to the sale of that building, and has been temporarily deposited in an inconvenient private house, until better quarters can be found for it. In the grounds around the house have been placed certain sculptured marbles, remarkable for the delicacy of their finish, from the ruined temple of Amrawuth, which was dedicated to the worship of Buddha. In the entrance hall are specimens of Indian sculpture, casts of faces of different races, statues, and busts of eminent persons connected with India. Above stairs, there is a room with specimens of the metals, precious stones, and soils of India; and a suite of rooms exemplifying her vegetable productions, cereals, starches, oils, fruits, fibres, etc., also the animal productions connected with manufactures, with specimens of textile fabrics. Glass cases are resplendent with weapons, jewellery, works in gold and silver, and gorgeous dresses, with cashmere shawls, and Dacca muslins, carvings in ivory, horn, and wood, will be noticed. A number of clay figures illustrate the races, castes, and employments of the people. In another department is a collection illustrating the natural history of the country, of which the birds form the best part. Here also are huge fossil bones from the Sewalik Hills.

Notice a model of the car of Juggernaut; Runjeet Singh's golden chair of state; Hindu idols in precious metals; gauntlets of elaborate workmanship made at Lahore; Tippoo Sultan's tiger, represented as devouring a man; a State Howdah; and a model of a Kutcherrie, or Law Court.

About Fife House, there is a curious story to this effect. The terrace fronting the Thames is wholly made of gravel and earth, brought by sea from Banffshire, by the directions of an Earl of Fife, who, when he was made a British peer about a century back, declared that if he was compelled to live in London half the year, he would at least walk on Scotch soil.

MISSIONARY MUSEUM, Bloomfield Street, Finsbury. Here are many objects of natural history collected by missionaries in various parts of the world, and amongst other curiosities may be seen examples of war implements, and of the idols worshipped by uncivilized man. Notice the household gods of Queen Pomare of Tahiti, simple logs of wood, or formed of grass and rags; a large wooden figure from an ancient building on one of the Sandwich Islands; a wooden figure covered in parts with children representing Tauroa, Upao, Valore, the supreme deity of Polynesia; Teriapatura, the protector of the Society Islands; Inquaddatra, the mother of the world, according to the superstition of Hindostan, standing on a lion, which is stationed on an elephant; Kulec, the black goddess of cruelty, a hideous figure with a necklace of human heads, and a robe formed of hands and arms; the Burmese idols glittering with tinsel and gilding. There are numerous articles for domestic use; personal ornaments; propitiatory offerings to the gods; the Chinese Bible with the blocks cut at one of the missionary stations from which it was printed; the club with which Williams the missionary was killed, etc., etc. The inspection of the objects by visitors is facilitated by their being labelled. Open free on Tuesdays, Wednesdays, and Saturdays, during the summer half of the year from 10 to 4; and from 10 to 3 during the rest of the year.

CHAPTER THE ELEVENTH.

SOCIETIES CONNECTED WITH SCIENCE, LITERATURE, AND THE ARTS.

Royal Society—Royal College of Physicians—Society of Antiquaries—
    Society of Arts—Royal Academy of Arts—Royal Institution—
    Linnæan Society—Geological Society—Royal Geographical Society
    —Royal Asiatic Society, Sion College—Institution of Civil En-
    gineers—Royal Institute of British Architects—Royal Society of
    Literature—Royal Agricultural Society—Smithfield Club—Lib-
    raries.

THE societies in London connected with science and literature are
of course very numerous, and it will not be expected that we can
do more than mention the principal of them here. It will be
observed that most of them affect the title of Royal. We begin
with the oldest, which also stands highest.

The ROYAL SOCIETY, Burlington House, Piccadilly, received
its charter of incorporation in 1663, from Charles II., who presented a silver gilt mace to it, still in its possession, and always
laid on the table at meetings. This is not the "bauble" of the
Long Parliament as traditionally asserted. Charles signed himself as "Founder," in the charter book, where also appear the
signatures of his brother James and Prince Rupert as "Fellows."
Their places of meeting have been numerous. For several years
they had rooms in Somerset House, before removing to their
present quarters. Most persons of scientific eminence in this
country, for the last 200 years, have belonged to it. Newton
was a member, and presented to it the manuscript of his Prin-
cipia, which is carefully preserved by it. The members are at
present upwards of 750, and consist chiefly of medical men and
mathematicians. They are elected by ballot, on being proposed
by six members. Each on admission pays £10 as an entrance
fee, and £4 annually. The annual meeting takes place on the
30th November. Major-General Sabine is the present President.

The library is a valuable one, and it possesses several portraits of eminent persons, of which a good catalogue with annotations has been drawn up; three of Sir Isaac Newton, one of which, by C. Jervas, is placed over the presidential chair; two portraits of Halley; two of Thomas Hobbes; Sir Hans Sloane; Sir Christopher Wren; Robert Boyle; Pepys, the diarist; Benjamin Franklin; Sir Humphrey Davy, by Laurence, and several others. Also busts of Charles II. and George III., by Nollekens; Sir Joseph Banks, by Chantrey; Sir Isaac Newton, by Roubiliac; James Watt, Cuvier, and others. The following relics of Newton are preserved by the society: a solar dial made by him when a boy; his gold watch with a medallion portrait of him, presented to him, as shewn by the inscription, by Mrs. Conduit, in 1708; the first reflecting telescope of his invention, made by his own hands; the mask of the philosopher's face, from the cast taken after his death; a lock of his silver white hair. Amongst other curiosities is the original model of Sir H. Davy's safety lamp, made by his own hands, and a MS. of Wren.

Four gold medals are distributed annually by the society. The memoirs read at its meetings, when published, are known as the "Philosophical Transactions." The fellows place the letters F.R.S., after their names.

THE ROYAL COLLEGE OF PHYSICIANS, Pall Mall, East, corner of Trafalgar Square, was erected in 1824-5 from the designs of Sir R. Smirke, at the cost of £30,000. The college was founded by Linacre, physician to Henry VII. and Henry VIII. He was the first president, and he bequeathed to it his own house in Knight-Rider Street, where the members had been in the habit of meeting. The buildings afterwards designed for them by Wren, in Warwick Lane, Newgate Street (described by Garth in his poem "The Dispensary"), are still standing, but have been converted partly into a meat market, and partly into shops. The style of the present college buildings is Grecian-Ionic. Amongst the portraits preserved here are those of Sir Thomas Browne, author of the *Religio Medici*, Sir Samuel Garth by Kneller, Dr. Radcliffe by Kneller, Harvey by Jansen, Sir Hans Sloane (whose collections were the nucleus of the British Museum, "Sloane's wondrous shelves"—Pope) by Richardson, and William Hunter. In the lecture-room are several busts of eminent physicians, a picture of Hunter lecturing on anatomy before the Royal Academy, by Zoffany. In a gallery in the library are various anatomical preparations, including some used by Harvey to illustrate his lectures on the circulation of the blood. The order of a physician, a member of the college, will admit persons to see the objects above mentioned.

THE SOCIETY OF ANTIQUARIES has rooms in Somerset House, Strand. It was founded in 1707, and has had many migrations before it settled in its present quarters. The society was incorporated in 1751, by George II. An applicant for the fellowship must be proposed by three fellows, and will then be balloted for. Five guineas are paid on admission, and two guineas annually. Their meetings are held weekly on Thursdays, beginning with the third Thursday in November, and ending with the third in June, and the anniversary meeting takes place on the 23d of April. Fellows are entitled to write F.S.A. after their names. The transactions of the Society are published under the name of *Archæologia*, and they date from 1770. It has also issued many independent works, as well as prints. It possesses a valuable library and collection of MSS., and museum. Here are portraits of distinguished antiquaries, portraits of Henry V., Henry VL, Edward IV., Richard III., Henry VII., Henry VIII., and Mary (by Lucas de Heere); also of Schoreel, a Flemish artist, by Sir Antonio More his pupil; and the Marquis of Winchester, Lord High Treasurer, who died 1572. Amongst other curiosities are a folding picture of Preaching at St. Paul's Cross (1616); Porter's map of London, time of Charles I.; prescriptions of the physicians for Charles II. on his death-bed; Cromwell's sword; brass-gilt spur from the battle-field of Towton, "the bloodiest field between the white rose and the red," with a rhyming posy on the shanks, "en loial amour tout mon coer;" Bohemian astronomical clock made in 1525 for Sigismund, King of Poland; early proclamations; early ballads and broad-sides; Roman antiquities found in Britain; coins, medals, and provincial tokens. For permission to see these things apply to the secretary, at Somerset House.

THE SOCIETY OF ARTS, John Street, Adelphi, is one of the most useful associations in London, established 1754, incorporated 1847. It styles itself the Society for the Encouragement of Arts, Manufactures, and Commerce. With this end in view, it offers prizes for new inventions and memoirs on subjects deserving of investigation. It publishes a weekly journal. Recognizing the great value of competitive examinations, it holds one annually, and grants certificates and prizes on the awards of the

Board of Examiners. In the spring there is an exhibition of new inventions, of which an illustrated catalogue is published. In the council-room are six large pictures, illustrating the progress of the arts, by James Barry, "interesting and remarkable." The society has taken a deep interest in the subject of international exhibitions, and it is doubtful whether, without its exertions, those of 1851 and 1862 would have taken place. It is supported by the subscriptions of members, who pay two guineas a year.

THE ROYAL ACADEMY OF ARTS occupies the east wing of the National Gallery, but as the rooms are required for the exhibition of the national collection of pictures, it is proposed to send the Academy elsewhere. It was established in 1768, and it consists of forty Royal Academicians, who attach the letters " R.A." to their names, twenty associates " A.R.A.," and six associate engravers. The Academicians elect a president from their own body, and appoint a secretary and keeper. Vacancies in the body are filled up from the associates. The Council consists of eight members, and they elect from " the forty," professors of painting, sculpture, and architecture. The professor of anatomy must be a surgeon. These professors deliver lectures to the students without charge. Medals are distributed annually as prizes amongst the sudents, and the most deserving of the latter are sent to Rome free of expense to study their art in that city. Sir Joshua Reynolds was the first president, and West the second. Their collection of prints, and library of books, is open to students. Persons wishing to be admitted as students should apply to the secretary. They also possess a good collection of casts, as well as some paintings, the most noticeable of which is an old Italian copy of Leonardo da Vinci's Last Supper, the size of the original. This is the oldest and best copy that has been made of that celebrated fresco, and it has become of great value, in consequence of the decay of the original. Here are also two cartoons by L. da Vinci, and a bas-relief in marble of the Holy Family, by Michael Angelo.

It is a rule that each Academician, on his election, shall present to the Academy a work of art of his own execution. These diploma-pictures and sculptures are placed in the council-room, and may be seen on application to the secretary. They include a portrait of George III., by Reynolds ; a rustic girl, by Lawrence ; boys digging for a rat, by Wilkie ; portrait of Gainsborough, by himself ; portrait of Sir W. Chambers, the architect, by Reynolds ;

and of Sir Joshua, by himself. Amongst the sculptures are Cupid and Psyche, by Nollekens ; bust of Flaxman, by Nollekens ; and a bust of West, by Chantrey.   The palettes of Hogarth and Reynolds are preserved here.

THE EXHIBITION OF PAINTINGS

by living artists, which annually takes place in the rooms of the Royal Academy, is open from the beginning of May to the end of July, and is one of the great sights of the London season. Many hundred pictures are hung on the walls, and a room is appropriated to sculptures. The Academy realizes a large income (and this is the only source of their income) from this exhibition, by charging 1s. admission for each person, and selling a catalogue at 1s.   As to the conditions on which works of art are admitted to the exhibition, these may be ascertained from the secretary.

ROYAL INSTITUTION OF GREAT BRITAIN, 21 Albemarle Street, Piccadilly, established 1799 ; the objects in view being the diffusion of knowledge, and the facilitating the general introduction of useful mechanical inventions, and the teaching by courses of philosophical lectures and experiments the application of science to the common purposes of life. This institution has taken a leading part in the great work of popularizing science, and applying its discoveries to the benefit of mankind. Benjamin Thomson, Count Rumford, was one of the early promoters ; and here Sir Humphrey Davy and Faraday have worked with such excellent result. There is a well selected library of about 30,000 volumes ; a theatre where lectures are delivered ; a laboratory for the promotion and advancement of the chemical and physical sciences ; a mineralogical museum ; and a reading-room, in which are found the principal newspapers and periodicals of Britain and the Continent. Certain professorships have been founded, which have been held by such men as Owen, Huxley, and Tyndal. who have delivered their lectures in the theatre. The institution is entirely supported by the subscriptions of members and the bequests of generous benefactors. Dr. Bence Jones is the present secretary.

THE LINNÆAN SOCIETY, Burlington House, Piccadilly, was founded in 1788 by Dr. (afterwards Sir James Edward) Smith, and received its charter in 1802. The object of the society is the study of zoology and botany in all their departments, and it is well supported by the scientific men of the country. They possess a museum and excellent library. The nucleus of the museum and herbarium was formed by the collection of Linnæus himself. When Smith was a young man he was breakfasting with Sir Joseph Banks, who informed him that Linnæus' collections had been offered to him for 1000 guineas, but that he had no intention of purchasing them. Smith conceived the desire of acquiring them, and with some difficulty prevailed on his father to supply him with money for the purpose. The King of Sweden, Gustavus III., happened to be absent from the country when the negotiations were proceeding, and hearing on his return that a vessel with the collections on board had just sailed for England, he immediately despatched a ship to intercept it. It was too late, and the collections reached England in 1784 in twenty-six cases. The society publishes its transactions, on which many valuable memoirs have appeared. The anniversary meeting is held on the 24th May. Applicants for the fellowship must be proposed by three fellows. The admission fee is £6, and the annual subscription £3. Fellows annex the letters F.L.S. to their names.

THE GEOLOGICAL SOCIETY, Somerset House. Instituted in 1807, incorporated in 1826. This society has been of eminent service to the science of geology, and is well supported by the subscriptions of nearly 900 fellows (F.G.S.), who pay an admission fee of six guineas, and an annual subscription of three guineas. They have a large collection of fossils, and a good library. They publish a quarterly journal, and they have a fortnightly meeting of fellows to hear papers read.

THE ROYAL GEOGRAPHICAL SOCIETY, 15 Whitehall Place. Established in 1830. Fellows (F.R.G.S.), admitted by ballot, pay an entrance of £3, and an annual subscription of £2. The society possesses a good collection of books and maps, and publishes a quarterly journal.

THE ROYAL ASIATIC SOCIETY, 5 New Burlington Street. Founded in 1823 for the investigation and encouragement of art, science, and literature, in relation to Asia. Their library is rich in oriental MSS. and Chinese books. The museum contains a collection of oriental arms and armour, which may be seen any day, except Saturday, by a member's order. Members resident in the British Isles pay an admission fee of five guineas, and an annual subscription of three guineas. Certain societies in India are branches of this. It publishes its transactions.

SION COLLEGE, London Wall, City, was founded in 1623 for the benefit of the clergy of London, the incumbents of parishes within the city and liberties of London being the fellows. In connection with it are almshouses for twenty poor persons. The library contains upwards of 35,000 vols. This library was one of those that received gratuitously a copy of every book published, but this privilege was abolished, and the library now has an annual treasury grant of £363 instead. An order from a fellow will admit to this library daily from 10 to 4. There are several pictures here, the most noticeable of which is a costume portrait of a citizen's wife of William and Mary's time.

INSTITUTION OF CIVIL ENGINEERS, 25 Great George Street, Westminster. Incorporated 1828, having been established ten years previously. It is supported by the subscriptions of persons connected with the various branches of civil engineering. Telford, the engineer of the Menai bridge, was the first president, and there is a portrait of him here. There is a good professional library, part of which was the bequest of Telford, who also bequeathed a sum of money, directing the interest to be expended in annual premiums.

ROYAL INSTITUTE OF BRITISH ARCHITECTS, 16 Lower Grosvenor Street, Grosvenor Square. Incorporated in 1837. Supported by the subscriptions of fellows and associates. Here is a good library of architectural works, including the works of Piranesi and Canina, and a large collection of original drawings of ancient and modern buildings.

ROYAL SOCIETY OF LITERATURE, 4 St. Martin's Place, Charing Cross. Incorporated 1826. Valuable library. Transactions published occasionally.

In addition to the societies already mentioned there are the Royal Astronomical Society, Somerset House.

Statistical Society, 12 St. James' Square.

Zoological Society, whose gardens are described elsewhere in this volume.

Entomological Society, 17 Old Bond Street.

Numismatic Society, 41 Tavistock Street, Covent Garden.

Geologists' Association.

Microscopical Society.

Chemical Society.

Pharmaceutical Society, etc. etc.

There are also several societies for the publication of scientific works, and the reprinting of old books, such as no publisher could undertake without loss; such are the Ray Society, the Cavendish Society, and the Camden Society.

THE ROYAL AGRICULTURAL SOCIETY, 12 Hanover Square, was established in 1838, and incorporated by charter in 1840, for the purpose of improving the agriculture of the country. One annual meeting is held in London, and another in the country. At the latter there is a cattle-show, an exhibition of agricultural implements, and a trial of cultivating machinery. Prizes are awarded, and the affair excites so much interest that crowds of people are attracted from all parts. A quarterly journal is published. The society is supported by the subscriptions of the governors (who pay £5 each annually) and members (who pay £1 each annually). It has been of signal advantage to British agriculture by pointing out improved systems of cultivation, and explaining the principles to be attended to.

THE SMITHFIELD CLUB is an agricultural association, founded about seventy years ago, which annually in December has an exhibition of cattle and sheep. Hitherto this exhibition has taken place at the Baker Street Bazaar, but this place is too small for its increased importance, and a structure, to be called the Agricultural Hall, is being erected in the Liverpool Road, near the Angel, Islington, at which future cattle-shows will be held. The exhibition hall will have an area of 384 feet by 217 feet, be covered with a roof of iron and glass having a span of 130 feet, and have a gallery 36 feet wide all round it. There will be a tower of 95 feet high at each side of the front. In addition, there will be a place for the exhibition of pigs, 100 feet square. First and second class refreshment rooms, lavatories, etc., will be attached. The façade, of red and white brick, is Italian. A company finds the funds for this structure, which is estimated to cost £25,000, and Mr. Peck of Maidstone has furnished the designs. This spacious hall will in every respect meet the requirements of the club, and that body has agreed to lease its exhibition to the company for twenty-one years.

LIBRARIES.

Besides the libraries which have been spoken of in other parts of this volume we must mention—

THE LONDON INSTITUTION LIBRARY, occupying a handsome

building (opened in 1819) in Finsbury Circus, which also contains a theatre where lectures are delivered. The library contains about 62,000 vols. The institution was established by the issue of £100 shares, and is supported by annual subscriptions. Porson, the learned Greek scholar, was the first librarian.

THE RUSSELL INSTITUTION, Great Coram Street, Brunswick Square, has been established somewhat on the plan of the London Institution, but on a smaller scale, the library only containing about 16,000 vols.

THE LONDON LIBRARY, 12 St. James' Square, is simply a library with about 80,000 vols., which are lent out to subscribers paying £3 a year, or £2 a year with an entrance fee of £6. There are about 850 members, and the late Prince Consort was patron.

CHAPTER THE TWELFTH.

Gardens belonging to Scientific Societies.

Royal Horticultural Society's Gardens—Royal Botanic Society's Gardens, Regent's Park—Zoological Gardens.

THE ROYAL HORTICULTURAL SOCIETY'S GARDENS, South Kensington, are situate on a quadrangular plot of ground about 500 yards in length by nearly 300 in width, abutting, south, on the Great Exhibition buildings of 1862, and west, on Exhibition Road, where the principal entrance is placed. There is a temporary roadway for admission from Kensington Gore, leading to the back of the conservatory. The ground is part of that purchased out of the surplus fund of the Great Exhibition of 1851, and has been leased by the commissioners of that Exhibition to the Royal Horticultural Society upon certain conditions, one of which was that the society should expend at least £50,000 upon the Garden, the commissioners binding themselves to lay out an equal sum on ornamental arcades. The garden occupies about 22 acres, and the arcades around it afford a sheltered walk of three-quarters of a mile. Here will be held flower-shows and fetes similar to those for which the Chiswick Gardens were renowned. The garden lies on three levels, and is decorated with terraces, waterworks, and cascades, the principal of which is 20 feet wide, and with a fall of 10 feet. When the trees have extended themselves, the effect of these gardens, with their embroidered beds and geometrical flower-plots, will be very good. Amongst the statuary there are two copies in bronze of Rauch's Victory, 9 feet in height. The four *terra-cotta* statues representing Strength, Temperance, Justice, and Truth, placed at the sides of the entrance to the maze, were given by the late Prince Consort, of whom a marble statue, the gift of the Prince of Wales, is to be placed here. At the north end is a grand conservatory, 270 feet long, 75 feet high, and 100 feet wide. The cost, including the engine-house, was about £16,000. The north and central arcades were designed by Mr. Sydney Smirke. The north arcade, in the style of that of the Villa Albani at Rome, is 600 feet long, 22 feet high, and 26 feet wide. The capitals and shields are in *terra cotta*. The central arcades are after the Milanese brickwork of the fifteenth century. They are 630 feet long, 20 feet high, and 24 feet wide. In both sets of arcades red brick has been chiefly employed on account of the colour harmonizing with the gardens. Captain Fowke, R.E., designed the south arcades after the cloisters of St. John Lateran at Rome, which were erected in the twelfth century. Their length is 1980 feet, with a height of 20, and a width of 27 feet. Here the pillars are of *terra cotta*. Upon the highest terrace are two circular houses for musical bands ; and near them are the trees planted by the Queen and the late Prince Consort.

The Horticultural Society was founded in 1804, and formed the garden at Chiswick in 1822. Five years later began those exhibitions of horticultural produce which for many years were among the most attractive events of a London season. Of late, however, the attendance of visitors, from one cause or other, materially diminished, and the income of the society was consequently much lessened. The society, indeed, was almost on the point of being broken up, when the late Prince Consort stepped forward, and under his patronage it has been brilliantly resuscitated, at a spot more conveniently situate for the meeting of pleasure-seekers. It was formally opened on the 5th June 1861. From the great benefits already conferred on the community by the society, it deserves every encouragement. Collectors of plants and seeds were sent into all quarters of the world ; and the experiments of plant-growing conducted at Chiswick have been attended with highly valuable results. As at present constituted, the society's affairs are managed by a council, assisted by a secretary, who is at present the eminent botanist Dr. John Lindley.

Every candidate for fellowship must be proposed by at least three fellows, one of whom must be personally acquainted with him. A fellow paying an entrance fee of 2 guineas, and an annual subscription of 2 guineas (compounded for by a single payment of 20 guineas), is entitled to admission at all times, and has the right of personally introducing two friends, except on certain great show days. A fellow paying an entrance fee of 2 guineas, and an annual subscription of 4 guineas (compounded for by a single payment of 40 guineas), is entitled, in addition to the preceding privileges, to a transferable ticket, the bearer of which has precisely the same privileges. A fellow subscribing 2 guineas annually is also entitled, on payment of 10 guineas, to an extra transferable ticket for life, admitting one person both on ordinary days and show days. A subscriber of 4 guineas may have three such tickets on paying the same amount. Fellows are entitled to free admission to the garden at Chiswick every day except Sunday from nine to six, and each fellow can introduce by written order four friends a day to the Chiswick Garden.

A person not being a fellow may, on payment of 5 guineas, obtain a joint ticket admitting him both to the International Exhibition and to the Horticultural Garden on every day when they are open to the public, from the 1st of May to the 18th of October.

The prices of admission to the public on single days must be ascertained from the advertisements in the newspapers.

THE ROYAL BOTANIC SOCIETY'S GARDENS are in the inner circle, Regent's Park, where they occupy about 18 acres. The society was incorporated in 1839 for the promotion of botany, but its principal attention is directed to making the gardens an agreeable rendezvous for the gay world. There is a spacious conservatory well stocked with beautiful plants. During the spring months promenades are held, at which military bands attend. There are also splendid exhibitions of fruit and flowers, which are very attractive, and at which prizes to a large amount are distributed. The gardens are supported by the subscriptions of fellows and members, as to which the secretary, Mr. De Carle Sowerby, who resides in the grounds, will give information. The exhibition days are advertised in the newspapers.

THE ZOOLOGICAL GARDENS, REGENT'S PARK, are amongst the most interesting and attractive sights of London. During the year 1860-61, the visitors amounted to 293,995. They belong to the Zoological Society, which was instituted in 1826 under the auspices of Sir H. Davy, Sir Stamford Raffles, and other eminent persons. The gardens were opened in 1828, and since that time a very large number of animals from all quarters of the world have been sent here ; some presented by foreign potentates, colonial governors, and travellers, but chiefly purchased. Fellows pay a fee of £5 on admission to the society, and an annual contribution of £3. Annual subscribers pay £3.

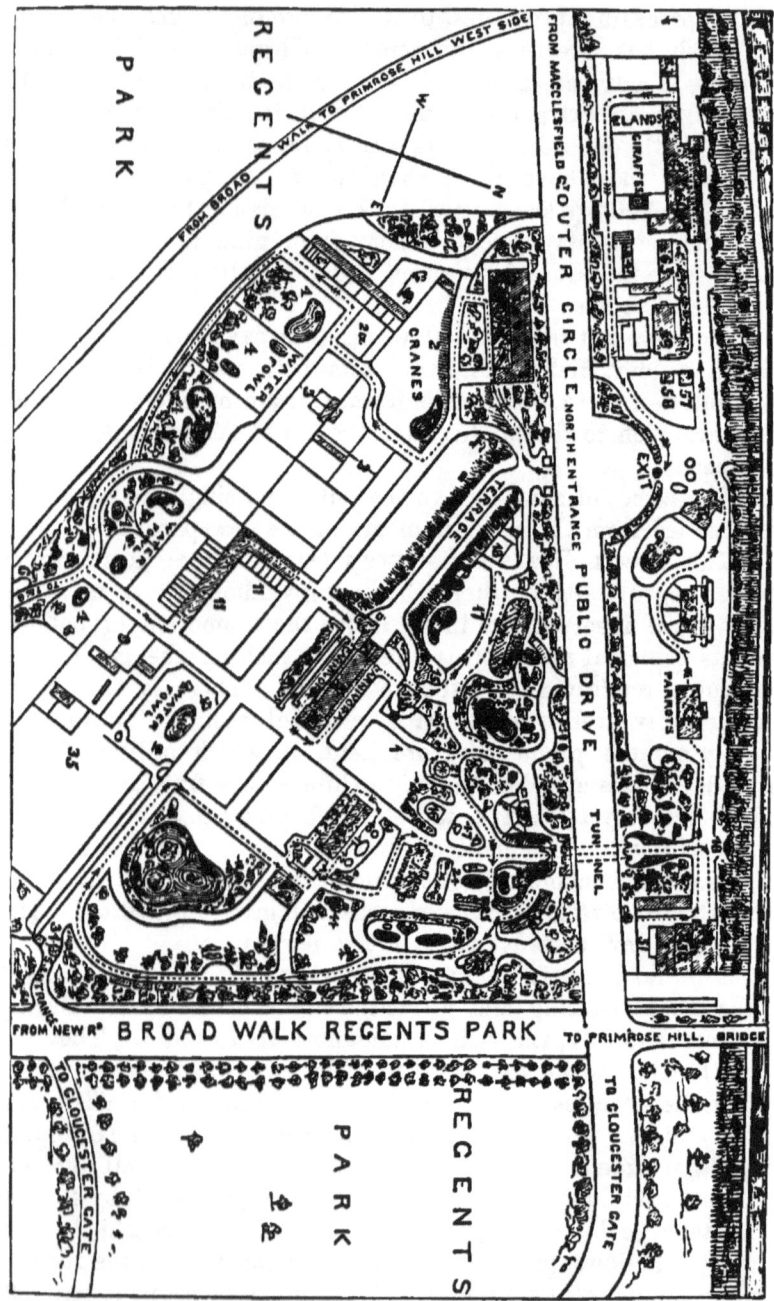

EXPLANATION OF FIGURES ON THE PLAN.

1. New Aviary.	18. Pelicans' Inclosure.	42. Armadillo Inclosure.
2. Crane Inclosure.	19. Old Aviary.	43. Coypu's Cage.
2 a. Impeyan Pheasants' Inclosure.	20. North Pond.	44. REFRESHMENT ROOM.
	21. Falcon Aviary.	45. Monkey House.
3. Swine-House.	22. Bison House.	46. Porcupine Inclosure.
4. Southern Ponds.	23. Mandarin Ducks' Pond	47. Rock-Rabbits' House.
5. Young Pheasants' and Emeus' Inclosure.	24. Seal Pond.	48. Virginian Owls' Cage.
	25. Kites' Aviary.	49. Reptile House.
6. Brush-Turkeys' Inclosure.	26. Winter Aviary.	50. Paradise House.
	27. Small Mammals' House	51. Kangaroo Inclosures.
7. Small Carnivora House	28. Racoon's Cage.	52. Sheep Sheds.
8. Pheasant & Pea-Fowl's Aviaries.	29, 30. Garganeys' Ponds.	53. Parrot House.
	31, 32, 33. Dens of Wolves	54. Sambur Deer House.
9. Alpacas' Inclosures.	and Foxes.	55. Wapiti House.
10. Waders' Inclosure.	34. South Entrance.	56. Elephant House.
11. Zebra & Antelope Ho.	35. Antelope Inclosure.	57, 58. Small Deer's Inclos.
12. Cages of Grt. Carnivora	36. Three-island Pond.	59. Superintendent's Office
13. Bear Pit.	37. Fish-House.	60. Hippopotamus Houses
14. Bear Pond.	38. Harpy's Aviary.	61. Giraffe House.
15. Eagle Owls' Aviary.	39. Eagles' Aviaries.	62. Eland House.
16. Camel House.	40. Beaver Pond.	63. Ostrich House.
17. Water-Fowls' Lawn.	41. Otter Cage.	64, 65. Goat & Deer Sheds.

Visitors are admitted to the gardens on Mondays on payment of 6d. each, and on the other days of the week on payment of 1s. each ; children pay 6d. only. Open from nine to sunset. On Saturday afternoon there is usually a military band performing in the gardens. The office and library of the society are at 11 Hanover Square. Dr. P. L. Sclater, the ornithologist, is the secretary, whose official guide (price 6d.) contains a plan of the gardens and several illustrative woodcuts. Refreshments may be obtained in the gardens at prices specified in a printed tariff. Enter at the north entrance in the outer circle of the park, and turn to the right to the New Aviary, where some of the most interesting birds in the collection are kept. Here are the sacred ibis, the scarlet ibis, and the American mocking bird ; close by is the crane inclosure, where numerous specimens of this long-legged tribe may be seen, the handsomest being perhaps the crowned crane. Near at hand is the swine-house, where many species of this dirt-loving family are preserved. Passing ponds where water-fowl are living, we arrive at the inclosures where the llamas and alpacas are confined ; adjacent to which is the inclosure of the wading birds. Opposite this are the new houses containing gnus, antelopes, and zebras. Amongst the latest additions are specimens of the sable antelope, and the hartebeeste, both from Africa ; the latter from the Cape Colony, where it has now become rare in the inhabited districts. Proceeding, we reach the terrace below, in which are found the great

carnivora—lions, tigers, leopards, and hyenas.   Close at hand are
the bear pit and the bear pond.   Two species of camel will be
found near the clock tower ; and a little beyond are inclosures
where water-fowl and pelicans are confined.   Not far from the
clock tower is a house where the Brahmin bulls and some yaks
from Thibet live.   Near the seal pond are aviaries containing kites
and vultures.   In a neighbouring house are some carnivorous
animals, including the beautiful clouded tiger, and some mar-
supials, including the Tasmanian devil, whose singular habits
will attract attention.   Making our way to the fish-house,
where fishes and many specimens of the lower aquatic animals,
such as sea-anemones, are living in large tanks, eagles and vultures are placed in a house close by ; and near them will be
found beavers, otters, and armadillos.   In the monkey-house
are many curious species of baboons, apes, and monkeys, those
caricatures of humanity.   Passing to the north part of the gardens, by means of a tunnel carried under the public road, and
turning to the right, we arrive at houses tenanted by snakes and
other reptiles, amongst which the gigantic salamander from Japan
is particularly to be noticed.   The great python lately laid a
number of eggs, which it incubated.   Such an event never occurred before in this country in the case of a large serpent.   This
reptile came from West Africa, and has been eleven years in the
garden.   The kangaroos are close at hand.   Passing through a
house containing a remarkably rich collection of parrots, we
reach a house tenanted by several foreign species of deer ; a
house where Indian elephants and rhinoceroses are living ; and
the tank where the hippopotami like to disport themselves.   In
this part are the giraffes and the elands, animals which have now
been established in the parks of some noblemen in our island.
The last house in this portion of the garden is tenanted by
ostriches, emus, mooruks, and the curious apteryx or kiwi, from
New Zealand, which has purely nocturnal habits, and is therefore only seen by the visitors when brought out by the keeper.

It may be well to mention that the pelicans, etc., are fed at
half-past two o'clock ; the otters, at three ; the eagles (Wednesdays excepted), at half-past three ; and the lions, etc., at four.

In addition to the entrance where carriages can set down visitors, there is the south entrance in the Broad Walk, only available
to pedestrians.   This is distant about 300 yards from Gloucester
Gate, near which an omnibus passes every ten minutes.

CHAPTER THE THIRTEENTH.

Public Picture Galleries.

National Gallery—South Kensington Museum—Soane Museum—National Portrait Gallery—Annual Exhibitions of Pictures, etc.

In addition to the public galleries, the subject of this chapter, the lover of pictures ought to visit the galleries at Windsor Castle, Hampton Court, and Dulwich, which are described elsewhere in this volume.

THE NATIONAL GALLERY is on the north side of Trafalgar Square, one of the finest sites in Europe, according to Sir Robert Peel. The eastern half is in the temporary occupation of the Royal Academy, the other half contains the national collection of pictures by the old masters, and the paintings bequeathed to the nation by J. W. M. Turner, the works of his own pencil. The pictures are very much crowded, but the arrangement is only temporary. Many plans for the enlargement of the gallery have been put forward, but nothing has been hitherto decided on.

Open free to the public on Monday, Tuesday, Wednesday, and Saturday, of each week, from 10 to 6, from the beginning of May to the end of September, and from 10 to 5 from the beginning of November to the end of April. During the month of October it is closed. Students are admitted on Thursdays and Fridays.

Speaking now of the ancient masters, the nucleus of the collection was acquired in 1824 by the purchase for £57,000 of 38 pictures brought together by Mr. John Julius Angerstein, a London banker. Two years later Sir George Beaumont presented a collection of 16 pictures to the nation ; and in 1831 the Reverend W. H. Carr left to the nation 31 pictures. Subsequently, 17 pictures were bequeathed by Lieutenant-Colonel Ollney, 15 by Lord Farnborough, 14 by R. Simmons, Esq., and 8 by Lord Colborne—honour to their names ! The nation has had many other generous benefactors in this way, and a large number of pictures have been purchased with public money, until the collection now amounts to upwards of 400 paintings. This is only a small number for a national collection, and it is far exceeded in extent by several galleries on the continent, but then ours promises to increase much more rapidly than those ; and in course of time we may hope to possess a gallery worthy of the nation. At present some of the leading schools are inadequately represented. Of Raphael, for example, we have a first-rate specimen ; of the Spanish and the Dutch schools the specimens are extremely few. On the other hand, in Correggios, Claudes, Gaspar Pousins, Nicolo Pousins, and Paul Veroneses, we are fairly rich.

The late J. W. M. Turner bequeathed to the nation a large collection of oil paintings and water-colour drawings, executed by his own hand, upon the condition that a suitable place for their exhibition should be provided for them within a certain time. At first they were placed in Marlborough House, then they were removed to the South Kensington Museum, and within the last few months they have been brought to Trafalgar Square. There are to be seen about 125 oil pictures in the artist's various styles, as well as a number of water-colour drawings and unfinished studies. These are placed in the great western room, which has been named the Turner Gallery.

In the entrance hall of the National Gallery are placed a marble statue of Sir David Wilkie, by S. Joseph (the painter's palette is let into the pedestal) ; a marble alto-relievo, by Thomas Banks, of Thetis and her Nymphs ; and a bust in bronze of the Emperor Napoleon, the bequest of P. C. Crespigny, Esq. Of the attendants in this hall may be purchased at various prices official catalogues of the pictures. These are hung on the walls of five saloons, the largest of which, only recently constructed, is 75 feet long and 30 feet wide. We shall now mention those pictures amongst the old masters that best deserve the visitor's attention, arranging them with reference to their schools.

Italian.

FRA ANGELICO : Christ surrounded by angels, saints, etc., the predella of an altar piece, in five compartments, cost £3500. GIOVANNI BELLINI : portrait of a Doge ; and Madonna and child. BRONZINO : portrait of a lady ; Venus, Cupid, Folly, and Time. CANALETTO : two views in Venice. ANNIBALE CARACCI : Christ appearing to St. Peter ; St. John in the wilderness ; Pan teaching Apollo. CARACCI LODOVICO : Susannah and the Elders. CIMA DA CONEGLIANO : Infant Christ on the knees of the Virgin. CORREGGIO : Mercury instructing Cupid ; Ecce Homo—for these two pictures £10,000 were given to the late Marquis of Londonderry ; Holy Family, cost £3800 ; Christ's agony in the garden, a repetition of the picture in the Duke of Wellington's collection. FRANCESCA : Virgin with the Infant Christ ; Virgin and two angels weeping over the dead body of Christ ; Virgin and child with two saints. GUERCINO : Angels weeping over Christ. GUIDO : Perseus and Andromeda ; Venus attired by the Graces ; the Magdalen ; the coronation of the Virgin ; Ecce Homo. FRA FILIPPO LIPPI : Madonna and child enthroned ; the Annunciation ; St. John the Baptist and saints. CARLO MARATTI : portrait of a Cardinal. PONTORMO : portrait of a knight. RAPHAEL : St. Catherine of Alexandria, cost £5000 ;. portrait of Pope Julius II. SEBASTIAN DEL PIOMBO : Resurrection of Lazarus, very fine, " the most important specimen of the Italian school in England" (Dr. Waagen)—£15,000 were offered for it by Mr. Beckford to Mr. Angerstein, and refused ; the composition and drawing are by Michael Angelo, and it was painted in competition with Raphael's celebrated Transfiguration, now in the Vatican. SALVATOR ROSA : landscape. TITIAN : the Music Lesson ; Bacchus and Ariadne, a picture finely criticised by Elia ; Madonna and child ; the Tribute Money, cost £2604 ; portrait of Ariosto. PAUL VERONESE ; adoration of the Magi ; Family of Darius at the feet of Alexander, cost £14,000. LEONARDI DA VINCI : Christ disputing with the Doctors.

Spanish.

MURILLO : `Holy Family, cost £3000 ; St. John and the lamb. VELASQUEZ : Philip IV. of Spain hunting. ZURBARAN : a Franciscan Monk.

Flemish and Dutch.

BAKHUIZEN : Dutch shipping. BERGHEM : Crossing the Ford. CUYP : landscape. GERARD DOW : the Painter's Portrait. VAN EYCK ; portrait of a Flemish Merchant and lady, painted 1434, cost £630 ; and two portraits of men. N. MAAS : Dutch Housewife ; the Idle Servant. MABUSE : Man's portrait. MORETTO : portrait of an Italian nobleman. MORO : portrait of a lady. REMBRANDT : Woman taken in Adultery, cost £5250 ; adoration of the Shepherds ; portrait of a Jew merchant ; portrait of a Capuchin Friar ; portrait of a Jewish Rabbi ; his own portrait ; the Amsterdam Musketeers. RUBENS : Abduction of the Sabine Women ; Peace and War ; the Brazen Serpent ; landscape with Rubens' Chateau ; the Judgment of Paris, cost £4200. RUYSDAEL : two landscapes with waterfalls. TENIERS : Music party ; Boors regaling ; the Money Changers ; Players at Tric-trac. A. VAN DER NEER : River Scene by Moonlight. VAN DER WEYDEN : portraits of himself and his wife. VANDYCK : the Emperor Theodosius refused admission into the Church by St. Ambrose ; portrait of Gevartius.

French.

CLAUDE : landscape, Cephalus and Procris ; Seaport at sunset ; landscape, David at the cave of Adullam ; the Chigi Claude ; Seaport ; the Embarkation of the Queen of Sheba ; the Bouillon Claude; Seaport, morning, Embarkation of St. Ursula ; small landscape, death of Procris ; landscape, a study of trees ; small landscape, given to the nation by Sir George Beaumont, but so admired by him that he asked leave to retain it during his life, and he made it his travelling companion. GASPAR POUSSIN : landscape, Abraham preparing to sacrifice Isaac ; a Land Storm ; landscape, Dido and Æneas taking refuge from the storm ; view of La Riccia ; Italian landscape, town on the side of a hill. NICOLO POUSSIN : Nursing of Bacchus ; Bacchanalian Festival ; Dance of Bacchanals in honour of Pan.

THE SOUTH KENSINGTON MUSEUM at Brompton is about one mile distant from Hyde Park Corner, in near neighbourhood to the Great Exhibition Buildings of 1862. It stands upon part of the ground which was purchased by the commissioners of the Exhibition of 1851 with the surplus funds derived from that Exhibition. About twelve acres of land were obtained from the commissioners at a cost of £60,000. Public money to the amount of nearly £140,000, has been further laid out here on buildings, and on those parts of the collections that have been purchased. · The cost of management is about £7000 a year.

Admission free on Monday, Tuesday, and Saturday of each week, the whole day from 10 A.M. till 10 P.M. In the evening the galleries are lighted with gas ; students are admitted on Wednesday, Thursday, and Friday. On these days the public must pay 6d. each person—hours from 10 A.M. till 4 P.M. Here are refreshment rooms, waiting rooms with lavatories, etc. In 1860, the visitors to this museum amounted to 610,696.

The collections here are so large that a careful examination would occupy some days. They consist of—

1. Objects of ornamental art, as applied to manufactures, with an art library.

2. British pictures, sculpture, and engravings.

3. Architectural examples, models, casts, etc.

4. Appliances for teaching in schools, school furniture, books, maps, diagrams, models, and apparatus used in primary education.

5. Materials for building and construction, stone, bricks, tiles, glass, etc.

6. Substances used for food.

7. Animal products employed in the arts, leather, furs, feathers, wools, hair, etc.

8. Models of patented inventions, machines, etc.

9. Reproductions, by means of photography and casting, of antique sculpture and paintings.

The two last named collections have entrances distinct from that leading to the other collections. The photographs are sold at cost price to the public. The collections of materials for building and construction, and animal products, have been almost wholly presented by private individuals, without cost to the state. The food collection is very interesting. Here may be seen the various articles used as human sustenance, from all quarters of the world, with analyses of those which are chiefly employed, shewing their comparative values as feeding agents. A collection

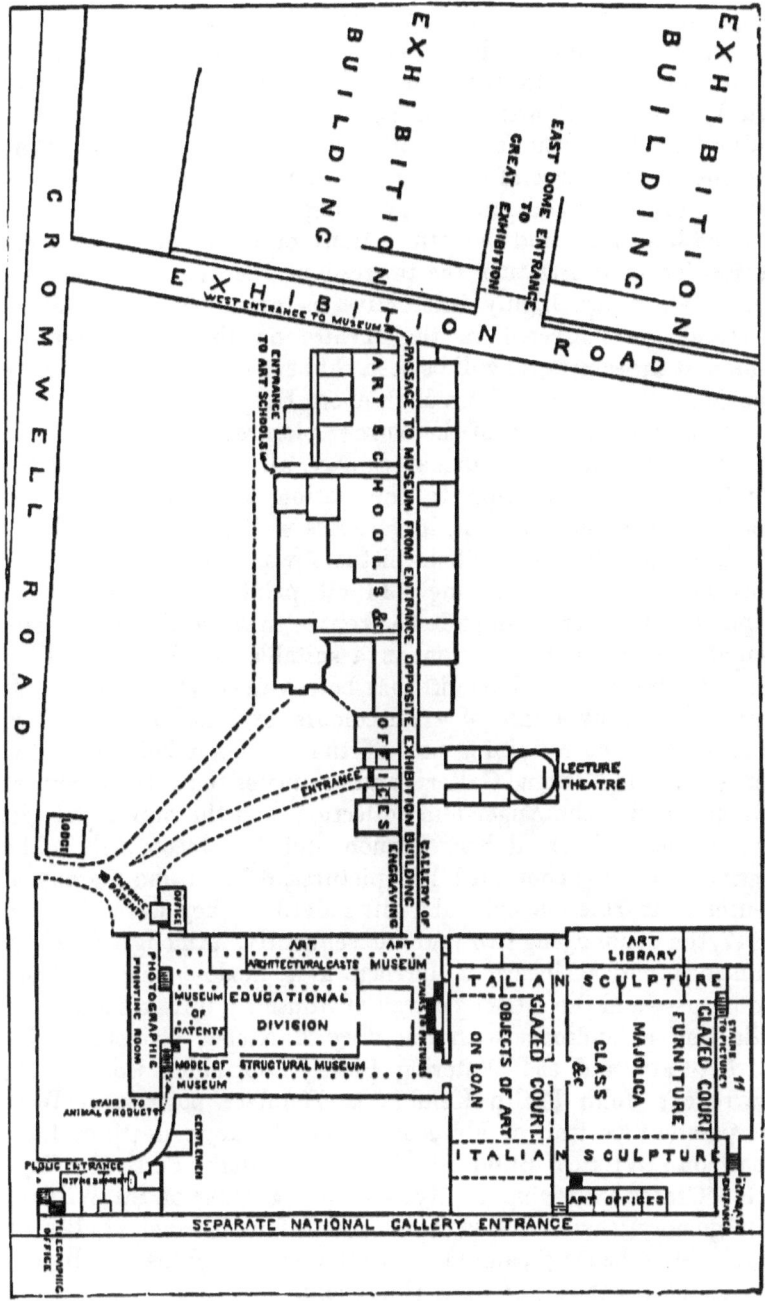

of preserved articles from China, will give some insight into the nature of a Chinese dinner; and there are curious collections from Siam and Japan, including rhinoceros' hide, and elephant's trunk. In the department of useful art, many articles of great value have been lent for exhibition with the best results. Here are shewn specimens of China and pottery ware, glass, jewellery, fancy work in metals, mosaics, carvings in wood and ivory, etc. etc., both antique and modern. Many of these things are mere curiosities, or illustrating the progress of the arts, but there are many which are highly instructive as examples for imitation. Lectures are delivered in the theatre on the art collections. Amongst the sculptures will be seen Cibber's statues of Melancholy and Madness, removed from Bethlehem Hospital.

With the exception of the Turner pictures, which are now in the National Gallery, Trafalgar Square, all the paintings of the English school belonging to the nation are exhibited at the South Kensington Museum, in galleries well lighted from above.

The collection of British pictures was commenced by Mr. Sheepshanks, who, on giving 234 oil paintings to the nation, stipulated that they should be kept either in the immediate neighbourhood of Kensington, in a suitable building, or failing this, at Cambridge. This gift has been valued at £52,595. It was followed by a gift of water-colours by Mrs. Ellison, valued at £3000. The remaining part of the collection belongs to the trustees of the National Gallery, and comprises the British pictures purchased with the Angerstein collection, and the munificent gift and bequest of Mr. Robert Vernon and Mr. Jacob Bell. The Vernon collection contained 162 pictures, 6 busts, and a group of figures in marble—a splendid gift indeed. They were given in 1847, the donor dying two years subsequently. Amongst the older paintings, notice Hogarth's Marriage à la mode—a series of six paintings—and the artist's portrait of himself; Wilson's Mæcenas' villa, and a landscape with the story of Niobe; Gainsborough's Market-Cart, and the Watering Place; Constable's Corn-Field; Lawrence's John Philip Kemble as Hamlet; portrait of West the painter; portrait of Mr. Angerstein; Copley's death of Lord Chatham; Wilkie's Blind Fiddler, and Village Festival; Reynold's Graces sacrificing to Hymen (the daughter of Sir William Montgomery) the Banished Lord, the Infant Samuel, studies of angels—five heads "painted with astonishing lightness, delicacy, and feeling," portrait of Lord Heathfield.

In the Vernon and Sheepshanks collections will be found many excellent specimens of the artists of the modern British school, including pictures from the easels of Wilkie, C. R. Leslie, Edwin Landseer, Mulready, Webster, Maclise, E. M. Ward, D. Roberts, Creswick, Stanfield, E. W. Cooke, and other painters. Notice amongst the Vernon pictures, Sir Joshua Reynolds' Age of Innocence, which cost £1522 : 10s. ; a landscape by Gainsborough; Wilkie's bagpiper; and Leslie's Sancho and the Duchess.

THE SOANE MUSEUM, on the north side of Lincoln's Inn Fields (No. 13), is distinguished from the neighbouring houses by some architectural embellishment. This was the residence of Sir John Soane, the founder of the museum, who, born the son of a bricklayer, died a knight in 1837, at the age of 84, after having amassed a large fortune as an architect. He vested £30,000 stock in trustees, to apply the dividends in support of the museum, and obtained an Act of Parliament for settling it for the benefit of the public.

In ordinary years, the museum is open free between the hours of 10 and 4, on Wednesdays, Thursdays, and Fridays, during the months of April, May, and June. Also to foreigners, and others having special reasons for soliciting admission, on Tuesdays in February, March, July, and August. Those who wish to obtain admission should apply by letter to the curator, or personally at the museum, a day or two before the day of the visit. The name and address of the person requiring admission, with the number of the proposed party, must be stated, and the caller's card is expected to be left. If there be no reason against complying, the curator will forward by post a card of admission for the next open day. To obtain access to the books, drawings, MSS., or permission to copy pictures or other works of art, special application must be made to the trustees or the curator. It is highly probable, however, that hereafter the museum will be more freely open to the public than it has hitherto been.

"There is no institution in London (says Mrs. Jameson) in which a few hours may be more pleasantly whiled away, or even more profitably employed, than in this fairy collection of virtû, where the infinite variety of the objects assembled together in every department of art—many, indeed, sufficiently trivial, some also of peculiar beauty and value—suggest to the intelligent mind and cultivated taste a thousand thoughts, remembrances, and associations, while the ingenuity shewn in the arrangement amuses the fancy in a very agreeable manner."

The objects are distributed over 24 rooms, every corner being crammed, every inch of wall turned to account. In the entrance hall is a bust of Sir Thomas Lawrence, and in the first room is a portrait by that artist of Sir John Soane, as well as a picture by Sir Joshua Reynolds, the Snake in the Grass, which cost 510 guineas. Passing Banks' model of a sleeping child, we reach a room, the capabilities of which for exhibiting pictures are considerably enlarged by the employment of shutters moving on hinges. In this room are placed Hogarth's four pictures, representing the scenes of an election with his accustomed humour. The successful candidate, whose chairing is depicted on the fourth, was Bubb Doddington, afterwards Lord Melcombe Regis, who, in his self-complacent diary, gave a specimen of the political morality of that day. These pictures were purchased from the painter by Garrick. Soane bought them for 1650 guineas when the effects of the actor's widow were sold. The Rake's Progress is delineated in another series of eight pictures by the same painter. Repeated engravings have made these paintings well known. In the same room is a very fine view on the Grand Canal at Venice by Canaletto, and two smaller works by the same artist; also a large work by Calcott, and several other paintings by Fuseli, Danby, and others. In a lower storey are numerous relics of antique sculpture, painted glass, and cinerary urns. The most interesting object, however, is an Egyptian sarcophagus, discovered by Belzoni in 1816 in a royal tomb at Thebes, 9 feet 4 inches long, 3 feet 8 inches wide, and with an average depth of 2½ feet. It has been cut out of a single piece of arragonite, so transparent that the rays of a candle penetrate through it even where it is three inches thick. It is sculptured within and without with hundreds of hieroglyphical figures, and bears the name and titles of the father of Rameses the Great. The lid was found in another place broken in many pieces. The fragments now lie underneath the sarcophagus. Soane paid £2000 for this curious relic after it had been refused by the trustees of the British Museum. In the gallery under the dome is a bust of Sir John Soane, by Chantrey, and a good cast of the Apollo Belvidere. Ascending the stairs to the first floor we pass Flaxman's model of the Archangel Michael overcoming Satan, a noble composition, and then a Mercury in bronze by Giovanni de Bologna. In the south drawing room are a series of medals, 140 in number, struck in France during the consulate and reign of Napoleon. They were once in the possession of Josephine, having been selected for her by the Baron Denon. Here are an ivory table and four ivory chairs brought from Tippoo Sahib's palace at Seringapatam ; Sir Christopher Wren's watch ; a piece of jewellery found amongst the royal baggage after the battle of Naseby. In the next room are several modern pictures, the best of which is Turner's Van Tromp's Barge entering the Texel. In glazed cases are gems, cameos, and intaglios. At the foot of the next flight of stairs is Flaxman's bust of the younger Pitt ; and in a recess is a cast of the shield executed in silver gilt for George IV., at a cost of 2000 guineas, after the designs of Flaxman, who in not less than a hundred figures has endeavoured to display the shield of Achilles, as described in the Iliad. Amongst the objects, which are only shewn by special permission, are the manuscript of the Jerusalem Delivered in Tasso's autograph ; a Latin manuscript embellished with exquisite miniatures by Giulio Clovio ; and a missal of the fifteenth century, with miniatures by Lucas van Leyden and his scholars.

The NATIONAL PORTRAIT GALLERY is a collection of about 100 portraits and busts of persons famous or infamous in our history and literature, brought together since 1858, and placed temporarily in a house, 29 Great George Street, Westminster, to which the public has free access on Wednesdays and Saturdays, between the hours of twelve and five in summer, and twelve and four in winter. The collection is being gradually increased by gifts and purchases. Here may be seen the Chandos Shakspere, with rings in the ears ; Mary Queen of Scots, the Fraser-Tytler portrait ; Elizabeth, the unfortunate Queen of Bohemia, daughter of our James I., by Mirevelt ; John Locke, at the age of 72 ; Pope, by Jervas, a painter to whom the poet addressed some lines :—

> Alas ! how little from the grave we claim ;
> Thou but preserv'st a face, and I a name.

Judge Jeffries, by Kneller ; Sir Robert Walpole by Vanloo (a painter whose success Hogarth styled " an inundation of folly and puff ") ; Hogarth himself, a terra cotta bust by Roubiliac ; Handel, by Hudson ; Reynolds, by himself, shading his face with a hand ; Wilkie, by himself ; Dr. Jenner, by Northcote ; Burns, by Nasmith ; Pitt, a bust by Nollekens ; John Hunter, by Jackson ; George IV., Wilberforce, and Mackintosh, by Sir Thomas Lawrence, the first, a study for the coinage ; Moore the poet, a bust ; Wordsworth, by Pickersgill ; John Wesley, preaching, by Hone ; and Sir Richard Arkwright, by Wright of Derby.

ANNUAL EXHIBITIONS OF PICTURES.

During the spring and summer there are several exhibitions of pictures, chiefly modern, to which the price of admission is one shilling. Those marked † are the best worth visiting.

† Royal Academy, east wing of National Gallery, Trafalgar Square. Sculpture as well as oil paintings.

British Artists, Suffolk Street, Pall Mall.

British Institution, 52 Pall Mall. (February, March, and April.)

French Gallery, 120 Pall Mall.

German Gallery, 168 New Bond Street.

† Exhibition of the Old Society of Painters in water colours, 5 Pall Mall, East.

Exhibition of New Society of Painters in water colours, 53 Pall Mall.

At the rooms of the British Institution, 52 Pall Mall, during the months of June, July, and August, there is an exhibition of paintings by the old masters, and deceased British artists, lent by noblemen and gentlemen from their galleries. Here may be inspected excellent pictures which it would be difficult to see at any other time. Admission, one shilling.

There are also one or two exhibitions of photographic works, which will be seen advertised in the newspapers.

CHAPTER THE FOURTEENTH.

Apsley House—Argyle House—Bridgewater House—Chesterfield House—Devonshire House—Grosvenor House—Holland House—Lambeth Palace — Lansdowne House — Northumberland House — Stafford House—Other Private Galleries.

APSLEY HOUSE, Hyde Park Corner, the residence of the Duke of Wellington. Here lived the first Duke for many years previous to his death in 1852. It was built by Lord Chancellor Bathurst. When the late Duke purchased it in 1820, it was a plain edifice of brick ; he caused it to be faced with Bath stone, and built the portico, the west wing, and a picture gallery 90 feet long, laying out, it is said, £130,000. He afterwards purchased the Crown's reversion in the property for £9530. The Duke celebrated the victory of Waterloo by a grand banquet every 18th of June in the picture gallery. The house contains a good collection of pictures, and many valuable objects presented to the Duke by foreign sovereigns and public bodies, e.g., a dessert service, painted with the Duke's victories, given by the King of Saxony ; services of china, presented by the Emperor of Austria, the King of Prussia, and Louis XVIII. ; and a silver plateau, to hold 106 wax tapers, given by the King of Portugal. The Duke's bedroom, with its simple furniture, is preserved in the state in which he left it. Amongst the pictures is the famous " Christ on the Mount of Olives," by Coreggio, of which there is a duplicate in the National Gallery. This picture was found in Joseph Buonaparte's carriage when captured in Spain. It was restored by the Duke to the King of Spain, and by him presented to the captor.

The interior of the house can only be seen by special permission.

ARGYLE HOUSE, Argyle Street, a plain mansion at the middle

of the east side of the street, is the residence of the Earl of
Aberdeen. It formerly belonged to the Dukes of Argyle, but
was sold to the present earl's father, the premier of the Aberdeen
ministry, which was planned here in 1852. We call attention to
the house, however, for the purpose of mentioning that the
dining-room wing which overlooks the garden at the rear has
been lately converted by the direction of the earl into an industrial school for about sixty boys. There is a class-room, a mess-
room, work-rooms in which various useful trades are taught, and
a lecture-room, where lectures will be delivered to the poor of
the neighbourhood. The coach-house in Marlborough mews has
been fitted with baths and lavatories. Sleeping accommodation
will be afforded to some of the boys, whilst the others will leave
in the evening and return in the morning. The boys are also to
be fed and clothed. The most destitute children of the neighbourhood will be selected. This is making a noble use of money,
and we trust so good an example will be followed by other
wealthy people.

BRIDGEWATER HOUSE, Cleveland Row, St. James', the residence of the Earl of Ellesmere, was erected by the late Earl (once
well known as Lord Francis Egerton) from the designs of Sir
Charles Barry, the style being Italian palazzo. It has a front
122 feet long towards the Green Park, and on this side it is seen
between the Duke of Sutherland's and Earl Spencer's mansions.
The picture gallery, 110 feet long, contains the Bridgewater collection, which was a portion of the celebrated Stafford gallery.
The last Duke of Bridgewater, who died in 1803, bequeathed his
pictures, valued at £150,000 to his nephew, the first Duke of
Sutherland, during whose life the collection, added to one formed
by himself, was known all over Europe as the Stafford gallery.
On the death of the duke in 1833, his second son Lord Francis
succeeded to the Bridgewater estates and pictures, the other part
of the Stafford gallery going to the eldest son, father of the present Duke of Sutherland. Here are about 320 pictures, and this
is the most accessible of the private collections in London.
" Whether we love pictures as representations of beauty, or as
emanations of mind, in every province of ideal or imitative
painting, there is here sufficient to form the uncultivated or en-
chant the cultivated taste. Yet not merely because of the value,
variety, and interest of its contents, does this collection take the
first rank, but its history is so connected with the history of the

progress of art in England as to render it peculiarly interesting. Of all the private collections, it will be found to be one which has had the most favourable, the most refining influence on the public and individual taste."—*Mrs. Jameson.* Here are 4 Raphaels, 2 Guidos, 6 Ludovico Carraccis, 7 Annibale Carraccis, 5 Domenichinos, 4 Claudes, 4 Gaspar Poussins, 5 Titians, 5 Berghems, 6 Cuyps, 3 G. Douws, 3 Hobbemas, 6 Adrian Ostades, 5 Rembrandts, 6 Ruysdaels, 8 Teniers, 7 Vanderveldes, etc., besides several pictures of the modern English school, and a master-piece of Paul de la Roche.

For cards to view apply to Messrs. Smith, 137 New Bond Street, and Messrs. Colnaghi, 15 Pall Mall, East. There is a separate entrance for the public, who are admitted on Mondays, Tuesdays, Thursdays, and Fridays, from 10 to 5.

CHESTERFIELD HOUSE, South Audley Street, opposite Great Stanhope Street, was built (1749) for the fourth Earl of Chesterfield, the author of the well-known letters, and the ancestor of the present owner. His favourite rooms remain as they were, when he boasted of them. The gardens are particularly fine. The pillars of the court-yard screen, and the marble staircase, each step a monolith 20 feet long, came from Cannons, the seat of the Duke of Chandos.

DEVONSHIRE HOUSE, Piccadilly, the residence of the Duke of Devonshire, was built on the site of Berkeley House by William Kent for the third duke. It is a plain brick structure, and cost £30,000. The modern portico ill agrees with the main building. The late duke (the seventh) built a state staircase of marble, and refitted the whole interior, except a small room decorated by the duchess, his mother, a lady renowned for her beauty and political zeal. The grounds are large. In addition to a few interesting pictures, this mansion contains the Devonshire gems, a celebrated collection of cut stones and medals, Claude's *Liber Veritatis*, outlines drawn by his own hand of the pictures he had painted, and the Kemble plays, a series of English dramas, with examples of the first editions of Shakspere's plays. These were brought together by John Philip Kemble, and were sold at his death for £2000.

GROSVENOR HOUSE, Upper Grosvenor Street, the residence of the Marquis of Westminster, is recognizable by the colonnade with double archway before the street front, and by the colonnade with six statues in the front facing Hyde Park. The first Earl

Grosvenor began in 1750 the celebrated collection of pictures which is to be found here. The next earl made splendid additions, and of the gallery as it now appears Mrs. Jameson has said that no private gallery in this country exceeds it in point of *variety*. " The fascination of the Claudes, the imposing splendour of the Rubenses, and the interest attached to a number of English pictures, long contributed to render this gallery quite as popular as the Bridgewater gallery as a resort for the mere amateur, and not less attractive and improving to the student and enthusiast." Unfortunately it has been less accessible of late years to the public. Here are three Murillos, two Titians, five Guidos, ten Claudes, 11 Rubenses (four of them brought from the convent of Loeches, near Madrid, cost £10,000), seven Rembrandts, one Paul Potter, " a very miracle in its way ;" then, of the English school, two Hogarths, Sir Joshua's Mrs. Siddons as the tragic muse, Gainsborough's Blue Boy, and West's *chef d'œuvre*, the Death of General Wolfe.

HOLLAND HOUSE, Kensington, a fine old mansion of the time of James I., around which cluster pleasant associations, with several generations of arts, politicians, and literary men. It was built for Sir Walter Cope in 1607, and passed on his death to his son-in-law Henry Rich, Earl of Holland, the son and father of Earls of Warwick. The Earl was beheaded by the Parliament in 1649, and the house was then occupied by Fairfax as his headquarters, but was afterwards restored to the Riches. William and Mary resided here a short time before going to Kensington Palace. Addison marrying the widow of the son of the decapitated earl, lived and died here ; it was, consequently, the scene of the interview between the young earl and Addison on his death-bed, unless that story be apocryphal. The Rich family having become extinct in the male line, Henry Fox was created Baron Holland, and purchased the mansion from Lord Kensington, to whom it had descended through female heirs. Here lived in his youth and early manhood Charles James Fox, the baron's second son. In the time of Henry Richard, third baron, C. J. Fox's nephew, the house was famous for the hospitality shewn there to literary men. Here met Rogers, Moore, Mackintosh, Hallam, Macaulay, Sydney Smith, and George Selwyn. They have all passed away with their host, and that host's son. " Where be your gibes now ? your gambols, your songs, your flashes of merriment that were wont to set the table in a roar ?" The property has gone into the hands of another family, and the time prognosticated by Sir Walter Scott has come, when rows and crescents lord it over the place. The seclusion of the park has been broken in upon, and parcelled out for "villa residences;" the end of the house itself cannot be far off. It is of red brick, embellished with turrets, gable-ends, and mullioned windows. A stone gateway on the east of the house was designed by Inigo Jones. In the house are several busts, and some pictures of value. The eastern wing of the house is formed by the long gallery, 102 feet in length by 17 feet, used as a library, where, besides books, many curiosities are or were stored.

LAMBETH PALACE, the residence of the Archbishops of Canterbury, Primates of all England, is on the south bank of the Thames, opposite the Houses of Parliament. This property was acquired in 1197, by the then Archbishop. Since that time large sums have been spent here, either in enlarging or rebuilding. A late Archbishop (Howley), laid out £60,000 in erecting the inhabited part of the palace, and restoring other parts, from the designs of Edward Blore. The garden front, in the Tudor style, is much admired. The gardens and grounds occupy eighteen acres. The *gate house*, of red brick, was built by Archbishop Morton, about 1499. Spiral staircases on the towers lead to the record room, where many of the archives of the see are preserved. In the small prison-room adjoining the gateway, are three iron rings, and the walls bear figures made by prisoners. On the left of the outer court is the *Lollard's Tower*, of red brick, faced with stone. Archbishop Chicheley was the builder (1434-5). The "post-room" in this tower has a curious flat panelled ceiling, with angels and scrolls. The river front bears the builder's arms, above a niche where an image of St. Thomas à Beckett was formerly placed. Passing by a spiral staircase into an adjoining tower, we reach a chamber 15 feet by 11 feet, and only about 8 feet high, which is called the *Lollard's Prison*, though it is more than doubtful whether any Lollards were confined in it. That the cell has been used as a prison is plain enough, for there are eight heavy iron rings fixed in the wall, and on the oaken wainscotting are inscriptions and figures, cut by the captives. "Nosce teipsum," "I.H.S., cyppe me out of all il compane, amen," may be deciphered amongst others. The entrance is guarded by two doors, each 3½ inches thick. Amongst the persons confined at Lambeth, were Queen

Elizabeth's Earl of Essex, Sir Thomas Armstrong, who suffered
capital punishment for sharing in Monmouth's rebellion, and
Lovelace the poet. The *Chapel* is early English; its lancet
windows are filled with stained glass, of Archbishop Howley's
time. The oldest part of the chapel was built by Archbishop
Boniface (1244-70). The roof is modern. Notice the primate's
stall; the marble slab over Archbishop Parker's remains, which
were taken up and indignantly treated by the Parliamentarian
soldiers, but re-interred at the Restoration. All the Archbishops
of Canterbury, since Boniface, have been consecrated here, as
well as more than 150 bishops. The west side of the inner
court is formed by the *Great Hall*, and the *Great Dining Room*.
The former is of red brick, 93 feet by 38 feet, and upwards of
50 feet in height. It was built by Archbishop Juxon about
1622. The oaken roof has eight main ribs, with pendants
and a central lantern. Notice in the glass of the bay window,
an ancient portrait of Archbishop Chicheley, also the arms of
Philip II. of Spain, Mary's husband, and those of some archbishops. The archi-episcopal collection of books is kept in this
hall. Archbishop Bancroft began it. Amongst the 25,000
volumes are some rare editions of the Bible, some early printed
books, black letter tracts, and many other curiosities. There is
also a valuable collection of MSS. The only known portrait of
Edward V. is here, in an illumination of Lad River's MS. trans-
lations from the French, from the Notable Wise Sayings of
Philosophers, in which Caxton is represented as being brought to
Edward IV., his queen, and prince Edward.

The Guard Chamber, 58 feet long and 27½ feet wide, contains a number of portraits of archbishops, the series since 1633
being complete. In the *Picture Gallery* are many more portraits
of more or less value, including Luther, Queen Catherine Parr,
and Henry Prince of Wales (son of James I.), in a very curious
dress. The entrance to the new buildings of the palace is
between two octagonal towers on the north side of the inner
court. In the archbishop's private library is a portrait by
Holbein, of Archbishop Warham, consecrated in 1504; and in
an ante-room is a portrait of Charles I., attributed to Vandyke.

The history of this interesting place would fill a volume.

The adjoining church with a perpendicular tower is St.
Mary's, the mother church of the parish. The oldest part dates
from about 1375, and it contains the tombs of seven archbishops.

Here also are the tombs of Dollond the well-known optician, and Elias Ashmole the antiquary. In the churchyard lie, under an elaborate mausoleum, the elder and younger Tradescant, the gardeners.

LANSDOWNE HOUSE, south side of Berkeley Square, was erected for George III.'s Marquis of Bute, but was sold before completion to the Lord Shelburne, afterwards first Marquis of Lansdowne, for £22,000. Priestley made the discovery of oxygen when living in the house as Lord Shelburne's librarian, in 1774. Here is a good collection of ancient sculpture, chiefly placed in the gallery, 100 feet long. The greater part of it was formed by Gavin Hamilton, who resided many years at Rome. A statue of Mercury, heroic size, was pronounced by Canova to be " not only the finest in the collection, but finer and more perfect than the Mercury of the Vatican." There are also works by Rauch and Canova, including the Sleeping Woman, the Italian artist's lost work, and a duplicate of the Venus in the Pitti Palace. The present Marquis came to the title in 1809, and has himself entirely formed the valuable collection of pictures, about 160 in number. These are divided between this mansion and Bowood, the Marquis's country residence, and are frequently changed from one place to the other. " The collection is quite miscellaneous in character; every school, every style, every age, every country, is here represented by one genuine specimen at least; of a few favourite painters the examples are numerous. It is strictly a private collection, the pictures being distributed through the family apartments. Of the most distinguished masters in the different schools of art, we find here sometimes a single good and genuine specimen, sometimes two or three. But the painter whose works so predominate that they may be said to impart a certain colour and character to this charming collection—the painter whose presence is most *felt* as we look around us, is Sir Joshua Reynolds "—*Mrs. Jameson.* Of that painter there are twelve examples, and amongst them are the celebrated strawberry girl, and the portraits of Sterne and Mrs. Sheridan. Here also are Hogarth's portraits of Peg Woffington and himself; Gainsborough's Dr. Franklin, and three Wilkie's.

NORTHUMBERLAND HOUSE, Charing Cross, the residence of the Duke of Northumberland, is concealed from the view by a high screen, over the gateway of which is the lion (cast in lead) of the

Percies. The house* was built by Henry Howard, Earl of Northampton, son of the poet Earl of Surrey, from whom it went to a
nephew, whose granddaughter took it on marriage to Algernon
Percy, tenth Earl of Northumberland (whose portrait by Vandyke
is in the house), and it then received its present name. General
Monk, a guest of the earl, planned here the restoration of Charles
II. The proud Duke of Somerset, who married the earl's grand-
daughter, kept great state here. From him it has descended
through a female heir to its present occupant. Very little of the
old house remains, the greater part having been rebuilt in the
last century. The interior contains a noble double staircase
with marble steps, a state-gallery 106 feet long and 27 wide, and
some good paintings, amongst which is Titian's picture of the
Cornaro family, bought from Vandyke by Algernon, Earl of
Northumberland. There is a copy at Hampton Court.

STAFFORD HOUSE, the residence of the Duke of Sutherland,
stands near St. James' Palace, with the west front looking into the
Green Park, and the south front into St. James' Park. The greater
part of the mansion was built for the late Duke of York, on
whose death the Crown lease was sold to the first Duke of Sutherland for £72,000, and a ground rent of £758 a-year. Sir Charles
Barry, who planned the interior, added the upper storey. The hall
and state staircase, 80 feet square, extend through the whole height
of the house. There are eight state rooms ; the great dining-
room, 70 feet by 30, contains a Ganymede by Thorwaldsen ; the
picture gallery, 126 feet by 32 feet in width, is " not only the
most magnificent room in London, but is also excellently adapted
to its purpose in the management of the light and the style of
decoration." Altogether, this mansion, whether as regards size
or splendour, has not its equal in London, and is worthy of the
residence of a noblemen who is reported to be the wealthiest of
the English aristocracy. The collection of pictures is large, and
includes that part of the famous Stafford Gallery which was
brought together by the first Duke of Sutherland, as well as many
paintings acquired by the late duke. They are not only hung in
the picture gallery, but in many of the other rooms. Amongst
them is " The Return of the Prodigal Son " by Murillo, of which

---

* On the site once stood the Hospital of Rouncevall, built upon land given by
William Mareschall, Earl of Pembroke, in the reign of Henry III., to the Prior of
Rouncevall in Navarre—

" With him there rode a gentil Pardonere
Of Rouncevall."—*Chaucer.*

Mrs. Jameson has said, that "in point of truth of expression, and in execution, Raphael himself never exceeded it;" a portrait of a Jesuite, called Titian's Schoolmaster, by Moroni, "which every painter must look at with a sort of desperation;" a portrait, by Giorgione, "exceedingly fine;" Correggio's Muleteer, "a celebrated little picture, in a style of composition quite unusual with the painter;" a wood scene, by Hackert, "a most charming picture;" a landscape, by Van Goyen, "eminently beautiful, soft, clear, and light;" St. Grisogono borne aloft by angels, by Guercino, forming the centre of the ceiling of the picture gallery, "a celebrated picture, painted with powerful effect." Amongst the modern pictures are portraits, in one canvas, of the present Duchess Dowager of Sutherland and her eldest daughter, by Lawrence, "beyond comparison the first of his works;" a Festival before the Flood, by Etty, "one of his very finest works, in conception most poetical, Titian-like;" the Day after the Battle of Chevy Chase, by Bird, "one of the best and most expressive pictures left by that painter;" Lady Evelyn Gower and the present Duke of Sutherland, by Sir Edwin Landseer, "beautifully painted." Lord Strafford going to Execution, by Paul de la Roche, "has transcendent merit in conception and execution." Dr. Johnson by Sir Joshua, and Lord Chancellor Thurlow by Romney.

In addition to the principal collection of about 200 ancient and modern paintings, there is a very interesting assemblage of 150 portraits illustrating French history, memoirs, literature, and art, during a period of three centuries. These formed the well-known *Cabinet le Noir*, which was purchased entire by the late duke when the French Government was hesitating on account of the price.

In addition to the private galleries previously mentioned, the following noblemen and gentlemen possess collections of pictures of more or less extent. Special permission must be obtained from their respective owners before they can be seen:—

Ashburton, Lord, Bath House, 82 Piccadilly—large and very good collection, especially of the Dutch and Flemish schools.

Barker, Alexander, Esq., Piccadilly.

Bedford, Duke of, 6 Belgrave Square—small, but very choice; chiefly Dutch pictures.

Bromley, Rev. Davenport, 32 Grosvenor Street.

Caledon, Lord, 5 Carlton House Terrace.

De Grey and Ripon, Earl, 4 St. James' Square.

Dudley, Earl of, Dudley House, Park Lane—large and good collection.

Eardley, Sir Culling, Bart., Belvidere, near Erith.

Garvagh, Lady, 31 Portman Square. Here is a *chef d'œuvre* of Raphael, a Madonna and child.

Hertford, Marquis of, Hertford House, 105 Piccadilly—a very valuable collection, to which the owner frequently adds. Here is Sir Joshua Reynolds' picture of Mrs. Hoare and child, for which the Marquis gave the largest sum ever paid for a work of this master, viz., 2550 guineas.

Holford, R. S., Esq., Dorchester House, Park Lane—a large and very handsome mansion, containing a collection of very good pictures, brought together by Mr. Holford.

Hope, H. T., Esq., M.P., Piccadilly, corner of Down Street. The house is new, and cost £30,000. The collection of pictures and sculptures divided between this mansion and Deepdene, Surrey, Mr. Hope's country seat, is very valuable.

Londonderry, Dowager Marchioness of, Holdernesse House, Park Lane—a handsome mansion, containing statuary, pictures, and articles of *vertu*.

Morrison, Charles, Esq., 57 Upper Harley Street.

Munro, H. A. J., Esq., Hamilton Place, Piccadilly.

Norfolk, Duke of, 21 St. James' Square.

Overstone, Lord, 2 Carlton Gardens—principally Dutch, very choice.

Peel, Sir Robert, Bart., 4 Whitehall Gardens, Whitehall—a collection of Dutch paintings, formed by the late baronet, the premier; "not only is there not one mediocre picture in the collection, but there is not one which is not of celebrity, and first rate."—*Mrs. Jameson*. Here is the Chapeau de Paille, by Rubens, which cost 3500 guineas.

Rothschild, Baron Lionel, Piccadilly, near Apsley House—collections of china, carved ivory, mediæval curiosities, besides pictures.

Wynn, Ellis, Esq., 30 Cadogan Place.

Yarborough, Earl of, Arlington Street, Piccadilly.

CHAPTER THE FIFTEENTH.

CLUBS.

Army and Navy Club—Athenæum Club—Carlton Club—City Club—
Conservative Club—Garrick Club—Guards' Club—Junior United
Service Club—Oriental Club—Oxford and Cambridge Club—Reform
Club—Travellers' Club—Union Club—United Service Club—Uni-
versity—White's—Brooks'—Boodle's—Chess Clubs.

THE CLUBS form a peculiar feature of London life, and their
houses as peculiar a feature in London architecture, not to be
paralleled in any foreign city. They consist no longer of a small
number of persons meeting at a tavern or coffee-house to spend
a social evening, and talk eloquently over their cups. They are
large assemblages of gentlemen, who, adopting one bond of union
or another, have subscribed their guineas, and built themselves
handsome houses, splendidly decorated, and luxuriously furnished,
where they can take their meals, read the papers, and discuss the
news of the day with their fellow-members. Some of the houses
are amongst the finest edifices in the metropolis. They are intended chiefly for bachelors ; and a man of moderate income may
enjoy comforts in them only otherwise to be commanded by a
large fortune. The two principal rooms on the ground-floor are
the morning room, where the members find a spacious sitting
room supplied with newspapers, and the coffee-room, in which
meals are served. On this floor is frequently a house dining-
room where set dinner parties can meet. On the upper floor
will be found a splendid drawing-room, a card room, and the
library well stocked with books. In some part of the building,
generally on the floor above the drawing-room, are billiard and
smoking rooms. It will thus be seen that all the appliances for
a comfortable existence are supplied, except as regards sleeping,
no beds being provided. The affairs of a club are in the hands
of a committee of management, appointed by the members out

of their own body. This committee acts in all respects as masters
of the house, appointing the servants, receiving subscriptions,
paying bills, and making regulations for the orderly ongoing of
the household. A complete establishment will embrace a secretary and librarian; a steward and house-keeper; groom of the
chambers, butler, hall-porter; clerk of the kitchen, chief cook,
under-cooks, with waiting and other servants of various kinds.
Viands are supplied at cost price, the general charges of the
establishment being defrayed from the fund arising from entrance-
fees and annual subscriptions. At some of the clubs a member
may entertain his friends at dinner, there being a strangers' room
provided for the purpose. Another convenience is that members
can have their letters addressed to them at their club. Gambling is not permitted; and deep drinking has long gone out of
fashion, moderation in wine being happily the order of the day.
In order to procure admission to a club, a gentleman must be
proposed by a certain number of members, and must then sub-
mit to the ordeal of the ballot-box, in which the presence of a
regulated number of black balls will exclude the candidate. The
entrance-fee varies from nine guineas to thirty-one guineas, but
it is usually about twenty-five guineas. The annual subscription
also varies, ranging from six to ten guineas.

The club-houses congregate in Pall Mall and the neighbouring streets, and Pall Mall derives its palatial aspect altogether
from them, for the real palace of St. James' is but a poor affair
by the side of the noble structures erected by the subscriptions
of a few gentlemen. The " city " possesses only one club. We
shall proceed to give a few details respecting the principal clubs,
and it will be seen that the bond of union has been furnished by
various circumstances: sometimes it is political, sometimes derived from the universities, and sometimes professional.

THE ARMY AND NAVY CLUB-HOUSE, a very handsome building, stands in Pall Mall, at the corner of George Street. It was
commenced in 1848 from designs by Messrs. Parnell and Smith,
who took for their models, to a considerable extent, two Venetian
buildings, Sansovino's Palazzo Cornaro, and the Library of St.
Mark. The entrance is in St. James' Square, by a loggia of
three arches, leading to a spacious hall, where hang an equestrian portrait of the Queen by Grant, which cost 400 guineas,
and a piece of Gobelin tapestry presented by the Emperor Louis
Napoleon, an honorary member. The coffee-room is 81½ feet by

30½ feet; the morning room 71 feet by 27½ feet. The site cost
£52,000! and the building £35,000. The number of members
is limited to 1450. The entrance-fee is £30; the annual subscription £6 : 11s.

THE ATHENÆUM CLUB, Waterloo Place, Pall Mall, was instituted in 1823 by Sir Walter Scott, Sir Humphrey Davy, Sir
T. Lawrence, Sir F. Chantrey, and others, for the association of
individuals known for their literary or scientific attainments,
artists of eminence, and noblemen and gentlemen, distinguished
as liberal patrons of science, literature, and the arts. The club-
house was built in 1829 from the designs of Decimus Barton.
The building cost £35,000; the furniture, plate, linen, and glass,
£7500; the library £4000. The library contains the best
collection of books of any club-house in London. In it is a portrait of George IV., on which Lawrence was working only a few
hours before he died. On the principal front is a frieze copied
from the Panathenaic frieze of the Parthenon; and over the
portico is a colossal statue of Minerva by Baily. The club
is limited to 1200 members; the entrance-fee is 25 guineas;
the annual subscription 6 guineas.

THE CARLTON CLUB-HOUSE, Pall Mall, is the head quarters of
the Conservatives. The building was originally in the Grecian
style, after designs by Sir R. Smirke, but was subsequently enlarged and refronted in a totally different style by his brother
Sydney Smirke. The present design owes much to Sansovino's
Library of St. Mark at Venice. The façade is 130 feet long, in
two orders—the lower Doric, the upper Ionic. Polished red
granite columns and pilasters adorn the Caen-stone front, and
catch the eye at once. The interior contains some splendid
rooms, one of which, the coffee-room, is 92 feet long by 37 feet
broad. The number of members is limited to 800, exclusive of
peers and members of the House of Commons. The entrance-fee
is 15 guineas, the annual subscription 10 guineas.

THE CITY CLUB is established at 19 Old Broad Street. It
was built in 1833, from Ph. Hardwick's designs, upon the site of
the old South-Sea House. Merchants, bankers, and professional
men, constitute the members, who pay an entrance-fee of 25
guineas, and an annual subscription of 6 guineas.

THE CONSERVATIVE CLUB-HOUSE stands on the west side, and
near the bottom of St. James' Street. It is a handsome Palladian
building, erected in 1845, from the designs of Sydney Smirke

and G. Basevi. The morning-room is 92 feet long by 28½ feet wide. The splendid drawing-room is of the same size, and its coved ceiling is supported by 18 Scagliola columns. The coffee-room has a length of 80 feet, and a width of 28½ feet, and the library has the same dimensions. The hall and staircase are richly decorated with encaustic embellishments by Sang. A gallery runs round the hall. The expenses of building and furnishing amounted to £73,000. Members limited to 1500. The entrance-fee is 25 guineas, the annual subscription 8 guineas.

The GARRICK CLUB meets at No. 35 King Street, Covent Garden, and derives its name from the celebrated actor. It was instituted in 1831, and consists of members of the histrionic art and patrons of the drama. Clarkson Stanfield, David Roberts, and Louis Haghe, have adorned the walls of the smoking-room with paintings. Members limited to 350. Entrance-fee 30 guineas ; annual subscription 6 guineas. Here is a collection of theatrical portraits, brought together principally by Charles Matthews. Strangers must be personally introduced by a member, and the pictures can only be seen on a Wednesday between eleven and three.

The GUARDS' CLUB-HOUSE, 70 Pall Mall, has the external appearance of a private house. Officers of the household troops alone can be members.

The JUNIOR UNITED SERVICE CLUB-HOUSE is a handsome edifice at the corner of Charles Street and Regent Street. It was rebuilt in 1857, from the designs of Messrs. Nelson and Innes. The members are limited to 1500. The entrance-fee is £30, the annual subscription £6.

The ORIENTAL CLUB, 18 Hanover Square, was instituted in 1824 for the convenience of gentlemen officially connected with our Indian empire, or who have travelled in Asia or Egypt, or at the Cape of Good Hope. It is limited to 800 members, who pay an entrance-fee of £21, and an annual subscription of £8.

The OXFORD AND CAMBRIDGE CLUB, Pall Mall, for members of the two universities. It was erected, 1835-8, from designs by Sir Robert Smirke and his brother. The façade is 80 feet in length, and 75 feet in height. Over the window of the upper floor are bas-reliefs in panels. The members are limited to 585 from each university. The entrance-fee is 25 guineas, the annual subscription 6 guineas.

THE REFORM CLUB, Pall Mall, stands between the Travellers'
and the Carlton. Sir Charles Barry furnished the designs, and
the building was erected in 1838-39. It has been greatly admired as a successful imitation of the Italian palazzo. It has a
front of 135 feet, 6 floors, and 134 rooms. A leading feature of
the interior is the grand hall, 56 feet by 50, covered with glass,
and surrounded by colonnades, the upper one forming a picture
gallery. The principal drawing-room is over the coffee-room in
the garden front, each about 130 feet in length. This is the
only club-house at which members can obtain sleeping accommodation. Soyer was chief cook here for some years. The
kitchen arrangements are very complete, and are shewn to
strangers as one of the admirable points of the establishment.
Water is obtained from an Artesian well 360 feet deep. The
number of members is limited to 1400, exclusive of peers and
members of the Lower House. The entrance-fee is 25 guineas ;
the annual subscription for the first five years 10 guineas, afterwards 8 guineas.

THE TRAVELLERS' CLUB is between the Athenæum and the
Reform. It was built in 1832, and is another of Barry's
designs in the Italian palazzo style. The garden front has been
highly eulogized. One of the rules of this club is, that no
person shall be eligible for a member who shall not have travelled out of the British Islands to a distance of at least 500
miles from London in a direct line—not so great a feat now-a-
days, as it was when the rule was instituted. Foreigners are
admitted to the privileges of this club during their temporary
stay in London, if properly recommended. Talleyrand was
accustomed to play whist in the card-room of the Travellers'.
Members are limited to 700 ; the entrance-fee is 20 guineas ;
the annual subscription 10 guineas.

THE UNION CLUB is at the corner of Cockspur Street, with
a front in Trafalgar Square. Sir Robert Smirke was the architect, and the building was erected in 1824. The stock of wine
is reputed to be larger here than in any other club-house.
Members limited to 1000. Entrance-money 31 guineas ; annual
subscription 6 guineas.

THE UNITED SERVICE CLUB have their house over against the
Athenæum, at the corner of Pall Mall, and the approach to St.
James' Park. It was built in 1826 from Nash's designs. Stan-
field's Battle of Trafalgar, and other pictures, adorn the interior.

P

Members limited to 1500 ; entrance-fee £30 ; annual subscription £6.

The University Club limits its members to 500 from Oxford and 500 from Cambridge, who pay an entrance fee of 25 guineas, and an annual subscription of £6. The club-house was built in 1824, in Suffolk Street, Pall Mall, east, from Wilkins' designs.

Besides these, the principal clubs, there are several others of more or less note, some of which boast of considerable age. For instance, White's, 37 and 38 St. James' Street, a Tory club which originated about 1736. It is written in its annals that the club in 1814 gave a ball to the allied sovereigns, then in London, which cost £9850 ; and three weeks afterwards a dinner to the Duke of Wellington, which cost £2480. Brooks' has always been a Whig club. It was founded in 1764 by Charles James Fox and the leading Whigs of the day ; the present house, 60 St. James' Street, was opened in 1778. Both this and White's were notorious for high play, as was Crockford's, 50 St. James' Street, at a later period, now converted into a public dining-room. Boodle's, 28 St. James' Street, also dates from the last century. Fox, and Gibbon the historian, were members.

Chess Clubs.—Strangers who may delight in the noble game of chess may like to know that, besides the public rooms where chess is played (amongst which Kilpack's Divan, 42 King Street, Covent Garden, and the Divan opposite Exeter Hall in the Strand, should be mentioned), there are two chess clubs in the metropolis—viz., the St. George's, meeting at 20 King Street, St. James' ; and the London, at the George and Vulture Tavern, Cornhill, City. For information respecting them, apply to the secretaries.

A great chess congress has been arranged for the summer of the present year, which is to comprise a grand tournament, blindfold chess play, consultation matches, and several other interesting events. Mr. Hampton of the St. George's Club, or Mr. G. W. Medley of the London Club, will give information and receive subscriptions.

CHAPTER THE SIXTEENTH.

THEATRES, CONCERT ROOMS, AND PLACES OF PUBLIC AMUSEMENT.

Adelphi Theatre—Astley's Amphitheatre—Covent Garden Theatre—
Drury Lane Theatre—Haymarket Theatre—Her Majesty's Theatre
—Lyceum Theatre—Marylebone Theatre—Olympic Theatre—Pa-
vilion Theatre—Princess' Theatre—Sadler's Wells Theatre—
Standard Theatre—Surrey Theatre—Victoria Theatre—Exeter Hall,
St. James' Hall, etc.—Polytechnic Institution—Tussaud's Exhibi-
tion of Waxworks, etc.—Bazaars.

THEATRES.

THOSE who intend to partake of theatrical and musical entertainments should consult the advertising columns of some of the
daily newspapers, where they will be kept advised from day to
day of the pieces to be performed, the actors and singers who are
to take part in them, and the hours of commencement, with the
prices of admission. Here we must confine ourselves to a short
description and history of the principal houses, which we shall
place alphabetically. Strangers must keep in mind that gentlemen are not admitted into either opera-house, who are not in
full evening dress, viz., dress-coat, black trowsers, and black or
white waistcoat, and tie.

THE ADELPHI THEATRE is opposite Adam Street in the
Strand. It is a most comfortable theatre, having been lately rebuilt on an enlarged scale, by the lessee Mr. Benjamin Webster,
who has long been known as a successful manager. The first
house on this site was called the Sanspareil. It was built about
sixty years ago by a Mr. Scott, a colour maker. The piece
called "Tom and Jerry" was brought out at this house some
forty years since, and the combined names have hardly yet died
out of recollection. Terry, Sir Walter Scott's friend, became joint

lessee and manager with Yates. Afterwards Charles Matthews
the elder took the house and brought out his popular "At
Homes." Since Mr. Webster has had the management, a number
of comic actors of note have assisted him in giving a high character to the house. There are seats for 1400 persons. The size of
the present theatre (of which Mr. T. H. Wyatt was the architect)
is about 70 feet in breadth and 107 feet in depth.

ASTLEY'S AMPHITHEATRE, Westminster Bridge Road, Lambeth, where equestrian performances take place. The present
house is the fourth house erected on the site, the three previous
houses having been destroyed by fire. Astley, after whom it was
called, was a cavalry soldier, whose first theatre was a structure
of deal boards, put up in 1773. The place afterwards passed
into the hands of Andrew Ducrow, and was called by his name.
During his proprietorship it was burned down, and he died in-
sane a few months subsequently.

CITY OF LONDON THEATRE, Shoreditch; principally for melodramas.

COVENT GARDEN THEATRE (Royal Italian Opera), Bow Street.
The first playhouse on this site was opened in 1733. This was
destroyed by fire ; and another theatre, erected from the designs
of R. Smirke, was opened in 1809, the cost having been about
£180,000. The prices of admission having been raised, there en-
sued the famous O. P. riots, which were only terminated at the
end of two months by a return to the previous charges. The
taste of the public running upon musical entertainments, the
theatre was converted into an Italian opera house in 1847.
Smirke's building was destroyed by fire in 1856. The present
handsome theatre is not quite so large as its predecessor. It was
designed by E. M. Barry, and was erected in the space of six
months (at a cost of nearly £80,000), being opened to the public
in May 1858. When used for the opera it will hold about 2300
comfortably-seated spectators; when otherwise fitted, 3000 or
more visitors can be easily accommodated. The statues of tra-
gedy and comedy, and the figures on the friezes in bas-relief at
the Bow Street front, are from Flaxman's chisel. The following
table will give some dimensions of the house in comparison with
those of other large theatres.

	Width of Proscenium.	No. of Boxes in each Tier.	No. of Tiers of Boxes.	Width between Boxes.	Length from Curtain to Centre Box.	Height from Pit to Ceiling.
	Feet.			Feet.	Feet.	Feet.
San Carlos, Naples . .	53	29	6	70	70	70
La Scala, Milan . . .	43	41	5	66	88½	69
Theatre at Bologna . .	51	25	5	57	78	63½
Theatre at Turin . . .	42½	29	6	52	61	53¾
Her Majesty's Theatre, Haymarket	37	43	6	59	88	51
Covent Garden . . .	50	36	4	63	81	65½

DRURY LANE THEATRE, near Covent Garden Market, is renowned in the annals of the British drama, the first house on this site dating from 1663. It was built for Thomas Killigrew, and others, " the king's servants," in Charles the Second's reign. When that theatre was burned down, Sir Christopher Wren designed its successor. Rich, Steele, and Garrick, were amongst the patentees ; and here the last took leave of the stage. Sheridan afterwards became one of the proprietors, and in his time the theatre was pulled down and rebuilt. The new house was destroyed by fire in 1809, and then succeeded the present building, designed by B. Wyatt, which was opened in 1812, Lord Byron writing the address. This occasion gave rise to that amusing production of the Smiths, " Rejected Addresses." The Doric portico in Brydges Street, and the iron colonnade in Little Russell Street, were added during Elliston's lessee-ship. The hall contains a cast of Scheemaker's statue of Shakspere, and a statue of Edmund Kean, by Joseph. Amongst the celebrated actors and actresses who have appeared at Drury Lane were, Nell Gwynne, Mrs. Siddons, John Kemble, Edmund Kean, and Macready.

THE HAYMARKET THEATRE, the name of which indicates its locality, was built from Nash's design, and opened in 1821. In a theatre which stood only a few feet distant from the site of the present one, the Beggar's Opera, that made Gay rich, and Rich gay, was produced in 1727. Foote afterwards became manager, and was succeeded by the Colmans. Mr. Buckstone is lessee of the present house.

THE ST. JAMES' THEATRE, King Street, St. James', was built by Braham the singer, at a cost of £26,000, and was opened in

1835. It proved a ruinous speculation for poor Braham. At present it is chiefly heard of as a place for the production of French dramas. Rachel and Ristori have appeared here.

HER MAJESTY'S THEATRE (Italian Opera House), Haymarket. Sir John Vanbrugh's was the first house on this site, opened in 1705. This having been burned down, the present house, designed by Novosielski, was built in 1790. The exterior arcades were added in 1820. The freehold of a box in this theatre has sold for £8000; and a rent of 300 guineas has been paid for a single season for one box. Very large sums have been expended by the management in keeping this theatre open, and it has been in difficulties for some years past. It will hold about 3000 persons. Its size, compared with other large theatres, will be seen from a preceding table.

THE LYCEUM THEATRE, Wellington Street, Strand, is so called from a former house having been erected (1795) as a lyceum or academy for a society of artists. Garrick afterwards bought the lease with the view of preventing its being converted into a rival theatre. After this time it was enlarged and English operas were performed in it. In 1816 it was pulled down and rebuilt ; the new edifice having been destroyed by fire, the present house was built from Beazley's designs in 1830 at a cost of £35,000. The much-admired decorations of the interior were executed in 1847 in Madame Vestris' management.

MARYLEBONE THEATRE, Church Street, Paddington, built in 1842, enlarged in 1854, will hold 2000 persons.

THE OLYMPIC THEATRE, Wych Street, Strand, stands on the site of a house built by Philip Astley for equestrian performances. That house having been burned in 1849, the present house was built the same year. This is the theatre at which Mr. Robson shews his great powers as an actor.

THE PAVILION THEATRE, Whitechapel Road, was erected in 1859. It will hold 3500 persons. Nautical pieces and farces chiefly performed here.

PRINCESS' THEATRE, Oxford Street, stands on ground belonging to the Duke of Portland, who has granted a lease of it for sixty years from 1830, when the theatre was built from Nelson's designs, at a cost of £47,000. When in the hands of Mr. Charles Kean, Shakspere's historical plays were brought out with great splendour at this theatre.

SADLER'S WELLS THEATRE, Islington, derives its name from

the fact that one Sadler built a music-house here in the neigh-
bourhood of a mineral spring, in the reign of Charles II. In
1764 the present house was built ; it is the oldest theatre in
London. The Grimaldis were clowns at this place ; and here
Belzoni was posture-master before setting out on his travels.
The New River, flowing close by, has been employed to fill a
tank under the stage, where aquatic performances were exhibited.
Mr. Phelps, the actor, is the present manager, and has won a
name for this little theatre by the excellent mode in which
Shakspere's plays, and other pieces of the classic drama, are re-
presented.

STANDARD THEATRE, Shoreditch, opposite the Eastern Counties Railway station. Melodramas and nautical pieces are principally performed here.

THE STRAND THEATRE, 169 Strand, was originally built for
the exhibition of a panorama, but was altered in 1831 into a
theatre.

THE SURREY THEATRE, Blackfriars' Road, was erected in
1806 on the site of an older house, which dated from 1782,
and was originally used for equestrian performances.

VICTORIA THEATRE, Waterloo Bridge Road, Lambeth, originally styled "the Cobourg," from the first stone having been
laid in the name of Prince Leopold of Saxe-Cobourg, 1817.
Some of the stones from the old Savoy Palace was employed in
its construction. The name was changed to its present form in
1833, and the Queen, then the Princess Victoria, visited the
house. The gallery is very large.

CONCERT ROOMS.

EXETER HALL, Strand, erected 1831, from the designs of
Gandy Deering, is a proprietary establishment. In the Great
Hall, 131½ feet long, 76½ feet wide, and 45 feet high, oratorios
by Handel, Haydn, and other great composers, take place, performed by the Sacred Harmonic Society, to whom the organ and
orchestra at the east end belong. The hall will accommodate
about 3000 persons. There are also two other halls here, one
accommodating about 600 persons, the other 250 ; twenty-one
other rooms, used as offices and committee-rooms, and also an
extensive range of vaults. The whole cost about £36,000.
During the months of April and May, annually take place the

meetings of religious and benevolent societies, one of the leading features of the London season.

HANOVER SQUARE ROOMS are now perhaps the most comfortable concert-rooms in London, having been recently refitted ; here is a concert-room 90 feet by 35 feet, where the concerts of the Philharmonic Society and of the Royal Academy of Music take place. Balls are also occasionally given here.

ST. JAMES' HALL (entrances both from Piccadilly and Regent Street) is 139 feet long, and 60 feet high. It was designed by Owen Jones, and is lighted by gas drops from the roof. It is a proprietary establishment, and is let for concerts, and other public entertainments.

ST. MARTIN's HALL, Longacre, designed by R. Westmacott, was opened in 1850. It was lately much damaged by fire, but has been repaired. It will accommodate 3000 persons. Mr. Hullah's concerts were given here.

WILLIS' ROOMS, King Street, St. James', were built in 1765, from designs by Robert Mylne. For a considerable time they were called " Almack's," after the original proprietor, a Scotchman. The great ball-room is about 100 feet long by 40 feet wide. It was here that the well-known exclusive balls took place. The rooms are let for concerts, lectures, etc.

The principal musical performances, in additition to the opera, are—

The Philharmonic Society's Concerts, at the Hanover Square Rooms. Addison and Co., 110 Regent Street, agents.

The Sacred Harmonic Society's Oratorios at Exeter Hall.

The Crystal Palace Opera Concerts.

Ella's Musical Union Concerts. Instrumental music.

The Popular Concerts at St. James' Hall.

The following are the principal places of public entertainment which exist in or near the metropolis, in addition to those already noticed :—

POLYTECHNIC INSTITUTION, 309 Regent Street, and 5 Cavendish Square, open, on payment of 1s., daily from twelve to five, and from seven to ten. Contains small machines in motion, scientific apparatus, a tank with diving-bell, a collection of pictures, etc. Here is a theatre capable of holding 1500 persons, where dissolving views are exhibited, and musical entertainments take place.

A smaller theatre, where lectures with experiments on chemistry, electricity, etc., are delivered. Mr. J. H. Pepper is the managing director and lecturer.

CREMORNE GARDENS, Chelsea (formerly the property of Lord Cremorne), occupy a large piece of ground, and are laid out with shrubberies, winding walks, etc. Dancing, concerts, rope-walking, balloon ascents, and fireworks, are amongst the entertainments. Dinners and suppers are served in public or private rooms. Admission to the gardens 1s.

SURREY GARDENS, Kensington Road, are a large piece of ground, ornamentally laid out with a sheet of water, etc. Here is a music hall, where concerts are given. Rope-walking, fireworks, etc., take place here. The wild animals, for which the gardens were once renowned, have been disposed of.

THE ALHAMBRA PALACE, east side of Leicester Square, a building in the Moorish style, with minarets, and a dome 150 feet high, was originally intended for a place of popular scientific entertainment. There is a small theatre where lectures are delivered. Music, dancing, rope-walking, etc., are now the stock performances. Open every evening.

BURFORD'S PANORAMA, Leicester Square. Open from ten to dusk. Admission 1s.

COLOSSEUM, Regent's Park (east side), is a building forming a polygon of sixteen faces, commenced in 1824, from the designs of Decimus Burton. It is lighted by an immense dome. Here are exhibited dioramas, and there are conservatories, fountains, waterfalls, casts after the antique, etc., with concerts, and scientific lectures, to please the varied tastes of visitors. Open daily, admission 1s.

CANTERBURY HALL, AND FINE ARTS GALLERY, Westminster Road, Southwark. Musical entertainments, chiefly operatic concerts, and a good collection of modern pictures. Open every evening, admission 6d.

ROYAL GALLERY OF ILLUSTRATION, 14 Regent Street. Musical performances. Various charges for admission according to accommodation.

POLYGRAPHIC HALL, King William Street, Charing Cross, where Mr. Wooden amuses his audience in the evening by acting in various characters.

"THE OXFORD," 6 Oxford Street. Musical entertainments every evening. Refreshments obtainable. Admission 6d. and 1s.

There are also several "Music Halls" in various parts of London, which will be seen advertised in the newspapers.

TUSSAUD'S EXHIBITION OF WAX WORK, Baker Street, Portman Square. Admission 1s. Open daily from 11 to 6, and from 8 to 10 in the evening. Here are upwards of 200 well modelled figures, in appropriate costume, of many celebrated persons of modern times. One of the rooms is 240 feet long by 49 feet. There is also a curious collection of relics of Nelson, Napoleon, and others. George IV.'s coronation robes, that cost £18,000, are shewn. This is one of the most popular exhibitions of London.

BAZAARS and ARCADES for the sale of millinery, table ornaments, toys, music, and other small articles, are to be found at various places at the west end of London. Admission free ; usually open from 9 to 6. The stalls are mostly attended by young women. Singing and fancy birds are on sale at the Pantheon and Portland Bazaars ; and photographic establishments are attached to some of them. At the Pantheon there is a collection of pictures, chiefly copies, but containing some originals of B. R. Haydon.

Soho Bazaar, west side of Soho Square.

Pantheon Bazaar, 359 Oxford Street, with an entrance in Great Marlborough Street.

London Crystal Palace Bazaar, north side of Oxford Street, near the Circus, with an entrance in Great Portland Street. Chiefly built of glass and iron, from the designs of Owen Jones, with a roof of coloured glass.

Portland Bazaar, or German Fair, Regent Street, nearly opposite the Polytechnic Institution.

Baker Street Bazaar, Baker Street, Portman Square.

Burlington Arcade, between Piccadilly and Burlington Gardens, west of Burlington House ; 600 feet long, with shops at each side. Closes at 8 in the evening.

Lowther Arcade, between West Strand and Adelaide Street ; 245 feet long, with stalls on each side.

CHAPTER THE SEVENTEENTH.

The City Corporation—Guildhall—Mansion House—City Companies
and their Halls.

THE " CITY" is the oldest part of London, and forms as it were
the nucleus of the whole metropolis, which from this point has
spread out in all directions, adding house to house, and street to
street, absorbing neighbouring villages, and covering the inter-
vening fields and gardens, until it has become one of the wonders
of the world.   The "City" extends from Aldgate on the east to
Temple Bar on the west, and from the river Thames on the south
to an irregular boundary on the north.   Within these limits
there are only 631 acres, 6367 inhabited houses, and 45,550
resident people; and yet all the great foci of commerce are here—
the Bank of England, the chief joint-stock and private banks, the
General Post Office, the Mint, Lloyd's, the Royal Exchange, the
Corn and Coal Exchanges, the Custom House, together with the
counting-houses of the principal merchants.   Here also are the
Tower and St. Paul's Cathedral, and here is the residence of the
Right Honourable the Lord Mayor, president of the Corporation
of London.

THE CORPORATION.

For municipal purposes, the city is divided into twenty-six
wards, each returning an alderman, and subdivided into precincts,
each returning a common councilman.   At the head of the corporation is the Lord Mayor, who is annually chosen by the livery
on the 29th of September.   He is usually the senior alderman
who has served the office but has not passed the chair, i. e., who
has not already been mayor.   Now and then, however, the same
gentleman is elected a second time, as in the case of the present
Lord Mayor.   The liverymen are select persons of the trade companies, about which we shall have something to say presently.

They are about 10,000 in number. With them rests the choice of the principal city officers. The freemen, a larger body, are persons who by various ways (inheritance, admission to a company, payment, etc.) have obtained the freedom of the city; they are about 20,000 in number. Any male person of the age of 21 may be made a freeman on paying £6. It is not an unusual thing to present the freedom of the city to persons who have distinguished themselves in the service of the state. The chief officers after the Lord Mayor are—two sheriffs, a recorder who is a barrister and officiates as judge, chamberlain, common serjeant, and town clerk. The style of the corporation is the Mayor, Commonalty, and Citizens of London. The chief is addressed as My Lord, and styled Right Honourable. After the King, he holds the first place within the city, even before the heir-apparent, a privilege disputed by but maintained against George IV. when Prince of Wales. He is at the head of the military force of the city, is a judge of the criminal court, and presides in all the civic courts. He is lodged in the Mansion House, which is splendidly furnished for him, where he is supplied with plate, jewels, and servants. He has an allowance of £8000 for his year, but he spends £4000 or £5000 out of his own pocket in addition, and the expenses of the office are not far short of £15,000. When installed in his office, on the 9th of November, "Lord Mayor's Day," he is conveyed to Westminster, to be sworn in before a Baron of the Exchequer, in a state coach, accompanied by the sheriffs in their state coaches, and by a showy retinue, aldermen, recorder, chaplain, chamberlain, bailiffs, sword-bearer, etc.

> " How London doth pour out her citizens !
> The Mayor and all his brethren in best sort,
> With the plebeians swarming at their heels."
> SHAKSPERE'S *Henry V.*

He wears a gold chain and badge, with rich gowns varying with the occasion. His state carriage was built in 1757, from Cipriani's design. It is one of the few remaining pompous vehicles of the last century, is richly carved and gilt, and adorned with paintings, good for their place. It cost originally £1065, and it is said £100 is laid out on it annually. He lives in a style of lavish hospitality, and entertains, several times in the year, the ministers, judges, and other distinguished personages. The great gold mace was given by Charles I.; the sword of state with a scabbard set with pearls, by Queen Elizabeth.

The freemen—householders of a ward paying £10 a year rent—elect the alderman of that ward, and he retains his seat until he chooses to resign it. He is a justice of the peace, a judge of the central criminal court, chairman of the ward meetings, and wears a state robe with a gold chain. The two sheriffs for London, who are also sheriffs for Middlesex, are chosen by the livery. It is said that the expenses of the office exceed the receipts by £2000 for each. The privileges and jurisdiction of the city have been granted or acknowledged by several royal charters. It has its own magistrates and police. It has often been proposed by those who do not like to see money wasted, to reduce the corporation to that of an ordinary municipal body, but so far it has borne a charmed life. The arms of the city, which will be seen everywhere, from the parapets of bridges to the collars of policemen, are the cross of St. George with the sword of St. Paul.

The conservancy of the Thames having been taken away from the corporation, to be vested in a special board, and there being no longer any pretence for preserving the city state barge (which had originally cost £3000, and was continually a source of expense), it was sold not long ago by public auction. It was forty-three years old, and had seen during this lengthened existence, much feasting and conviviality, when the Mayor, Aldermen, and their friends, proceeded in it to view officially the upper part of the Thames.

There are many curious customs connected with the City Corporation, to which we have no space to do more than allude. We may, however, mention that until quite lately the sheriffs were bound to attend once a year in the Court of Exchequer at Westminster, there to perform suit and service in respect of certain lands held by the corporation, the said suit and service consisting of chopping faggots with a bill hook and adze, and of counting six horse shoes, and sixty-one nails, all which was done in sober seriousness, before the judges and a crowd of spectators. It actually required an Act of Parliament to modify this absurd custom (to abolish it would have been a too dangerous tampering with the institutions of our forefathers), and the proceedings are now transacted with the utmost gravity once a year, between the *under*-sheriffs and the Queen's Remembrancer, at the official chambers of the latter.

CORPORATION BUILDINGS.

GUILDHALL, end of Cheapside, King Street, City, is the town-hall of the City of London. The first hall on this site was built in 1411, but only a few fragments of that edifice remain. The present building was erected in 1789, from the designs of the younger Dance. It is in decidedly bad taste. Over the entrance are the city arms and motto " *Domine dirige Nos.*" The great hall is 153 feet long, 50 feet wide, and 55 feet high, illuminated with windows of painted glass, and having at the west end two gigantic grotesque wooden figures (carved in 1708), called Gog and Magog, of the origin of which little is known. Around the hall are several marble monuments. 1. Lord Mayor Beckford, father of the author of Vathek, with his bold speech (said never to have been spoken) to George III. 2. Lord Nelson; the inscription was written by Sheridan. 3. The Duke of Wellington. 4. The Earl of Chatham; the inscription was written by Burke. 5. His son, William Pitt; the inscription was written by Canning. At the back of the dais, are statues of Edward VI., Elizabeth, and Charles I. These came from the old Guildhall Chapel, pulled down some years ago. This hall is used for civic banquets, elections, and other city meetings. It is open to the public every day. In the lobby leading to the Common Council Chamber is a portrait of Major-General Sir W. F. Williams of Kars. At the upper end of the Common Council Chamber is Chantrey's statue of George III., with his words " Born and bred a Briton," inscribed ; and at the opposite end is Copely's large picture of the siege of Gibraltar. Another large picture is Northcote's Sir William Walworth, the Lord Mayor, killing Wat Tyler. Here are portraits of several British warriors, judges, and aldermen, with busts of the Queen, Nelson, Granville, Sharp (by Chantrey, good), and others. The room where the Court of Aldermen transacts business is rich, and is adorned with paintings by Sir James Thornhill. The windows contain the arms of the Lord Mayors. In an adjoining committee-room is a picture by Opie, representing the murder of James I. of Scotland. The library contains a valuable collection of early printed pageants, tracts of the time of the Civil war, and the Commonwealth, and papers connected with the city. Here are preserved antiquities, pottery, glass, etc., found in various parts of the city, a large stone coffin from Guildhall Chapel no longer in existence, coins, etc. In glass cases may be seen autographs of kings and queens, of Cromwell, Sir C. Wren, Sir Robert Walpole, Dr. Johnson, and other eminent people. The most interesting object of this class, and one that will receive particular attention, is an autograph signature of the author of Hamlet, attached to the deed of purchase of a house in Blackfriars, dated the 10th of March 1613, in which deed he is described as " William Shakespeare, of Stratforde upon Avon, Gentleman." The signature is unmistakeably " William Shakspere." The city gave £142 for this document. The mortgage of the same property, which Shakspere executed shortly afterwards, was purchased by the trustees of the British Museum, for 300 guineas. Adjoining Guildhall are some inconvenient law courts, where the superior judges preside.

THE MANSION HOUSE is the residence of the Lord Mayor during his year of office. It stands in the neighbourhood of the Bank of England and the Royal Exchange, and was erected from George Dance's designs in 1740, but was not inhabited until 1753. The principal feature of the front is a Corinthian portico with six fluted columns, and a pediment of allegorical sculpture by Sir Robert Taylor. The chief room is called the Egyptian Hall, on account, it is said, of being an imitation of that which Vitruvius described under that name. Here the Lord Mayor gives his grand banquets, and it can accommodate 400 guests. It contains some marble statues by British artists, amongst which notice Caractacus and Egeria, by J. H. Foley ; Genius and the Morning Star, by Bailey ; Comus, by Lough ; and Griselda, by Marshall. About £8000 have been laid out on the statuary here. The edifice contains other dining-rooms, with drawing-rooms and a ball room. The Venetian Parlour and some other of the rooms have been recently redecorated in a costly manner. There is also a justice-room, where the Lord Mayor sits as a magistrate daily to hear police cases.

THE CITY COMPANIES AND THEIR HALLS.

The City Companies, of which there are about 82, are the relics of the trading companies that in old time were omnipotent within the city in their respective occupations. Most of their privileges, however, have disappeared, as not being in conformity with the spirit of the age—in other words, as being injurious to the community. In several cases their very names relate to branches of trade that have ceased to exist, for example, the loriners, the girdlers, the patten-makers, and the bowyers. It will be inferred that they now retain little of the influence they once possessed. Only about forty of them have halls. Of these, twelve are known as the Great Livery Companies. They are wealthy associations, whose halls are for the most part conspicuous amongst city edifices, where the members meet, not only to transact the business of the companies, the great bulk of which relates to charitable trusts, but to enjoy good eating and drinking. Most of them have founded alms-houses, where decayed members may retire in the evening of life, protected from want, and free from anxiety as to the morrow. Their annals contain curious records of their feasts, revels, and pageants, in bygone centuries. It must be remarked that the majority of the members of any company do not exercise the trade indicated by the company; and that it is only in one company, the stationers, that the members are restricted to the craft.

The halls of the twelve companies will now be mentioned :—

1. MERCERS' HALL stands on the north side of Cheapside, between Ironmonger Lane and Old Jewry, on the site of an ancient hospital which had been erected on the spot where stood the house of the father of Thomas à Becket, Archbishop of Canterbury. The hospital was built by his sister after the murder, and fell a victim to the great fire. Wren designed the chapel, but only the front of his work remains, a richly decorated façade. The hall is over the ante-chapel. Here are original portraits of Sir Thomas Gresham and Dean Colet. The Mercers' ranks first of the city companies, and can boast of having had amongst its members kings and princes. Richard II., who granted the first charter, was a mercer, and Queen Elizabeth was free of this company; also Caxton, Whittington, and Gresham. The last made the company joint-trustees with the corporation, of the funds with which he founded his college. The Golden Lectureship is in their gift. Amongst their treasures are the silver-gilt election cup, and some other silver-gilt vessels of the sixteenth century.

2. GROCERS' HALL, in the Poultry, only dates from the beginning of this century. It was erected on the site of older halls, in one of which Cromwell and Fairfax were feasted. The statue and portrait of Sir John Cutler (Pope's " sage Cutler"), who was four times master of the company, are in the hall. Sir

Philip Sidney was free of the Grocers, who attended his public burial in St. Paul's, preceded by Lord Mayor, aldermen, and sheriffs in purple. Charles II. and William III. were masters of the company, originally termed Pepperers, and afterwards united with the Apothecaries !

3. DRAPERS' HALL is in Throgmorton Street. It was erected after the great fire on the site of a house built by Cromwell, Earl of Essex, after whose attainder the company (in 1541) purchased it from the crown. Alterations and additions were made by the brothers Adam. The company itself dates from 1332. Notice Beechy's portrait of Lord Nelson, George IV. by Lawrence, and a whole-length, attributed to Zucchero, of Mary Queen of Scots, and her son James I. when four years old. According to tradition, this picture was thrown over the wall into the Drapers' garden during the great fire, and never afterwards claimed. In the hall is a curiously carved screen, and an old but not cotemporary portrait of Fitz-Alwin, the first Mayor of London.

4. FISHMONGERS' HALL, at the north-west foot of London Bridge, was built in 1832 on the site of an older hall. The basement contains fire-proof warehouses, and the river front has a balustraded terrace. The banqueting hall is 73 feet long by 38 feet. The company claims to possess the dagger with which Sir William Walworth, a member, stabbed Wat Tyler, and a funeral pall of cloth of gold, called Walworth's, but really of the period of Henry VIII. Notice Pierce's statue in wood of Walworth ; portraits of William and Mary by Murray ; of George II. and his Queen by Shackleton ; the Duke of Kent, Queen Victoria's father, by Beechy ; Admiral Earl St. Vincent by Beechy, and Queen Victoria by Herbert Smith. In the court dining-room is a silver chandelier weighing 1350 ounces. Dogget, the actor, was a member of this company, and bequeathed to its care a coat and silver badge to be rowed for on the Thames on the 1st of August annually, in commemoration of the accession of George I. The present company was founded by the incorporation, in Henry VIII.'s reign, of two older companies—the Salt Fishmongers and the Stock Fishmongers. Its head is styled Pume Warden. Grand banquets are occasionally given in their hall to the ministers or distinguished individuals.

5. GOLDSMITHS' HALL is in Foster Lane, Cheapside, at the back of the General Post-Office. It is a handsome structure, built

in 1834, from the designs of Ph. Hardwick, but in a situation so bad, being almost hidden from view, that one is left to wonder how they could bring themselves to place it there. It has a frontage of 180 feet, and the style is Italian. The grand staircase is one of the finest in the metropolis. Here is a portrait bust of William IV. by Chantrey, and portraits of George III. and his Queen by Ramsay, and George IV. by Northcote. The banqueting hall is a superb room, 80 feet by 40, having busts of George III. and George IV. by Chantrey, and portraits of Queen Adelaide by Shee ; of William IV., Queen Victoria by Hayter, and Prince Albert by Smith. In the court-room is preserved, under glass, a Roman altar, bearing figures of Apollo, a dog, and a lyre, discovered when the foundations of the hall were being excavated. Here also is a portrait by Janssen of Sir Hugh Middleton, who brought the New River to London ; a portrait of Sir Martin Bowes, Lord Mayor in 1545, with the cup he bequeathed to the company, which is still preserved ; a painting of St. Dunstan, the patron saint of the goldsmiths. The marble chimneypiece was brought from Canons, the Duke of Chandos' mansion ; its terminal busts are attributed to Roubiliac. In the livery tearoom is a conversation piece by Hudson (Sir Joshua's master), with portraits of six Lord Mayors, members of the company. The plate possessed by the company is very valuable. Amongst it is a gold chandelier, weighing 1000 ounces. The goldsmiths acquired the site of the hall so far back as 1323, and were incorporated by Edward III. seven years later. They have altogether fifteen charters. From 1641 to the Restoration, the hall was employed by the Parliamentarians to receive the money obtained by sequestrations. Under several Acts of Parliament all articles of gold and silver manufacture must be assayed and stamped by the company before being sold. When plate is passed it is stamped with certain marks indicating the place of manufacture, the payment of the duty, the date of the assay, and the quality of the metal.

6. SKINNERS' HALL, Dowgate Hill, Upper Thames Street, was a building subsequent to the great fire, and since refronted. It contains a drawing-room lined with cedar, and a portrait of Sir Andrew Judd, a member of the company, and Lord Mayor in 1551, who founded Tunbridge School, and made the Skinners trustees. They were incorporated in 1327. The chief officer is called Master, and next under him are four wardens, in whose election a singular custom is pursued. A cap of maintenance,

made to fit a particular individual, is brought with great formality into the hall, and being tried on by the retiring master, to pronounce that it does not fit him, trials are then made by other persons until it reaches the person for whom it was made, who declares it to be a fit, and is thereupon inducted into the office. A similar proceeding takes place with regard to the wardens.

7. MERCHANT TAILORS' HALL is in Threadneedle Street, but is not seen from the street. It was built shortly after the great fire of 1666. Upon the walls of the banqueting hall, the largest of the halls possessed by city companies, are portraits of several of our sovereigns ; including a head of Henry VIII. by Paris Bordone, head of Charles I., three quarters and full length of Charles II., James II., Queen Anne, and George III. and his Queen, by Ramsay. There are also the Duke of York by Lawrence, Lord Chancellor Eldon by Briggs, the Duke of Wellington by Wilkie, Mr. Pott by Hoppner, and an old picture of Sir Thomas White, Master of the Company in 1561, the founder of St. John's College, Oxford, besides of several Lord Mayors who have been merchant tailors. This company was originally incorporated by Edward IV. in 1466, and was then styled "Taylors and Linen Armourers." They can boast of having had sovereigns and many distinguished persons amongst their members. Several grand political dinners have been given by them to the conservative party. In the old hall James I. and his son Prince Henry were entertained, for which occasion Ben Jonson had "devised" some verses. For admission apply to the clerk at the hall.

8. HABERDASHERS' HALL, Gresham Street, West, was rebuilt in 1855. The site was acquired in 1478, a year after their incorporation. They were then called Hurrers. Several portraits hang in the hall, but none of much value.

9. SALTERS' HALL, St. Swithin's Lane, Cannon Street, was opened in 1827, being the fifth hall of the company. In the election hall are portraits of several sovereigns, and of Adrian Charpentier, painted by himself in 1760. The Salters, i.e., Drysalters, were not regularly incorporated until 1558, but they had existed as a company for a considerable period before that date.

10. IRONMONGERS' HALL, north side of Fenchurch Street, was erected in 1748. The banqueting hall has been decorated of late years with papier mâché and carton pierre ornaments in the

style of Louis Quatorze.   Amongst the portraits there is one of
Mr. Thomas Betton, who, in 1724, left the company £26,000,
and directed that half the interest should be laid out in ransoming
British subjects, captives in Barbary or Turkey.   Also a portrait of Admiral Hood by Gainsborough, presented by the
admiral when admitted an ironmonger in testimony of his distinguished naval services.   This company was incorporated in
1464.

11. VINTNERS' HALL, Upper Thames Street, near Southwark
Bridge, was rebuilt by Wren after the great fire, and it has since
been refronted.   In the court room are some portraits of royal
personages.   The Wine Tunners, afterwards Vintners, were incorporated in 1437.

12. CLOTHWORKERS' HALL, in Mincing Lane, Fenchurch
Street, has been lately rebuilt, and is an elegant edifice, with a
noble banqueting hall 80 feet long by 50 wide, and 40 high.
The Shearmen were incorporated in 1482 ; and when they united
with the Fullers, and received another charter from Henry VIII.,
they were styled Clothworkers.   James I. was admitted into the
company ; and Pepys, the diarist, was master in 1677, which
time he presented a silver cup, which is still used at the company's banquets.   A Mr. Thwaites left £30,000 to this company
a few years back, and directed half the income to be laid out in
charities, and half on feasting.

Amongst the halls of the minor companies the following
deserve notice.

APOTHECARIES' HALL, in Water Lane, Blackfriars, was erected
in 1670 ; and here pure drugs are sold to the public on behalf
of the company.   All the drugs for the army and navy are procured at the hall.   Here are some portraits of James I. (good),
Charles I., and others.   The apothecaries were at first joined
with the grocers, but they obtained a charter as a separate company in 1617.   The company has a botanic garden at Chelsea.

ARMOURERS' AND BRAZIERS' HALL, Coleman Street, a modern
building.   In the banqueting-hall, which is decorated with armour,
is Northcote's painting representing the Entry of Richard II.
and Bolingbroke into London, painted for Alderman Boydell.
This company has a fine collection of mazers, hanaps, and silver
cups.   It was incorporated in 1422 by Henry VI., a member.

BARBER-SURGEONS' HALL, Monkwell Street, was built after
the great fire which destroyed the old hall.   In the Court-room

hangs a celebrated picture of Holbein, Henry VIII. presenting the charter to the company, 10 feet 6 inches by 7 feet, containing 18 figures. The king is on his throne ; Thomas Vicay, the master of the company, is kneeling before him and receiving the charter. The members of the court are also kneeling. All the details are very carefully finished. This admirable painting is the finest of Holbein's works in Britain. Sly Mr. Pepys tried to buy it for £200, " it being said to be worth £1000," as he notes. There are also some curious portraits of Sir Charles Scarborough (chief physician to Charles II., James II., and William III.) and other physicians. The chests of the company contain a silver-gilt cup, richly embossed, given by Henry VIII. ; a silver cup given by Charles II. ; two chaplets in silver, and a silver punch-bowl, presented by Queen Anne. In olden time the same person practised the arts of shaving and surgery. An act was passed in 1512 forbidding any except barbers from practising surgery within the city and seven miles round, save such persons as had been examined by the Bishop of London ! In 1540 the barbers and the surgeons were made one corporation, but the barbers were interdicted from practising surgery, except so far as drawing teeth and bleeding were concerned. The surgeons were separated in 1745, and have now a college of their own in Lincoln's-Inn-Fields. The designation of barber-surgeons, however, is still retained. Close by are the clothworkers' almshouses. Underneath the chapel are the remains of a Norman crypt. The short columns have embellished capitals ; the ribs of the groining have zig-zag and spiral ornaments. This crypt belonged to the hermitage of St. James. The church of St. Giles, Cripplegate, is in the neighbourhood. For an account of it see another page.

PAPER-STAINERS' HALL, Little Trinity Lane, Upper Thames Street, rebuilt after the great fire, contains a picture of St. Luke writing the gospel, by Vansomer ; a landscape, by Lambert, with figures by Hogarth ; Charles II. and his queen, by Huysman ; Queen Anne, by Dahl ; William III., by Kneller ; and some other portraits. Camden, the historian, bequeathed money to buy a silver cup, which is now employed at the election feasts. The company was incorporated in 1582 by Queen Elizabeth. This company has very commendably commenced an annual exhibition, open during the summer, of specimens of marbling, graining, arabesque, glass-work, and other ornament. It takes place in their hall, and prizes are awarded to the most successful exhibitors. This proceeding ought to have a beneficial effect on the arts of decoration, and is deserving of imitation by other city companies.

SADDLERS' HALL, No. 143 Cheapside, has a handsome great hall. Here is an ancient funeral pall of crimson velvet, embroidered with gold. In the hall is a portrait of the father of George III., a master of the company, which was incorporated by Edward I.

STATIONERS' HALL, Stationers' Hall Court, Ludgate Hill, was erected after the great fire (in which the company are said to have lost £200,000) on the site of the old hall then destroyed. The stationers existed as a guild in 1403, but were not incorporated until 1557, in the reign of Philip and Mary, the existing charter being dated in 1690. Under their charters all printers were obliged to serve their time to a member of the company ; and publications of all kinds were required to be entered at Stationers' Hall. The register of works commencing in 1557 has been published. James I. granted them the monopoly of printing almanacs, which they retained until late years, and this branch of business they still carry on, though subjected to competition. The bible printed by them in 1632 is classed amongst bibliographical curiosities from its omitting the word " not" from the seventh commandment. Archbishop Laud made a star chamber of it, and the company had to pay a heavy fine. Under the copyright act the proprietor of every published work must register it in the books of the company before he can prosecute any claim at law in respect of it ; and assignments must also be registered. In the Court-room is some carving, attributed to G. Gibbons ; also West's painting of King Alfred sharing his loaf with the pilgrim St. Cuthbert, given by Alderman Boydell, a former master, whose portrait as Lord Mayor, by Graham, hangs here. Other portraits are those of Prior, Steele, Richardson the novelist and his wife, John Bunyan, Bishop Hoadley, and Vincent Wing the astrologer. In the hall used to take place musical performances on St. Cecilia's day, for which Dryden wrote his well known ode.

WATERMEN'S HALL, St. Mary at Hill, built 1786. This company was incorporated by Philip and Mary in 1555. Under various Acts of Parliament it is empowered to make regulations with reference to the watermen, barge owners, and others connected with the navigation of the Thames from Teddington to Gravesend.

WEAVERS' HALL, Basinghall Street, contains an old picture representing William Lee, a Cambridge M.A., directing the attention of a knitter to his loom for weaving stockings. This company is allowed to have been earlier incorporated than any other of the city companies.

CHAPTER THE EIGHTEENTH.

The Thames : its Origin, Tides, etc.

Port of London—On the River from Chelsea to Hungerford—From Hungerford to London Bridge—From London Bridge to Greenwich —River Steamers.

This river, so intimately connected with all our associations of London, has its rise near Cirencester in the county of Gloucester. In its course of 220 miles it crosses or touches nine counties. Its basin is estimated to have an area of 6600 square miles, and it extends into fifteen counties. The source of the Thames is thought to be about 280 feet above low-water mark at London Bridge. Its navigation commences at Lechlade on the borders of Gloucestershire and Berkshire, but its navigable property for many miles below this point, as far indeed as Teddington in Middlesex, is obliged to be kept up by means of locks and weirs. Small steamers occasionally make their way up to Hampton Court. At London itself the river is alive with them, and they afford a cheap and ready means of passing from point to point, of which thousands daily avail themselves. The first steamer was placed on the river in 1814. Large vessels are stopped at London Bridge, ships of 800 tons burden come up to St Katherine's docks, and vessels of 1400 tons burden can get as far as Blackwall. Vessels of any burden may reach Woolwich.

At London Bridge the river is about 300 feet wide ; at Woolwich it is about a quarter of a mile ; at Gravesend it has widened —it is more than half a mile ; and at its mouth it has a width of eighteen miles. The upper part of its course abounds with pretty scenery, but below London Bridge it is extremely uninteresting in this respect, except at one or two points.

At low water there is a depth of about twelve feet at London Bridge, but the influence of the ocean tide causes the water to rise twice a day to the height of seventeen feet at London Bridge, or at the extreme springs to the height of about twenty-two feet, and this influence is perceptible, though in a less degree, as far as Teddington, between Richmond and Kingston. The salt water itself keeps many miles away from London, but once, in Henry VIII.'s reign (1542), there occurred such a drought, and the Thames fell so low that the salt water flowed above London Bridge. The flow of the river at ebb tide is about 3½ miles an hour between Westminster and London Bridges; the tidal flow is about thirteen miles an hour.

On rare occasions the tide rises to such a height that all the low-lying places on the banks of the river are flooded, and much damage is done. On the 7th and 8th of March 1860 the river rose to an unusual height; the Temple Gardens were flooded to the depth of several feet, and the pleasure grounds attached to the mansions in Privy Gardens, Whitehall, were inundated. The water covered the Horseferry Road, Westminster, to a considerable depth, and prevented all thoroughfare, so that persons proceeding in that way had to be ferried in boats along the street. The open spaces in front of Lambeth Palace and Bishop's Walk were likewise covered with water. In this neighbourhood the houses of the poor inhabitants were flooded, and much mischief was done. Lower down the river, on the south shore, and at Limehouse, Blackwall, and Wapping, on the north shore, there was much destruction of property, and in many granaries, warehouses, and cellars near the banks, very great damage was done. The marshes of Battersea, Greenwich, Woolwich, and Essex, were converted into great lakes.

Formerly there were several state barges kept on the Thames, but they are being gradually laid down. The Lord Mayor's barge and the barge of the Goldsmith's Company have been sold. The Sovereign has, or had until lately, a state barge, a curious specimen of boat building, constructed 150 years ago. The Elder Brethren of the Trinity House retain their barge, and so do the Lords of the Admiralty.

Rowing in light pleasure boats on the Thames, from Chelsea upwards, is a favourite amusement with young men, and matches take place during the summer which excite great interest among the Londoners, who are attracted to the river in large numbers on these occasions to witness the contest. Large sums are staked in bets on the event, *more Anglorum.* The most interesting of these matches is that between the Universities of Oxford and Cambridge. On the first of August every year a coat and silver badge are rowed for by Thames watermen in pursuance of the will of Dogget the actor (d. 1721), who left a sum of money for the purpose.

The cold is sometimes so severe that the Thames is frozen from bank to bank, and there are records from ancient times of carts having crossed over the ice, and of fairs being held upon it. Thus Evelyn, under date of the 24th of January 1684, writes, "The frost continuing more and more severe, the Thames before London was planted with boothes in formal streetes, all sorts of trades and shops furnished, and all full of commodities, even to a printing presse, where the people and ladies tooke a fancy to have their names printed on the Thames. Coaches plied from Westminster to the Temple, and from several other staires, as in the streetes ; sliding with skeetes, and bull-baiting, horse and coach races, puppet plays, and interlades, cookes, tipling, etc., so that it seemed to be a bacchanalian triumph or carnival on the water." At the beginning of 1814 similar occurrences and scenes took place on the frozen river, and there is a book in existence which has this title page :—" Frostiana, or a History of the river Thames in a frozen state, with an account of the late severe frost, etc., printed and published on the ice on the river Thames, February 5, 1814." So lately as January 1861 the river was ice bound.

THE PORT OF LONDON extends from London Bridge for six miles and a half down the river to a place called Bugsby's Hole. The part where vessels lie is divided into the Upper Pool, which consists of the reach from the bridge nearly as far as the tunnel, and the Lower Pool, extending thence to Cuckold's Point. Colliers lie chiefly in the Lower Pool, a clear way of 300 feet being left for other vessels. The amount of business done in this port is very great. (See the notice of the Custom House in this volume.) As many as 244 vessels have been known to enter it in one day, but this was after bad weather. Many fatal accidents occur in the port in the course of the year ; there being about 500 lives lost here annually. A vigilant police force keeps depredators in check. At Wapping is a place called Execution Dock, where pirates and sailors guilty of murder were executed in former days.

As the " silent highway " of the Thames is greatly frequented, and as it is highly desirable that the stranger who wishes to

examine London thoroughly should see not only various objects
lying on the banks of the river, but the bridges spanning the
current, which can be done nowhere so well as from the stream
itself, we propose to take him to the bridge that connects
Battersea with Chelsea, and then conduct him in three stages to
Greenwich. The first division of this river route will be that
from

BATTERSEA AND CHELSEA BRIDGE TO HUNGERFORD BRIDGE.

Battersea Church, where Lord Bolingbroke, Pope's friend, was
interred, stands on the south bank, a little above the first-men-
tioned bridge. Cremorne Gardens, a popular haunt of pleasure
seekers, lies almost opposite on the north bank. A little below
it on the same bank is Chelsea Church. Sir Thomas More lived
in a mansion in this neighbourhood, the gardens of which extended to the river ; and here Henry VIII. has been seen to walk
with him " by the space of an hour, holding his arm about his
neck," that neck which his gracious majesty was in course of
time to order the executioner to sever with his axe. In the
church is a black marble tablet to More, with a Latin inscription,
placed there by More himself three years previous to his judicial murder. In the churchyard is a curious monument to Sir
Hans Sloane, egg-shaped, with serpents entwined round it. At
Chelsea have lived several eminent persons in former days, when
country retirement was to be had here. Swift, Addison, Steele,
Locke, and Smollett, made it their residence. Between the
church and Cadogan Pier is Cheyne Walk, and a little below is the
Apothecaries' Botanic Garden, and then comes *Chelsea Hospital*,
for our old soldiers, built by Wren. On the opposite bank is
Battersea Park, a place only recently laid out. Between the
hospital and the park the river is 790 feet wide. From the
north end of Mr. Page's elegant *Suspension Bridge* a new road
leads to Sloane Street, in the direction of Hyde Park. Nearly
adjacent to this bridge is the bridge by which the railway is
taken northwards to the *Victoria Station*, Pimlico. On the south
bank below these bridges are the Nine Elms Station Warehouses
of the South Western Railway Company, the Belmont and Vauxhall Works of Price's Patent Candle Company, and near the end
of Vauxhall Bridge, the Phœnix Gas Works. Not far distant are
the once celebrated Vauxhall Gardens, but their glory has de-
parted ; their ten thousand lamps have been extinguished for

ever, and they have become common-place building ground, which
any one may purchase at so much a foot. Behind Pimlico Pier,
on the north bank, are the Government Military Clothing Stores.
Trinity Church is opposite to the end of the bridge. We now
pass under *Vauxhall Bridge*, and are in the near neighbourhood
of the huge building once called Millbank Penitentiary, now
Millbank Prison. On the other bank are the towers of Lambeth
Palace and St. Mary's Church, opposite St. John's Church (north
bank), which has been compared to an elephant on its back, with
its four legs in the air. Beyond are the grand front and the lofty
towers of the *Houses of Parliament*, and behind stands *Westminster
Abbey*. Passing under the *new Westminster Bridge*, another of
Mr. Page's iron structures, we may see the building lately used
by the extinct Government Board of Control in Indian affairs,
then the end of Richmond Terrace, near which is the Duke of
Buccleuch's new and spacious mansion. Then come Privy
Gardens, Whitehall, with their private houses, in one of which
Sir Robert Peel died. Soon afterwards we arrive at the new
railway bridge at Hungerford.

HUNGERFORD BRIDGE TO LONDON BRIDGE.

Soon after leaving Hungerford Bridge behind, we see at the
end of Buckingham Street the rustic Watergate, the work of
Nicholas Stone, the sculptor of many monuments in Westminster
Abbey. It is the last relic of a mansion known as York House,
from having been the town residence of the Archbishops of York.
It came, however, to be let to the keepers of the great seal, and there
Lord Bacon was born, and there he was living when the great
seal was taken from him. It passed into the hands of Villiers,
the first Duke of Buckingham, and he it was who built the
Watergate, two years before his assassination. The adjoining
Adelphi Terrace was erected, with other streets, by the brothers
Adam in 1768. David Garrick died in the centre house (1779),
and there his remains lay in state previous to interment in the
Abbey. The vaults under the terrace are used as cellars and coal
wharfs. Before gas was, these vaults were the mighty haunt of
thieves and profligates. A little beyond the terrace is the SAVOY.
On the opposite bank of the river will be seen the Lion Brewery
and a tall shot tower, which some one has ventured to say is of
finer design than Wren's London Monument. We now pass under
one of the arches of WATERLOO BRIDGE, and emerge in front of

SOMERSET HOUSE. The eastern angle of the noble front is King's College. From some parts of the river the towers of St. Mary le Strand and St. Clement Danes are caught. The three streets that come down to the river are Surrey Street, Norfolk Street, and Arundel Street, which occupy the site of the Earl of Arundel's mansion, where he assembled his famed marbles in the first half of the 17th century. Peter the Great lodged in Norfolk Street, in a house near the river, and at the south-west corner William Penn the quaker lived. Essex Street is on the site of the mansion where the Earl of Essex was living when he made his attempt to dethrone Queen Elizabeth. He fortified the house and only surrendered when he saw that defence against the artillery, by which it was threatened, was hopeless.

The Temple Pier is at the end of Essex Street, and close by is a new and handsome building, the MIDDLE TEMPLE LIBRARY, standing at one side of its patch of garden, and near the HALL. The larger garden of the Inner Temple is a little beyond, with its halls and various buildings occupied as lawyers' chambers. Further on are the unsightly buildings of the City Gas Works, erected on part of the site of Whitefriars which acquired the cant name of Alsatia. It was the haunt of the worst class of people, and has been often mentioned in works of fiction, early and modern. (See Sir Walter Scott's " Fortunes of Nigel" for example.) The elegant spire of St. Bride's is seen behind. Passing Blackfriars Bridge—on the east side is the city steam-boat pier— we shall see on the north bank the City Flour Mill, said to be one of the largest establishments of the kind in the world. The buildings cover an acre of ground, and the principal one is eight stories high. This bank of the river is a region of active commerce, lined with warehouses that extend to Upper and Lower Thames Street. The Dome of St. Paul's is seen towering over all meaner edifices. Behind St. Paul's pier is St. Bennet's church, where Inigo Jones, the architect of the beautiful banqueting-house, Whitehall, was interred. Notice the handsome steeple of Bow Church. An indentation of the river is called Queenhithe dock, hithe being the Saxon name for a wharf. This spot has been used as a landing-place from very ancient times, and is frequently mentioned in our early dramatists. It derives the first syllable of its name from having been part of the dowry of Eleanor, queen of Henry II. In Stow's time it was the chief watergate of the city. At this time it is chiefly used by barges bringing grain and flour from the west country. On the opposite side of the river is Bankside, where stood some old theatres which have long since disappeared. At SOUTHWARK BRIDGE the river is at its narrowest, being only about 650 feet wide. On the south side is that great establishment BARCLAY'S BREWERY, and hereabouts, in Shakspere's time, stood the famous Globe Theatre. Beyond, on the same side, is ST. SAVIOUR'S CHURCH, the interior of which is well worth inspecting. On the north bank close upon London Bridge is FISHMONGERS' HALL, above which are several piers for landing and taking up passengers. But if the London Bridge Railway Station be the reader's destination, he should land on the opposite (north) side of the river.

LONDON BRIDGE TO GREENWICH.

Stepping on board a steamer from a pier on the west or upper side of London Bridge (steamers bound for Greenwich and Woolwich call here every quarter of an hour), we pass through an arch of the bridge, and are soon in front of Billingsgate market, standing on the left, and marked by an Italian campanile; behind which is the dome of the Coal Exchange. Next to the market is the great front of the Custom House, and behind it is seen the church steeple of St. Dunstan-in-the-East, copied by Wren from one at Newcastle-on-Tyne. The Tower of London, with its lofty keep, is conspicuous; the low arch under the esplanade is Traitor's Gate. At this spot the Thames is 860 feet in width. The high walls of St. Katherine's Docks succeed, and a church tower indicates the classic district of Wapping. We now enter the Pool, which, with its vast crowd of ships, will give some idea of the immense commerce of the Port of London, and must strike all foreigners with astonishment. The London Docks lie, like all the preceding objects, on the north bank of the stream. The tower of Rotherhithe Church, on the opposite bank, will point out the position of the south entrance into the Thames Tunnel, that costly and nearly useless work, over which the steamer insensibly glides, having previously stopped to land and receive passengers at a pier on the north side, known as the Tunnel Pier. "Prince" Le Boo, from the Pellew Islands, was interred at Rotherhithe Church. The Commercial Docks are on the Surrey side, in the angle formed by the river bending to Limehouse Reach, and over against them are the immense West

India Docks, which have entrances at both sides of the Isle of Dogs, as the large horse-shoe piece of land round which the river winds is called, from Henry VIII. having kept his hounds upon it. Its western shore is known as Millwall, and here are placed some large manufacturing and engineering establishments, to wit, Burnett's timber-preserving works, the white-lead works of Messrs. Pontifex, the engineering yards of the Napiers, Swayne and Bovill, Mare, and Scott Russell. In the last mentioned establishment the mighty but unfortunate Great Eastern was constructed. Deptford, with its royal dockyard, indicated by low buildings and vast sheds, is on the south bank. It was here that Peter the Great studied ship-building. The Navy Victualling Offices are an immense establishment here. A little further on are Messrs. Rennie's engineering works. Shortly after passing the Dreadnought hospital ship (where the sick sailors of all nations are received for treatment), we are in front of that magnificent group of buildings forming Greenwich Hospital, backed by the trees of Greenwich Park and the Observatory. Here, if our design be to inspect the interior of the hospital, we land, but if Woolwich be our destination, we proceed. In a few minutes we are abreast of the pier at Blackwall, noted for its iron ship-building establishments and for its hotels, to which the Londoners resort, in the proper season, to eat their favourite dish of whitebait, a small fish taken abundantly in the Thames, and formerly supposed to be the young of the shad, but now established in books of natural history with a scientific name of its own (*Clupea alba*). The ministers of the crown have a curious custom of coming here or to Greenwich to feast on whitebait at the end of the session. Near the pier is the terminus of the Blackwall Railway. Behind Blackwall are the East India Docks, and a little lower down the river the Victoria Docks, the last construction of these artificial basins. Charlton, a pretty village, with a manor-house of James I.'s time, is seen on the south bank ; and shortly afterwards we are at the Woolwich pier, with a not very attractive prospect of houses, and high walls, and tall chimneys, before us. Behind Woolwich, Shooter's Hill, a mound of London clay capped with drift gravel, rises to the height of 412 feet. On the opposite side of the river is the terminus of the North Woolwich Railway. Our return to London may be made, if thought desirable, either by this line (the London terminus of which is at Shoreditch) or by the North Kent line to London Bridge.

RIVER STEAMERS.

HALFPENNY STEAM-BOATS between Adelphi Pier and Dyer's Hall Pier, London Bridge.

PENNY STEAM-BOATS between Westminster Bridge (Surrey side), Hungerford Bridge, and London Bridge, every ten minutes, not calling at intermediate piers.

CITIZEN AND IRON STEAM-BOAT COMPANY's BOATS start every five minutes from piers on both sides of London Bridge, and call at Paul's Wharf, Doctors Commons, Blackfriars Bridge, Temple Pier, Essex Street, Strand, Waterloo Bridge, Hungerford Bridge, Westminster Bridge, Lambeth, Vauxhall Road, Vauxhall and Nine Elms, Pimlico, West London and Crystal Palace Railway Pier, Battersea Park Pier, Cadogan Pier, Chelsea, and Battersea Bridge. *Fares*, from London Bridge to Lambeth, 1d.; to Pimlico Piers, 2d.; to Chelsea and Battersea, 3d.

WATERMEN's COMPANY STEAM-BOATS start during the summer months for Greenwich and Woolwich every fifteen minutes from Hungerford Bridge, calling at the Temple Pier, Blackfriars Bridge, London Bridge (upper side), Cherry Gardens, Rotherhithe, Thames Tunnel, north bank, and Commercial Dock, and calling at Blackwall every half hour.

DIAMOND FUNNEL PACKETS leave, during the summer, Hungerford, London Bridge, Greenwich, Blackwall, and Woolwich, for Erith and Gravesend, every half hour throughout the morning, and at two and half-past four from London Bridge in the afternoon; for Southend and Sheerness at half-past eight, and ten from Hungerford, and nine and half-past ten from London Bridge, returning the same day. *Fares*, Sheerness and back, 2s. 6d.; Gravesend and back, 1s. 6d.

STEAMERS TO KEW, from London Bridge, calling at the other piers, every half-hour throughout the summer. *Fare*, there and back, 1s. From Cadogan Pier, Chelsea, by the Citizen and Iron Steam-boats every half-hour, calling at intermediate piers; fare there, 4d. Return from Kew Bridge every half hour.

STEAMERS TO KEW AND RICHMOND from Hungerford Bridge at half-past ten on Sundays and Mondays.

R

CHAPTER THE NINETEENTH.

THE BRIDGES.

Battersea Park Bridge—Blackfriars Bridge—Charing Cross Bridge—
Lambeth Bridge—London Bridge—Southwark Bridge—Vauxhall
Bridge—Waterloo Bridge—New Westminster Bridge—The Tunnel.

BETWEEN Chelsea and the Tower the Thames is crossed by ten
bridges, of which seven are constructed of iron, and the rest of
stone. Two of them are railway bridges, the others are for foot
passengers and ordinary vehicles. The following account of the
London Bridges is arranged alphabetically :—

BATTERSEA PARK OR VICTORIA BRIDGE is an elegant iron
structure, erected in 1857, from the designs of Mr. T. Page, at a
cost of £88,000. It crosses the river in the neighbourhood of
Chelsea Hospital, and the new park at Battersea. Including the
abutments, it is 915 feet long, the distance between the two suspension towers being 347 feet. Toll is levied ; foot-passengers
pay a halfpenny, vehicles various rates. Close by is the viaduct
by which the Crystal Palace and West End Railway is carried
over the Thames from the Victoria Station, Pimlico.

BLACKFRIARS BRIDGE.—The old bridge was commenced in
1760, and opened in 1769, Portland stone being the material
employed in its construction. Robert Mylne was the architect,
and its total cost, including the approaches, was about £262,000.
It had nine semi-elliptical arches, the largest having a span of
100 feet. Its total length was 995 feet, and its width 45 feet.
Large sums have been expended upon repairs, but the foundations having given way, a new iron bridge is about to be erected
from the designs of Mr. Page. It has only three spans, with a
width of 80 feet within the parapets.

CHARING CROSS (HUNGERFORD) BRIDGE.—This bridge has
been lately erected for the purpose of extending the South-Eastern
Railway from London Bridge to the station built on the site of

Hungerford Market. It has taken the place of the suspension bridge for foot-passengers, which was erected by Mr. Brunel only a few years ago at this point, where the river is 1350 feet wide, and 30 feet deep at high water. It is wholly of wrought iron, supported on cast iron columns sunk deep into the river's bed. It crosses the Thames in eight spans, with a width of 70 feet, sufficient for four lines of rails, with a footpath on each side seven feet wide. Mr. Hawkshaw is the engineer of the bridge and railway.

LAMBETH BRIDGE, a new bridge half way between Vauxhall and Westminster Bridges, intended to connect Lambeth with Pimlico and Chelsea, is in progress, and is expected to be completed in the course of 1862, at the low cost of £40,000. It will have three equal spans of wire cables, each 280 feet wide, supporting a wrought-iron platform. It will have a double carriage-way and two footways, the total width being 34 feet. Mr. Barlow is the engineer.

LONDON BRIDGE was commenced in 1824, from the designs of John Rennie, and continued after his death by his sons Sir John Rennie and George Rennie. It is the first bridge met with on coming up from the sea. The building occupied nearly seven years and six months. The bridge was opened on the 1st of August 1831, with great state by William IV. and his Queen, who partook of a banquet served upon the bridge itself, Lord Mayor Key presiding. The total cost, including the approaches, was £1,458,000. The stone employed was granite. It is 928 feet long, and consists of five semi-elliptical arches, two of 130 feet, two of 140 feet, and the centre of 152½ feet span ; the roadway being 52 feet wide. The masonry is from 8 to 10 feet below the bed of the river. About 120,000 tons of stone were used in the structure. Cannon taken in the Peninsular war are said to have furnished metal for the lamp-posts. The old bridge, which had stood through nearly six centuries and a quarter, was about 100 feet to the eastward. There were houses upon it at each side like a continuous street, and at each end a gate-house, upon which it was the barbarous custom to place the heads of persons decapitated for political offences. So late as 1598 thirty heads were counted on the bridge. In the middle of the bridge was a Gothic chapel dedicated to St. Thomas of Canterbury ; and in its crypt, within a pier of the bridge, were found the bones of the architect Peter of Colechurch, when the bridge was taken down in 1832.

In consequence of the proximity of a great railway station, or rather an aggregation of stations, the traffic across this bridge is immense ; and, notwithstanding the excellent arrangements made by the police (one of which is, that the quick vehicles shall take the middle part of the roadway, and those with heavy burdens the sides), there are frequently "dead locks" upon it.

SOUTHWARK BRIDGE is an iron bridge designed by John Rennie, and erected, 1813-19, at a cost of about £800,000, including the approaches. It is badly placed, and it would require a large additional expenditure to make the approaches what they ought to be. There are three arches, the middle one having a span of 240 feet, and two side arches, each with a span of 210 feet. About 5700 tons of iron were used. The total length is 708 feet. Toll, one penny.

VAUXHALL BRIDGE connects Millbank with Kennington. Nine cast-iron arches of 78 feet span rest upon stone piers. Clear of the abutments, the bridge is 806 feet long ; its centre arch is 27 feet above high-water mark. It was begun by a public company in 1811, but in consequence of disagreements with the engineers, it was not finished until 1816, the total cost being upwards of £300,000. The tolls for the year 1860-61 produced £9556.

WATERLOO BRIDGE, the admiration of all beholders, was also designed by John Rennie for a public company. It was begun in 1811, and was opened with great pomp by the Prince Regent in 1817, on the 18th of June, the anniversary of the battle of Waterloo. The cost was large, more than a million sterling, and the tolls yielding a very small dividend, the value of the shares has been much depreciated. The company would be glad to dispose of it for a small sum to the government to be thrown open as a free bridge. The total length is 1380 feet, to which must be added 1070 feet for the approaches. It is built of granite, and consists of nine semi-elliptical arches, each having a span of 120 feet. The façades are embellished with Grecian-Doric columns between the piers, and by a Doric entablature beneath the balustrade.

WESTMINSTER BRIDGE.—In place of a stone structure built in the first half of the last century, a new bridge has lately been erected at the cost of about £250,000. The arches are iron, the piers granite, and its appearance is light and elegant, harmonizing well with the Houses of Parliament, near which it crosses the river. It has a length of 1160 feet, with a width of 85 feet, of which 50 feet are allotted to the carriage-way, and 15 feet on each side to the foot-ways. The arches are elliptical in shape, and seven in number ; the centre arch has a span of 120 feet, and has a height of 20 feet above high-water mark ; the two arches on each side of the central one have each a span of 115 feet, the two next on each side 115, and the shore arch at each side is 94½ feet. The foundation is sunk 30 feet below low-water mark, entering 20 feet into the London clay. It was commenced in 1856 from the designs of Mr. Page, and in building it one longitudinal half was completed and opened for traffic before beginning the other half. The difficulties encountered in pulling down the old bridge and constructing the present one were considerable, and much work was done by divers. The tidal rise compelled the labourers to woik at night, and at one time the " electric light " was used as the mode of illumination, but gas was afterwards employed. The spectacle presented by the nocturnal operations was curious in the extreme—crowds of labourers actively employed, divers in their wild costumes, the shouts, the clang of hammers, the blows of the pile driver, the rush of the river amongst the obstructions, and the flickering of the bright gas flames, made up a scene that was singularly strange and interesting.

In addition to those previously mentioned, bridges cross the Thames at Chelsea and at Battersea, Fulham and Putney, Hammersmith, Barnes, and Chiswick (railway), Kew, and Richmond.

THE THAMES TUNNEL.—This is a tunnel under the Thames connecting Rotherhithe and Wapping, about two miles below London Bridge, and is most readily reached by a steam-boat. This expensive and useless undertaking was commenced from the designs of Sir I. K. Brunel in February 1835. A shaft on the Rotherhithe side was first sunk, and then the excavation of the nearly horizontal tunnel commenced. A large apparatus called a shield was employed to facilitate the work. This consisted of 12 great frames placed close together. Each frame was 22 feet high and 3 feet wide, and was divided into three chambers or cells, in each of which a workman was placed. As the work of excavation advanced, the bricking of the tunnel proceeded. In May 1827 the river broke into the tunnel. When the bed of the river was examined with the help of a diving bell, it was found that a large cavity had been formed, through which the tunnel had been filled. Bags of clay and gravel were thrown into the hole, and in this way it was filled up. The water was then pumped out of the tunnel, and the work proceeded. When the tunnel had advanced 600 feet, the water from the river again entered, and with such violence that six men were drowned. Mr. Brunel himself had a narrow escape. The water carried him up the shaft along with timber and casks. This injury was repaired in the manner previously described. On both occasions, after the water had been drawn out, the brickwork was found uninjured. The works were stopped from 1828 to the beginning of 1835 from want of funds. A supply having been obtained from Government, the excavation went on slowly, until a third irruption of the river occurred in August 1836. Measures similar to those already mentioned were taken. A vertical shaft having been constructed, the tunnel was finally completed and opened to the public the 25th of March 1843. Its total cost has been £468,000, of which £250,000 have been advanced by Government. It was originally contemplated to have a carriage entrance at each end of the tunnel, but these have never been made. Their estimated cost was £180,000.

There are two parallel archways (of which, however, one only is used), with arched communications between them. The dividing wall was built entirely solid, and then the cross archways were cut through the wall. The section of each arcade is horse-shoe shaped. The bottom of the tunnel falls in slightly from each end. There are about 100 steps in each staircase in the vertical shafts. The tunnel is lighted with gas, and is traversable night and day. Permission to pass through it costs one penny. The total length is 1200 feet. Each archway is 14 feet wide and 17 feet high. About 5500 bricks were used in each foot of length, and altogether about seven millions of bricks were consumed. The number of persons who have passed through it up to the present time is about 19½ millions. It will be readily conceived from the enormous cost that it pays small interest on the money invested. In 1860, the total receipts amounted to £5755, whilst the expenses had been £3432, so that the company to which it belongs had very little to divide.

CHAPTER THE TWENTIETH.

THE DOCKS.

Commercial Docks—East India Docks—London Docks—St. Katherine's Docks—Surrey Docks—West India Docks—Victoria Docks.

THESE vast works, for the accommodation of shipping, are all situate on the east side of London, and have been entirely formed during the present century by joint-stock companies. Previous to their formation, merchandise was kept in barges on the river, and was subject to much depredation. The docks are seven in number, and occupy between 700 and 800 acres.

THE COMMERCIAL DOCKS, at Rotherhithe, on the south of the Thames, were opened in 1807. They contain about 50 acres, with five basins, and are chiefly occupied by vessels from the Baltic, and for east country trade. The grain stores will hold 100,000 quarters. The office is at 106 Fenchurch Street.

THE EAST INDIA DOCKS are at Blackwall, near the termination of the Blackwall Railway. They were opened in 1806, having been formed for the use of the East India Company. The basins comprise about 32 acres, and have been made very deep to hold vessels of heavy burden. The cast-iron wharf, 750 feet long, is said to weigh 900 tons.

THE LONDON DOCKS, opened in 1805, comprise 90 acres, of which about 35 are water, in four docks. There are three openings from the Thames. The mere walls enclosing these docks cost £65,000; the total capital of the company is four millions. One dock, and one huge warehouse, covering five acres, are devoted to tobacco. The tea warehouse is capable of holding 120,000 chests. Altogether there are 20 warehouses, 18 sheds, and 17 vaults, for the reception of goods. The wine entering the port of London is chiefly kept here; there is accommodation for 60,000 pipes, but not more than from 40,000 to 45,000 pipes is to be found there at one time. The liability to loss by the

fraudulent dealing of persons who have access to the wine vaults
is very great. In 1855 the loss on the stock of wine deposited
in the east vault was upwards of 3400 gallons. What is known
amongst the merchants as the Osborn fraud was the mysterious
change of 22 pipes of Italian or Spanish red wine into very excellent port wine, which could only be explained by supposing
that the inferior wine had been abstracted by some means never
discovered, and that the loss had been made good by pilfering
wine from port wine casks. The loss of one firm in two years
amounted to 567 gallons, but when they sought to recover the
value of the wine, estimated at £2800, from the Dock Company,
they failed in doing so.

For an order to see the vaults and warehouses apply to the
secretary of the company at the London Dock House, in New
Bank Buildings. To see the wine vaults to advantage, secure the
assistance of a wine-merchant, who will procure a "lasting order."

ST. KATHERINE'S DOCKS are close to the Tower, and are nearer
the centre of London than the other docks. They were commenced in 1827, and opened the following year, Telford having
furnished the plan. Besides St. Katherine's Hospital, which was
reconstructed in the Regent's Park, 1250 houses were pulled
down, and 11,300 inhabitants were displaced in carrying out
this great undertaking, which cost £1,700,000. The walls enclose about 24 acres, of which between 11 and 12 are covered
with water. The earth removed by the excavations was taken
up the river to Millbank to fill up reservoirs, which were afterwards built over. The annual gross earnings of the company are
about £230,000, and their expenses about £124,000. It is
said that the cats, which are kept to destroy vermin, cost £100
a year ! There is accommodation in the warehouses, etc., for
110,000 tons of goods.

THE SURREY DOCKS are near the Commercial Docks, on the
south side of the Thames. They are chiefly used for timber.

THE WEST INDIA DOCKS are the most extensive on the river,
and perhaps have no equal in the world. They are situate at
the bend of the river, opposite Greenwich, called the Isle of
Dogs. The Blackwall Railway has a station where passengers
can alight. They were commenced in 1800, William Pitt, the
minister, laying the first stone, and were finished in two years.
Their area is said to be 295 acres. The wall surrounding them
is five feet thick. The basins are connected with the river on

each side of the bend, that is, both above and below Greenwich. The great import dock has a length of 170 yards, and a breadth of 166 ; it is capable of containing 250 vessels, each of 300 tons. The export dock has the same length, but the width is only 135 yards ; this is calculated to hold 195 such vessels. There is besides a canal-shaped dock, almost three quarters of a mile in length, which is used for timber vessels. The warehouses are sufficiently spacious to hold 180,000 tons of goods. Colonial produce to the value of twenty millions sterling has been stored here at one time. These docks, and the East India Docks, belong to the same company, and receive shipping from all quarters. The capital of the company invested on the West India Docks is £1,200,000. The greatest revenue these docks ever realized was in 1813, when £449,000 was the gross return, but since that time the returns have much decreased. The office is at 8 Billiter Square.

VICTORIA DOCKS are the most modern, and the most distant from London. They are below Blackwall, and their walls inclose 200 acres. Persons desirous of visiting them may either take the railway to Blackwall, and then a steamboat to the docks, or go down by the North Woolwich line, which has a station at the docks. Graving docks in connection with the Victoria docks were added 1856-8, at a cost of £116,000, furnished by a distinct company.

CHAPTER THE TWENTY-FIRST.

The Courts of Law.

Civil Courts.

THE law of England is divided, for the benefit of the lawyers, into two great branches, the Common Law and Equity, each with its own rules, modes of procedure, and judges. The only persons who have the right of speaking in these courts on behalf of clients are barristers, gentlemen who have been called to the bar by one of the four INNS OF COURT, and from them the judges are selected, on the occurrence of vacancies, by the ministry of the day. These persons appear in court in black gowns and gray wigs. Of barristers there are three grades; viz. 1. *Serjeants-at-law*, gentlemen who, after having been a certain number of years at the bar, have induced the Lord Chancellor to advance them to this dignity. As this step is a costly one, and as the serjeants have no longer exclusive audience in the Court of Common Pleas, their numbers are becoming small. They are always addressed as " Mr. Serjeant ——," and are to be known in court by the black patch on the crown of the wig, and by the judges always styling them " brother," in consequence of the occupants of the bench being invariably made serjeants when they take their seats, if they were not of this dignity previously. On the appointment of a serjeant, it is the custom for him to distribute gold rings, with an appropriate motto, to the Sovereign, the Lord Chancellor, the Judges, and others. 2. *Queen's Counsel*, who wear silk gowns, and have seats *within* the bar. The Chancellor has the privilege of making queen's counsel of barristers after a certain number of years. The dignity has no salary attached to it, and involves the inability of supporting a client against the crown without permission to do so, which permission, however, is invariably given on application. Queen's counsel have precedence over their seniors at the bar who have not arrived at this rank, and they are entitled by the etiquette of the profession to higher fees. 3. *Barristers* below the bar, who wear stuff gowns. The judges are taken indiscriminately from the three ranks, though it is rarely that a stuff gown is elevated to the bench. The Attorney and Solicitor-General, officers appointed by the Crown as its representatives, are considered the chiefs of the bar in the common law and equity courts respectively. They have seats in Parliament, and are the official legal advisers of the Government. The remuneration they receive in the shape of fees is very large, the income of the Attorney-General from his whole business, public and private, averaging £20,000 a-year. On the occurrence of a vacancy on the bench, the offer of the place is always made to them in the first instance, but the Attorney-General will only accept the highest prizes of the profession.

The chief administrator of equity law is the Lord Chancellor, who is assisted by the Master of the Rolls and three Vice-Chancellors, each of whom has a separate court. From their decision an appeal lies to the two Lords Justices, who sit together, and their judgments may be reviewed by the Lord Chancellor, who now-a-days seldom or never hears cases except in the way of appeal. Lastly, the ultimate court of appeal is the House of Lords. The whole house nominally hears and decides the appeal, but in point of fact the Law Lords (*i. e.*, such peers as have been lawyers) decide the case.

The Chancellorship is a place of great dignity. The holder of it, though usually only a baron, ranks next after the royal family and before every other peer of the realm. He is speaker of the upper house of Parliament, where he sits on a particular seat called " the woolsack." He receives his appointment by delivery to him, by the hands of the sovereign, of the Great Seal of England, of which he is the custodian. This seal, placed in an embroidered bag, is deposited, along with the silver-gilt mace, upon the table when he takes his seat in court or in the House of Lords. This seal consists of two dies six inches across, one of which is engraved with the figure of the sovereign on the throne, the other with her figure on horseback. The mode of using the seal is to close the dies, placing between them the ribbon or slip of parchment intended to receive the seal. The wax is poured in through a channel left for the purpose. On the death of the sovereign the old seal is cut into pieces, which are deposited in the tower, and a new seal is prepared.

The Mastership of the Rolls is an office of ancient date. The holder, besides being an equity judge, is the *custos rotulorum* of the realm, and the new Record Office has accordingly been built on the Rolls Estate in Chancery Lane. During term all the equity judges sit in courts at Westminster ; in vacation they sit in courts at Lincoln's Inn, except the Master of the Rolls, who sits in his own court in Chancery Lane.

There are three superior courts of common law, the Queen's Bench, the Common Pleas, and the Exchequer, all of which date from a very ancient period. The bulk of the business is of the same general nature in all, but the Queen's Bench has exclusive jurisdiction in criminal cases which belong to the *crown side* of the court, whilst civil business is taken on the *plea side ;* and the Exchequer has exclusive jurisdiction in revenue cases. There are five judges in each of these courts, all of whom, though only knights, are styled " My Lord." The chiefs of the Queen's Bench and the Common Pleas are styled " Lord Chief Justice," the junior or puisne judges, " Mr. Justice." The head of the Court of Exchequer is styled " Lord Chief Baron," and the puisne judges, " Mr. Baron." The courts in which these judges and the equity judges sit, are on the right hand side of Westminster Hall ; they were built from Soane's designs, and are so inconveniently small that new courts have been long talked of.

Appeals from the decisions of any one of these courts lie to the Court of Exchequer Chamber, which is constituted of the judges of the other two courts ; and from the Court of Exchequer Chamber the appeal is to the House of Lords.

The Court of Probate and the Court of Divorce were constituted in 1857, and are presided over by the same judge. In the former, questions relating to the proof of wills are decided ; in the latter, where, we are sorry to say, the business is large, applications for the dissolution of the marriage tie are heard. Previous to the constitution of this court the only mode of obtaining a divorce *a vinculo matrimonii,* was through the House of Lords, and the proceeding was so expensive that only very rich people could avail themselves of it.

Appeals from the Indian and Colonial Courts, and from the Maritime and Ecclesiastical Courts, lie to the Queen in Council, and are heard before the *Judicial Committee of the Privy Council*, sitting at the Privy Council Office, Whitehall. This committee consists of persons filling or who have filled the office of judge in some other court.

THE COUNTY COURTS, constituted under a modern Act of Parliament, are minor courts distributed over England under the presidency of judges who are appointed by the Lord Chancellor from amongst the barristers, for deciding cases where the debt or demand does not exceed £50 ; and of these there are eleven in the metropolis.

CRIMINAL COURTS.

THE CENTRAL CRIMINAL COURT in the Old Bailey was established in 1834 for the trial of offences committed in the metropolis and certain parts of the adjoining counties. The Sessions take place twelve times a year before two of the common law judges. The lighter charges are disposed of by the recorder and common serjeant, officers of the corporation.

THE SESSIONS HOUSE, Clerkenwell Green (now only a paved roadway), is the building where the magistrates for the county of Middlesex hold their quarterly sessions with the aid of the assistant judge. It was built in 1780, and refronted with Portland stone in 1860. One of the rooms contains a carved oak chimney-piece brought from Hicks' Hall, and bearing an inscription recording the gift of it in 1612 by Sir Baptist Hicks, a city mercer, afterwards Viscount Campden, who in that year presented to the justices and their successors for ever, for their meetings, a house which he had erected for that purpose in the neighbouring St. John Street. This building received the name of Hicks' Hall, and was a noted landmark from which distances were measured. There are milestones still remaining inscribed with the number of miles " from the spot where Hicks' Hall formerly stood."

CHAPTER THE TWENTY-SECOND.

INNS OF COURT.

Lincoln's Inn—The Inner Temple—Gardens—Church—The Middle Temple—Old Hall—New Library—Gray's Inn—Minor Inns.

THE INNS OF COURT comprise the four honourable societies of Lincoln's Inn, the Inner Temple, the Middle Temple, and Gray's Inn. Their common designation is derived from the fact of their having been at one time held in court of the king's palace. Each society is governed by Benchers, the principal of whom is the treasurer, who is annually elected from amongst the benchers. By them alone is the privilege of calling to the bar exercised. Before a student can be called, he must dine a certain number of days in each term in the hall of the society to which he belongs. When he has "kept" twelve terms (*i.e.*, eaten his commons in the hall along with his brother students), and has attended a year's lectures, he is eligible to be called to the bar, if he has arrived at the age of twenty-one. The barristers, members of these inns, are upwards of 3000 in number. Beyond compelling a student to attend the lectures of two of the five readers for a year, and offering prizes to those who most distinguished themselves at the non-compulsory examinations, the Inns of Court do nothing to further the legal education of students. It would not be amiss, if some other portion of their vast revenues were devoted to this end. The chief part of a student's learning is obtained in the chambers of some practising barrister.

Ben Jonson dedicated his drama of "Every Man out of his Humour," to the "noblest nurseries of humanity and liberty in the kingdom, the Inns of Court." In the dedication he says, he looks upon the members of the Inns "as being born the judges of these studies" (*i.e.*, dramatic literature); and he boasts of his friendship with divers in those societies. In those days, the lawyers formed a considerable portion of the auditors who as-

S

sembled in theatres, and hence it was worth the while of play-
writers to conciliate their good will by frequent allusions to
matters connected with the law.   In Shakspere we find a great
number of legal phrases which are introduced with such techni-
cal accuracy, as to have led some persons to suppose that he had
spent part of his youth in an attorney's office.

LINCOLN'S INN is situate on the west side of Chancery Lane,
and is called after De Lacy, Earl of Lincoln (d. 1312), who had
a house and garden here, and whose device, a lion rampant, has
been adopted by the Inn.   The great gate-house in Chancery Lane
was built in 1518.   The *Old Hall* was rebuilt in 1506, on the
site of an ancient hall.   It is about 71 feet long, 32 feet broad,
and about the same height.   At one end is a screen put up in
1565, and curiously carved, a hundred years later, with the
achievements of Charles II., and some of his lords.   The ceiling
is a modern disfigurement.   This hall is no longer used as a
dining room since the completion of the new buildings, of which
the society may well be proud.   These were erected in 1843-5,
from the designs of P. Hardwick, in the late Tudor style, and are
well seen from all sides.   The *Hall* is 120 feet in length, and
45 feet in width.   The windows are filled with stained glass,
enriched with arms and mottoes.   In canopied niches are life-size
figures of several eminent members.   The roof of oak is handsome, and the entire effect of the interior very striking.   Here is
Hogarth's picture of Paul before Felix, curiously characteristic of
the painter.   On the upper part of the north wall is a large
fresco painting, 45 feet wide, by 40 high, representing in 30
figures the early lawgivers, from Moses down to Edward I.   It
was the gratuitous work of Mr. G. F. Watts, and was completed
in 1860.   In the drawing room are many portraits.   The *Library*,
80 feet long, 40 feet wide, and 44 feet high, has an open oak
roof, with a collection of upwards of 20,000 volumes, and many
valuable MSS., chiefly bequeathed to the society by Sir Matthew
Hale.   The library was founded in 1497, and dates from an
earlier period than that of any other library in London.   Some
of the books retain the iron rings by which they were secured to
the shelves.   Other books are in their original oak bindings.
For a single odd volume of Prynne's Records, the society gave
£335 at the Stowe sale.   The new hall and library were inaugurated in 1845 by the Queen and Prince Consort, who were
entertained at a banquet given by the benchers.   The Prince was

made a bencher of the Inn. The society counts amongst its eminent members, Sir Thomas More, Sir Matthew Hale, John Selden, and Lords Mansfield and Hardwicke. The extent of the *Garden* was much diminished by the erection of the new buildings, and " the walks under the elms," spoken of by Ben Jonson, have disappeared. Rare Ben is said to have worked as a bricklayer at some of the old buildings here, holding a trowel in his hand, and having a book in his pocket. The pile on the east of the garden is occupied as chambers, and is known as Stone Buildings. The *Chapel* was built in 1621-3, by Inigo Jones, the first stone having been laid by Dr. Donne, who preached the consecration sermon. There is an open cloister under the chapel, where in former times lawyers met their clients, but it is now inclosed by an iron railing, and is used as a place of interment for the benchers. The chapel bell is said to have been brought from Cadiz by the Earl of Essex, about 1596. The oaken seats date from the time of James I. On the ascent to the chapel will be seen a marble tablet to the memory of Lord Brougham's only child, with an inscription written by the Marquis Wellesley. The preachership is considered a high appointment, and has been held by Donne, Usher, Tillotson, Warburton, Hurd, and other eminent men. The equity judges sit here in vacation in courts provided for them, in place of sitting at Westminster.

NEW SQUARE and LINCOLN'S INN FIELDS form no part of the Inn, which is an extra-parochial district. ˙ The houses around the former entirely, and those around the latter in great part, are used as chambers by lawyers.

THE TEMPLE is a district lying between Fleet Street and the Thames, and divided by Middle Temple Lane into the Inner and Middle Temple, belonging to separate societies, each with its hall, library, and garden. The Outer Temple no longer exists. The name is derived from the Knight Templars, who removed hither from Holborn in 1184. The Knights Hospitallers of St. John of Jerusalem, to whom the forfeited property of their rival brotherhood was granted by the Pope, demised it to certain law students who wished to live in the suburbs, out of the noise of the city. In the sixth year of James I., royal letters patent granted the Temples to the Chancellor of the Exchequer and other persons, whence originated the incorporated society of the " Students and Practisers of the Laws of England ; " in whom the property is now vested. The two Temples are separated by a wall from the rest of the city, and have entrance gates, which are locked at night. The district is extra-parochial, being exempt from the operations of the poor law, and maintaining their own poor.

In a by-gone age the gentlemen of these societies were famous for the masques, revels, and banquets which they gave in their halls. To these entertainments their are many allusions in the old poets. Kings have attended them ; the benchers joined in them, and directed the students to dance, as the exercise made them more fit for their books at other times. Nay, on one occasion at Lincoln's Inn, the under barristers were put out of commons, because they had not danced on a day when the judges were present! In the hall of the Inner Temple, in 1733, a play and farce were acted, songs were sung, and dancing took place. Of these doings the only relics are on what are called Grand Days, when the judges dine in hall with the benchers. The Inner Temple has for its device a winged horse, the Middle Temple a lamb. These devices (the latter derived from the old Templars) called forth some satirical verses :

> Their clients may infer from thence
> How just is their profession ;
> The lamb sets forth their innocence,
> The horse their expedition !

THE INNER TEMPLE. Passing through the archway, built in the time of James I., into Inner Temple Lane, a new pile of chambers will be seen on the right. These have been erected on the site of a set, in one of which Dr. Johnson lived for five years, and the new pile is now called after him, Dr. Johnson's Buildings. We then arrive at the western doorway of the Temple Church ; and beyond are cloisters built by Wren, after the fire of 1678, for the students to walk in and discuss law points. On a broad terrace facing the garden is the library (where an autograph manuscript of Lord Bacon is preserved), and adjacent to it is the hall, both of which are of modern date. In the latter are portraits of those pillars of the law, Coke and Littleton, who were members of this Inn, as well as Selden, the poets Beaumont and Cowper, with many chancellors and judges. The *Garden* is a quadrangular piece of ground, about three acres in extent, prettily laid out, and looking very ornamental from the river. It is hemmed in between piles of chambers, and is noted for its autumnal show of chrysanthemums. The public are admitted on summer evenings between six and nine, and strangers may like to avail themselves of this permission to walk in a spot whence originated (according to Shakspere, 1st part of Henry VI., act ii., sc. 4) the Wars of the Roses. At 5 King's Bench Walk, Lord Mansfield ("How sweet an Ovid Murray was our boast"—*Pope*) had chambers when practising at the bar.

THE TEMPLE CHURCH. This highly interesting edifice belongs to the two Temples. The members of the Inner Temple occupy the southern half, and those of the Middle Temple the northern half, as indicated by their devices. The porter at the top of Inner Temple Lane has the keys, and strangers may easily procure admission should the church not be open. The plan of the Church of the Holy Sepulchre at Jerusalem has been copied to the extent of combining a rotunda with an edifice of rectangular form. The entrance doorway is fine. The round part remains as it was built in 1185 (saving that externally it has been refaced with stone), but the remaining portion replaced one previously built, and was dedicated to St. Mary in 1240. The *Round Church*, 58 feet in diameter, is said to afford one of the earliest examples in this island of pointed arches, which are still intermingled with round arches. The clerestory is pierced by six Romanesque windows over interlaced Norman arches. The vaulting is supported by six clustered pillars of Purbeck marble, having boldly sculptured capitals. On the floor are two groups of monumental effigies, cross-legged knight-templars, whose names are uncertain. A figure between two columns on the south-east is said to represent William Mareschall, Earl of Pembroke, the Protector *temp.* Henry III. In former times the lawyers waited for clients in this part of the church, as a merchant now-a-days meets his customers on 'Change, and there is a passage in Hudibras referring to them walking " the round about the cross-legged knights." Notice the prismatic or ridge-like coffin-stone of the twelfth century. Such cope stones, *en dos d'asne*, are not very common. The *Rectangular Church*, or choir, is in the Early English style. It is 82 feet by 58 feet, with a height of 60 feet. The roof is painted with arabesques ; triple lancet-headed windows admit light. The great east window is ornamented with modern stained glass ; the altar, choir-stalls, and benches, are all new. The hymn of St. Ambrose is inscribed on the wall, beneath the windows. Left of the altar is Selden's white marble monument ; his remains are below. On the south side of the church is the effigy of a bishop in pontificals ; and in the south-west angle is a bust of the "judicious" Hooker, who was master of the Temple. In a recess under the organ-gallery is a tablet, recording that Oliver Goldsmith lies interred in the burial-ground outside. The organ was built by one Schmydt, after a competition with another builder, which Judge Jeffries was called on to decide. In the north-west angle of the choir is a well-staircase, leading past what has been called a penitential cell to the Triforium, where monuments, formerly scattered about the church, have been collected. The most noticeable of these are the memorials of Plowden the jurist ; Anne Littleton, with a quaint epitaph ; Howell, the old letter-writer ; and an ancestor of Gibbon the historian. Here is a bust of Lord Chancellor Thurlow. The walls are inscribed with texts from the Latin Scriptures. In 1839-42, £70,000 were laid out in restorations. The preacher at this church is termed the Master of the Temple, formerly an office of more consideration than at present. His house is north-east of the choir, and has a small garden attached to it.

THE MIDDLE TEMPLE is entered from Fleet Street through a gateway built by Wren. The *Hall* was built 1562-72, but since that time it has been refaced and has had external additions. It is 100 feet long, 40 feet wide, and 47 feet high. The roof is of open timber, and is without the principal arched rib. By increasing the pendants and smaller curves a handsome effect has been obtained. At the lower end is a carved Renaissance screen and Muric gallery. The side-windows are emblazoned with arms of eminent members, on the dais are marble busts of the brothers Lord Eldon and Stowell (members of the Inn), and on the wall hang some royal portraits, including a large equestrian portrait of Charles I. by Vandyke. The benchers dine at the table on the dais, the barristers and students at the tables on the floor. *This hall is the only edifice now standing in which a play of Shakspere was acted in the poet's lifetime.* The play was Twelfth Night. This Inn boasts of having had amongst its members Sir Walter Raleigh, John Ford the dramatist, Wycherley, Congreve, Blackstone, Dunning, Burke, Sheridan, and Lords Chancellor Clarendon, Somers, and Eldon.

A fountain of elegant design has lately been erected at the top of the steps leading to the Middle Temple Garden, in place of an old single jet fountain.

THE LIBRARY, a recently erected Gothic structure in the perpendicular style, is best seen from the river, and is a conspicuous object amongst dingy hall and chambers, standing at one side of the small garden. It has a high steep roof, a tower, and a number of grotesque gargoyles. The library room measures 85 feet by 42 feet, and has a height of 63½ feet. It is illuminated with 14 windows filled with stained glass blazoned with heraldic devices. The roof is of open timber work, the principal ribs of which rest on massive stone corbels. The books here are nearly 30,000 in number. This library, the building of which cost about £14,000, was opened by the Prince of Wales in November 1861, on which occasion his Royal Highness was made a bencher, and a grand banquet took place in the noble old hall.

Goldsmith had chambers on the second floor of No. 2 Brick Court (a pile pulled down within the last few months), over chambers occupied by Blackstone, then writing his famous commentaries. "I have been many a time in Goldsmith's chambers (says Thackeray), and passed up the staircase which Johnson and Burke and Reynolds trod to see their friend, their poet, their kind Goldsmith—the stair on which the poor women sat weeping bitterly when they heard that the greatest and most generous of all men was dead within the black oak door."

"I was born," says Charles Lamb in his delightful essay on The Old Benchers of the Inner Temple, "I was born, and passed the first seven years of my life in the Temple. Its church, its halls, its gardens, its fountain, its river, I had almost said—for in those young years, what was this king of rivers to me but a stream that watered our pleasant places?—these are my oldest recollections. I repeat, to this day, no verses to myself more frequently, or with kindlier emotion, than those of Spenser where he speaks of this spot :—

'There when they came whereas those bricky towers,
The which on Themmes brode aged back do ride,
Where now the studious lawyers have their bowers,
There whylome wont the Templer knights to bide
Till they decayed through pride.'

Indeed it is the most elegant spot in the metropolis. What a transition for a countryman visiting London for the first time— the passing from the crowded Strand or Fleet Street, by unexpected avenues, into its magnificent ample squares, its classic green recesses ! What a cheerful, liberal look hath that portion of it, which from three sides overlooks the greater garden ; that goodly pile ' of building strong, albeit of paper hight,' confronting with massy contrast the lighter, older, more fantastically shrouded one named of Harcourt ! What a collegiate aspect has that fine Elizabethan hall ! What an antique air had the sundials with their moral inscriptions seeming coevals with that time which they measured !"

GRAY'S INN stands on the north side of Holborn and abuts on Gray's Inn Lane. It derives its name from the family of Gray of Wilton, to whom the property formerly belonged. It came into the possession of " certain students of the law" in the 16th century. The chief entrance is from Holborn, by a gateway of brickwork erected in 1592. There are two squares with chambers around them, divided from each other by the hall, chapel, and library, the last erected in 1861. The hall was finished in 1560. The open roof is of oak, and the windows are emblazoned with arms. The garden was first laid out when Francis Bacon was treasurer, and in Charles II.'s time they were a fashionable place of promenade. Here is a catalpa tree, cuttings of which are much sought after, for it is traditionally asserted that it was raised from a tree planted by Lord Bacon. Chief Justice Holt, Lord Burghley, and Sir Samuel Romilly, were members of this Inn ; and Bradshaw, who presided at the time of Charles I., was a bencher. But the most eminent name connected with the Inn is that of Lord Bacon, who was a bencher and reader. His celebrated essays are dated from "my chamber at Graie's Inn." After his disgrace he returned to his old chambers, and was residing here at the time of his death, which, however, took place at Highgate. His chambers are thought to be no longer in existence.

In addition to the four principal Inns there are several minor Inns nominally attached to the others. They are scattered about in the neighbourhood of the parent Inns, and some of them are quaint places with halls. It will be recollected that Justice Shallow was once of *Clement's Inn* (a dependency of the Inner Temple), where Falstaff remembered him " like a man made after supper of a cheese-paring." In *Staple Inn*, Holborn, a dependency of Gray's Inn, Dr. Johnson wrote his *Idler* in 1759. *Serjeant's Inn*, Chancery Lane, is the Inn of the serjeants, of whom mention has already been made.

CHAPTER THE TWENTY-THIRD.

CRIMINAL PRISONS.

Bridewell — Holloway Prison — Coldbath Fields Prison — Middlesex
House of Detention — Millbank Prison — Newgate — Pentonville
Prison — Debtors' Prisons.

THE FLEET PRISON, in Farringdon Street, and the COMPTER,
Giltspur Street, have been pulled down. There remain for
notice the following places of incarceration.

CRIMINAL PRISONS.

BRIDEWELL HOSPITAL, in Bridge Street, Blackfriars, is marked
by a bust of Edward VI. over the entrance. It stands on the
site of an ancient royal palace, which site was granted by Edward
VI. to the city as a workhouse and house of correction. To
this use it was applied for many years, but it is now unoccupied.
There is a hall 85 feet long by 30 feet wide, and over the
chimney-piece is a picture attributed to Holbein, but spoiled by
being painted over, if really his, representing King Edward
handing the endowment charter to the mayor. The room contains a full-length of Charles II. by Lely ; of George III. and his
Queen by Reynolds, as well as portraits of several presidents of
the institution. Hogarth laid in Bridewell the scene of the
fourth plate of the Harlot's Progress. The name Bridewell,
which has been transferred to other prisons, is derived from the
parish in which it is situate.

THE CITY PRISON, Holloway, was opened in 1852, having
been built by the city at a cost of £100,000. The walls
include a space of ten acres. Mr. Bunning designed the prison,
which, by its castellated style, resembles a fortress. It contains
436 cells, which are disposed in six radiating wings.

COLDBATH FIELDS' PRISON, between Gray's Inn Road and
Bagnigge Wells Road, covers nine acres of ground, and will hold
1500 prisoners. It is the prison for Middlesex.

THE FLEET PRISON, infamous for nearly 800 years, was abolished by Act of Parliament, and the corporation bought it from the Government for £25,000. It stood on the east side of Farringdon Street, where the vacant site may still be seen, for it was pulled down in 1846, and the materials sold. It derived its name from the river Fleet, which ran hard by, and is at this day hidden under the pavement of Farringdon Street.

HORSEMONGER LANE GAOL, Newington Causeway, is the prison for the County of Surrey. It was built 1791-9, upon the plan of John Howard, and has accommodation for 400 prisoners. Colonel Despard, the Mannings, and other criminals, have been hanged here. Leigh Hunt was imprisoned for two years for libellously styling the Prince Regent an Adonis of fifty, and here Lord Byron made his acquaintance.

MIDDLESEX HOUSE OF DETENTION, Clerkenwell, erected in 1846, with 286 cells, to receive prisoners detained for trial.

MILLBANK PRISON, a very large structure near Vauxhall Bridge, Westminster, built on the plan devised by Jeremy Bentham, who had described something like it in his work on prison discipline, entitled the " Panopticon, or the Inspection House." But Bentham's plan, if properly carried out, would have cost about £30,000 for 1000 prisoners, whereas this building cost about £500,000—about £500 for each cell. Six lines of building radiate from a centre, where the governor's house is placed. The average number of persons confined in this, the largest prison in London, is about 700, but there is accommodation for 1200. The outer walls enclose sixteen acres, seven of which are covered with buildings. The corridors are said to be more than three miles in length, and the staircases almost as long. Convicts sentenced to transportation are lodged here until they are removed out of the country. For permission to inspect the prison, apply to the Home Secretary of State ; or to the Directors of Convict Prisoners, 45 Parliament Street, Westminster.

NEWGATE, in the Old Bailey, has become a celebrated name in the annals of crime. Its name originated from the first prison on the site having been adjacent to the then latest built of the city gates. Here are confined persons who have been guilty of offences on the high seas ; those upon whom sentence of death has been passed ; and persons who are awaiting trial at the Central Criminal Court in the Old Bailey. In the old prison. many persons who have made figures in history or literature have been confined. George Wither, the poetical Earl of Dorset, William Penn, Titus Oates, Defoe, Dr. Dodd, and Jack Sheppard, were imprisoned in Newgate. The present building, which has received commendation for its appropriate style of architecture, was commenced in 1770 from the designs of George Dance. In 1780, when still unfinished, it was set on fire by Lord George Gordon's rioters, and 300 prisoners set free from the inhabited portion. In 1782 it was repaired and completed. Soon afterwards the sentence of hanging was carried out in front of it, instead of at Tyburn. John Howard was opposed to the plan of the prison, and it is now seen to be utterly unfit for the purposes of a jail, except that of securing the persons of its inmates. Fevers have often raged within its walls, from the want of ventilation and the small space. Lord George Gordon died here in 1793 of fever, after several years' imprisonment. About 2500 persons are committed to this place in the course of a year. To inspect the prison, apply to the Home Secretary of State, the Lord Mayor, or the sheriffs. Next to the prison stands the Sessions' House, mentioned in another part of this volume.

PENTONVILLE PRISON, frequently called the Model Prison, stands in the Caledonian Road, Islington, not far from the New Cattle Market. It contains 1000 cells, and was erected, 1840-42, at a cost of £85,000. Nearly seven acres are enclosed by the wall. The system of management is a modification of the silent and solitary systems. In plan, five wings radiate from a central hall, and a lofty clock tower rises from the main building. The cells are each 13 feet long, 17 feet wide, and 9 feet high. The prisoners are made to work at various handicrafts—tailoring, shoemaking, weaving, etc. ; and the cultivation of their minds is attended to. A library of 2000 volumes is placed at their use. Everything is kept in admirable order, and the place well deserves the inspection of those who take an interest in such things. For permission to see it, apply to the Directors of Convict Prisons, 45 Parliament Street, Westminster, or to a visiting magistrate.

DEBTORS' PRISONS.

Of these there are only two in the metropolis—The QUEEN'S PRISON, Borough Road, Southwark, and the DEBTORS' PRISON, in Whitecross Street, Cripplegate.

CHAPTER THE TWENTY-FOURTH.

CHARITABLE INSTITUTIONS, HOSPITALS, ETC.

Chelsea Hospital—Foundling Hospital—General Hospitals for Diseases
—St. Bartholomew's — St. Thomas'—University College—West-
minster—Charing Cross—Great Northern — St. George's —Guy's
—King's College—St. Mary's—Middlesex—Royal Free Hospital
—Hospitals for Special Diseases—Bethlehem Hospital—Cancer
Hospital—Consumption Hospitals—Fever Hospital—St. Luke's—
Ophthalmic—Orthopædic—Small Pox—Spinal Hospitals.

CHELSEA HOSPITAL.—Open daily from 10 to 4 ; it is usual to
pay a small gratuity to the pensioner who conducts visitors
round.

This hospital, for the reception of old and disabled soldiers,
occupies the site of a college commenced in James I.'s reign, for
the purpose of maintaining a body of clergy who were " to answer
all the adversaries of religion," and hence Laud nicknamed it
Controversy College. That scheme fell through, and in the reign
of Charles II. the present establishment was founded. Nell
Gwynne it is said used her influence to effect this laudable work.
Sir Christopher Wren was the architect. Charles himself laid
the first stone, and the buildings were finished in 1690, the cost
having been £150,000. They are of red brick with stone dress-
ings, shewing towards the Thames a recessed centre and two
wings. The centre forms a square, open towards the river, and a
bronze statue of Charles II., executed by Grinling Gibbons for
Tobias Rustat, occupies the middle. The north front is long, and
has before it an avenue of limes and horse-chestnuts. The Roman-
Doric portico in this front is four columned. Between the two
fronts are two spacious quadrangles. The wards of the pensioners
are on the wings of the river front; and the governor's residence
is at the end of the eastern wing. The state apartment contains
portraits of Charles I., Henrietta Maria, and the two sons who

succeeded him, of Charles II., William III., and George III., and
his queen.   In the chapel is an altar-piece of the Ascension,
painted by Seb. Ricci ; the communion plate was given by James
II.   Here are thirteen French eagles, and many colours taken by
our armies.   In the great dining hall is an equestrian portrait of
Charles II. by Verrio and H. Cooke, and an allegorical picture of
the Duke of Wellington's victories by James Ward.   Here are
more colours captured by our armies in various campaigns, and
some staves of the colours won at Blenheim.   The Duke of
Wellington's body lay in state in the hall.   The establishment is
managed by a board of commissioners and a governor, under
whom are subordinate officers.   The resident pensioners are from
400 to 500 in number, and the cost of their maintenance is
about £36 a year for each man.   Several of them will be seen
about Chelsea wearing their hospital costume, a long red coat
lined with blue, and a three-cornered hat.   There are besides
about 70,000 out-pensioners who receive money at various rates,
chiefly from sixpence to a shilling a day, though some have as
much as three shillings and sixpence a day.

THE ROYAL MILITARY ASYLUM, where the children of soldiers
are supported and educated, is to the north of the hospital.
Friday is parade day for the boys.

Near Chelsea Hospital, and on the north-eastern side of the
road leading to Battersea Park Bridge, new and handsome barracks for 1000 men of the Guards have recently been erected.
These barracks are on an improved plan, and have been specially
designed by Mr. George Morgan, with a view to the comfort and
well-being of the soldiers.   They have a frontage of upwards of
1000 feet.   There is a detached building for the officers, and
one for the serjeants ; a separate house for the married privates,
well ventilated quarters for privates, schools, baths, washhouses,
reading room and library, lecture room, gymnasium, etc.

THE FOUNDLING HOSPITAL, Guildford Street, bears an incor-
rect name, for it is a place for the maintenance of illegitimate
children, whose mothers are known.   When originally established
in 1739 by Thomas Coram, it was intended for the reception of
exposed and deserted children.   So numerous were the children
sent hither, and so indiscriminate the admission, that far more
infants were received than could be properly attended to.   Out
of 14,934 received in three years and ten months, 10,389 died.
Such wholesale slaughter called for the interference of the legis-

lature, and in 1760 the establishment was placed nearly on its present footing. The site of the hospital was purchased for £5500 in 1741 from Lord Salisbury, who compelled them to buy the whole estate, refusing to sell a part only. It is fortunate they did so, as the rents now produce every year more than the original purchase-money. The building, erected from Jacobson's designs, was opened in 1754. Hogarth was an intimate friend of Coram, painted his portrait, and helped him in carrying out his design. He has recorded that he painted this portrait with more pleasure than any other man's. The painter became a governor and guardian, and presented not only the portrait of Coram, but others of his portraits, viz., the march to Finchley (one of his best works), and Moses brought to Pharaoh's daughter. There are other paintings worth notice, viz., Handel by Kneller, Dr. Mead by Allan Ramsay, Lord Dartmouth by Sir Joshua Reynolds, George II. by Shackleton, views of the Foundling and Guy's Hospitals by Richard Wilson, and the Charter-house by Gainsborough. Here will be seen Roubiliac's bust of Handel, who was a great benefactor to the hospital. He frequently performed his "Messiah" on the organ in the chapel. The musical performance of divine service has always been a source of revenue, as a collection is made at the door, and the good singing attracts a large number of persons. The altar-piece, Christ presenting a little child, is by West. After service visitors may inspect the building; this may also be done on Mondays from ten to four. From three to four a band, formed of boys belonging to the establishment, executes pieces of music. It is an interesting sight to witness the children, of whom there are 500 of both sexes, in the act of dining. Coram lies in the chapel vaults, as well as Chief-Justice Tenterden, whose bust will be seen near the eastern entrance of the chapel. Preachers of celebrity are selected to deliver sermons here. Sterne preached in this chapel in 1761; Sydney Smith, another humourist, was also a preacher. The children are well cared for, and their general health is very good. At a proper age the boys are put out to trades, and the girls to service. The donation of £50 qualifies for a governor.

HOSPITALS FOR THE TREATMENT OF DISEASES.

No application of money is more to be commended than that which attempts to relieve the poor when suffering from disease or accidental injury. London may boast not only of having numerous institutions for this object, but of their magnificent scale. The twelve principal hospitals of the metropolis possess a permanent annual income of £110,000, exclusive of voluntary contributions. They have upwards of 3500 beds, and the out-patients attended to in the course of a year are not far short of 400,000. We have only space to mention the chief institutions of this nature, which the benevolence of the rich has founded for the relief of the needy ; but it may here be stated that, in addition to the hospitals about to be noticed, there are upwards of thirty dispensaries where medical assistance is afforded to applicants. The art of nursing has been much improved of late years. In the larger hospitals a " sister" takes charge of each ward, and sees that the nurses do their duty, besides exercising a vigilant superintendence over the patients themselves, the result of which is communicated to the medical officer.

General Hospitals.

St. Bartholomew's Hospital, Smithfield, occupies the site of part of the ancient priory of St. Bartholomew, whereon Rahere founded an hospital. At the Dissolution, Henry VIII. refounded it, and gave the charge of it to Thomas Vicary, his serjeant-surgeon, who wrote the first anatomical work published in English. Harvey was physician to the hospital for many years, and lectured in it on his discovery as to the circulation of the blood. The buildings having become much decayed were taken down, and the great quadrangle was built in 1730, the architect being Gibbs, who built St. Martin's-in-the-Fields. The entrance had been erected nearly thirty years previously. The new surgery was built in 1842, and the year after, a collegiate establishment for the abode of students within the walls was founded, and is placed under the superintendence of a warden. This hospital is under the management of the Corporation, and the president is an alderman who has served the office of Lord Mayor. Persons who present 100 guineas become governors. Dr. Radcliffe, Queen Anne's physician, gave a considerable sum towards the building ; he also bequeathed to the hospital £500 a year, to aid in improving the diet of patients, and in addition £100 a year to be laid out in linen. The income of the hospital is about £35,000 a-year. Cases of all kinds are treated at this hospital, and patients are admitted on presenting a formal petition. In urgent cases, such as accidents, the patients are admitted at once, either in the day or at night, the resident medical officers being on the spot to attend to such cases. There are 650 beds, and a large number of out-patients. The in-patients treated in the course of a year are between 6000 and 7000 ; whilst the out-patients during the same space amount to more than 70,000. Destitute patients are relieved from the " Samaritan fund." The annual expenditure in an establishment of this magnitude is of course very large ; about £2600 being laid out on drugs alone. With regard to the education of students, clinical lectures are delivered, and other lectures in the theatres on the various branches of medical science and art. Several scholarships have been founded with the view of encouraging and assisting students. Prizes are bestowed on those who best acquit themselves at the annual examinations. The library is large, and there are museums containing anatomical preparations and specimens of *materia medica.* In the great staircase are some pictures painted by Hogarth in the grand historical style. The work was gratuitous, and he was made a life-governor in return. In the court-room is an old portrait of Henry VIII. ; Dr. Radcliffe, by Kneller ; Percival Pott, by Reynolds ; and Abernethy, by Lawrence.

St. Thomas' Hospital, Wellington Street, Southwark, near the London Bridge railway stations, opened in 1552 ; rebuilt, 1701–6. Guy the bookseller, who founded the hospital that bears his name, built and furnished three wards of this hospital ; he also gave the large iron gate and the house on each side, which cost him £3000. In the first court is a bronze statue of Edward VI. by Scheemakers. The income of the hospital is about £25,000 a-year, and between 50,000 and 60,000 patients are annually treated. An arrangement has been made with the authorities of this hospital by the committee of the " Nightingale fund" for educating women as hospital nurses, who, on the satisfactory completion of 'one year's training, will be considered eligible to receive appointments as nurses in other hospitals. As shewing the value of land in this part, it may be mentioned that the hospital sold the site of two houses to the city at the rate of £70,000 an acre. This hospital has lately been sold to the Charing Cross Railway Company, which required part of the site, but was obliged to take the whole. It will be pulled down and

T

rebuilt elsewhere. The Governors claimed £750,000 as the value of the grounds, and as a compensation for purchasing land elsewhere, and for the expense of rebuilding. On reference to arbitration, the sum of £296,000 has been awarded to them.

UNIVERSITY COLLEGE HOSPITAL, Upper Gower Street, founded 1833, in connection with University College. The building is capable of containing 200 beds, but want of funds has hitherto limited the committee to a much less number. Relief is afforded to about 21,000 patients in the course of a year.

WESTMINSTER HOSPITAL, near the Abbey ; a handsome embattled building, in a style more suitable for a jail than a hospital. Messrs. Inwood were the architects. It has a frontage of 200 feet, and the windows amount to 260 in number. This hospital boasts of being the oldest subscription establishment of the kind in the Metropolis.

CHARING CROSS HOSPITAL, Agar Street, West Strand. This charitable institution was founded in 1818 ; the present buildings were erected in 1831. There is accommodation for about 100 in-patients ; and from 2000 to 3000 cases of accidents and dangerous emergency are annually relieved. A large number of out-patients are also attended to.

GREAT NORTHERN HOSPITAL, King's Cross.

ST. GEORGE'S HOSPITAL, Hyde Park Corner, was founded in 1733 ; rebuilt by Wilkins in 1831. It is supported by voluntary contributions. John Hunter was surgeon here ; he died, in the hospital, of disease of the heart in 1793. There are about 350 beds.

GUY'S HOSPITAL, Southwark, near the London Bridge Railway Stations, was founded by Thomas Guy, a bookseller, who by speculating in South Sea stock had accumulated a large fortune. The hospital was built from the designs of Dance in 1722–24, at a cost of £18,800, and he left for its endowment £219,500. Another benefactor, Mr. Hunt of Petersham, left £119,000 to the hospital, the income of which is now upwards of £25,000 a year. The management of the hospital is vested in governors, who are about sixty in number. There is a statue of Guy in brass in the front court ; another statue of him in marble by Bacon in the chapel, and a portrait of him by Dahl in the court-room. Sir Astley Cooper was interred in the chapel. Attached to the Hospital are lecturing and operating theatres, laboratories, a museum, library, etc.

KING'S COLLEGE HOSPITAL, Portugal Street, Lincoln's-Inn-Fields, has lately had an addition on an immense scale made to it. The wards are very spacious and airy, with excellent ventilation. This hospital was established in 1839 in connection with King's College.

LONDON HOSPITAL, Whitechapel Road ; instituted 1740, chiefly for seamen, watermen, and labourers on the river.

ST. MARY'S HOSPITAL, Cambridge Place, Paddington—opened 1850.

MIDDLESEX HOSPITAL, Charles Street, Berners Street ; established 1745. The nucleus of the present buildings was erected in Marylebone Fields in 1755, and great additions and improvements were made in 1848.

ROYAL FREE HOSPITAL, Gray's Inn Road, a very useful institution, where every patient that applies is admitted so long as there is room, without the necessity of producing a recommendation. It is supported by voluntary contributions, which amount to from £6000 to £7000 a year, and are the means of relieving 30,000 patients in the course of that time.

THE DREADNOUGHT HOSPITAL is a ship moored on the Thames near Greenwich, where sick and diseased seamen of all nations are received, and their cases attended to without requiring a recommendatory letter. Between 2000 and 3000 sailors are received on board in the year (about 200 being on board at one time), and from 1500 to 2000 out-patients receive attention. This hospital is supported by voluntary subscriptions, and several foreign potentates contribute. Visitors may inspect the ship daily, except on Sundays, between 11 and 3. The original Dreadnought, fitted up as an hospital in 1831, was engaged at Trafalgar, where she made capture of the Spanish three-decker the San Juan.

HOSPITALS FOR SPECIAL DISEASES.

BETHLEHEM (Bedlam) HOSPITAL, St. George's Fields, Lambeth, is a great establishment for the reception of lunatics. There was an hospital bearing this name, and applied to the same purpose, in Moorfields, as far back as 1402, the buildings having been a priory. Having become dilapidated, a new structure was erected in the neighbourhood in 1675, and this in turn falling into a bad condition, the site was exchanged for a much larger piece of ground in St. George's Fields. The present edifice was erected in 1812, at a cost of £122,500. Various additions have since been made, including a lofty dome. The building is three storeys high, and 897 feet long. It covers, with the offices and garden, eight acres of ground, and there is accommodation for nearly 400 patients. This institution is under the management of the governors and officers. The house is warmed by means of hot air and water. The system of treatment is admirable, the patients being allowed every possible indulgence. They are kept scrupulously clean, and are decently attired. Those who can work at any sedentary employment, are encouraged to do so. Both sexes have musical instruments, books, and writing materials. Billiard and bagatelle tables are supplied to the men, who play at cricket and other games in the grounds. Balls are occasionally given, as well as musical performances. Refractory patients are confined in cells lined with cork and indiarubber. Restraint is dispensed with as much as possible, which is quite the reverse of the old method of treatment of chains and straight-waistcoats. One division of the building is appropriated to criminal lunatics, who are supported by Government. They cost the country about £4000 a year, the rest of the establishment is maintained at an annual cost of about £20,000 a-year. A governor's order will admit visitors to see the hospital on Tuesdays and the three following days of the week. At *Hanwell*, 7½ miles from town on the Great Western Railway, is an asylum for the reception of 1000 pauper lunatics. At *Colney Hatch*, 6½ miles from London on the Great Northern Railway, is another asylum for pauper lunatics, where upwards of 1200 patients can be accommodated. About 118 acres are included by the walls. Here are 14 wards for men, 18 for women, a hall for exercise 112 feet long and 58 feet wide, a chapel to hold 600 persons, workshops, school-rooms, etc., the whole costing £200,000.

CANCER HOSPITAL, Brompton, a well-designed building of recent erection.

CONSUMPTION HOSPITAL, Fulham Road, Brompton, opened in 1846, and since enlarged. One-eighth of the entire mortality of the country ensues from chest-diseases. All classes of the community are attacked by these insidious diseases, and no specific has yet been discovered which does much more than mitigate the symptoms. The importance of hospitals where the several modes of treatment may be put to the test, and the several remedies administered under the most favourable circumstances to ascertain their real value, must be apparent, to say nothing of the benefit afforded to the afflicted poor. Machinery, actuated by a steam-engine, is employed to ventilate the building, which is warmed by hot water. The male and female patients are lodged on opposite sides of the hospital. Long corridors afford places for exercise during inclement weather. On the staircase is placed a bust of Madame Lind-Goldschmidt, who contributed £1606 to the Hospital funds.

THE CITY OF LONDON HOSPITAL FOR DISEASES OF THE CHEST, Victoria Park, founded in 1851, is another institution of the same nature.

THE FEVER HOSPITAL, Liverpool Road, Islington, instituted on another site in 1803, opened here in 1849, cost in its erection £19,500.

ST. LUKE'S, Old Street, City Road, another large establishment for lunatics. It was begun in 1782, Dance the younger being the architect, and the cost was £40,000, obtained by subscription. There is accommodation for 260 patients, but there is usually not more than 200 in the hospital at one time. The improved system of treatment adopted at Bethlehem Hospital is carried out here, and with the best results, kindness being substituted for harshness, and amusement for restraint.

OPHTHALMIC HOSPITALS are established in Calthorpe Street, Gray's Inn Road; in Blomfield Street, Moorfields; and in Chandos Street, Charing Cross, for the treatment of eye diseases and accidents. About 20,000 cases are treated annually in these hospitals.

ORTHOPÆDIC HOSPITAL, Oxford Street, established in 1838 for the treatment of clubfoot and spinal curvature. About 1400 cases are treated in the year. There is another hospital for the treatment of the same complaints in Hatton Garden.

SMALLPOX AND VACCINATION HOSPITAL, Highgate-Hill, a handsome building, erected in 1850 for the accommodation of 70 patients, at a cost of £20,000.

SPINAL HOSPITAL, Portland Road, Regent's Park, instituted in 1836. About 1400 cases come under treatment in a year.

CHAPTER THE TWENTY-FIFTH.

EDUCATIONAL ESTABLISHMENTS.

Charter-House—Christ's Hospital—Gresham College—King's College and School—Merchant Tailor's School—New College—St. Paul's School—Westminster School—University College—University of London.

THE CHARTER-HOUSE, Aldersgate Street, City, was founded in 1611 by Thomas Sutton, a wealthy London merchant, for the reception and support of 80 poor gentlemen, and for the free education of 40 poor boys. It has an income of about £29,000 a year. It is under the management of the Queen, and the Archbishops of Canterbury and York, and thirteen other governors. The master has a salary of £800 a year, besides a house within the walls, which inclose an area of upwards of thirteen acres. The name is a corruption of Chartreux, there having been a monastery of Carthusians founded on this site in 1371. Howghton, the last prior, and several of the monks, venturing to deny Henry VIII.'s supremacy, were executed at Tyburn in 1535. Their heads were planted on London Bridge, and the prior's mangled body was suspended over the monastery gate. After the suppression of religious houses it passed through several hands. Queen Elizabeth stayed here on two occasions, and James I., on his accession, kept his court and made 200 knights at the Charter-House, when it was in the possession of Lord Howard de Walden, from whom, when Earl of Suffolk, Sutton purchased it for £13,000. Sutton died in the year he bought it, and was buried in the chapel, where his handsome tomb is still to be seen. It was opened in 1842, and the body was found wrapped in lead. Not much of the old monastery remains. The Ante-Chapel and the Evidence Room above bear the date of 1512. The Great Chamber, or Old Governor's Room, was built, or at all events decorated, by the fourth Duke of Norfolk, father of the Earl of Suffolk before mentioned, and is thought to be the most perfect Elizabethan apartment in the metropolis. It was restored in 1838. Here are an elaborate chimney-piece of wood, and an ornamental ceiling. The walls are hung with tapestry. In the Great Hall notice the screen, music gallery, chimney-piece, and lantern in the roof. In the Governor's Room, in the Master's Lodge, are several portraits which deserve notice : Sutton, the founder, at the age of 79 ; Charles II. ; Shelden, Archbishop of Canterbury ; William, Earl of Craven, in armour ; George Villiers, second Duke of Buckingham ; James, Duke of Monmouth ; Lord Chancellor Shaftesbury ; Sheffield, Duke of Buckingham ; Talbot, Duke of Shrewsbury ; Lord Chancellor Somers ; and a very fine portrait, by Kneller, of Dr. Thomas Burnet, author of *Telluris Theoria Sacra*, and a master of the house.

The eighty pensioners live together in collegiate style, being furnished with good rooms, food, and £14 a year to buy clothing. They are nominated by the governors in rotation. The scholars on the foundation are 44 in number, and they are supported as well as educated without charge. They are nominated, like the pensioners, by the governors. Other boys are educated along with them, and the whole number is about 200. Amongst the eminent persons educated here may be mentioned : Crashaw the poet, Dr. Isaac Barrow, Sir William Blackstone, Addison, Sir Richard Steele, John Wesley, Lord Chief-Justice Ellenborough, Lord Liverpool the Prime Minister, Bishop Thirlwall, and George Grote, the historian of Greece.

Christ's Hospital, Newgate Street, City, is a noble establishment for the education of poor fatherless children, between 800 and 900 in number, founded on the site of the monastery of the Grey-Friars by Edward VI., in 1553, shortly before his death. A few arches, part of a cloister, are the only remains of the monastery ; and all the buildings of Edward and his sisters have been " restored." The great hall, seen through a double railing from Newgate Street, was erected 1825-9 from the designs of John Shaw. In the hall are a few portraits : Edward VI. granting the charter of incorporation to the hospital, sometimes attributed to Holbein ; James II. with his courtiers receiving the mathematical pupils at the annual presentation, by Verio, presented by him to the hospital ; the Queen and late Prince Consort, by F. Grant ; and some others. In the counting-house there is also a portrait of Edward VI., attributed to Holbein. This is often called the Blue Coat School, from the dress of the scholars, some of whom in their quaint ancient costume may frequently be seen in the streets. They wear a blue gown, and yellow stockings. The flat caps supplied to them are so small that they are seldom worn, the boys preferring to go about bare-headed. In 1672, Charles II. founded the mathematical school for 40 boys, called King's Boys. Twelve more have since been added, and all are distinguished by a badge on the shoulder. There are 17 wards or dormitories, to each of which a nurse and two or more monitors attend. Four boys are annually sent to the universities. On the Thursdays, between Quinquagesima Sunday and Good Friday, the public are admitted by tickets obtained from the governors to see the children sup in their great hall, a curious and interesting sight. On New Year's day, the king's boys are presented at Court ; on Easter Monday all the boys walk in procession to the Royal Exchange ; on Easter Tuesday they pay a visit to the Lord Mayor at the Mansion House ; and on St. Matthew's day, the 21st September, the head boys deliver orations in their hall before the Mayor, corporation, and governors. The hospital has an income of about £40,000 a-year ; and its management is vested in the governors. The president has always been an alderman, until the Duke of Cambridge was elected in 1854. The boys are admitted by presentations, of which the Lord Mayor has two annually ; the aldermen one each, and the other governors have a presentation once in three years. At the time of his admission, a boy must be between seven and nine years old. The younger children, about half of the whole number, are kept in a branch school at Hertford. Any one may qualify for a governor by paying £500 to the hospital. The school can reckon amongst its former pupils, Camden the historian, Richardson the novelist, S. T. Coleridge, Mitchell the translator of Aristophanes, Charles Lamb the author of the Essays of Elia, and Leigh Hunt.

GRESHAM COLLEGE, Basinghall Street, City, was founded by Sir Thomas Gresham, who gave certain property to the Corporation of London, and the Mercers' Company, upon trust that they should jointly name seven professors (viz., on astronomy, physic, law, divinity, rhetoric, and music) to lecture successively one on each day of the week, and to pay them each a yearly salary of £50. The lectures were first delivered in Gresham's mansion in

1597.   Afterwards a room in the Royal Exchange was used, but when that was last rebuilt the present edifice was erected in 1843 at a cost of £7000.   Over the portico Gresham's arms are sculptured between those of the City and the Mercers' Company.   It contains a large library, professors' rooms, and a theatre capable of holding 500 persons.   In this theatre the professors deliver their lectures, gratis to the public, during term time, daily (Sundays excepted), first in Latin ! at noon ; then in English at one in the afternoon ; those on geometry and music being delivered at seven P.M.   The professors' salaries are now £100 each.

KING'S COLLEGE AND SCHOOL are vested in a body of shareholders who, in 1828, subscribed £100 a-piece to found a place where boys might be educated in connection with the Established Church.   The buildings adjoin Somerset House, of which they may be considered the east wing.   Sir Robert Smirke was the architect.   The façade (north to south) is 304 feet in length. Two grand staircases ascend from the hall to the museum (where Mr. Babbage's first calculating machine is deposited) and library. In addition to the school, to which boys are admitted on the presentation of the proprietors from nine to sixteen years of age, there are four departments : 1, Theological ; 2, General Literature ; 3, Applied Sciences ; 4, Medical.   The great hospital in Portugal Street, Lincoln's-Inn-Fields, is in connection with the last.

MERCHANT TAILORS' SCHOOL, Suffolk Lane, City, was founded in 1561, by the Merchant Tailors' Company.   The school and head master's house, both of brick, were built in 1675, the old buildings having been destroyed in the great fire.   About 260 boys are educated here at a charge of £10 a year each, the company supplying the remaining funds.   Thirty-seven fellowships at St. John's College, Oxford, and several exhibitions at that university and at Cambridge, are prizes that make this an attractive place of education to city people.   Amongst the persons educated here were Shirley the dramatist, Titus Oates of infamous memory, and Lord Clive of Indian celebrity, with many bishops and writers on theology.

NEW COLLEGE, St. John's Wood, was erected 1850-1 by the Independent Dissenters for the education of their ministers. The building is a handsome structure of Bath stone, in the Tudor style, 270 feet long, with a central tower 80 feet high.   Here is a library of 22,000 volumes.

St. Paul's School is on the east side of St. Paul's Church-yard. It was founded in 1512 by Dr. John Colet, dean of the cathedral, for 153 children, the sons of poor men. The number was adopted from the number of fishes taken by St. Peter. The lands given by Colet for the maintenance of the school are now worth more than £5000 a year. The education is altogether classical. Lilly, the author of a well known Latin grammer, was the first master. Amongst the persons educated here were Leland the antiquary, John Milton, the first Duke of Marlborough, Halley the astromoner, and Samuel Pepys. Colet's school-house was destroyed by the great fire. The present building was erected in 1823.

Westminster School.—The chief buildings in connection with this ancient establishment are the school-house, with the library, the dormitory of the college, the college hall, and the boarding houses of the town boys.

The school stands in Little Dean's Yard, and is approached from Great Dean's Yard through a low worn Gothic arch of the thirteenth century, and a doorway attributed to Inigo Jones. It was formerly the dormitory of the monks of St. Peter's. The roof is of chestnut, and at the upper end there is a semicircular apse. On certain parts of the walls the boys of several genera-tions have carved or painted their names, interesting records when their owners have become afterwards famous. The dormi-tory of the college adjoins the entrance to the school. It is 161 feet long and 25 feet broad. Here the boys annually act a play of Terence in the presence of bishops and ladies. The college hall is 47 feet long by 27½ feet wide, and dates from the time of Edward III., when it was erected as a refectory. The tables are said to have been formed of wood taken out of some of the wrecked vessels of the Spanish Armada.

Amongst the eminent persons who have been educated at this school may be enumerated—Ben Jonson, Cowley, Dryden (whose name, until lately, was to be seen cut by his own hand in one of the benches), Locke, Wren, Warren Hastings, Cowper the poet, Gibbon, and Southey, with judges and bishops beyond number.

University College, Gower Street, was founded in 1828 by a number of subscribers "for the general advancement of litera-ture and science, by affording to young men adequate opportuni-ties for obtaining literary and scientific education at a moderate expense." Lord (then Henry) Brougham, Campbell the poet, and

Dr. Birkbeck, were the chief inaugurators, and the Duke of Sussex laid the first stone of the building, which was designed by W. Wilkins, but only the central portion has yet been erected. The principal feature is a Corinthian portico, so large that it dwarfs the dome behind. The building is 400 feet long. In the library is a marble statue of Locke. On the stairs is a statue of Flaxman the sculptor, the original models of whose principal works are placed in the hall under the cupola, amongst which notice the composition of St. Michael and Satan, and the Pastoral Apollo. There is no divinity chair, and consequently young Jews and Mahommedans who would not be admitted at King's College are usually amongst the pupils. There is a junior school, to which boys are not admitted after the age of 15. Corporal punishment forms no part of the discipline, the extreme penalty for misconduct being expulsion. The library contains 45,000 vols., including 10,000 vols. of Chinese books left by Dr. Morrison, and the collection of books on political economy bequeathed by David Ricardo. *University College Hospital* is over against the College, and is in connection with the medical school. Behind the college, in Gordon Square, is *University Hall*, erected in 1849, where theology and moral philosophy are taught.

THE UNIVERSITY OF LONDON consists of an examining body, with a chancellor, senate, and subordinate officers, and the graduates. It was instituted in 1836 for the purpose of rendering academical honours accessible without distinction to every class and denomination, and its place of assembling is Burlington House, Piccadilly. It does not undertake the office of instruction; its sole duty is to examine the persons who present themselves for examination, and to confer degrees on those who prove to be deserving. There are two matriculation examinations in each year, at Burlington House, two B.A. examinations, and one M.A. examination. There are also provincial examinations for matriculation, and for the degree of B.A. These examinations are carried on simultaneously with the examinations in London, on the same days and at the same hours, before a sub-examiner, named by the senate and sent down expressly for the occasion. The answers are taken to London in sealed packets, to be reviewed by the London examiners at the same time with the answers of the London candidates.

Amongst other noteworthy places of education must be mentioned the *City of London School*, Mill Street, Cheapside, founded

1835 ; the *Wesleyan Normal College*, Horseferry Road, West-minster, established 1850 ; *Mercers' School*, College Hill, Dow-gate, founded before 1447, since which time the school has been often removed—Sir Thomas Gresham was educated here ; *St. Mark's Training College*, Chelsea, established for training school-masters for the National Society ; and *Queen's College*, 67 and 68 Harley Street, for the general education of ladies, and for granting certificates of knowledge.

CHAPTER THE TWENTY-SIXTH.

PUBLIC MARKETS.

Covent Garden—Floral Hall—Smithfield—Billingsgate—Metropolitan
Cattle Market—Tattersall's.

MARKETS.

COVENT GARDEN MARKET, the chief market in London for fruit,
flowers, and vegetables, dates from Charles II.'s reign, and occupies the site of a convent garden, whence the present name. The
existing buildings were erected for John, Duke of Bedford, in
1830, by Mr. W. Fowler, architect. The area is about three
acres, and the Duke of Bedford derives about £5000 a year
from the place. It is well worth while to walk along the central
arcade any day before five o'clock to see the articles exposed for
sale on the stalls. Hither is sent fresh produce, not only from
many parts of the British Isles, but from France, Belgium, Portugal, even from Azores, the Bermudas, and the West Indies.
Extravagant prices are paid occasionally for early produce : green
peas at £2 the quart, fifteen shillings for a bundle of asparagus,
and strawberries at one shilling an ounce. Early in the
morning, from four to six o'clock in summer, the market is
crowded with carts bringing in vegetables from the neighbourhood of London, or from the railway stations. At each end of
the arcade, a flight of steps leads to a terrace with conservatories.
Here Ward's cases, ferns, aquariums, ornamental fish, greenhouse
plants, etc., are sold. Beneath the market are spacious store-
cellars ; and an artesian well, 280 feet deep, furnishes the needed
supply of water.

THE FLORAL HALL, a structure of iron and glass, contiguous
to the Royal Italian Opera House, Covent Garden, was erected in
1859, from the designs of E. M. Barry, for the purpose of affording a suitable place for the sale of flowers and objects connected

with their cultivation when alive, or their reception when cut. The structure has a frontage of 75 feet in Bow Street, and its total length is 280 feet. Cast-iron columns, 27 feet high, support the arches of the roof. The crown of the arch is 52 feet from the floor. A dome 50 feet in diameter ornaments the south end of the building, having a height of 91 feet from the floor of the hall. Access to the interior is obtained both from the Covent Garden Piazza, and from Bow Street. When well filled with flowers, the appearance of this hall is very beautiful, and it looks well when lighted up at night, when the visitors to the theatre are promenading in it. Balls are occasionally given here, for which, from the abundance of space, it is well suited.

SMITHFIELD MARKET, Newgate Street, City (frequently styled West Smithfield, to distinguish it from East Smithfield, Tower Hill), was until the last few years the only market for live stock in London. Although, after the erection of the Metropolitan Cattle Market in the north of London, it ceased to be so used, the pens until lately still encumbered the place, and the surrounding objects were anything but sightly. Operations, however, are now in progress for the construction of a metropolitan meat and poultry market on this site. It is to be 30 feet in height, 625 feet in length, by 240 feet wide, and will contain 100,000 feet of shop space. A carriage road will bisect it from north to south, with avenues occupying 50,000 superficial feet. There will be roads 60 feet wide on the east, west, and north sides, where vehicles can be accommodated without interfering with the street traffic. Meat and poultry will be brought direct from the country and from the Metropolitan Cattle Market, near the Caledonian Road, by means of rails laid under the market, by which it will be connected with the Metropolitan and other railways. A new street, 60 feet wide, will lead into Victoria Street. The cost of these improvements is estimated at £180,000. The nuisance occasioned to the streets of London by the droves of cattle and sheep that were brought here for sale was intolerable, and but for the strenuous opposition of the Corporation would not have been suffered to continue so long. The Corporation derived from £5000 to £6000 a year, tolls being charged on the beasts exposed for sale, and a rental for the use of the pens. The space, only about six acres and a quarter, was much too small for the accommodation of the stock, and this led to the infliction of many cruelties on the animals. The business transacted was very large, the payments

being estimated at seven millions a year. The name appears to
to have been originally *smooth field* (campus planus). This, before
the days of Tyburn, was the place of public executions. Mortimer suffered death here, and Wallace. Here Walworth the mayor
stabbed Tyler the rebel ; and here Jack Straw was hanged. Tournaments were held on the spot. Edward III. celebrated the deeds
at Cressy and Poictiers by mimic feats of arms at Smithfield.
Richard II. gave a tournament on three days to celebrate his marriage in 1396. A more terrible page of history tells of those
murders by way of burning which took place here in the name
of religion from 1555 to 1611. Ashes and charred bones have
been found in various spots beneath the pavement.

Bartholomew Fair, mentioned so often in our literature, was
held at Smithfield. The Lord Mayor went in his gilt coach, attended by city officers and trumpets, to open it. Mountebanks,
conjurors, giants, and dwarfs, rope dancers, punchinello, exhibited themselves ; wild beasts, dancing dogs, and all the other
marvels of a fair, were shewn to the crowd. The licence of the
carnival became too great ; the fair was gradually curtailed of its
attractions, and finally abolished in 1853, after having existed
from the time of Henry I.

BILLINGSGATE MARKET, Lower Thames Street, City, is the great
wholesale market for fish of the Metropolis. It is a neat Italian
structure of red brick, open at the sides, and with a campanile towards the river, designed by Mr. Bunning. The market commences,
six days in the week, at five o'clock, A.M., all the year round. The
vessels that bring the river-borne fish are moored alongside the
floating quay during the night, the oyster boats lying apart. The
fish are brought to land in baskets, and immediately sold to the
large retail fishmongers, who carry off their purchases at once in
the carts they have in readiness. Then come the " bomarees," or
middle men, who buy large lots, which they divide and re-sell.
And these are succeeded by the costermongers, the fishmongers of
the poor, who hawk the fish about London. In the market,
oysters and other shell-fish are sold by measure, salmon by
weight, all other fish by number. The traffic in the course of a
year is enormous, for not only does fish pour in by the river, but
large quantities are now brought by railway. Billingsgate is worth
seeing at an early hour, but "let the visitor beware," says Dr.
Winter, " how he enters it in a good coat, for as sure as he goes
in broadcloth, he will come out in *scale* armour. They are not

polite at Billingsgate as all the world knows, and ' by your leave'
is only a preliminary to your hat being knocked off your head by
a bushel of oysters or a basket of crabs.   In the early part of the
morning it would gladden the heart of a Dutch painter to see the
piled produce of a dozen different seas glittering with silver and
brilliant with colour."   The east coast sends herrings and sprats ;
Devonshire and Cornwall, mackerel, pilchards, and red mullet ;
Scotland, salmon ; the Doggerbank, cod and turbot ; Norway,
lobsters ; the North Sea, soles ; Holland, smelt and eels ; the
mouth of the Thames, and the English Channel, oysters.   The
use of this locality as a quay can be traced to a very early period
—as far back as the Anglo-Saxon kings.   It was appropriated as
a fish market in 1699.   The origin of the name is very doubtful.   Some conjecture that a British king, Belin, built a gate
here ; others that a later owner of the property may have been
named Beling.   The name has long become the proverbial designation of a certain kind of fluent discourse—viz., " opprobrious
foul-mouth language," as a dictionary has it.

At certain taverns in the neighbourhood, notably at " Simpson's," a table d'hote dinner at one and four is to be obtained for
eighteenpence.   Several kinds of fish are followed by joints.

The METROPOLITAN CATTLE MARKET, Copenhagen Fields, in
the north of London, was built in 1854, in order that Smithfield might cease to be what it had long been, the greatest
nuisance in the metropolis.   Live stock and dead meat are
brought for sale, the transactions in the course of a year here
reaching a very large amount.   The market covers about 30
acres, and cost £300,000.   Mr. Bunning was the architect.
Early on Monday morning is the time for seeing the greatest
bustle of business.

The other markets of London may be summarily treated, as,
however extensive their business, they are anything but models
for neatness or orderly arrangement.   *Newgate Market*, for flesh
meat, between Newgate Street and St. Paul's ; *Leadenhall Market*,
Leadenhall Street, for poultry, game, butcher meat, vegetables,
etc.; *Farringdon Market*, Farringdon Street, where water-cresses
predominate over other articles.   The site and buildings cost
£250,000, opened in 1829 ; *Hungerford Market*, Strand, a
general market, which will probably be shortly removed, to make
way for a railway station.   The market buildings were erected
by Mr. Fowler in 1832-3 for a public company.   The name is

derived from Sir Edward Hungerford, who in 1680 had property here.

For *horses* the great mart is *Tattersall's*, Grosvenor Place, Hyde Park Corner, where they are disposed of by auction on Mondays throughout the year, and on Thursdays in spring. Tattersall's is also the head-quarters of racing men, there being a subscription room here where turfites of all grades meet to make and settle bets. The betting on the most interesting "events" is regularly quoted in the newspapers.

"CAVEAT EMPTOR."

CHAPTER THE TWENTY-SEVENTH.

BREWERIES AND OTHER INDUSTRIAL ESTABLISHMENTS.

STRANGERS interested in industrial operations would, if properly introduced, have no difficulty in obtaining permission to inspect some of the great engineering works, such as Maudslay and Field's in Westminster Road, Lambeth, or some of those at Millwall. The manufacture of gas on a large scale, as conducted by some of the great companies, is also an interesting sight. The great drainage works, now being carried on by the Metropolitan Board of Works, may be seen by application to the chief clerk, at the office in Spring Gardens, who should be asked which, for the time being, is the most available point to visit. The printing establishment of the *Times* newspaper, in Printing-House Square, Blackfriars, is highly deserving of a visit, and may be seen by ticket obtained from the printer. Messrs. Clowes' printing office in Stamford Street, Blackfriars, is one of the largest in London, and may be inspected by an order obtained from the proprietors. Then there are the great BREWERIES, so remarkable for the vast amount of their operations. Taking the twelve largest concerns, the annual consumption of malt ranges from 15,000 quarters to 140,000. The establishments of Messrs. Barclay, Perkins, & Co., Park Street, Southwark, and Messrs. Hanbury, Buxton, & Co., Bricklane, Spitalfields, are larger than the others. By procuring a letter of introduction to either firm, there will be no difficulty in obtaining permission to view the brewery. Barclay's covers about 12 acres of ground. Steam-engines are employed to work the machinery. The water is obtained from an artesian well 367 feet in depth. The brewhouses, the cooling-floors, the fermenting "squares," the storehouses with their tuns, are on a gigantic scale. One vat holds about 3500 barrels, the value of the porter being about £9000. The horses, of which there are upwards of 180 employed, are striking creatures, and will be often noticed in the streets pulling drays. They are chiefly

Flemish, and cost from £50 to £80 each. This brewery, in a much less developed state than at present, belonged to Thrale, Dr. Johnson's Streatham friend. On his death, it was sold to a descendant of Barclay, the author of the well-known "Apology for the Quakers." Perkins, his partner, was a clerk in the establishment, and the descendants of these two gentlemen are at this day possessed of the property. The brewery is thought to cover the site of the Globe Theatre, Bankside, with which Shakspere was connected.

In Haydon Square, Minories, is the ale depot of Messrs. Allsopp of Burton, covering 20,000 square feet. Another vast manufacture is that of candles, as conducted by Price's Patent Candle Company. These are amongst the most interesting manufacturing establishments in the metropolis. The company has works both at Belmont, Vauxhall, and at Battersea. At the latter place the works cover 11 acres ; the capital invested in apparatus and machinery is £200,000, and 800 persons are employed, although machinery is used as much as possible. For permission to inspect the works apply by letter to the managing director.

CHAPTER THE TWENTY-EIGHTH.

THE PARKS.

Battersea Park—The Green Park—Hyde Park—Kensington Gardens
—St James' Park—Kennington Park—Victoria Park.

NOTHING in London pleases a foreigner more than our parks,
and to the Londoners themselves they are, in a sanitary point of
view, of the utmost value. Large sums are ungrudgingly laid
out upon them, whilst they are jealously guarded from encroach-
ment. These "lungs of London" are seven in number : Hyde
Park with Kensington Gardens, the Green Park, St. James' Park,
and the Regent's Park, in the west of London ; Victoria Park in
the east ; and Kennington and Battersea Parks on the south of
the Thames. We will speak of them alphabetically.

BATTERSEA PARK lies on the south bank of the Thames over
against Chelsea Hospital. It is of recent formation, and contains
about 185 acres ornamentally laid out with trees, shrubs, flower-
plots, and a sheet of water. For the land £246,500 were paid,
and the laying out made the total cost amount to £312,900.
The best mode of approaching this park from the north is by the
new iron suspension bridge called *Battersea Park Bridge.* The
orator and statesman, Viscount Bolingbroke, lies interred in the
family vault of the St. John's at St. Mary's church, Battersea.
The monument, with a bust of himself and his second wife, was
executed by Roubiliac ; the epitaphs were written by Bolingbroke himself.

THE GREEN PARK, on the south side of Piccadilly, contains
about 70 acres. It adjoins St. James' Park, and is separated by
the road called Constitution Hill from the private gardens of
Buckingham Palace. At its western termination, near Hyde
Park Corner, is a gateway in the form of an arch, imitated from
the arch of Titus at Rome. Upon its top has been placed M. C

Wyatt's colossal equestrian statue in bronze of the Duke of Wellington. It was cast in eight pieces, which were fastened together with screws. The weight of the whole is 40 tons, and a good deal of difficulty was encountered in placing so heavy an object in its present position, which took place in August 1846. The height of the group is nearly 30 feet, its length 26 feet. It cost £30,000. On the east side of the Park are several handsome mansions of the nobility. Stafford House, the Duke of Sutherland's, is at the corner next to St. James' Park, then comes Bridgewater House, the Earl of Ellesmere's, succeeded by Spencer House, Earl Spencer's, ornamented with finial statues. The poet Rogers had a house a little higher up, looking into the Park (22 St. James' Place), where he had a valuable collection of pictures, which have been dispersed since his death. The reservoir in the north-east corner belongs to the Chelsea Waterworks Company, and contains a million and a half of gallons.

HYDE PARK derives its name from the ancient manor of Hyde, situated here, and conveyed to Henry VIII. in 1530. After Charles I.'s death the Parliament sold the park to one Anthony Dean, who levied tolls on all carriages that entered it. It seems to have been early the haunt of the gay and fashionable, for the Puritans complained that it was the resort of " most shameful powdered hair men and painted women ;" and, after the Restoration, when it was bought back to the Crown, it was, in De Grammont's words, " the rendezvous of fashion and beauty." Queen Anne and George II.'s queen took away a considerable portion of it to increase the size of Kensington Gardens, and the latter caused the sheet of water now called the Serpentine to be formed. It now contains about 390 acres. Footpaths cross it from gate to gate for the convenience of the public, and there is a carriage drive round it. The fashionable drive is on the north bank of the Serpentine ; the ride for equestrians, called *Rotten Row*, a name of uncertain derivation, is at the other side of the water, and is nearly a mile and a half in length. Here let strangers come between five and six on a fine afternoon in the height of the season, and they will see something that no other city in the world can shew them—beautiful women, splendid equipages, and fine horses, in astonishing numbers. In this park reviews take place, and afford the Londoners the sight of as large an army as they are ever likely to see. The number of troops collected here is however small, in comparison with that which can be massed together in Paris and other continental cities, a fact which need not be deplored. There are eight gates into the Park, viz., Kensington, Prince's, and Albert Gates, and the gate at Hyde Park Corner, all on the south side ; Stanhope and Grosvenor Gates on the east side ; Cumberland and Victoria Gates on the north side. The gate at Hyde Park Corner is very handsome. It consists of three carriage archways in a colonnaded screen, designed by Decimus Burton, and erected in 1828 at a cost of £17,000. The Green Park Arch, surmounted by the bronze equestrian statue of the Duke of Wellington, is on the opposite side of the road. The two gateways, together with Apsley House and St. George's Hospital, form a striking architectural group. At Cumberland Gate, on the north-east corner of the Park, stands the *Marble Arch*, which was built for George IV. at a cost of £80,000, and placed in front of Buckingham Palace, from which it was removed when the east front was added to that palace. Its taking down and rebuilding here cost £4300. The bronze gates, which cost £3150, deserve notice for the elegance of their design. Park Lane, on the east side of the park, contains several handsome houses : Holdernesse House (the Marchioness of Londonderry), near the south end, Dorchester House (R. S. Holford, Esq.), near Stanhope Gate, and Grosvenor House (the Marquis of Westminster), are the most noteworthy. In the south-east angle of the park is a colossal statue in bronze, cast from cannon taken at the battles of Salamanca, Vittoria, Toulouse, and Waterloo. It was erected on the 18th of June 1822, and was " inscribed by the women of England to Arthur Duke of Wellington and his brave companions in arms." Its cost, £10,000, was subscribed by ladies. The statue is miscalled Achilles ; it is a copy of one of those on Monte Cavallo, Rome, named by antiquarians Castor and Pollux.

The Serpentine is the resort of a vast number of early bathers during the summer months ; and during a hard frost, the ice attracts a great crowd of skaters. Pleasure-boats are kept for hire. The Royal Humane Society have a receiving-house close by, which is frequently put to use by the carelessness of persons resorting to the lake. The present structure was designed by J. B. Bunning, and the first stone was laid by the late Duke of Wellington in 1834. The society was founded in 1774 ; it is said that £3000 a year are expended in supporting the receiving-houses in the parks. Near this house is a Government magazine of gunpowder and ammunition, to which it would be a mistake to apply the motto inscribed above the entrance to the receiving-house—" *Lateat scintillula forsan*" (perhaps a spark may be concealed), illustrating the device of a boy attempting to rekindle an almost extinct torch.

This park has been the scene of many duels, the usual place of encounter being the Ring about the middle of the park. One of the most fatal of these duels was that between the Duke of Hamilton and Lord Mohun, in which both were killed. " They fought at seven this morning," writes Swift in his Journal on the 15th of November 1712. " The dog Mohun was killed on the spot ; and while the Duke was over him, Mohun shortened his sword and stabbed him at the shoulder to the heart. The Duke was helped to the cakehouse, by the ring in Hyde Park, where they fought and died on the grass, and was brought home in his coach by eight, while the poor Duchess was asleep." Lord Mohun was the last of a very ancient race.

The site of the great house of glass and iron which formed the exhibition building of 1851, is near Prince's Gate. Nothing remains to shew that it stood in this park, save some beautiful gates of wrought-iron placed at the west end of Rotten Row ; these formed the entrance gates to the south transept of the building.

KENSINGTON GARDENS adjoin Hyde Park, and have been principally formed at the expense of that park, from which they are divided by a ha-ha fence. They comprise about 360 acres, of which 300 were added by Caroline, Queen of George II., who intrusted the laying out to Kent. Here we have long avenues of tall trees, offering delightful promenades in the summer. They are best seen from the neighbourhood of the palace. Standing on the Broad Walk, a promenade 50 feet in breadth, extending from the Bayswater Road to the Kensington Road, we see three diverging avenues beyond a round pond. Walking down any of these, we shall perceive that other avenues cross them in different directions. About half the Serpentine is in the gardens, and this sheet of water is crossed by an elegant bridge, designed by Sir John Rennie, which connects the gardens with Hyde Park. Not far distant from this bridge is the station of the military band that plays once or twice a week during summer, and attracts a crowd of fashionable people. In another part are shrubberies and a flower garden, where the plants are labelled with their botanical names, and the places whence they have been brought. A seated statue of Dr. Jenner, formerly in Trafalgar Square, has been placed on the border of the new ornamental basin at the head of the Serpentine on the Bayswater side.

A road for carriages has recently been made across the gardens in the neighbourhood of the Serpentine, to facilitate communication between the districts north and south of Hyde Park. Tolls will be levied upon vehicles and foot passengers until the cost of constructing the road is repaid.

ST. JAMES' PARK is triangular in plan, and contains about 83 acres. Henry VIII. drained the swampy fields hereabouts to make pleasure-grounds for his newly acquired residence ; and at their eastern limit next Whitehall, he had a tilt-yard, cockpit, tennis court, and bowling green. Charles II. added to the park, and employed Le Nôtre to lay it out. Pepys has recorded his visits to the park, which he found " every day more and more pleasant by the new works upon it ; " and on another occasion, " it being a great frost, did see people sliding with their skeates, which is a very pretty art." Waller did not omit to pen some flattering lines on the park, " as lately improved by his Majesty." The broad walk planted with limes, elms, and planes, on the north side, is called the Mall, from the ancient game of *pale-maille* that was played here. Pepys records having seen the Duke of York playing at *pall-mall* in the park. St. James' Palace and Marlborough House look into the Mall ; and further east is Carlton House Terrace, houses built on the site of Carlton House. A broad flight of steps in a line with Regent Street leads up to the York column. At the east end of the park is the Parade, on one side of which is a Turkish gun taken from the French in Egypt, and on the other a mortar left behind by the French at Salamanca. The Horse Guards and other Government offices stand between the Parade and Whitehall. Near this park is the State Paper Office in Duke Street, one of Sir John Soane's best works. At the north-east corner are some foot-roads through Spring Gardens to Charing Cross, in one of which stand the newly erected offices of the Board of Works. On the south side of the park is Birdcage Walk, communicating at one end, through Storey's Gate, with Great George Street, and at the other, through Buckingham Gate, with Pimlico. Near Storey's Gate is a brick house with some stone steps, in which the execrable Jeffreys lived. Wellington Barracks and the military chapel are on Birdcage Walk. Milton had a house in Petty France, and his garden extended to the Walk. The new east front of Buckingham Palace looks down the Mall and into the park. And now, turning out of the roads into the green enclosure, we may admire the fresh sward, the shrubberies, tall trees, and winding piece of water, variegated with islets, and alive with aquatic fowl. Charles II. planted here acorns from the Boscobel oak, which grew into trees, but none now remain. From the walls, many pleasing glimpses of fine buildings may be obtained between the trees. A chain bridge has been thrown across the water about the middle. The bed of the lake has been heightened, and the depth does not anywhere exceed four feet. The gossip about St. James' Park would fill a volume, of which the sayings and doings of Charles II. would form no short chapter.

KENNINGTON PARK, formerly Kennington Common, is a small piece of ground on the south side of the Thames, enclosed only a few years ago with iron railings. It contains no more than about twelve acres, but having been planted with shrubs, it is a great ornament to the neighbourhood. One of the late Prince Consort's model lodging-houses is placed at the principal gate. It is passed by the Kennington and Clapham omnibuses.

THE REGENT'S PARK, in the north-west of London, comprises about 450 acres. In Elizabeth's reign there was a royal hunting ground here called Marylebone Park. Like Regent Street, it derives its name from having been planned during the regency of George IV. It was not opened to the public until 1838, although it had been laid out some years before by John Nash, the architect of most of the house-terraces around it, in which the Crown has some valuable reversions. George IV. contemplated, it is said, the building of a palace here. The trees must grow higher before the park will be seen in its full beauty, still that part near the ornamental water is pretty, but perhaps the most pleasing portion is that near the north end, in the neighbourhood of the canal, where there are some old thorns. In the park, the Zoological Society occupies a large piece of ground. The drive round the park is not much short of two miles, and there is in addition the drive round the inner circle, where the gardens of the Royal Botanic Society are situate. Footpaths traverse the park in various directions. Very little can be said in favour of Nash's terraces ; the style, like that of Regent Street, also designed by him, is decidedly mean.

Near Gloucester Gate is *St. Katherine's Hospital*, which consists of a chapel and dwellings for the brethren and sisters, erected in 1828. The master's residence is at the opposite side of the road. This hospital formerly stood near the Tower, but that site was sold for the use of St. Katherine's Docks for £125,000, and £36,000 were paid for the rebuilding, together with £2000 for the purchase of a site. In the chapel is the tomb of John Holland, Duke of Exeter, and his two wives, removed hither from the old building, like the octagonal wooden pulpit given by Sir Julius Cæsar, master in Queen Elizabeth's time. A school where thirty boys and twenty girls are educated and clothed is attached to the hospital. This institution has an income of £6000 a year, and the master's salary is £1200, each brother has an allowance of £300 a year, and each sister £200. There are several villas inside the park—St. Dunstan's, the Marquis of Hertford, near Hanover Gate, where the clock with automaton strikers, removed from St. Dunstan's, Fleet Street, has been placed; St. John's, Baron Goldsmid, and the Holme, in the inner circle; the Baptists' College, formerly Mr. Holford's villa, and South Villa, the residence of the late Mr. Bishop, whose observatory, under Mr. J. R. Hind's management, gained so much distinction by the discovery of asteroids and variable stars. The *Coliseum* is conspicuous at the south-east corner of the park.

Primrose Hill, another piece of public ground of about fifty acres, is to the north of Regent's Park, and only separated from it by a road. The view from the top, which has an elevation of 206 feet above the Thames, is very good, extending over the whole of London, and the country to the north. In a ditch at the foot was found the body of Sir Edmondsbury Godfrey, whose murder in 1678 was asserted by Titus Oates to have been committed by the papists. Through the ridge adjoining the hill, the North Western Railway passes by a tunnel of 3493 feet long.

VICTORIA PARK, Bethnal Green, in the east of London, has been formed within the last few years at a cost of £130,000, part of which was supplied by the Duke of Sutherland's payment of £72,000 for Stafford House. It has been ornamented with three pieces of water, and has been planted with shrubs. A gymnasium has been built, and cricket and archery grounds formed. In a few years its appearance will be greatly improved by the growth of the trees, and it will be of essential advantage to the inhabitants of this part of the world of London.

CHAPTER THE TWENTY-NINTH.*

PRINCIPAL STREETS IN THE CITY.

Fleet Street—Temple Bar—Ludgate Hill and Street—St. Paul's Churchyard—Chancery Lane—Holborn—Newgate Street—Aldersgate
Street—Cheapside, and the Poultry—Streets by the Bank of England—Moorgate Street, and Finsbury—Threadneedle Street—Cornhill—Bishopgate Street, and Crosly Hall—Lombard Street—Fenchurch Street—King William Street—London Stone—Old City
Mansions.

WITHIN a radius of six miles from Charing Cross there are 2637
miles of street. Immense sums have been laid out from time to
time in improving London. Regent Street cost upwards of a
million and a half, of which more than a million was expended
in purchasing property. Improvements in Regent's Park (where
the land belonged to the crown, and was not paid for) cost
£120,000. Those at Charing Cross cost upwards of a million.
New Oxford Street cost £290,000, of which £114,000 was paid
for land to the Duke of Bedford. Cannon Street (1166 yards),
in the City, was opened at an expense of £589,470. Battersea
Park cost upwards of £300,000, and Victoria Park about
£130,000. The cost of 5659 yards of new street was
£2,034,872, or £359 per yard of length of street.

Works are now in progress by which new streets are being
formed, or old ones widened, in various parts of the metropolis.
Improvements in the thoroughfares of the city, particularly Ludgate Hill, St. Paul's Churchyard, and Cheapside, have long been
pressingly needed. The crowding becomes greater, and the stoppages more numerous, every day. Many plans have been put
forward, but the immense expense attending them has hitherto

* The reader will find, by reference to the index, some further description of
those places the names of which are printed in capital letters in the succeeding
pages.

prevented any one being adopted. The plan already mentioned in connection with the Thames embankment seems to offer the most feasible mode of relief.

FLEET STREET.—This street, one of the most crowded thorough-fares in London, derives its name from a stream called the Fleet, which now runs under Farringdon Street. It abounds with banks, insurance offices, printing offices, and newspaper offices. Several of the early printers were established here, and many an old volume prized by collectors was "emprynted in Flete Strete." The modern printers have their presses up narrow courts.

TEMPLE BAR, which divides it from the Strand, and the City of London from the liberty of Westminster. This gate was erected in 1670 by Wren, on the site of a house of timber which was consumed in the great fire of 1666. Two niches on the west side contain statues of Charles I. and Charles II., in Roman costume. It was the custom to place the heads of persons exe-cuted for high treason upon iron spikes on the top of the bar. The last heads thus exhibited were those of Townley and Fletcher, who were implicated in the rebellion of 1745, and they remained there until 1772. The original oak gates remain. They are usually closed when the sovereign pays a visit to the city, and only opened after parley on a formal demand by a herald. The Lord Mayor is in attendance, and presents the city sword to the sovereign, which is immediately returned. This ceremony can be traced back to Queen Elizabeth's time, on the occasion of that Queen paying a visit to St. Paul's to return thanks for the de-struction of the Spanish Armada. The room over the gateway is hired from the city by Messrs. Child, the bankers, as a place of deposit for their account books. That this gate, destitute as it is of all beauty, and possessing but little historical interest, should remain in these days to obstruct a crowded thoroughfare, is a striking instance of the tenacity with which the English cling to what is old, however inconvenient it may be.

Just inside Temple Bar (N.) is a narrow passage called Lower Serle's Place, formerly Shire Lane, in which Sir Charles Sedley, the poet of Charles II.'s time, was born, where Elias Ashmole the antiquarian lived, and where one Christopher Katt had a house, in which the kit-kat club began. A carved doorway marks the house in which Grinling Gibbons, the sculptor and wood-carver, once resided.

Soon after passing through Temple Bar we arrive at *Middle Temple Gateway* (S.), and a little farther on is Inner Temple Gateway, opposite which is *Chancery Lane* (N.), leading up to Holborn. Then *St. Dunstan's Church*, built by John Shaw, 1831-3, on the site of an old church. The heads of Tyndall the reformer and John Donne the poet, vicar of the church, are cut over the door. The old church had a curious overhanging clock, and two wooden figures of savages that struck the quarters with their clubs. *Fetter Lane* (N.), is a narrow street leading to Holborn; in it may be seen part of the New Record Office. Opposite Fetter Lane is a passage to *Mitre Court*, where there is a tavern, at which Dr. Johnson, Goldsmith, and other celebrities met. In *Crane Court* (N.), is a house, now belonging to the Scottish Hospital and Corporation, in which the Royal Society met for seventy years; the room in which Sir Isaac Newton sat as president is preserved as it was in his time. In *Johnson's Court* the doctor lived for eleven years, and in the neighbouring Gough Square he compiled the larger part of his dictionary. He died in Bolt Court. In the same court Cobbett wrote and printed his Political Register. In Wine Office Court Goldsmith lodged, and commenced his Vicar of Wakefield. *Whitefriars' Street* (S.) leads to Whitefriars, the once notorious Alsatia, a privileged sanctuary, where the scum of London collected (see Sir Walter Scott's " Fortunes of Nigel "). In Salisbury ~~Street~~ (S.), Richardson wrote Pamela, and printed others of his novels. Bride's Passage leads to *St. Bride's,* one of Wren's churches, famous for its steeple. Fleet Street terminates at Farringdon Street. Here New Bridge Street leads to Blackfriars' Bridge.

LUDGATE HILL and STREET take their name from an old city gate that once stood hereabouts, said to have been built by a British king named Lud. In the OLD BAILEY (N.) are the Central Criminal Court and NEWGATE PRISON. *St. Martin's* was one of Wren's churches. At 32 Ludgate Hill, the celebrated jewellers, Rundell and Bridge, had their shop, where Flaxman's silvergilt shield of Achilles was executed for George IV., Mrs. Rundell wrote a book which has brought a fortune to the publisher, " The Art of Cookery." Notice the west portico of St. Paul's, seen through the vista of houses. STATIONERS' HALL is up a court (N.), to which it gives a name. *Ave Maria Lane,* (N.) opposite Creed Lane, and leading to Paternoster Row, the head quarters of the booksellers, indicates, with Amen Corner,

x

the route taken by religious processions in Roman Catholic times.

St. Paul's Church Yard.—The north side is reserved for foot passengers, and is connected by several narrow passages and one broad thoroughfare with Paternoster Row and Newgate Street. The entrance to the cathedral is on this side. On the south side are streets leading to *Doctors Commons* (where wills are proved and preserved) and to Heralds' College. At the south-east angle of the churchyard a new street, called *Cannon Street*, leads to London Bridge. This street, which was opened in 1854, cost £200,000. Hereabouts are some large new warehouses ; one of them, Messrs. Cook's, contains 1,100,000 cubic feet of space, and is equal to 25 ordinary dwelling-houses. St. Paul's School is over against the east end of the cathedral.

Chancery Lane is a narrow street connecting the west end of Fleet Street with Holborn. Charles I.'s Lord Strafford was born in this street. On the west side, near the bottom, lived Izaac Walton, where he had a draper's shop. *Serjeant's Inn*, rebuilt in 1838, is on the opposite side. Here are the chambers where the judges sit to decide minor points of practice. The *Law Institution*, the head quarters of attorneys and solicitors, is a little higher on the west side. Here young attorneys have to pass an examination before being admitted to practice. There are also a library and a club. On the east side of the street, nearly opposide Carey Street, is the entrance to the *Rolls Buildings*, which consist of a court presided over by the Master of the Rolls, who ranks as the second judge of the Court of Chancery, and to whom is intrusted the custody of the imperial records or rolls, a residence for that judge, and a chapel of the early part of the seventeenth century, which contains several monuments, the most noticeable of which are Torrigiano's monument to Dr. John Young, M.R., in the time of Henry VIII., with a well modelled recumbent figure in terra cotta ; and the monument of Lord Kinloss, M.R., *temp.* James I. The kneeling figure in armour is supposed to be his son, killed in a duel with Sir Edward Sackville. Bishops Burnett, Atterbury, and Butler, were preachers in this chapel, which occupies the site of a house founded by Henry III. for converted Jews. In the *New Record Office*, not yet completed, are preserved the official records of Parliament, of the Courts of Chancery, Common Law, etc., which were previously scattered about in upwards of sixty places of deposit. The style of the building is a late Gothic or Tudor-esque, with a north front and two wings containing 228 rooms. Mr. Pennethorne is the architect. " The records of this country (says Sir F. Palgrave, late deputy-keeper) have no equal in the civilised world in antiquity, continuity, variety, extent, or amplitude of facts and details. From Domesday they contain the whole materials for the history of this country, civil, religious, political, social, moral, or material, from the Norman Conquest to the present day. Of the decisions of the law courts a series is extant from the beginning of the reign of Richard I. With the public records are now united the state papers and government archives, and by their aid may be written the real history of the courts of common law and equity ; the statistics of the kingdom in revenue, expenditure, population, trade, commerce, and agriculture, can from the above sources be accurately investigated. The Admiralty documents are important to naval history, and others afford untouched mines of information relative to the history of private families. Perhaps the most interesting documents preserved here are William the Conqueror's Domesday book, written on vellum, and bound in two volumes ; the deed of resignation of the Scottish crown by David Bruce to Edward II. ; and the treaty of peace between Henry VIII. and Francis I. The gold seal attached is in high relief, and is supposed to be Benvenuto Cellini's work. Quite lately have been acquired the official orders, decrees, and reports in chancery for the sixteenth and seventeenth centuries, including the cases heard and decided by Lord Bacon, many of them signed by his hand, and having notes in his writing upon them. Permission to examine documents must be obtained from the deputy-keeper, who will allow inquirers for literary purposes to inspect papers without payment of fees. State papers dated subsequent to 1688, cannot, however, be seen without the express license of the Secretary of State for Home Affairs. The Master of the Rolls is publishing a series of the most interesting documents, with the assistance of competent editors.

Pursuing our way up Chancery Lane, and passing the gloomy chambers and gateway of *Lincoln's Inn*, we arrive at a street on the east called Southampton Buildings, where stood Southampton House, obtained by Lord William Russell on his marriage with Rachel, daughter of Thomas, last Earl of Southampton. Some of Lady Rachel's letters were dated from this house. Several of the modern houses on the site contain portions of the old mansion. Here is a large building formerly used by the Masters in Chancery, but now by the Commissioners of Patents. Near the top of Chancery Lane, in a pile of stone buildings, are the offices of the Chancery Registrars and the Accountant General ; the Chancery Inrolment Office is also here.

HOLBORN, one of the main east and west arteries of London, derives its name from a stream or bourne which anciently ran in open view, but which now traverses an underground sewer. It is a long street of varying width and direction. Commencing on the west at the north end of Drury Lane (which part is called High Holborn), it soon reaches Southampton Street (N.), which leads to Bloomsbury and Russell Squares. A little further on (S.) is Little Queen Street, leading into Great Queen Street, in which is Freemason Tavern, a place for public dinners. Some narrow passages (S.), called Turnstiles, lead into *Lincoln's Inn Fields*, in which are the *College of Surgeons* and *Sir John Soane's Museum*. A good street into the Fields is much wanted. At No. 67 (N.) is Day and Martin's Blacking Manufactory, a handsome building that cost £12,000. Mr. Day was blind, and left £100,000 for the benefit of poor persons similarly circumstanced. The Blue Boar, 270 High Holborn (S.), is an old inn, where it is said Cromwell and Ireton, disguised as troopers, intercepted an important letter of the king, but the story is not generally credited. Red Lion Street (N.) leads to the *Foundling Hospital*. Further east on the south is *Chancery Lane*, which conducts past *Lincoln's Inn Gateway* to *Fleet Street*. The entrance to *Gray's Inn* (N.) is near a pile of old unsightly buildings, called Middle Row, standing in the middle of the street at the end of Gray's Inn Lane (N.), that leads up to King's Cross and the *Great Northern Railway Station*. Hereabouts are *Holborn Bars*, the limits of the city, at which toll (1d. and 2d.) is levied by the corporation on vehicles not belonging to freemen entering the city. The amount annually obtained is upwards of £5000. *Furnival's Inn* (N.) presents a good front to Holborn Hill, where we have now arrived. Staple Inn, where Dr. Johnson wrote his Idler ; Barnard's Inn and Thavie's Inn, minor inns, dependencies of the *Inns of Court*, are on the south of Holborn Hill. On the north are Hatton Garden,* where the Bishops of Ely had a large

---

* " My Lord of Ely, when I was last in Holborn, I saw good strawberries in your garden there."—RICHARD III.

garden attached to a house, which came into the possession of Sir Christopher Hatton in Queen Elizabeth's reign. In Ely Place (N.) is St. Ethelreda's Chapel, almost the only relic of the bishops' palace. St. Andrew's (S.) was Dr. Sacheverell's church. The wheels of vehicles are locked in descending the steep part of the hill, which it has often been proposed to bridge over. At the bottom, Farringdon Street (the river Fleet underneath it) runs southward to Fleet Street and Blackfriars' Bridge, and Victoria Street northward. Here is a terminus of the METROPOLITAN UNDER-GROUND RAILWAY. Proceeding eastward, and climbing Skinner Street, we pass the end of Snow Hill (N.), leading to Smithfield Market. At No. 41, William Godwin, the author of the famous novel "Caleb Williams," and the father of the poet Shelley's second wife, kept a bookseller's shop. John Bunyan died in this street in 1688. It was in this street that a picture by William Dobson attracted the attention of Vandyck, and induced him to recommend the painter to the attention of Charles I., whose serjeant-painter he became. *Cock Lane*, the scene of the trick that excited so much noise in the last century, the agent of which made the credulous Londoners believe that a ghost was really revisiting "the glimpses of the moon," is in the immediate neighbourhood of Skinner Street. At the top of Skinner Street St. Sepulchre's Church (N.) at the corner of Giltspur Street, which leads to *St. Bartholomew's Hospital* and *Smithfield Market*. The drinking fountain in the wall of St. Sepulchre's was the first erected in the metropolis. The great bell of that church is tolled on the morning when an execution takes place at *Newgate*, which is at the diagonally opposite corner of the Old Bailey. At this spot many a criminal has suffered the extreme penalty of the law. The *Central Criminal Court* is in the last-mentioned street, which leads down to Ludgate Hill. We now enter

NEWGATE STREET,

which had a city gate at its east end, whence the name. In *Warwick Lane* (S.) is the edifice surmounted by a dome which Wren built for the College of Physicians, and where the fellows met until 1825. Vendors of meat and brassfounders have now possession of it. *Newgate Market* for butchers' meat is on the same side, and Paternoster Row lies behind. *Christ's Hospital* (N.) has near it *Christ's Church*, built by Wren, which has a

tower and steeple 153 feet high.   Sir Kenelm Digby, the husband
of the beautiful Venetia, was buried here ; and here, since the
end of the last century, the " Spital Sermons " have been annually delivered on Easter Monday and Tuesday by a bishop or by
a preacher appointed by the Bishop of London.   The Lord
Mayor attends the church in state, and the boys of Christ's
Hospital walk in procession.   The discourses now relate to certain charitable institutions of London.   In Ivy Lane (S.), over
against Christ's Church, Dr. Johnson formed one of his clubs.
Above the entrance to Bull Head Court (N.) is a stone bas relief
representing the gigantic porter of Charles I., and Jeffrey Hudson
his dwarf, whose portrait is at Hampton Court.   In Panyer Alley
(S.) there is a pedestal, with an old sculpture in stone of a boy
upon a pannier.   The inscription runs—

> When ye have sought the city round,
> Yet still this is the highest ground.
> August the 27th, 1688.

The height of the spot is about 48 feet above Trinity high-water
mark.

We now reach St. Martin's-le-Grand, at the corner of the
General Post Office, and at the west end of Cheapside.

Aldersgate Street.

St. Martin's-le-Grand is continued by Aldersgate Street and
Goswell Road to Islington, where the thoroughfare enters the City
Road near that well known landmark the Angel Inn.   Opposite
the General Post Office, marked by a quaint sign, is the Queen's
Hotel, formerly the Bull and Mouth, much frequented in the
palmy days of stage coaches.   The old designation was a corruption of Boulogne mouth, and referred to Henry VIII.'s naval victory in 1544.   At the corner of Bull and Mouth Street (W.),
where a city gate once stood, and where Aldersgate Street commences, is a new church of the French protestants, opened 1842 ;
and adjoining this is the *Money Order Office,* an establishment in
connection with the General Post Office.   At 15 Aldersgate
Street is Saull's Museum, which is free to the public on Thursdays after 11.   Its contents are antiquities chiefly found in London, and geological specimens.   *Little Britain* (W.) was once
famous for its booksellers.   The Spectator dated from this place.
Milton lodged here, and so did Franklin when working for a

printer in the adjoining St. Bartholomew's Close. Washington Irving has described the place in his Sketch Book. The *Albion Tavern*, west side of Aldersgate Street, is frequently the scene of large public dinners. Opposite is Shaftesbury House, built by Inigo Jones, and inhabited by Shaftesbury, Lord Chancellor in Charles II.'s reign, one of the cabal. In Jewin Street Milton resided. The Barbican (E.), a street named from a watch-tower which anciently stood here, leads to Finsbury Square ; Long Lane, the opposite street, leads to Smithfield. Carthusian Street (W.) leads to the CHARTERHOUSE.

CHEAPSIDE AND THE POULTRY.

At the west end of Cheapside is *Sir Robert Peel's statue*, and here meet Aldersgate Street (with the *General Post Office*, standing in the lower part called St. Martin's-le-Grand), Newgate Street and Paternoster Row. We are now in the very thick of London business. In Foster Lane (N.), which leads to *Goldsmiths' Hall*, is *St. Vedast's Church*, erected by Wren, and having a handsome three-storeyed spire. Cheapside in old times was famed for its goldsmiths ; it was the street that passed along the side of the chepe or market. Opposite the end of Wood Street (N.) stood one of the nine crosses erected by Edward I. to the memory of Queen Philippa ; it stood there until 1643. In Milk Street (N.) Sir Thomas More was born ; in Bread Street, opposite, Milton ; and in this street stood the Mermaid tavern, the scene of " wit-encounters" between Shakspere, Ben Jonson, Raleigh, and others. *Bow Church* is about half way down (S.) Nearer the Bank are *Mercers' Hall*, and Saddlers' Hall, No. 143 (N.), with their balconies for viewing street pageants. King Street (N.) leads to *Guildhall* and Queen Street, opposite to Blackfriars' Bridge. Off Queen Street is Budge Row, in which stands the church of *St. Antholin*, rebuilt by Wren in 1682. The carpentry of the roof is thought an eminent example of the architect's skill. The octagonal spire, 154 feet high, is also admired. The stone-fronted house, No. 72 Cheapside, was built by Wren, and occasionally used by the Lord Mayor before the Mansion House was erected. The *Poultry* commences at the divergence (S.) of Bucklersbury, a short street, noted for its dining-rooms, and equally noted in Shakspere's day for its druggist's shops. " Like Bucklersbury in simple time," is a comparison in the " Merry Wives of Windsor." *Grocers' Hall* is on the north side of the Poultry. At the bottom of Charlotte Row (S.) is *St. Stephen's, Walbrook*, the interior of which is considered one of Wren's masterpieces. We are now arrived at the large open space into which look the *Mansion House*, the *Bank of England*, the *Royal Exchange*, and the church of St. Mary Woolnoth. Hence diverge Princes Street (west side of the Bank), Threadneedle Street (between the Bank and the Exchange), Cornhill (south side of the Exchange), Lombard Street, and King William Street, leading to *London Bridge*.

STREETS BY THE BANK OF ENGLAND.

Princes Street on the west side, and *Lothbury* on the north, contain several banks, and in the latter is St. Margaret's Church, rebuilt by Wren in 1690, with a steeple 140 feet high. Its beautifully sculptured font is ascribed to Gibbons. This neighbourhood is populous with stock and share-brokers, whose place of meeting, the *Stock Exchange*, is in Capel Court, *Bartholomew Lane*, on the east side of the Bank. At the corner of this lane and Throgmorton Street is the *Auction Mart*, where much house and landed property is disposed of yearly. *Throgmorton Street*, in which stands (N.) *Drapers' Hall*, leads into *Old Broad Street*, where the church of *St. Peter-le-poor* (N.) (" sometime peradventure a poor parish" says Stow) occupies the site of one known to exist as far back as 1181. A narrow passage (N.) leads to *Austin Friars*, the site of an establishment of monks of the order of St. Augustine, founded in 1243. Here is the *Dutch Church*, containing some good decorated windows. The worshippers are protestant and the service in French. The use of the building was granted by Edward VI. in 1550 to refugees from the Netherlands, France, and other foreign parts. In Old Broad Street (E.) are the *City Club*, several joint-stock banks, and a large building occupied as Commercial Chambers, on the site of the old Inland Revenue Office. This street terminates at London Wall, a street on the site of the Roman wall round old London.

MOORGATE STREET AND FINSBURY.

Moorgate Street is a new street leading northward from the north-east corner of the Bank. It is lined with offices and shops, and at its north end is intersected by London Wall. Passing on into Finsbury Pavement, Fore Street is on the east side, with which is connected Milton Street, formerly Grub Street of literary renown, so cruelly treated by Pope, Swift, and their compeers.* Dr. Johnson in his dictionary says that Grub Street had been "much inhabited by writers of small histories, dictionaries, and temporary poems ; whence any mean production is called Grub Street." On the east side of the Pavement is Finsbury Circus, where the *London Institution* is situate. Proceeding northward we reach Finsbury Square, which, like the Circus and the surrounding streets, was built upon a tract of ground called Moorfields, of which we first hear as a *fen*, whence Finsbury. In 1415 a gate was made through the city wall, whence Moor-gate. At the time of the great fire the houseless people sought a refuge in these fields, in wretched hovels, and under tents. Immediately afterwards buildings began to be erected on them, and in 1675 *Bethlehem Hospital* was built. That institution has since been removed to Lambeth. On the west side of Finsbury Square is *The Artillery Ground*, the place of exercise of the Royal Artillery Company of the City of London, a body composed of merchants and others. This company was first heard of as the City Trained Band in 1585, when Spain threatened to invade this country. In 1610 the body was re-established, and in 1622 they acquired their present exercising ground. In the Civil War they took the side of the Parliament. Since that time their services in the field have not been needed, but in 1780 they helped to protect the Bank of England in the mob riots. On certain state occasions they have made their appearance to increase the effect of the pageant, and they have frequently attended the sovereign as a guard of honour when paying a visit to the city. The sovereign or some member of the royal family has held the chief command for the last 150 years ; the late Prince Consort was Captain-General at the time of his death. They bear as a motto the words *Arma pacis fulcra*. Their armoury contains some fine pieces of ordnance, and some curiosities in the shape of specimens of the ancient accoutrements of the corps.

Adjoining the Artillery ground is *Bunhill Fields Burial Ground*, the great place of interment for the dissenters, which

---

* "O Grub Street ! how do I bemoan thee,
  Whose graceless children scorn to own thee ;
  Yet thou hast greater cause to be
  Ashamed of them than they of thee."—*Swift.*

was originally a common burial-ground for those who died during the Great Plague in 1665. The land within the walls is less than four acres, and yet within the last 150 years probably 150,000 bodies have been laid here. John Bunyan, George Fox, the founder of Quakerism, Daniel Defoe, and Dr. Isaac Watts, were interred at Bunhill Fields.

Here commences the City Road. In Tabernacle Row (E.) is the TABERNACLE, a meeting house of the Methodists. Not far off in Old Street is ST. LUKE'S HOSPITAL for lunatics.

THREADNEEDLE STREET is thought to derive its name from the three needles which the Needlemakers' Company bore on their arms. It formerly commenced at the spot where the Mansion House stands, and the Bank of England is supposed to stand in it, whence that establishment has been facetiously termed " the Old Lady of Threadneedle Street."

Passing the ROYAL EXCHANGE, and the point where Old Broad Street diverges, we reach the *Hall of Commerce* (N.), built in 1843 for Moxhay the biscuit-maker, who expended upon it and the site upwards of £60,000. It was intended to be used as a mercantile club house, but this plan did not succeed, and it now serves for the offices of two joint-stock banks. On the façade is a frieze 73 feet long, with bas reliefs. In the vestibule is a statue of Whittington. The larger of its halls has a length of 130 feet, and a width of 44 feet. On the south side of the street is *Merchant Tailors' Hall*, and a little further on (N.) is the once famous *South Sea House*, the history of which belongs to the romance of commerce.* The year of 1720 is marked by the blowing and bursting of the great bubble, when £100 stock was sold at £1200, and within three months it would hardly fetch £86. One of the largest speculators and severest sufferers was the Duke of Chandos (the Timon of Pope) who lost £300,000.

> " Yet since just heaven the Duke's ambition mocks,
> And all he got by fraud is lost by stocks,
> Since he no more can build and plant and revel."

Thus wrote Swift, to whom the wild speculation of that time was

---

* " Reader, in thy passage from the Bank—where thou hast been receiving thy half-yearly dividends—to the Flower Pot, to secure a place for Dalston or Shackle-well, or some other thy suburban retreat northerly—didst thou never observe a melancholy-looking, handsome brick and stone edifice to the left, where Thread-needle Street abuts upon Bishopsgate? I daresay thou hast often admired its mag-nificent portals ever gaping wide and disclosing to view a grave court with cloisters and pillars."—*The South Sea House*, by Elia.

a fertile source of sarcastic remark. Threadneedle Street enters Bishopsgate Street Within, opposite the *Wesleyan Centenary Hall.*

CORNHILL extends eastward from Mansion House Street to the corner of Bishopsgate Street, and was named, according to old Stow, of " a corn-market time of mind there holden." In 1748 occurred a great fire that destroyed upwards of ninety houses, including that in which Gray the poet was born, and which belonged to him at the time. The house rebuilt on the site is No. 41. The street contains several well-stored shops of jewellers and silversmiths. On the south side, opposite the Royal Exchange, is *'Change Alley,* the scene of the South Sea Stock gambling.

> " There is a gulf where thousands fell,
> Here all the bold adventurers came ;
> A narrow sound, though deep as hell—
> 'Change Alley is the dreadful name."

So wrote Swift in his ballad, " The South Sea Project." And thus Gay, in his " Panegyrical Epistle to Mr. Thomas Snow"—

> " Why did 'Change Alley waste thy precious hours
> Among the fools who gaped for golden showers?
> No wonder they were caught by South Sea schemes
> Who ne'er enjoyed a guinea but in dreams."

In *Finch Lane* (N.) are Ned's and Joe's chophouses. *St. Michael's Church* and *St. Peter's* are on the south side of the street ; the latter, one of Wren's churches, has a tower and spire 140 feet high, with a great key, the emblem of St. Peter, at the top. Near the east end of Cornhill stood the *Standard*, a structure connected with a conduit supplying water. From it distances were measured for some time. From this end of Cornhill, Bishopgate Street strikes northward, Gracechurch Street southward to London Bridge, and Leadenhall Street eastward. Gracechurch Street is the starting place of omnibuses crossing London Bridge.

LEADENHALL STREET was so named from an ancient manor-house of Leadenhall. In the angle between it and Gracechurch Street is *Leadenhall Market,* where much butchers' meat and poultry are sold. In this street (S.) stands the old *East India House*, an edifice erected in 1800. It is no longer occupied by the Government of India, having been lately sold to persons who intend to pull it down, and the business relating to Indian affairs is now transacted in a portion of the Westminster Hotel. The museum has been removed to Fife House, Whitehall (see *India Museum*).

Hoole, the translator of Tasso; Peacock, the author of " Headlong
Hall," " Crotchett Castle," and other stories; Charles Lamb, the
essayist; James Mill, the historian of India; and John Mill, his
son, the author of valuable works on logic and political economy,
held clerkships at the India House.

North, are the churches of *St. Andrew Undershaft*, and *St.
Catherine Cree*, rebuilt in 1629, and consecrated by Laud, whose
proceedings on the occasion savoured so much of superstition
that they were made a formal charge against him, and helped to
bring about his fate. Holbein is said to have been buried in the
old building. A sermon is preached here annually on the 16th
October, in pursuance of the will of Sir John Gager, Lord
Mayor in 1646, to commemorate his escape from a lion which
he encountered in his travels in Asia Minor. Leadenhall
Street terminates at *Aldgate*, where formerly stood one of
the city gates. In the triangle, formed by Bishopgate Street,
Leadenhall Street, and Houndsditch, the Jews are very numerous.

BISHOPSGATE STREET commences at the junction of Cornhill,
Gracechurch Street, and Leadenhall Street. Its southern portion
is known as Bishopsgate Street Within (the walls), and in this
part (W.) is the London Tavern, where great public dinners
take place. Opposite the end of Threadneedle Street (where the
South Sea House is seen over against the church of St. Martin
Outwich) is the *Wesleyan Centenary Hall* (E.) A little beyond
(E.) is *Crosby Hall*, highly interesting as the only relic in
London of ancient domestic architecture on a large scale; Crosby
Place, as it was anciently called, was originally built in 1466 by
Sir John Crosby, alderman. It came afterwards into the possession of Richard, Duke of Gloucester, afterwards Richard III.
Readers of Shakspere will remember that one of the scenes of
the drama, bearing that king's name, is laid here, but it is
believed that the poet had no authority for supposing that the
property belonged to Richard at the date in question. After
passing through several hands, including Sir Thomas More, it
came into the possession (1564) of Sir John Spencer, ancestor
of the Marquis of Northampton, who greatly improved it.
Readers of our poets may like to know that when in the hands
of Lord Compton, Sir John's son-in-law, the Countess of Pembroke (the lady to whom Sir Philip Sidney, her brother, dedicated his Arcadia, and Spenser addressed one of his sonnets)`

lived here several years, and when she died, Ben Jonson wrote her epitaph. About the middle of the seventeenth century it was so injured by fire that it was never afterwards used as a dwelling-house. The Presbyterians, however, met here for religious worship for upwards of 100 years. Some 30 years ago, what remained of the old mansion attracted public attention, and subscriptions were raised for the purpose of restoring it. It was opened with a musical performance in 1838. The repairs have been very extensive, and much of the edifice has been rebuilt. What we now have are the Hall, the Council Chamber, and the Throne Room above, with vaults of early brickwork below. The hall is 54 feet long, 27½ broad, and 40 feet high. It is lighted by lofty windows and a beautiful oriel; there is a minstrels' gallery, and the roof is a very fine specimen of timber work. The fire-place is considered a very curious feature in a hall of this date. The roof of the Throne Room is oak-ribbed rounded. This building may be recognised on the east side of Bishopsgate Street, by the front which is new, but composed in the style of the timber houses of the period. The door is in the entrance to Crosby Square, which is formed by houses built on the ruins of the old place. The hall is let for musical performances, lectures, etc. To see it, apply to the porter.

Behind Crosby Hall is *St. Helen's Church*. Before arriving at Wormwood Street, on the east, is the Bull Inn, an ancient hostelry with a galleried yard, in which, before the building of theatres, the actors placed their stage. This was the inn of Hobson the carrier. In one of Milton's humorous pieces of verse upon him, we are told that he died because he had nothing to do, being forbid to make his usual journeys "betwixt Cambridge and the Bull" by reason of the plague. Further north is *St. Botolph's Church* (W.), which yields the largest income of any of the city churches, the incumbent deriving £2290 a year from it. It escaped the great fire, but was rebuilt 1725-9. Hereabout stood the city gate, which gave its name to the street; and now commences Bishopsgate Street Without, a thoroughfare of irregular width, which leads through Shoreditch to the *Eastern Counties' Railway Station.*

LOMBARD STREET abounds in banks and insurance offices. It derives its name from the Lombards, who settled here as goldsmiths at a very early period. Their device, the three gold pills of the Medici family, or, as some think, the three pieces of gold, the emblem of the benevolent St. Nicholas, is now in possession of the pawnbrokers. The expression, a china orange to all Lombard street, indicates the wealth of the place in popular estimation. The church of *St. Mary Woolnoth* stands at the west end, on the site, it is said, of a pagan temple. It was rebuilt in 1716 by Hawksmoor. The Rev. John Newton, Cowper's friend, was rector here for twenty-eight years. Pope, " the little Queen Anne's man," was born in this street, but in what house is not known. Thomas Guy, the founder of Guy's Hospital, kept a bookseller's shop in Lombard Street. Sir Thomas Gresham's shop was on the site of No. 68, where Martin, Stone, and Co. carry on business. Here are two churches on the north side : *St. Edmund the King and Martyr*, a church rebuilt by Wren, with a steeple 90 feet high ; over the altar are two paintings by William Etty, representing Moses and Aaron : and *All-Hallows*, also rebuilt by Wren after the Great Fire. Lombard Street terminates at Gracechurch Street, over against the commencement of Fenchurch Street.

FENCHURCH STREET is a long thoroughfare, which meets the end of Leadenhall Street at Aldgate. *St. Benet's Church*, at the east end, has a spire 149 feet high. In Rood Lane (S.) is St. Margaret Pattens, rebuilt by Wren in 1687, containing an altar-piece attributed to Carlo Maratti, and around it are flowers well carved in wood. In this church is a large monument to Sir P. Delme, Lord Mayor in 1723, by Rysbrack. In Mincing Lane (S.) are the new *Clothworkers' Hall* and the *Commercial Salerooms*, where an enormous amount of property is disposed of in the course of the year, the articles principally dealt in being tea, coffee, sugar, tobacco, indigo, spices, and drugs. *Ironmongers' Hall* (N.) is opposite the end of Mark Lane (S.), which abounds in wine merchants ; and here is the *Corn Exchange*, where more extensive transactions in grain take place than anywhere else in the world. The chief day is Monday, from ten to three, but Wednesday and Friday are also business days. It is notorious that much hazardous speculation takes place amongst the frequenters of this exchange. The corn merchants have a newspaper, the Mark Lane Express, devoted to their interests. A few steps from the Corn Exchange, in Hart Street, Crutched Friars, is St. Olave's Church, one of the few city churches that escaped the Great Fire. Its clustered columns and pointed arches are highly interesting. Pepys the diarist was buried here, and there are several brasses and figure tombs. Passing Mark Lane, the next turn on the south, out of Fenchurch Street, brings us to the *Blackwall Railway Station,*

KING WILLIAM STREET.

Starting once more from the Bank, and aiming at London Bridge, we enter King William Street, a new and wide thoroughfare. At the point where this street, Cannon Street, Eastcheap, and Gracechurch Street meet, there is a statue of William IV. by S. Nixon. Mrs. Quickly's house, the Boar's Head Tavern, was in Eastcheap. The *Monument* is close by on Fish Street Hill. As we approach *London Bridge*, Upper Thames Street strikes westward, Lower Thames Street eastward, under the archway. In the latter, which leads to the *Tower*, are *Billingsgate Market* and the *Custom House.*

On the west side of the north end of the bridge is the *Hall of the Fishmongers*, one of the great City Companies ; and on the east side the church of *St. Magnus the Martyr*, built by Wren. The tower with its spire is classed amongst his best works. The base is open and used as a thoroughfare, thus contrived by Wren, although not freed from the masonry that filled it up until 1730. The tower of Christ Church, Newgate Street, is similarly contrived.

LONDON STONE. On the north side of Cannon Street, City, and against the wall of St. Swithin's Church, which stands at the corner of St. Swithin's Lane, will be observed a worn fragment of stone, protected by iron bars. This is the famous London Stone, which is supposed to have formed part of the *Lapis milliaris*, the pillar set up in the forum of Agricola's station, from which distances were reckoned by the Romans. It is referred to in Saxon charters as a landmark of immemorial antiquity, and it has been again and again mentioned in later chronicles. When Jack Cade entered London, he struck his sword on this stone, and exclaimed, " Now is Mortimer lord of this city ;" as will be found duly stated in Shakspere's drama, following Holinshed. Wren caused the stone, by his time much worn, to be cased with a new stone, hollowed for the purpose. The place of the stone was originally on the south side of the street, but its position causing it to be an inconvenience there, it was removed in 1742 to the north side ; but it was again found to be in the way, and had been doomed to demolition as the best method of getting rid of a nuisance, when a worthy printer prevailed on the churchwardens of St. Swithin's to fix it against the wall of the church. This was in 1798, when the church was undergoing repair.

᾽ In or near several of the streets that have been mentioned the stranger will unexpectedly come upon houses erected by wealthy merchants for their residence two hundred years ago. These are all occupied now-a-days as commercial chambers, for at the present time the City, so thronged during the day, is deserted at night. It is a vast mart whither men come to buy and sell ; but the wealthy merchants and dealers who make their money in close counting-houses or shops, hasten in the evening to their airy houses at the west end or in the country. It is a curious fact that the resident population of the City is decreasing, for the census ascertained that it was less by upwards of 10,000 in 1861 than in 1851. The old houses to which we allude have been mentioned by Lord Macaulay in some graphic words which we transcribe :—

"Those mansions of the great old burghers which still exist have been turned into counting-houses and warehouses ; but it is evident that they were originally not inferior in magnificence to the dwellings which were then inhabited by the nobility. They sometimes stand in retired and gloomy courts, and are accessible only by inconvenient passages ; but their dimensions are ample, and their aspect stately. The entrances are decorated with richly carved pillars and canopies. The staircases and landing-places are not wanting in grandeur. The floors are sometimes of wood, tesselated after the fashion of France. The palace of Sir Robert Clayton, in the Old Jewry, contained a superb banqueting-room, wainscotted with cedar, and adorned with battles of giants and gods in fresco. Sir Dudley North expended £4000, a sum which would have been important to a duke, in the rich furniture of his reception-rooms in Basinghall Street. In such abodes, under the last Stuarts, the heads of the great firms lived splendidly and hospitably. To their dwelling-place they were bound by the strongest ties of interest and affection. There they had passed their youth and had made their friendships, had courted their wives, had seen their children grow up, had laid the remains of their parents in the earth, and expected that their own remains would be laid. That intense patriotism which is peculiar to the members of societies congregated within a narrow space, in such circumstances, strongly developed. London was to the Londoner what Athens was to the Athenian of the age of Pericles ; what Florence was to the Florentine of the fifteenth century. The citizen was proud of the grandeur of his city, punctilious about her claims to respect, ambitious of her offices, and zealous for her franchise."

CHAPTER THE THIRTIETH.

Principal Streets and Squares West of the City.

Trafalgar Square—The Strand—Lincoln's-Inn Fields—Leicester Square —Whitehall—Westminster—Pall Mall—St. James' Street—Piccadilly—Bond Street—Regent Street—Oxford Street.

TRAFALGAR SQUARE, named after Nelson's great victory, was commenced in 1831. On the north side is the *National Gallery;* on the west, the *College of Physicians,* and the *Union Club-house,* which stand between Pall Mall and Cockspur Street ; on the east, hotels and private houses ; on the south-east, *Northumberland House,* with the lion of the Percies on the top of the screen ; and the south side is open towards Whitehall. The square is paved with granite, and contains two fountains, the design of which has been much criticised. At the north-east corner is a bronze equestrian statue of George IV. by Chantrey, the horse being represented standing with its four legs on the ground, instead of in the act of pawing the air, as is usual with equestrian statues. At the south-east corner is a recently erected statue of General Havelock, who died in the service of his country in India. At the corner next Cockspur Street is a statue of Sir Charles Napier, another Indian general. The great feature of the square is the *Nelson Column.* On the south of the square is *Charing Cross,* one of the landmarks of London, where stands Le Sœur's statue of Charles I., cast in that monarch's reign, but not erected until the reign of Charles II. Horace Walpole says :—" This noble equestrian statue, in which the commanding grace of the figure, and the exquisite form of the horse, are striking to the most unpractised eye, was cast in 1633 ; and, not being erected before the commencement of the civil war, it was sold by the Parliament to John Rivet, a brazier, with strict orders to break it in pieces. But the man produced some fragments of old brass, and concealed the statue and horse under ground till the Restoration. There is a story that the brazier made handsome profits by selling to both Royalists and Parliamentarians a number of brazen handles of knives and forks, asserting that they were made out of the metal of the statue. After the Restoration, legal proceedings were taken against Rivet to compel him to deliver up the statue, which was set up in 1674. For many years it was customary to decorate the statue with oak boughs on the 29th of May. It measures 9 feet 2½ inches in height, and the horse is 7 feet 9 inches from head to tail. The pedestal is 13 feet 9 inches high. The sculptures on the pedestal were not by Gibbons, as was long thought, but by Joshua Marshall, master mason to the crown. At Charing Cross formerly stood one of the highly decorated stone crosses erected by Edward I. (1291), on the spots where the corpse of his Queen Eleanor rested on its way to Westminster Abbey. It was removed by the Parliament in 1647. The site was afterwards used as a place for the execution of capital punishments, and here some of the regicides suffered. It has been customary for many years past to read royal proclamations here.

On the west side of Charing Cross are Spring Gardens, through which there is a foot road to St. James' Park. In years gone by, there was a garden here attached to the palace of Whitehall, which was thrown open to the public as a bowling green and place of diversion. Here John Evelyn " treated divers ladies of my relations." " The enclosure is not disagreeable," says a writer in 1659 ; " for the solemness of the grove, the warbling of the birds, etc., as it opens into the spacious walks of St. James'." After it was built over, Prince Rupert had a house in Spring Gardens, and died here in 1682.

THE STRAND, an ancient thoroughfare connecting the City with Westminster, and deriving its name from lying on the bank of the river, from which it is now separated by houses. The river side came to be occupied by the houses of the nobility and bishops, which have entirely disappeared, but the names of the streets record their situations. On the south side lay the gardens of the convent of Westminster, and some fields.

The first street east of *Northumberland House* is Northumberland Street. In a house in this street occurred the murderous rencontre which excited so much sensation in London in the summer of 1861. In the same street Ben Jonson lived when a boy. Benjamin Franklin lived at No. 7 Craven Street for several years, and many of his published letters were dated from this street. Hungerford Market is to be diverted from its original purpose, and made into a railway station. At the corner of Adelaide Street (N.) is an office of the Electric Telegraph Company, marked by a ball at the top, which drops at one o'clock every day. Villiers and Buckingham Streets (S.) were built on the site of York House, where Lord Bacon and then the Duke of Buckingham lived. The water gate, at the foot of the latter Street, is the only relic of the edifice. Opposite the same street is the Lowther Arcade (N.), a popular place for cheap toys, etc. *Charing Cross Hospital* is in Agar Street (N.) Coutts' Bank is at 59 Strand ; and behind are the streets of the Adelphi, built by the brothers Adam, of which Adam Street forms the main communication with the Strand. In John Street is the house of the *Society of Arts*. The mansion of the Bishops of Durham stood at this place. After it went from them, Lady Jane Grey was married in it ; and Raleigh had it for twenty years. The *Adelphi Theatre* (N.) is opposite Adam Street. Salisbury and Cecil Streets occupy the site of Cecil House, built in 1662 by Lord Treasurer Cecil. Southampton Street (N.) leads to Covent Garden Market. Beaufort Buildings (S.) stand on the site of a mansion inhabited by Bishops of Carlisle, Earls of Bedford, and the first Duke of Beaufort ; also by Lord Chancellor Clarendon, at the time his daughter Anne was married to the Duke of York. *Exeter Hall* (N.) is marked by a Greek inscription over the portico. Savoy Street (S.) leads to the old church of *St. Mary-le-Savoy*. We now arrive at Wellington Street, which leads (S.) to Waterloo Bridge, passing the new wing of Somerset House, and (N.) to Bow Street, passing the *Lyceum Theatre*. Jacob Tonson, Dryden's publisher, lived " at Shakpere's Head, over against Catherine Street, in the Strand." No. 141 has been built upon the site. Catherine Street leads to *Drury Lane Theatre*.

Nearly in front of SOMERSET HOUSE (S.) is the church of St. Mary-le-Strand, the earliest built of Queen Anne's fifty churches (1714-17). It was erected from the design of Gibbs on the site of the old Maypole—

> " Where the tall Maypole once o'erlooked the Strand ;
> But now, so Anne and Piety ordain,
> A church collects the saints of Dury Lane."

Superabundance of ornament is said to be the fault of this

church, but it certainly looks handsome at a distance, in walking eastward up the Strand, with its steeple of three receding storeys.

KING'S COLLEGE adjoins Somerset House on the east. In the next narrow alley, called Strand Lane, is an old Roman bath—a vaulted chamber with clear, cold water. Between this alley and Surrey Street is the *Strand Theatre*. In Surrey Street (N.) lived and died William Congreve the dramatist, and here he received a visit from Voltaire, to whom he expressed a wish to be considered only " as a gentleman who led a life of plainness and simplicity." In Norfolk Street, Peter the Great, when lodging there, received a visit from William III. Here too dwelt William Penn, and Ireland the forger of Shaksperean manuscripts, which Dr. Parr kissed on his knees. Arundel Street (S.) stands on the site of a mansion belonging to the Howards, in which the Arundel marbles, now in the British Museum, were deposited for some years. It had been originally the town house of the bishops of Bath. Here is the Whittington Club. St. Clement's Dane's church stands in the middle of the Strand ; the body was designed by Wren, the tower, 116 feet high, by Gibbs, the latter built in 1719. Otway and Lee, the play writers, were buried here. A brass tablet, placed against a column, records that Dr. Johnson was in the habit of attending divine service at St. Clement's. From the east end of St. Mary's to the west end of St. Clement's runs an old alley called Holywell Street, filled with dirty, unwholesome shops. In Wych Street, a nearly parallel street to the north, are several old house fronts. Here is a cluster of four of the minor inns—Lyon's Inn, New Inn, Dane's Inn, and Clement's Inn. At the west end of Wych Street stands the *Olympic Theatre*. Godwin, the author of Caleb Williams, had a bookseller's shop at 191 Strand. Essex Street is so called from a house belonging to Queen Elizabeth's rebellious Earl, which stood here, and where he was besieged. At the bottom is the Temple pier. There are two entrances to the Middle Temple from this street. The Strand terminates at *Temple Bar*, which is 1370 yards distant from Charing Cross. The shortest way for persons on foot from Temple Bar to Lincoln's-Inn is through Bell Yard.

LINCOLN'S-INN FIELDS, one of the largest squares in London, was formerly the resort of the idle and vicious, dangerous to be encountered after dark had set in. The fields were not enclosed with railings until about 130 years ago. Previous to that time they had been used as a place of capital punishment. Babington and his accomplices were hanged here in 1586 ; and in July 1683 Lord William Russell was beheaded here. Two narrow passages, called Great and Little Turnstile, communicate with Holborn. *Lincoln's-Inn* Hall and Library that stand on the east side, the *College of Surgeons*, a conspicuous edifice on the south side, and *Sir John Soane's Museum*, on the north side, have been described elsewhere in this volume. On the west side, an archway, built by Inigo Jones, leads into Duke Street, which connects the Fields with Drury Lane. About the middle of the same side is a house built by Inigo Jones for an Earl of Lindsay, and it was afterwards the residence of the proud Duke of Somerset. At the S.W. angle of the Fields is another of Inigo Jones's houses, built for an Earl of Portsmouth. At the corner of Queen Street is a large house built for a Marquis of Powis, and afterwards inhabited by Lord Chancellor Somers, and the Duke of Newcastle, the leader of the Pelham administration under George II. Several curious anecdotes are told of the Duke whilst living here. In *Queen Street*, Lord Herbert of Cherbury and Sir Godfrey Kneller lived at a time when it was a fashionable locality.

LEICESTER SQUARE, formerly Leicester Fields, was so called from a house built for an Earl of Leicester (*d.* 1677), which stood at the north-east corner. In that house lived Elizabeth, the unfortunate queen of Bohemia, daughter of James I., Colbert, and two Princes of Wales, after they had quarrelled with their fathers, George I. and George II. The square was enclosed about 1738 ; the houses around were built between 1630 and 1670. They, as well as those in the neighbourhood, are chiefly inhabited by foreigners. For ten years, 1851-61, a large building 90 feet across covered the enclosure, containing a model of the earth, erected by Mr. Wyld the map-seller. At No. 47, on the west side, is the house Sir Joshua Reynolds lived in ; it has been turned into book-auction rooms. At the opposite side of the square stands the *Alhambra*, a building in the Moorish style, where musical performances, rope-walking, etc., take place. In the northern wing of the Sablonière Hotel, Hogarth the painter lived and died. Sir Isaac Newton had a house in St. Martin's Street, on the south side of the square. The house was afterwards inhabited by Dr. Burney and his daughter, the authoress of " Evelina." In the north-east corner of the square is *Burford's Panorama ;* and at the middle of the north side is Savile House, at which exhibitions of various kinds have taken place, including Miss Linwood's curious needlework, imitating pictures that pleased our mothers and grandmothers so much. It had been the residence of Sir George Savile, whose books, paintings, and furniture were burned in the square by the rioters of 1780.

WHITEHALL is a part of Westminster, extending from Scotland Yard to Downing Street, and from the river to St. James' Park. It is so called from a royal palace of that name which stood here, and of which there only remains the banqueting house. Advancing from Charing Cross towards Westminster, the *Admiralty* is seen on the west, and on the opposite side is *Great Scotland Yard*, where are the head-quarters of the metropolitan police. Here the chief commissioner, Sir Richard Mayne, sits, and here application must be made for articles inadvertently left in cabs and omnibuses. The place is said to obtain its name from being the site of a residence for the Scottish kings, when they came to the Parliament of England. Here lived the crown surveyors, Inigo Jones and Wren; also Milton, when acting as Cromwell's Latin Secretary. Here Vanbrugh, the architect and play wright, built a house for himself out of the ruins of Whitehall, in which he died in 1726. Swift bantered "brother Van" in verse about his mansion, declaring it was "a thing resembling a goose pie," and that when harnessed to a horse, he might "take journeys in it like a chaise."

Opposite the *Horse Guards* (W.) is Whitehall Yard, where stand the *United Service Institution*, and Fife House now the *India Museum*. The noble *Banqueting House* will receive due attention as we proceed southward. Nearly opposite is Dover House (Viscount Clifden), where Lord Melbourne and the last Duke of York have resided. The handsome front of the *Treasury Buildings*, at the corner of *Downing Street* (W.), is opposite Montague House, the Duke of Buccleuch's new mansion, designed by William Burn. Close by are Priory Gardens, where at No. 4, Sir Robert Peel, the eminent statesman, lived and died. There is a very good collection of paintings here.

WESTMINSTER.—Passing through Parliament Street, we reach the turning which will take us to *Westminster Bridge*, and a few steps more bring us to the quadrangle called *New Palace Yard*, over which soars the lofty Clock Tower of the Houses of Parliament. The north end of *Westminster Hall* abuts on this quadrangle, which has been frequently used as a place of punishment.

Perkin Warbeck sat in the stocks; one Stubbs, a puritan attorney, having been convicted of a libel on Queen Elizabeth, had his hands cut off in 1580; in 1612, Lord Sanquhar was hanged for murder; in 1634, William Prynne was placed in the pillory; in 1649, the royalist Duke of Hamilton, the Earl of Holland, and Lord Capel were beheaded; in 1685, the infamous Titus Oates, and in 1765, the publisher of No. 45 North Briton, stood in the pillory; all of which punishments were inflicted in New Palace Yard.

In the green enclosure by *St. Margaret's Church*, is a bronze statue by Sir R. Westmacott, of George Canning, looking into New Palace Yard. Passing the courts of law (the entrances to which are through Westminster Hall) we arrive at Henry VII.'s Chapel and Old Palace Yard, where Marochetti's fine equestrian statue in bronze, of Richard Cœur de Lion, has been placed. In this space Guy Fawkes and his fellow conspirators were executed in 1606. Making our way across the graveyard attached to *St. Margaret's Church*, we shall find on the north side of the piece of ground into which the old abbey and the new palace look with such fine effect, the Guildhall of the City of Westminster, *Westminster Hospital*, and, behind, the Government Stationery Office, built in 1854 in the Italian style. At the west end of the abbey is the *Westminster School Monument*, and in the angle, between Tothill and Victoria Streets, the new Westminster Hotel, in part of which the India Office is located.

Passing through Princes Street we shall enter Great George Street, where at No. 29 the *National Portrait Gallery* is placed. At the upper end of this street a gate admits us into the Bird Cage Walk, leading to Pimlico. We may here enter *St. James' Park*.

PALL MALL.—The old French game of *paille maille*, played here in Charles II.'s time, gives its name to this, perhaps the most striking of the London streets in point of architecture. It swarms with curious associations with the history, art, and literature of the past, but the present must alone occupy us now. That part of it between Trafalgar Square and George III.'s statue is called Pall Mall, East. Here (S.) is the College of Physicians, and Colnaghi's print shop; on the north, the Gallery of the Old Society of Water-colour Painters, and the University Club. In Suffolk Street (N.) is the Exhibition of the Society of British Artists. The bronze equestrian statue of George III., at the junction of Cockspur Street, is a work of M. C. Wyatt. At the corner of the Haymarket, distinguished by an arcade, is *Her Majesty's Theatre*, a house for the performance of operas. The *Haymarket Theatre* is in the same street, on the east side. The Haymarket abounds with restaurants, oyster shops, etc. Over against the Opera House in Pall Mall is the *French Gallery*, where an annual exhibition of pictures takes place. We are now in the land of clubs. The *United Service Club* is at the corner of Waterloo Place, and on the opposite side is the *Athenæum Club*. In this place, at the top of the steps leading into St. James' Park, is the *Duke of York's Column.* The splendid houses of Carlton House Terrace, overlooking the Park, stand on the site of the palace, where George IV., when Prince of Wales, squandered millions. At the bottom of Regent Street, a granite memorial has been erected, from the design of John Bell, R.A., to the 2162 officers and men of the guards who perished in the disastrous Crimean war. In front is a group in bronze of three guardsmen, with suitable inscriptions. At the back are two heavy guns and a mortar, actual trophies from Sebastopol.

On the south side of Pall Mall come in succession the *Travellers' Club* (go round to the other side to see the garden façade which has been much admired), the *Reform Club*, and the *Carlton Club*, distinguished by its polished granite columns, and according to one critic, its " singular architectural antithesis, with a violation of all orthodoxy and rule." To the heterodox eye the effect is certainly superb. A little beyond, on the same side, is the *Ordnance Office*, where the Secretary of State for War has his office. The house was built as a residence for a brother of George III. At the opposite side of the street, at the entrance to St. James' Square, is the Army and Navy Club.

In the middle of *St. James' Square* is a bronze equestrian statue, by Bacon the younger, of William III. In this square (which was built between 1574 and 1690) several of the nobility have houses. At No. 21, now the residence of the Duke of Norfolk, the premier Duke, George III. was born. No. 22 is the episcopal residence of the bishops of London.

Returning to Pall Mall, the *Oxford and Cambridge Club* and the *Guards' Club* are seen on the south. On the opposite side are the galleries of the *New Society of Painters in Water-colours*, and the *British Institution.* The entrance to *Marlborough House*, lately fitted up as a residence for the Prince of Wales, is on the south. Opposite the end of *St. James' Street* is *St. James' Palace*, and at the end of Cleveland Row, the continuation of Pall Mall, is the Earl of Ellesmere's new mansion, *Bridgewater House.* The Duke of Sutherland's, *Stafford House*, is to the south, in the angle between St. James' Park and the Green Park.

ST. JAMES' STREET.—In this street have lived Waller, Wren, Pope, Swift, Steele, Gibbon, C. J. Fox, Crabbe, Moore, and Byron ; and this was the scene of Blood's attack on the Duke of Ormond. On a Drawing-Room day this street is crowded with persons who come to see the ladies on their way, in their carriages, to pay their respects to the Queen, who receives them in St. James' Palace.

On the west side, near the bottom, is the Thatched House Tavern, No. 85, where the Dilettanti Society meet. Here are a number of portraits of deceased members, and two fine conversation pieces by Sir Joshua Reynolds. The society originated in 1734. Close by is a handsome pile, the *Conservative Club ;* and a little higher up, at 69, is Arthur's Club House. In King Street (E) are the St. James' Theatre, Almack's (or Willis's) Assembly Rooms, and Christie and Manson's Auction Rooms, where valuable pictures are sold in the season. At 64 is the Old Cocoa-tree Club House (W.), and at 60 *Brooks's Club House*, and near the top of the street, what was once Crockford's Club, now the Wellington Dining Rooms. On the opposite side, at 28, is Boodle's Club House, and at 37 White's. In Jermyn Street (E.) the first Duke of Marlborough, Sir Isaac Newton, Gray the poet, and John Hunter have lived. In this street is the entrance to the *Museum of Practical Geology.*

PICCADILLY, a street about 1650 yards in length, which commences at the Haymarket, and, passing along the north side of the Green Park, terminates at Hyde Park corner. It is rich in interesting associations with many persons and events. The name is of uncertain origin, but it is supposed to be somehow connected with the word " pickadils," the ruffs worn in the time of James I. Crossing Regent Circus we shall see the Museum of Practical Geology on the south (the entrance is in Jermyn Street) and opposite to this, one of the entrances to *St. James' Hall. St. James' Church*, built by Wren, is opposite the end of Swallow Street, where there is a Scottish Episcopal Church. The Albany (N.) is let as residence chambers ; and here have lived George Canning, Monk Lewis, Lord Byron, Bulwer Lytton, and Macaulay.

Burlington House is hidden by a brick screen. Burlington Arcade, lined with shops, leads to the street called Burlington Gardens. Bond Street (N) is followed by Albemarle Street (opposite St. James' Street), in which stands the *Royal Institution*, and at No. 23 is the Alfred Club House. The Egyptian Hall, between Duke Street and St. James' Street, easily made out by the architecture of its front, is a place for lectures and exhibitions. It was originally built for Bullock's Museum of Natural History, and cost £16,000. At the gateway of the Three Kings' Inn, 75 Piccadilly, are two Corinthian pilasters, supposed to have been part of Clarendon House, which stood hereabouts. The building of this mansion by Lord Chancellor Clarendon made him very unpopular. After his flight to France, it was occupied by the Duke of Ormond at the time Blood attacked him. In Arlington Street (S.) are the mansions of several of the nobility, with fronts to the Green Park. Berkeley Street (N.) leads to Berkeley Square and to *Lansdowne House*. *Burlington House* is hidden by a high brick wall from Piccadilly, opposite the commencement of the Green Park, across which are good views of Buckingham Palace, Westminster Abbey, and the Houses of Parliament. On a clear day the Crystal Palace may be seen on its hill, glittering in the sun. At No. 1 Stratton Street lives Miss Burdett Coutts, who obtained the great wealth left by the Duchess of St. Albans, who began life as Miss Mellon the actress. Bath House, 82 Piccadilly (Lord Ashburton), contains a very good collection of pictures. Cambridge House, No. 94, is occupied by Lord Palmerston. Hertford House, No. 105, is the Marquis of Hertford's. When the Pulteney Hotel, Alexander, Emperor of Russia and his sister, the Duchess of Oldenburg, were lodged in 1814 ; but in 1851 that edifice was taken down, and rebuilt with a picture gallery, which will contain the Marquis's valuable collection of paintings. At the east corner of Down Street is Mr. H. T. Hope's new mansion, built from a French design. The iron railing was cast in Paris. The house has been splendidly finished throughout, and cost £30,000. It contains some good pictures, a portion of the celebrated Hope gallery, but the choicest part of that collection is at Deepdene, Mr. Hope's country seat. Gloucester House, corner of Park Lane (No. 137), long the residence of the late Duchess of Gloucester, the Queen's aunt, was bequeathed to, and is now occupied by the Duke of Cambridge. When tenanted by the Earl of Elgin, the Elgin marbles, now in the British Museum, were deposited here. Park Lane is lined with the mansions of the nobility facing Hyde Park. At No. 139, Lord Byron was living when his wife left him, and refused to return. The Baron Lionel de Rothschild (No. 148) has a valuable collection of mediæval art and old Ceramic ware. One candlestick of white clay cost £220. We now arrive at *Apsley House* (the Duke of Wellington's) and Hyde Park corner. Here the two park gateways (one crowned with the late Duke of Wellington's equestrian statue) and other buildings make a striking architectural group. *St. George's Hospital* stands at the corner of Grosvenor Place, which leads between Belgravia and the private gardens of Buckingham Palace to the new Pimlico Railway Station. The main road is continued alongside Hyde Park by Knightsbridge to Kensington. A turn to the left at Knightsbridge, near Albert Gate, leads to the *South Kensington Museum* and the *International Exhibition Buildings.*

BOND STREET acquired its name from Sir Thomas Bond, who bought Clarendon House from the second Duke of Albemarle, and pulled it down to form streets on its site, one of which was this. Its upper part, next Oxford Street, is known as New Bond Street, the lower as Old Bond Street; both are filled with shops of the first repute. At 41 Old Bond Street, in 1768, died the humourist Sterne, " vain, wicked, witty, false." The German Gallery, where there is an annual exhibition of foreign pictures, is at 168 New Bond Street (W.) At No. 141, Lord Nelson lodged in 1797.

REGENT STREET, only 30 yards less than a mile in length, is the handsomest shop street in London. Designed by Nash in 1813, and named after the Prince Regent, it begins at Waterloo Place, Pall Mall, where there are the offices of several Insurance Companies. The Junior United Service Club is at the corner of Charles Street (E.), and above this are the GALLERY OF ILLUSTRATION and the buildings lately occupied by the Parthenon Club. On the west side are the Club Chambers, a large house let off in residential chambers to gentlemen, and having a common coffee-room and dining-room. A steam engine is employed to raise water from a deep well, and to lift coals, furniture, etc., to the upper floors. The building cost £26,000. At the intersection with PICCADILLY is a *Circus*, and just above this the *Quadrant* commences. This is a sweep adopted for the purpose of joining the upper and lower parts of the street which were not in the same line. Some years ago the Quadrant had an arcade on each side, supported by 270 columns. In the Quadrant (W.) is an entrance to St. James' Hall. Nearly opposite New Burlington Street (W.) (in which the Royal Asiatic Society have rooms) is Archbishop Tenison's chapel (E.), built in 1702. On approaching Oxford Street, Hanover Chapel is seen with the portico over the footpath between Hanover Street and Princes Street, both of which communicate with Hanover Square. At the intersection with Oxford Street there is another *Circus*, to the north of which is, at No. 309, the POLYTECHNIC INSTITUTION (W.) between Cavendish Place and Margaret Street, both leading into Cavendish Square. In Margaret Street (E.) is ALL SAINTS' CHURCH. Opposite the Polytechnic is (No. 316) the Portland Gallery and Bazaar (E.) Regent Street ends at All Souls' Church, Langham Place, which has a fluted spire that has been a good deal ridiculed for its resemblance to an extinguisher. Further north is *Portland Place*, the broadest street in London, being 126 feet wide from house to house. At its northern end are Park Crescent and Park Square, surrounded by good houses.

OXFORD STREET.—*New* Oxford Street, opened in 1847, extends from High Holborn to Tottenham Court Road, and occupies part of a notorious district known as St. Giles's Rookery, inhabited by the lowest of the low. It is now a broad street of handsome shops, with ambitious façades in different styles. Near the Holborn end, Museum Street (N.) leads to the BRITISH MUSEUM, and in Hart Street is the church of ST. GEORGE's, Bloomsbury, the steeple of which is ornamented by a statue of George II. Bloomsbury Street (S.) contains the Bedford Episcopal Chapel, a Baptist Chapel (with a large rose window), and a French Protestant Chapel. Arthur Street (S.) leads to ST. GILES' CHURCH. At the north-east corner of Tottenham Court Road is Meux's great brewery.

Oxford Street begins at Tottenham Court Road (which is a main line for omnibuses to Camden Town and Hampstead, Kentish Town and Highgate), and extends westward to the northeast corner of Hyde Park, a distance of a mile and a half. Tottenham Court Road obtained its name from leading to the manor-house of Totten or Tottenhall, now removed. Hanway Street, leading from it into Oxford Street, is filled as of old with china dealers and curiosity-shops. Charles Street (S.) leads to

Soho Square (an old square with a history), in the middle of
which is a stone statue of Charles II. in armour, and at the west
side is the Soho Bazaar. Wardour Street (S.) abounds in curiosity-shops. The PRINCESS'S THEATRE (N.) is opposite the much
frequented PANTHEON BAZAAR, built in 1812 as a theatre, and
remodelled in 1835 for its present application. The LONDON
CRYSTAL PALACE, another bazaar, has an entrance near the Circus
(N.) Crossing REGENT STREET at the Circus, we continue westward along Oxford Street, and reach Hollis Street (N.) leading to
Cavendish Square, in which are the residences of the Duke of
Portland, and statues of the Culloden Duke of Cumberland, and
Lord George Bentinck. Byron was born at 24 Hollis Street.
On the other side of Oxford Street is Harewood Place, leading to
Hanover Square, where there is a statue of William Pitt. The
ORIENTAL CLUB, the Hanover Square Concert Rooms, and the
offices of the Royal Agricultural and Zoological Societies are in
this square. After passing the top of Bond Street we arrive at
Duke Street, which leads (N.) to Manchester Square, and (S.) to
Grosvenor Square, built about 1730, and now inhabited by seve-
ral of the nobility. Orchard Street (N.) leads to Portman Square,
also the haunt of the aristocracy ; and to Baker Street, in which
are Tussaud's Wax - Work Exhibition, and the Baker Street
Bazaar. This is a route for omnibuses to the north-west side of
London. Passing the top of Park Lane, which contains many
handsome houses of the nobility and wealthy gentry, we come
to the Cumberland Gate entrance to HYDE PARK where the
MARBLE ARCH has been placed.

A little west of the Marble Arch, and near the end of the
Edgware Road, there is a stone with an inscription recording that
Tyburn Turnpike stood at that spot, and within a short distance
was the site of the gibbet where many a criminal has come to an
untimely end. " What a change in a century ; in a few years !
(exclaims Thackeray.) Within a few yards of that gate the fields
began : the fields of the highwayman's exploits, behind the hedges
of which he lurked and robbed. A great and wealthy city has
grown over those meadows. Were a man brought to die there
now, the windows would be closed and the inhabitants keep their
houses in sickening horror. A hundred years back people
crowded to see that last act of a highwayman's life and make
jokes on it. Swift laughed at him, grimly advising him to provide a Holland shirt and white cap crowned with a crimson or

black ribbon for his exit, to mount the cart cheerfully, shake hands with the hangman, and so—farewell. Gay wrote the most delightful ballads and made merry over the same hero. Contrast these with the writings of our present humourists ! Compare those morals and ours—those manners and ours !"

CHAPTER THE THIRTY-FIRST.

COLUMNS AND STATUES IN THE OPEN AIR.

Monument—Nelson Column—York Column—Westminster Column—
Statues.

THE MONUMENT on Fish Street Hill, in the City, stands on the site of St. Margaret's Church, which was consumed in the great fire, to commemorate which it was erected by Wren at a cost of about £14,000. It is a fluted Doric column of Portland stone, and 202 feet high. On the pedestal are some sculptures, of little value as works of art, and some Latin inscriptions recording the destruction of the city and its restoration. Up to the year 1831, there was also to be read an inscription untruthfully attributing the fire of 1666 to " the treachery and malice of the Popish faction, in order to carry out their horrid plot for extirpating the Protestant religion and old English liberty, and the introducing Popery and slavery." It was to this inscription that Pope's couplet alluded—

> " Where London's column, pointing to the skies,
> Like a tall bully, lifts the head and lies."

A winding staircase of 345 steps passes up the interior to the balcony at the top. The charge for permission to ascend is 3d., and it is open from nine to dusk. A vase of flames, made of gilt bronze, 42 feet high, crowns the apex. Defoe has compared the structure to a candle, and the great vase " to a handsome gilt flame like that of a candle." Several persons having committed suicide by throwing themselves from the balcony, a height of 175 feet, it was thought prudent to encage it with iron work to prevent future attempts of that kind.

THE NELSON COLUMN, Trafalgar Square, commenced in 1839, is still unfinished! The design was furnished by Mr. W. Railton, who took for his model a column of the Temple of Mars

Z

Ultor at Rome. The order is Corinthian, the material Devonshire granite. At the base are four blocks, intended to receive four lions as soon as the painter to whom they have been entrusted shall have sculptured them. The four sides of the pedestal have bronze reliefs. On the north side, fronting the National Gallery, the relief (by W. F. Woodington) represents a scene at the battle of the Nile, when Nelson, on being wounded in the head, said to the surgeon, who was leaving a sailor to attend to the admiral, " No ; I will take my turn with my brave fellows." On the south side, facing Parliament Street, the relief was designed by C. F. Carew, and represents Nelson's death at the battle of Trafalgar. The hero is being carried from the quarter-deck to the cockpit, and is telling Captain Hardy that " they have done for him at last." The figures are life-size. Underneath is Nelson's ever memorable signal, " England expects every man will do his duty." On the east side, next the Strand, the relief, designed by Mr. Ternouth, pictures the bombardment of Copenhagen ; whilst that on the west side, facing Cockspur Street, designed by Watson and Woodington, represents the battle of St. Vincent. At the top of the fluted column is a statue of Nelson, 17 feet high, cut by E. H. Baily out of three blocks of Craigleith stone. The top of the statue is 162½ feet above the ground. The diameter of the column at its base is rather more than ten feet ; its summit has a height of 145½ feet. The column has cost £25,000, the statue, capital, and reliefs £5000, and the lions will cost about £3000 more, so that the whole expense of the structure will be about £33,000.

THE YORK COLUMN, Carlton House Terrace, St. James' Park, affords a striking instance of the extent to which party spirit will go in this country. It was erected in 1830-33 in memory of the Duke of York (second son of George III.) who died in 1827. One would think that the sooner such a man was forgotten the better for himself and for royalty. And yet he has a memorial equal to the hero Nelson's, and superior to those of the greatest benefactors of our nation. The cost was about £25,000, which sum was raised by subscription. It is of the Tuscan order, designed by B. Wyatt, and constructed of Aberdeenshire granite. On the summit is a bronze statue of the Duke in his robes of the order of the garter by Sir R. Westmacott. Inside the column there is a spiral staircase of 168 steps, leading to the top, 123½ feet above the ground, whence there is a good view of

London to be obtained on a clear day. The statue is 13½ feet high. The balcony of the summit has been enclosed by an iron cage to prevent persons throwing themselves over. Open daily from May to end of September, admission 6d.

WESTMINSTER COLUMN. At the Broad Sanctuary, the open space between Westminster Hospital and the west end of the Abbey, a granite pillar, surmounted by a statue of Victory, has been erected to the memory of those educated at Westminster School who died in the Russian and Indian wars, 1854-1859, by their old schoolfellows.

STATUES.

The following list of the principal statues erected in the open air in the Metropolis may be useful. They are all of marble except when otherwise stated. Eq. signifies equestrian :—

Statues.	Sites.	Sculptors.
Achilles, bronze	Hyde Park	Westmacott.
Alfred, King	Trinity Square, Newington.	
Anne, Queen	Queen Square, Bloomsbury.	
Anne, Queen	Queen Square, Westminster.	
Anne, Queen	St. Paul's Churchyard	F. Bird.
Bedford, Duke of	Russell Square	Westmacott.
Bentinck, Lord George, bronze	Cavendish Square	Campbell.
Canning, George, bronze	New Palace-yard	Westmacott.
Cartwright, Mayor	Burton Crescent	Clarke.
Charles I., Eq., bronze	Charing Cross	Le Sœur.
Charles II.	Soho Square.	
Charles II.	Chelsea Hospital	Gibbons.
Clayton, Sir Robert	St. Thomas' Hospital.	
Cumberland, D. of, Eq.	Cavendish Square	Chew.
Edward VI.	Christ's Hospital.	
Edward VI.	St. Bartholomew's Hospital.	
Edward VI.	St. Thomas' Hospital.	Scheemakers.
Fox, Charles James	Bloomsbury Square	Westmacott.
George I.	Steeple, St. George's Ch., Bloomsbury.	
George III., bronze	Somerset House	Bacon.
George III., Eq., bronze	Cockspur Street	M. C. Wyatt.
George IV., Eq., bronze	Trafalgar Square	Chantrey.
Guy, Thomas, brass	Guy's Hospital	Scheemakers.

Statues.	Sites.	Sculptors.
Havelock, Gen., bronze	Trafalgar Square.	
Henry VIII. . . .	St. Bartholomew's Hospital.	
James II., bronze . .	Whitehall	G. Gibbons.
Jenner, Dr.	Kensington Gardens . .	Marshall.
Kent, Duke of . . .	Portland Place	Gahagan.
Napier, Gen. Sir Charles	Trafalgar Square . . .	Adams.
Nelson, Lord, on column	Trafalgar Square . . .	Baily.
Peel, Sir Robert . .	Cheapside	Behnes.
Pitt, William . . .	Hanover Square . . .	Chantrey.
Richard I. Eq., bronze	Old Palace-yard . . .	Marrochetti.
Sloane, Sir Hans . .	Botanic Gardens, Chelsea	Rysbrach.
Victoria, Queen . .	Royal Exchange . . .	Lough.
Wellington, Duke of, Eq., bronze . . .	Green Park Arch . . .	M. C. Wyatt.
Wellington, Duke of, Eq., bronze . . .	Royal Exchange . . .	Chantrey.
William III., Eq., brass	St. James' Square . . .	Bacon, jun.
William IV.	King William Street, City	Nixon.

GREENWICH HOSPITAL.

CHAPTER THE THIRTY-SECOND.

Greenwich—Woolwich—Crystal Palace—Dulwich Picture Gallery—
Epsom—Kew Gardens—Richmond—Hampton Court—Windsor
Castle.

HAVING now described the principal objects of interest in the
Metropolis itself, we shall proceed to conduct the stranger to a few
places in the neighbourhood, which he will do well to visit before
travelling homeward. These places will be taken in the following
order :—

GREENWICH HOSPITAL AND PARK.
THE CRYSTAL PALACE, SYDENHAM.
DULWICH PICTURE GALLERY.
KEW GARDENS.
RICHMOND AND ITS PARK.
HAMPTON COURT PALACE.
WINDSOR CASTLE AND PARK, AND ETON COLLEGE.

GREENWICH HOSPITAL.

This noble establishment for the reception of old and disabled
seamen of the Royal Navy stands on the south bank of the river,
six miles below London Bridge, on the site of an ancient royal palace
called *Placentia*, or *La Plaisance*, where Henry VIII. was born,
and where he married Anne Boleyn and two others of his unlucky
wives, where his three children Mary, Elizabeth, and Edward,
were born, and where the last, when Edward VI., died. No part
of that palace, nor of that which James I. built, is now standing.
Charles II. proposed to build a vast mansion here, but only
finished a small part, designed by Webb, Inigo Jones' son-in-law,
and that forms the west wing of the present hospital. After the
battle of La Hogue, 1691, there being much difficulty in accom-

modating the wounded, Queen Mary desired to convert the building into a place for their reception, a design that William III.,
after her death, carried out, Sir Christopher Wren superintending
the work gratuitously. In Queen Anne's reign, a repetition of
the first building was erected, again under Wren's superintendence. When Lord Derwentwater's forfeited estates, worth £6000
a year, were given to the hospital, the buildings were completed
as we now have them, saving that the oldest part was in some
measure rebuilt in 1811, and that the present chapel was erected
to replace one destroyed by fire in 1779.

Greenwich may be reached either by railway from London
Bridge Station or by steam-boat.   Both railway and river route
are mentioned elsewhere in this volume.

The Hospital * is open free on Tuesdays and Fridays ; on
the other days, 4d. for each person, not being soldier or sailor, is
paid.   The Painted Hall and the Chapel may be seen on week
days from 10 to 7 in summer, and from 10 to 3 in winter ; on
Sundays after service.

The buildings, consisting of four masses, and forming " an
architectural group unparalleled in modern England," are best seen
for general effect from the river. A terrace 860 feet long stretches
by the water, and here may be seen a granite obelisk to the
memory of Lieutenant Bellot, the Frenchman who joined one of
our polar expeditions, and lost his life by an accident.   Of the
two piles that front the river, the one nearer London is of Charles
II.'s time, the opposite one was erected in Queen Anne's reign.
Each of these measures 175 feet by 290 feet.   In the middle of
the ground between them has been placed a statue of George II.
in Roman costume ; the marble was taken from the French by
Sir George Rooke.   Proceeding to the pile erected by Wren, behind Webb's building, we pass under the dome to the *Painted
Hall*, 106 feet by 56, and 50 feet high.   The walls and ceiling
were painted by Sir James Thornhill between 1708 and 1727,
his remuneration being £3 per yard for the ceiling, and £1 per
yard for the walls, by which arrangement he made £6685.   These
paintings are not to our taste in these days, but Sir Richard Steele
was of opinion that they were calculated to raise in the spectator
" the most lively images of glory and victory, and could not be
beheld without much emotion and passion."   In this hall are hung

* A fuller account than can be given here of Greenwich Hospital and the
neighbourhood will be found in " Black's Guide to Kent."

the portraits of many sea commanders, amongst which should be noticed Vansomer's Earl of Nottingham, Lely's Admiral Harman, and Captain Cook by Dance. There are many pictures representing naval engagements ; amongst which notice Zoffany's Death of Captain Cook ; Loutherbourg's Victory of Lord Howe of the 1st June ; Turner's Battle of Trafalgar ; and Sir W. Allan's Nelson boarding the San Nicholas. The state was at the expense of the statues of Sir Sidney Smith by Kirk, Lord Exmouth by Macdowell, and Lord de Saumarez by Steel. That of Sir William Peel (by Theed), who fell in the Indian mutiny, was given by his brother. A monument, designed by R. Westmacott, has been lately erected in memory of Sir John Franklin and his companions. It is of marble, 18 feet high. One of the statues represents an officer studying the route of the ships, the other a man in deep despondency near icebergs.

In the Upper Hall are preserved various relics of our seamen's idol, Nelson ; the coat worn at the battle of the Nile ; the coat and waistcoat which he wore when killed at Trafalgar, four stars of so many orders being sewn on the breast of the former, the undress-coat of a vice-admiral. In another case are some relics of the Franklin expedition. Notice also the astrolabe presented to Sir Francis Drake by Queen Elizabeth. The models of Anson's ship *The Centurion*, and *The Royal George*, which went down off Spithead in 1782, will interest the visitor.

In the Vestibule are some tattered flags, won in various hard fought combats, and pictures of Vasco de Gama and Columbus (copies).

Leaving this building and entering the opposite one, we pass under the dome to the chapel, a work in the Grecian style of " Athenian" Stuart. It is of the same size as the Painted Hall, and is richly decorated. In the Vestibule are four statues personifying Faith, Hope, Charity, and Meekness, designed by West. The portal has been highly praised ; the principal sculpture is by Bacon. The altar-piece, by West, depicts the shipwreck of St. Paul, and the same artist designed the pulpit and reading desk, both of lime tree, enriched with alti-relievi. Chantrey's monument to Sir R. Keats, and Behnes' to Sir Thomas Hardy, were given by William IV. Keats was lieutenant, and the king, when a boy, midshipman, on board the Prince George. Over the lower windows are monochrome paintings illustrating gospel history.

THE DINING HALLS are below the chapel and the Painted Hall. Here about 1500 persons meet daily, whilst 1000 live in the infirmary or beyond the walls. One of the *dormitories* in the N.W. wing is shewn to visitors, who will see a long chamber divided by partitions into little recesses, each containing a bed. In the colonnade is an alto-relievo commemorating Nelson's battles.

The officers of the establishment consist of a governor, a lieutenant-governor, four captains, four commanders, eight lieutenants, two masters, six surgeons, and two chaplains.

The civil department is under the control of five commissioners, assisted by a secretary. The income is about £130,000 a year, of which £20,000 is a Parliamentary grant. The cost of maintaining the establishment is frequently complained of as unnecessarily heavy, and unfavourable comparisons in this respect have been made between it and a similar establishment in France.

In the neighbourhood of the hospital is the *Royal Naval School*, where 800 boys and 200 girls are clothed, fed, and educated.

Some of the hotels at Greenwich, such as the Trafalgar and the Crown and Sceptre, are noted for their whitebait dinners.

GREENWICH PARK, a picturesque piece of ground of 174 acres, contains some magnificent old elm trees planted in Charles II.'s time, and some elevations whence good views are obtained. On one of these stands the *Royal Observatory* of world wide celebrity, at the head of which is the Astronomer Royal G. B. Airy, F.R.S. It was built in 1675, but various additions have since been made. The cost to the nation of this establishment is about £4000 a year. Meteorological observations are made here as well as astronomical, and the collection of instruments for both sciences is large. The longitude is calculated from this observatory, and marked on all maps of English construction. At one o'clock every day the exact time is notified by the descent of a large ball on the spire of the eastern turret. By electric agency this is conveyed to London, and to all the chief towns of the kingdom where it is desirable to know Greenwich time. The public have free access to the park but not to the observatory.

WOOLWICH

May be visited either by means of a steamboat from Hungerford, London Bridge, or Blackwall, or by the North Kent Railway from London Bridge. The objects which make Woolwich deserving of a visit, are—1. The *Dockyard*, 2. The *Arsenal*, and 3. The *Royal Military Repository*. 1. The *Dockyard* is open daily (Sundays excepted) from 10 to 4—admission free. Here ships of war will be seen in various stages of construction, with men and machinery actively at work sawing timber, casting metal, etc. There are here two dry docks of great size. The building and docks extend a mile along the river. 2. The *Arsenal*. Strangers are not allowed to enter the buildings without a signed order. Foreigners must apply for permission to the *Dockyard* and other establishments through their respective ambassadors. Here, in many buildings, is carried on the manufacture of implements of warfare. In the Foundry, cannon are cast and bored. In the Laboratory, cartridges, rockets, and other explosive articles, are constructed. In the Storehouses are the fittings for several thousand cavalry horses, and accoutrements. Within the Arsenal are 24,000 pieces of ordnance, and three millions of cannon balls in pyramidal piles. A vast quantity of weapons, powder, cartridges, etc. is preserved here. 3. In the *Royal Military Repository* and in the *Rotunda* are models of fortifications, and of barracks, batteries, and dockyards; cannon, and every kind of implement employed in warfare, with an immense number of curiosities, are to be seen here.

THE ROYAL MILITARY ACADEMY is not far from the Repository. Here cadets are educated for the artillery and engineers. The building, a castellated pile, built in 1805, cost £150,000. The average number of young men in the establishment is 160, but there is accommodation for nearly twice that number.

Another large building is the head-quarters of the Royal Sappers and Miners ; and not far off is the Field Artillery Depot. The Hospital is an extensive building with 700 beds.

THE ROYAL ARTILLERY BARRACKS have a frontage of 1200 feet, and are capable of holding 4000 men. The buildings include a chapel and library.

It will be seen from this summary that there is full employment for many hours at Woolwich.

THE CRYSTAL PALACE,

Open from Monday to Friday inclusively, on payment of 1s. each person (except on certain special days notified in the newspapers), and on Saturday on payment of 2s. 6d., except during August, September, and October, when the admission is 1s. Children under twelve half price. Non-transferable season tickets, admitting for a whole year, are issued at two guineas and one guinea each person, with different privileges. The two guinea tickets admit on all occasions when the palace is open. The one guinea tickets admit only when the price of admission is under 5s. When the price of admission is 5s. or upwards, holders will be admitted on an uniform payment of 2s. 6d. Tickets may be obtained at the Crystal Palace Office, near the Central Transept Entrance ; at the offices of the London and Brighton Railway Company, London Bridge ; at the Victoria Station, Pimlico ; at the Central Ticket Office, 2 Exeter Hall, Strand ; and at various other places in London. Persons not holding tickets may either pay at the entrance to the palace, or at the railway stations on paying their fare. Much more detailed information than can be given here will be found in the Shilling Official General Guide, illustrated with plans and views, sold at the railway stations and in the palace.

To those who do not drive, the railway, with many trains in the course of the day, from both the London Bridge Station and the Victoria Station, Pimlico, offers every facility for reaching the palace.

The Crystal Palace is seen from far, crowning Sydenham Hill with a structure of glittering glass, held together by iron. It owes its origin to the Exhibition building of 1851, a structure of the same materials, and designed by the same person, Sir Joseph Paxton, M.P. A joint-stock company, promoted by a number of gentlemen who believed that a permanent edifice might be of great service in furthering the education of the people, and affording them a large amount of innocent recreation at a cheap rate, purchased an estate which now comprehends about 200 acres, erected the buildings, and laid out the gardens, at an expense of nearly two millions sterling—a sum very much beyond that originally contemplated. The main building is 1608 feet long, with a width throughout the nave of 312 feet, increased to

CRYSTAL PALACE, SYDENHAM.

384 feet at the central transept. A striking feature of the interior is its great height, the nave rising to the height of 110 feet above the ground floor; the central transept to the height of 174 feet. Two spacious galleries extend at each side of the nave throughout its entire length, and round each end. From a distance the two towers, 284 feet high, are conspicuous objects. These can be ascended by a spiral staircase, and their roofs command, as may be imagined, a splendid view of the country, extending into six counties. They serve the double purpose of carrying off the smoke of the fires which heat the building, and of maintaining in tanks at their summits a supply of water for the high jets of the great fountains. Railway visitors alight at a covered station, and proceed along a wing (passing under rooms employed as dining-rooms) to the south end of the main building. The corresponding north wing was blown down by a violent storm in February 1861, and has not been rebuilt.

On entering the palace for the first time, the visitor is recommended to place himself at one end of the building, for the purpose of obtaining a view along the entire nave. He will be much struck by the length and height of the structure, its light and elegant appearance, the floods of daylight that pour in from all sides, the distant statues, the baskets of flowers suspended from the galleries, the green healthy plants growing on the level of the floor, and the large marble tanks, rendered gay by bright blossoms and beautiful ferns.

Then, with the view of taking things in detail, let him, after glancing at the screen of the kings and queens, turn to the left, and, passing the Crystal Fountain, make his way to the *Pompeian Court*, where he will see reproduced a house such as a well-to-do inhabitant of Pompeii resided in at the time Vesuvius potted it for posterity. Enter the court or atrium, with its tank in the middle, and observe the miserably small dens set apart for sleeping in. Into the ambulatory beyond, the dining-rooms, chief bed-chamber, and other apartments opened. In the middle is a small garden, and between this garden and the atrium is the tablinum, where were deposited the ornaments of the house.

We may then pass in succession through the *Sheffield, Birmingham*, and *Stationery Courts*, all elegantly and appropriately decorated and filled with objects displayed in cases or on stalls ; works for the most part appertaining to the useful arts. Issuing from the last named court we find ourselves in the central transept, at the foot of a flight of stairs leading to the western gallery. Over against these stairs is the Concert Room, where there is a daily performance of good music. At the west end of the great transept is the organ and grand orchestra, in which oratorios are executed. Behind it is the main carriage entrance from the road.

Now let us enter the *Egyptian Court*, with lions couchant keeping guard. The architecture is characterised by massive solidity, and the examples here given, selected from various temples and tombs, fully conveys that idea. Two courts are separated by a hall of columns, modelled from those at Karnak. The colouring is taken from actual remains in Egypt, and all the hieroglyphics have their meaning.

In the *Greek Court* the style is marked by far more elegance and symmetry. Models of temples, and sculptures copied from the finest remains of Greek art, are placed in the central court. The light colouring of this court is supposed to be justified by ancient examples. In the gallery beyond the pillared walk, at the back of this court, a copy of the frieze of the Parthenon has been placed, and this has been coloured, the tints employed being however purely conjectural. Here also will be seen a model of the western front of the Parthenon, about one-fourth of the size of the original ; and more statues and groups, including the famous Niobe group from Florence. This gallery is continuous with that behind the *Roman Court*, and we may compare the noble intellectual countenances of the Greeks with the more sensual faces of their Roman conquerors. In the court will be found copies of sculptures, all of them carved by Greeks under Roman rule, including many well-known masterpieces. The walls are coloured in imitation of the marbles with which the rich Romans were in the habit of adorning their houses. In the side court are placed the busts of generals and empresses.

The Alhambra Court, copied from the ruined Moorish palace of this name at Granada in Spain, must strike every eye by the gorgeousness of the colouring, the elaborateness of the ornamentation, and the quaint grace of the architectural style. The Court of the Lions, 75 feet long, is two-thirds the size of the original. Crossing what is here called the Hall of Justice, we enter the Hall of the Abencerrages, with its stalactite roof and its lateral divans.

We now come upon an avenue of Egyptian sphynxes leading

up to two *colossal seated figures*, copied from the temple of Rameses the Great in Nubia. They are 65 feet high, the size of the originals.

The *Assyrian Court*, like the Egyptian, is connected with a remote antiquity. Here we have copies of the sculptures and portions of the buildings which our countryman, Mr. Layard, has disinterred at Nimroud and elsewhere in the old empire of Assyria. This court, larger than any other in the palace, is 120 feet long, and it affords us an opportunity of studying that monstrous style of architecture, with its human-headed bulls and winged lions, in which the barbaric Sennacherib and Sardana-palus delighted, the remains of which have been so lately revealed to us. Notice those puzzling arrow-headed characters in which a people long passed away concealed their thoughts, and which, however, have yielded up their meaning to the acumen and perseverance of the moderns.

This is the last of the courts on the western side. Passing into the nave we may examine the plants, natives of warm regions, which are hereabouts to be found. The water plants look particularly healthy and happy. Opposite the middle of the tank is the bark from the lower part of the trunk of a Cali-fornian coniferous tree, named Wellingtonia gigantea. On its native mountains it rose to the astonishing height of nearly 400 feet, and its age has been estimated at 4000 years, that is far older than any of the ancient buildings whose copies we have been examining. Close by is the *Water Barometer*, 40 feet long, which was originally erected by Professor Daniel in the hall of the Royal Society's rooms, Somerset House, and has only lately been removed here. The top of the column of water may be seen from the first gallery. As the extent of its variation is twelve times greater than that of the barometrical column of mer-cury, it is very interesting to watch its oscillations in unsettled weather.

Not far off the *Library and Reading Room* offer their re-sources to the visitor. There is a fair collection of books, a large supply of newspapers, British and foreign, materials for writing letters, a postage box, etc. To non-subscribers the charge of one penny is made for admission.

Let us now enter the *Byzantine Court* by the middle of the three arches which communicate with the north transept, and turning to the right pass along the copy of a cloister, the original of which is at Cologne. The roof is decorated with Byzantine ornament in imitation of glass mosaic work. In the middle of the court is a copy of a fountain from a convent on the Rhine. Notice the Prior's doorway from Ely, in a late Norman style ; the curious Norman doorway with zigzag moulding from Kilpeck Church, Herefordshire ; the doorway from Mayence Cathedral— the bronze doors within being from Augsburg Cathedral—the effigies, near the fountain, of Henry II. and his queen Eleanor ; Richard I. and his wife Berengaria ; John, and his wife Isabella, all from ancient originals. There are many other copies of architectural subjects in this court and the adjoining vestibules which deserve attention.

The next court is a small one, exclusively devoted to speci- mens of Gothic art and architecture in Germany, and hence styled the *German Mediæval Court*, where, dividing court from vestibule, we shall see the copy of a celebrated church doorway at Nuremberg. St. George on horseback, from the cathedral square at Prague, and some tombs of bishops and others, are amongst the remarkable objects here. In the vestibule next the nave are several pieces of sculpture, some of it quaintly droll.

Passing into the nave, and proceeding to the *English Mediæval Court*, we enter beneath a pointed arch, and find ourselves in a cloister of the Decorated period, with a doorway from Worcester Cathedral at the north end, and a doorway from Ely at the op- posite end. The court itself contains many excellent examples from old churches. The rich doorway from Rochester Cathedral, leading to the vestibule, will catch the eye, and in the middle is a decorated font from Walsingham in Norfolk. Turn round and admire the arcades of the elevation towards the cloisters. Those who revel in the poetry of Gothic architecture will find much to delight them in the doorways, tombs, niches, and canopies placed before them here.

We now arrive at the *French and Italian Mediæval Court*, the details of which have been furnished by various foreign churches, much being taken from Notre Dame at Paris. The statue on the floor, and the subject towards the nave, are Italian.

The rich elaborateness of the *Renaissance Court* will fascinate the most careless eye. The façade towards the nave, copied from a mansion at Rouen, built at the beginning of the sixteenth cen- tury, is highly attractive. In the centre of the court is a foun- tain from a French chateau, and two bronze wells from the ducal palace at Venice, arranged as fountain basins. Amongst the numerous charming things, notice the copy of the Baptistery gates from Florence, so famous in art ; the cinque-cento doorways from the Doria palace, Genoa ; one with five bas-reliefs from the Florence museum, above it ; various compositions of cinque-cento work on the back wall ; the Louvre caryatides supporting Benvenuto Cellini's nymph of Fontainebleau ; a part of the interior of the principal entrance to the Certosa at Pavia, very elaborately carved ; and Donatello's two statues, St. John in marble, David in bronze. The adjoining vestibule contains the bronze monument of Lewis of Bavaria, remarkable for its finish, Pilon's Graces, and many beautiful bits of the period when the Renaissance style prevailed. In the gallery behind this court is the monument of Richard Beauchamp, Earl of Warwick, from Warwick, considered one of the finest Gothic monuments now existing in this country.

The small *Elizabethan Court* is indebted for its architectural details to Holland House, Kensington, mentioned elsewhere in this volume. Here are some tombs of the period, inlcuding those of Mary Queen of Scots, Queen Elizabeth, and the Countess of Richmond, Henry VII.'s mother, all from Westminster Abbey. Here also is a copy of Shakspere's bust from Stratford upon Avon.

The *Italian Court* succeeds and illustrates the style which the Roman nobility employed in their palaces, the Farnese palace being the type selected. Observe the statue of the Virgin and Child after Michael Angelo ; the monument of Giuliano de Medici from Florence on the south side, with the reclining figures of Night and Day on the opposite side ; M. Angelo's monument of Lorenzo de Medici, likewise from Florence ; Bernini's group of the Virgin with the dead Christ ; the same subject by M. Angelo ; the Fountain in the centre from Rome ; and the copies in the arcades from Raphael's frescoes in the Vatican. In the gallery behind, notice the painted ceilings partly after Raphael ; and Michael Angelo's Moses, the admiration of all lovers of art. In the adjoining *Vestibule*, next the great central transept, the decorations are copied from a mansion at Milan. On the extensive wall in the transept we shall find several interesting monuments.

Now let us turn aside for a few minutes to survey the beautiful prospect of the gardens and the country beyond, which is afforded by the open corridor at the end of the central transept.

Then, recommencing our survey of the courts, we may betake ourselves to the nearest one, which contains a large collection of *Fancy Manufactures*, a sort of bazaar, in short, where a good deal of money is expended in the course of the year by persons desirous of carrying away with them some memorial of the Palace. Then come the *Ceramic Court*, illustrating the art of pottery from early times to the present day, the *Glass and Porcelain Court*, and the Court containing *Foreign Glass Manufactures*, where Bohemian and Bavarian glass is exhibited and sold. This is the last of the courts on this side and in this direction. Issuing from it we may examine the illustrations of *Natural History* which are here to be found in the shape of figures representing man as he has been met with in different parts of the globe ; and the stuffed animals scattered amongst beds of plants that grow in the localities from which these animals have been brought. Here are also aquaria with fish, cases of birds, sponges, etc.

Scattered up and down the nave and transepts are many pieces of sculpture to which we have hitherto paid no attention. We shall now recommend the visitor to bend his steps down one side of the nave, examine the casts as he goes along, and on arriving at the transepts to survey each completely before proceeding As all the casts have been marked with their names it will be unnecessary here to repeat them. On arriving at the central transept look up at the *Orchestra* erected for the Handel Festival, and capable of accommodating 4000 performers. The organ built by Gray and Davidson for its present position, contains 66 stops, with four rows of keys. In the eastern portion of this transept is a large collection of casts from several of the most celebrated ancient and modern statues and groups ; and here also is the Choragic monument of Lysicrates, often called the Lantern of Demosthenes, one of the marvels of Greek architecture. Then working our way down the nave we reach the tropical end of the building divided by glass during the cold months of the year from the rest of the building.

At the extreme north end of the building are some colonial and other collections worthy of notice. One is of the products of Tasmania, another comes from Egypt. Into the botany of the Palace we shall not undertake to enter, partly because all the plants have been labelled with their names, but chiefly because to give even a short account of the interesting collection would occupy more space than we can command.

The Galleries, however, must not be passed by. In the gallery over the Stationery Court, and the other courts on that side, is a large collection of oil paintings, and the stairs to the south of the grand orchestra will lead us to them. At the north-western end of the central transept is deposited a collection of the staple and manufacturing products of Canada. Passing through the Picture Gallery we shall arrive at a series of stalls where a great variety of articles are exposed for sale, and continuing our course we work round to the garden end of the central transept. Climbing the spiral staircase we reach a gallery above, where is deposited the *Industrial Museum and Technological Collection,* illustrating our manufactures by the exhibition of the various materials employed therein. There are a vegetable, a mineral, non-metallic, a metallic, and an animal series, all deserving examination on the part of those who desire enlightenment as to the numerous articles with which the productive labourers of this country deal.

In the main gallery on the north-eastern side of the Mediæval Court are placed some hundreds of photographs of architectural and sculptural subjects, and a collection of busts of the eminent persons of all ages. A *Naval Museum,* with models of ships and boats, illustrating the naval architecture of all countries, is to be found in the north-eastern galleries on the garden side of the north transept ; and in the first gallery at the extreme north end of the nave, there is a collection of *Engineering Models,* including those of bridges, viaducts, and docks. In the gallery at the back of the Assyrian Court is a great number of articles from India, and hence this department has been termed the *Indian Court.* Here will be seen arms and armour, idols, musical instruments, textile manufactures, carvings in ivory and wood, etc.

Descending into the body of the building, we may cross the great central transept, and seek the stairs that lead down to the basement floor, which is on a level with the first terrace. Here we shall find a large collection of agricultural implements, and a number of manufacturing machines in motion, including cotton spinning machinery, steam engines, pumps, etc.

Let us now leave the building for the gardens. The first terrace is 1576 feet long, by 48 feet wide ; on its parapet are placed 26 allegorical marble statues, intended to represent important countries and industrial cities. Descending the flight of steps, 96 feet wide, we reach the lower terrace 1664 feet long, and 512 feet wide, affording a beautiful promenade, adorned by the six upper fountains, and by beds of flowers. The chief features of the picturesque grounds are the broad central walk, 96 feet wide, and 2660 feet long; the arcade of iron trellis work, and the rosery around, placed on a mound; the two grand fountain basins with the stone arcades; and the lake at the bottom of the gardens, with restorations of extinct animals upon its islands. These restorations are intended to give as accurate a notion as can now be formed of those animals, whose bony remains have been found fossilized in various ancient strata, the Hylæosaurus, Megalosaurus, Ichthyosaurus, and other monsters, with forms as ugly as their names, who lived in lakes and swamps in the age of reptiles. Near at hand are some illustrations of geology, ingeniously designed to explain the succession of rocks in the crust of the earth, and the principal geological phenomena. In other parts of the gardens are a rifle ground, a cricket ground, and an archery ground.

THE FOUNTAINS, which constitute a great attraction in the grounds, are in two series. The six fountains of the upper series, which are upon the lower terrace, throw their water to the height of 90 feet, whilst minor jets play round the bases of the principal one. Then there is a great circular fountain in the middle of the central walk, which can throw a jet of 150 feet in height, whilst many other jets are playing around. On each side is a smaller basin. These nine fountains comprise the upper series. Below are two water temples 60 feet high, placed at the head of a cascade on each side of the broad walk. Below these again are the great fountains, which throw a central column to the height of 280 feet, with a great number of jets around them. The effect of the display of the whole system of fountains is very striking, but of course this occurs but seldom, and on special occasions, for a grand display consumes about six millions of gallons, 120,000 gallons being thrown in a minute, through 11,788 jets. It may be well to state here that the lofty *towers*, 284 feet high, one of which stands at each end of the palace, are of cast iron, and each contains 800 tons of that metal. They need to be strongly built, for they hold when full, a body of water weighing 1576 tons. The water is obtained by means of an artesian well 575 feet deep, which penetrates the London clay to the greensand below. This well, which is at the bottom of the garden, is a brick shaft 8½ feet in diameter, for the first

247 feet; the remaining part is an artesian bore. Steam-engines of 320 horse power are employed to force the water into the garden basins, and the tower-tanks. The pipes which convey the water, and by which a great part of the garden is tunnelled, weigh about 4000 tons, and are ten miles in length.

It remains but to add, that all classes of visitors to the Crystal Palace may obtain refreshments in it at rates suited to their purses. There are private dining rooms, where first class dinners can be obtained; public dining rooms, where meals are furnished at a settled printed tariff; there are even third class rooms, where plain fare is supplied at a low charge; and lastly, stalls are scattered about the palace, where light refreshments are to be had as in a confectioner's shop. Those whose physical strength is not equal to the task of perambulating the palace, may hire bath-chairs, the stand for which is near the entrance to the building from the railways. Lifting chairs for carrying invalids from the railway station into the palace, or to the galleries, may also be procured. In short, the convenience of visitors is consulted in every possible way.

The Portuguese have a saying to the effect, that those who have not seen Lisbon have seen nothing. In the same spirit, we may say that those who have not seen the Crystal Palace have not seen London. A thousand interesting objects have necessarily been pretermitted in our hasty sketch, but even if the half only of those mentioned have been examined, every visitor must admit that he has had a marvellously cheap shilling's worth of enjoyment, for he will have seen something that no other age, and no other country has been able to produce.

THE DULWICH GALLERY

of pictures is at the pretty village of Dulwich, 5 miles from Waterloo or London Bridge. It is open to the public, free, and without tickets, every day except Friday and Sunday, from 10 to 5 during the months from April to November, and from 11 to 3 during the remaining months. Children under 14 are not admitted. Omnibuses run to Dulwich from the Elephant and Castle, a place easily reached by other omnibuses from all parts of London.

The pictures were collected by M. Noel Desenfans, for Stanislas, last King of Poland, with a view of forming a gallery at Warsaw, but troubles came on that monarch, and the pictures remained on the hands of the collector, who bequeathed them to his friend Sir Francis Bourgeois, an artist of Swiss extraction, and a member of our Royal Academy. Sir Francis died in 1811, leaving the whole collection, and some of his own landscapes, to Dulwich College, for the use of the public. He also gave £10,000 for a building to receive the pictures, and £2000 to provide for their care. Sir John Soane designed a gallery of five rooms, lighted from above ; and in 1812 the public was admitted. A few portraits were subsequently added, and the collection now consists of 360 pictures. It is rich in specimens of the Dutch masters, and there are some fine Murillos. Although there are many inferior pictures in the collection, it will, as a whole, afford high gratification to lovers of art.

The visitor's attention may be directed to the following pictures, the numbers being those on the frames.

First Room.

3. Opie, by himself. 9. Landscape, by Cuyp. 11 and 12. Small landscapes, by Wynants. 13. Landscape, by Cuyp in Wouvermans' style. 36. Landscapes, by Jan Both. 37. Sketch for the large picture in the Munich Gallery, the Traveller and the Satyr, by Jordaens. 50. Interior of a Guard-Room, by Teniers. 54. Interior of a Cabaret; Boors drinking, by Adrian Bronwer. 63 and 64. Landscapes, by Wouvermans, not in his usual style. 66. A bull, by Ommeganck. 68. Landscape, by Cuyp. 77. A Moorish Market, by Lingelbach. 78. Sketch of four saints, by Rubens. 79. Interior of a Cathedral, by P. Neefs. 83. Landscape, by Cuyp. 85. Woman eating Porridge, said to be a portrait of the artist's mother, by G. Douw. 86. Portrait, by G. Douw. 93. View on the sea-shore of Holland, by Ph. Wouvermans. 107. Interior of a Cottage, by Adrian Ostade.

Second Room.

116. Winter Scene, by Teniers. 124. Group of four figures, the principal one representing Charity, by Vandyck. 125 and 126. Landscapes, by Ph. Wouvermans. 130. Woody Landscape by Pynacker, the figures by Berghem. 131. Village Scene by Hobbema. 132. Farrier shoeing an ass, by Berghem. 135. Virgin and Child, by Vandyck. 136 and 137. Return from the Chase, and a Farrier, by Ph. Wouvermans. 139. Teniers' chateau, with himself and his wife, by Teniers. 141. Rocky landscape, by Cuyp. 144. Halt of Travellers, by Wouvermans. 145. Winter Scene, by Cuyp. 146. Sir Joshua Reynolds, by himself. 150. Landscape, by Pynacker. 152. Man smoking, by Adrian Ostade. 153. John Philip Kemble the actor, by Sir W. Beechey. 155. Sketch of a landscape with gipsies, by Teniers. 160. Wood Scene, by Berghem. 168 and 169. Landscapes, by Cuyp. 166. View on the Texel, by W. Vandervelde. 168. Samson and Dalilah, by Rubens. 173. Landscape, by Ph. Wouvermans. 179. Jacob's Dream, by Rembrandt. 185. Farm-Yard, by Teniers.

Third Room.

189. Man's Portrait, by Rembrandt. 190. Boors' merry-making, by A. Ostad

191. Judgment of Paris, by Vanderwerf. 192. Landscape, by Cuyp. 194. The Prince of the Asturias, son of Philip IV. of Spain, by Velasquez. 197 and 210. Fête and Ball in the open air, by Watteau. 199 and 205. Landscapes, by Jan Both. 200 and 209. Landscapes, by Berghem. 201. Landscape, by Hobbema. 202. View near Rome, by Joseph Vernet. 206. Girl leaning out of a Window, "wonderful for mingled power and simplicity," by Rembrandt. 213. Woman's Portrait, by Vandyck. 214. Portrait of Philip Herbert, fourth Earl of Pembroke, by Vandyck. 215. Mæcenas' Villa, near Tivoli, by Wilson. 217. St. Veronica, by Carlo Dolce. 218. Portrait of a man of rank, by Vandyck. 222. Head of a boy, by Velasquez. No number—Portrait of William Linley, by Sir T. Lawrence. 228. Landscape, by Ph. Wouvermans. 229. Farrier's Shop, by Karel du Jardin. 237. Lady buying game, by Gonzales Cocques. 239 and 243. Landscapes, by Cuyp. 241 and 245. Landscapes, by Ruysdael.

Fourth Room.

248. Flower Girl, a celebrated picture by Murillo. 250. Portrait of a Lady, by Vandyck. 259. Europa, by Guido. 261. St. Sebastian, by Fr. Mola. 264. Landscape, by Claude. 268. St. Catharine of Alexandria, by P. Veronese. 270. Embarkation of St. Paula, by Claude. 271. Soldiers Gambling, by Salvator Rosa. 278. View near the Hague, by Ruysdael. 279. Landscape, by N. Poussin. 283 and 284. Spanish Peasant Boys, the finest pictures in the collection, by Murillo. 286. The Infant Samuel, by Sir J. Reynolds. 291. Adoration of the Magi, by N. Poussin. 294. The Meeting of Jacob and Rachel, by Murillo. 299. The Locksmith, by Caravaggio or P. della Vecchia. 300. The Nursing of Jupiter, by N. Poussin. 309. Portrait of Philip IV. of Spain, by Velasquez. 315. Rinaldo and Armida, by N. Poussin.

Fifth Room.

329. Christ bearing his Cross, by a Spanish painter of the Seville School. 331. St. John the Baptist preaching, by Guido. 333. A Cardinal, by P. Veronese. 336. The Assumption of the Virgin, by N. Poussin. 337. The Mater Dolorosa, by Carlo Dolce. 339. The Martyrdom of St. Sebastian. 340. Mrs. Siddons as the Tragic Muse, by Sir J. Reynolds. 341. The Assumption of the Virgin, by Murillo. 345. The Adoration of the Magi, by P. Veronese. 347. Virgin and Child—the *Madonna del Rosario*, very fine, by Murillo. 348. The Woman taken in Adultery, by Guercino. 351. Venus, Mars, and Cupid, by Rubens. 353. Portrait of an old man, by Holbein. 355. The Mother of Rubens, by Rubens.

DULWICH COLLEGE was founded by Edward Alleyne, an actor and contemporary of Shakspere, in the early part of the seventeenth century, for the benefit of members of his own profession. He expended about £100,000 on land and buildings, and directed that the warden was to be an unmarried man, of the name of Alleyne or Allen. The annual income of the estate is now upwards of £11,000. For further particulars respecting the college, the reader may consult Black's Guide to Surrey. We may, however, mention here, that there is a good old Italian copy of Raphael's Transfiguration attributed to Giulio Romano over the altar of the college chapel ; and that in some of the rooms of the college are several portraits of old actors and poets.

EPSOM.

The races at Epsom, "our Isthmian games," as they were
styled by the Premier, are renowned all over the world, the
"Derby" being the great event of the British racing year. High
and low assemble on the course, and make up a crowd such as
can be witnessed nowhere else. The House of Commons invariably adjourns over the day, in order that honourable members
may have an opportunity of enjoying some excitement on another arena. "From every part of the metropolis and the surrounding country the roads which converge towards the great
centre of attraction are crowded with four-in-hands, barouches,
phaetons, gigs, chaises, carts, omnibuses, stage-coaches, trucks,
and equestrians. Upwards of 100,000 persons assemble to take
their part in this grand national gala."* The foreigner should
by no means omit to see London out for a holiday. Let him betake himself to Epsom on the day when "the blue ribbon of the
turf" is contended for, and he will come back with new ideas
about the English, their love of fun, their taste for betting, and
their splendid horses ; but let him take care of the champagne
and his pocket. The railways (starting either from London
Bridge or the Pimlico Station) convey large numbers to the neighbourhood of the course, but the proper thing (we suppose ourselves speaking to a bachelor) is to join with some friends in
driving down in a carriage-and-four, a hamper with potables and
comestibles being stowed somewhere out of sight. The town of
Epsom, an irregularly built place of about 4000 inhabitants, is
about fourteen miles distant from London ; the race-course is a
little further. The great annual meeting takes place on four
days (Tuesday to Friday) immediately before Whitsuntide. Wednesday is the *Derby* day, Friday the *Oaks* day. It must be explained that these races were named after a former sporting Earl
of Derby and his seat, the Oaks, in this neighbourhood. The
latter was established so long back as 1779, the former in the
following year. Great interest is attached to both races, but the
Derby takes the lead. Upon the course is a Grand Stand of
three storeys, capable of accommodating nearly 5000 persons,
who obtain a better view of the races from it than they could
elsewhere.

* **Black's Guide to Surrey.**

EPSOM RACE-COURSE.

The races at Ascot, in Berkshire, attract a more " select" company than those at Epsom, and the Queen has sometimes attended on the Cup day.

KEW GARDENS.

The Botanic Gardens are open free to the public daily from 1 P.M. to sunset. On Sundays the hour of opening is 2 P.M. The grand entrance is on Kew Green ; there is another entrance, the Unicorn Gate, in the Richmond Road. The adjacent park, or *Royal Pleasure Grounds*, which extend by the river side nearly to Richmond, are open daily from May to Michaelmas, and may be entered either from the Botanic Gardens, or by a gate on the river bank called the Brentford Gate, by the Unicorn Gate in the Richmond Road, or by the Lion Gate in the same road.

Visitors have the option of travelling to Kew (6½ miles by the road from Hyde Park Corner) by omnibus, steamboat, or railway. 1. By red omnibuses to Kew Bridge, alighting north of the bridge ; or by the white Kew Bridge and Richmond omnibuses, alighting south of the bridge. 2. The Kew steamboats start daily every half-hour from London Bridge and Hungerford, calling at the other piers. 3. The loop line of the Richmond railway (London terminus, Waterloo Station) has a station at Kew Bridge. The North and South Western Junction Railway, which is in connection with the North London Railway, has a station near Kew Bridge. The bridge is a stone structure, completed in 1789. A heavy toll is payable each way in crossing it in a carriage.

Kew Gardens are one of the few national establishments really worthy of the nation. They are not only most attractive for their picturesque beauty, but are rich with rare plants, brought from all quarters of the globe, and protected under glass for the study of the botanist and the gardener. Under the excellent management of the director, Sir William Hooker, they have increased in value year by year ; and their appreciation by the general public may be inferred from the numbers that now visit them in the course of a twelvemonth. Between four and five hundred thousand persons enter them during the year, and sometimes 14,000 in a single day. On a fine Sunday afternoon they are crowded with people, chiefly of the lower orders, neatly dressed and well behaved, a most pleasing sight to those who consider what these people might be doing if they had not a place like this to visit.

The visitor will do well to purchase at the gate Sir William Hooker's "Popular Guide," which contains a plan of the gardens; and his account of the contents of the museums; the price of each being sixpence.

The first of our royal family that became connected with Kew was the Prince of Wales, son of George II., who began to form the pleasure grounds, which were completed by his widow. Their son George III., taking a liking to the spot, took up his abode for several months a year in the old brick house, still standing, which is supposed to date from the reign of James I. or his son. His queen had a taste for gardening, and, assisted by Sir Joseph Banks, she got together a valuable collection of exotic plants, whilst Sir William Chambers was called upon to erect a number of strange buildings, pagoda, mosque, etc., many of which have since been removed. After George III.'s death the gardens languished, but in time it became plain either that they should be abandoned as a botanic garden or placed on a different footing, it was determined that the gardens, pleasure-grounds, and park should be transferred to the department of the Commissioners of Woods and Forests, with a view of establishing a national botanic garden, and opening the whole as a place of public recreation. The present director entered on the duties of his office in 1841, with instructions to carry out these designs, and very efficiently he has done so. The whole area where the public obtain healthful recreation consists of nearly 350 acres, of which about 75 acres are included within the limits of the botanic gardens.

Before entering, let us cast a glance across the Green, the prettiest in the neighbourhood of London, to the churchyard where lie the remains of the painters Zoffany and Gainsborough, and of Aiton, formerly gardener here, and the author of the *Hortus Kewensis*, a book well known to botanists. The Duchess of Cambridge has a house near the church. In a house passed on the right as we approach the garden gates, the late King of Hanover, when Duke of Cumberland, resided; it is now used as a place of deposit for Sir W. Hooker's vast herbarium, which, as added to of late years, is the largest in the world.

The elegant entrance gates were designed by Decimus Buron. The *Conservatory* on the right formerly stood in the ground of Buckingham Palace ; in it is placed a collection of Australian plants, many of which are distributed about the grounds during summer. Entering the main walk and turning at right angles to the path from the entrance, we see in the distance the ornamental chimney of the steam-engine which propels hot water into the palm house. At this point we are in the neighbourhood of the old palace, the red brick walls of which contrast well from various stations with the foliage. On our left is a house, 142 feet long, erected by Sir William Chambers in 1761, in which is deposited during the winter various delicate shrubs and young pines. Advancing between beds that are gay with flowers, massed and arranged so as to please the eye with the harmony of their contrasted colours, and passing near some fine groups of trees, we arrive at the small hothouse where the *Victoria regia* is enjoying its tepid bath along with the papyrus, the edible arum, the lattice-leaf plant from Madagascar, the rice paper plant from China, and other things that delight in warmth and moisture. We may then enter the great *Palm House*, quite a forest of vegetation, where splendid specimens of tropical plants will be observed, palms, dragon-trees, screw-pines, bananas (often to be seen in fruit), bamboos, sugar cane, bread fruit tree, Indian figs (including the banyan, the sacred fig, the caoutchouc fig), etc. etc. Observe from the west transept the vista into the pleasure grounds, planted with young deodar cedars. This house is 362 feet long ; the transept is 100 feet across, and 66 feet high, the rest of the house being 50 feet wide and 30 feet high. It is constructed of iron and glass, from the designs of Decimus Burton, the glass being slightly tinged green, in order to temper the too powerful rays of the sun. Across the piece of water outside will be seen the new Museum, to which we will now bend our steps. On the three floors of this building are preserved in glass cases, specimens of those vegetable products that are either eminently curious, or in anywise serviceable to mankind. The shipbuilder, the carpenter, the cabinetmaker, the general merchant, the weaver, the physician, the druggist, the dyer, the oilman, the colourman, the grocer, and many other productive members of the community, will here find systematically arranged the several objects in which they are interested, accompanied by their correct appellations, the countries whence they come, and the names of the plants from which they are procured. So valuable and extensive a collection of useful vegetable products has never before been brought together, and it is increasing rapidly by the contributions of travellers in all parts of the world. Leaving the Museum and winding round a knoll, on which is perched an ornamental building, known as the Temple of Eolus, we arrive at a cluster of small houses, in one of which will be found a collection of tropical plants of great beauty, revelling in a hot atmosphere saturated with moisture. Holding to the right on quitting this, we pass a fine walnut tree and come to the old Museum, where is stored another collection of vegetable products ; at the back of the Museum is a house containing some very fine tropical plants. Not far distant is the cool Fern House alongside a hothouse filled with valuable plants. After looking at these and the plants in a neighbouring house, we may find our way back to the large walnut tree, and pass on to the new house for succulent plants, 200 feet long and 30 feet wide. Here are placed cactuses, euphorbias, aloes, and other plants that like similar conditions. Some of these are very grotesque in figure, or in their mode of growth. Notice in particular the old man cactus, its top covered with white dishevelled hair ; and a great round urchin cactus (*Echinocactus*), weighing 713 lbs., which was brought from the interior of Mexico. Close by this house is one of the most attractive to the general eye in the gardens. It is filled in summer with fuchsias, geraniums, and other flowering shrubs of great beauty. Near this is a stove containing tree ferns, orchids, begonias, and other tropical plants of high interest. We are now in the neighbourhood of another round ornamental building called the Temple of the Sun. The noble trees around will doubtless attract the visitor's eye. A Turkey oak, a great cedar, and an oriental plane, are amongst the most conspicuous. Passing the trunk of a dead cedar of Lebanon, a great favourite, when in its prime, with George III., we are again at the great gates. A splendid specimen of the Douglas pine has been erected in the gardens as a flag-staff. The tree from which it was cut was 220 feet high, and is supposed to have been 200 years old. The staff is 157 feet long, its cubical contents 160 feet, and its weight 4 tons, 8 cwt., 2 qrs. Its lower end for the length of 11½ feet is sunk in a brick well below the surface of the ground. Curtailed as it is, it towers into the air twice as far as the tallest trees about it.

THE PLEASURE GROUNDS comprise about 250 acres, which are divided into the Arboretum, the Nurseries, a large lake, and

VIEW FROM RICHMOND HILL.

a piece of ground, 26 acres in extent, allotted to the private use of the Queen. The Arboretum contains about 3500 kinds of trees and shrubs, it being intended to exhibit specimens of all ornamental or useful trees that will flourish in our climate. The Pagoda, visible from most parts of the grounds, is 160 feet high and contains ten storeys. It was designed by Sir William Chambers, but since his time some of its objectionable features have been removed. The temple of Victory stands on a mound near the Unicorn Gate. It was designed to commemorate the battle of Minden, August 1, 1759. The two *Nurseries* are usefully devoted to the rearing of young trees, for the purpose of supplying the London parks and the grounds here; and many thousands are transplanted from them every year.

The large piece of ground lying between the pleasure grounds and Richmond is called the *Observatory Park*, from its containing an observatory, built by Sir W. Chambers for George III., and now supported by the British Association for the purpose of carrying on meteorological and magnetical observations. It was in this park that Sir Walter Scott laid the scene of the interview between Queen Caroline and Jeanie Deans. Neither it nor the observatory is open to the public.

The pedestrian after surveying the pleasure grounds may make his way out at the Lion or Pagoda Gate, and proceed to the railway station at Richmond; or he may prefer walking along the river side, here very pretty, and so return to Kew Bridge, where omnibus, steamer, or railway carriage will convey him back to town.

RICHMOND

may be visited either by steamboat, omnibus, or railway. The river route is interesting if the tide be in the steamer's favour, otherwise it is tedious. The railway (from Waterloo Station) is the quickest; there are many trains during the day. The omnibuses are well managed vehicles and are coloured white. They start from St. Paul's Churchyard, calling at Charing Cross.

The attractions at Richmond are the Park and the far-famed view from Richmond Hill; the town is uninteresting except historically. It was originally named Shene, but Henry VII. Earl of Richmond, gave its present name to it. Edward III. built a palace here, and several of his successors resided in it. Henry VII. held a great tournament at this place in 1492. A few years afterwards a fire destroyed a great part of the buildings, which the same king restored. His son feasted Charles V. of Germany here; that son's daughter Mary lived here a while, and her sister Elizabeth died here. Masques were performed before Charles I. in the palace, of which the only remains are a gateway and postern gate.

The bridge across the river, here about 500 feet wide, is not an inelegant structure. It was built in 1774, and cost £26,000. The road across it leads to Twickenham, where Pope lived, and to Hampton Court. The view up and down is very pretty, and many villas belonging to the nobility or to wealthy people are here to be seen nestling amongst foliage. Among them is the Earl of Shaftesbury's villa, which incloses within it the house occupied for some years by Thomson the poet, of whom various relics are preserved, including parts of the seasons in his autograph manuscript. If the visitor has not come by the river he will be much pleased by a row upon the stream as far as Kew Bridge, the park and gardens of Kew skirting the south bank all the way; and the grounds of Sion House (Duke of Northumberland) occupy much of the north bank. When gliding down the stream call to mind Wordsworth's remembrance of Collins, composed upon the Thames near Richmond,—

> " Now let us as we float along
> For him suspend the dashing oar;
> And pray that never child of song
> May know that poet's sorrows more."

Leaving the town for the park we ascend the hill and pass the Star and Garter Hotel, much resorted to on account of its excellent cuisine and wines, and the attractions of the view. Such is the profit derived from these visits, that when the place was sold in 1859 it brought £21,000. Louis Philippe and his family resided here for some months after their expulsion from France. The Castle is another excellent hotel.

RICHMOND PARK belongs to the Crown, and is open to the public. It is much frequented, especially on a fine Sunday afternoon. It contains 2253 acres, and parts of it are characterised by a picturesque wildness, that one is surprised to find so near London. Some of the trees are good studies for the artist. Entering at the gate near the Star and Garter, we soon reach the Terrace commanding a view over the Thames, winding below through a richly wooded country that extends towards Windsor

Castle, which may be distinctly seen crowning the brow of its hill.
This is the view that has received so much praise in prose and
verse, and it certainly is very pleasing in its soft style of beauty.
Close by this terrace is the house (Pembroke Lodge) inhabited
by Earl Russell by permission of the Crown. Professor Owen is
permitted to have the use of another house in the park near
East Sheen Gate. The house called the White Lodge is in the
occupation of the Prince of Wales. The sheets of water, about
18 acres in extent, near the middle of the park, were formed by
the Princess Augusta. The park is well stocked with deer, there
being about 1700 head feeding in it, a few being red deer, but
the majority fallow deer. The gates into the park at different
points are five in number, and there are several entrances for
foot passengers besides. Equestrians may ride over the turf, but
carriages are restricted to the roads. Pedestrians may wander at
their will and pleasure in search of sylvan beauty.*

The nightingales of this neighbourhood have been celebrated
in verse by Wordsworth, who has told us how he stood to
listen to

> " The quire of Richmond hill
> Chanting with indefatigable bill,
> Strains that recalled to mind a distant day ;
> Where haply under shade of that same wood,
> And scarcely conscious of the dashing oars
> Plied steadily between those willowy shores,
> The sweet souled poet of the seasons stood—
> Listening and listening long, in rapturous mood,
> Ye heavenly birds ! to your progenitors."

HAMPTON COURT.

The State apartments in the Palace are open free to the
public every day except Friday, from 10 to 6 from the 1st of
April to the 1st of October ; and from 10 to 4 during the remainder of the year. On Sundays they do not open until 2 P.M.
The Great Vine and the Maze may be visited every day until
sunset ; a small fee is paid to the gardeners.

Omnibuses start every morning from St. Paul's Churchyard,
calling at the Bolt-in-Tun, Fleet Street, and the White Horse
Cellar, Piccadilly ; but the most expeditious mode of reaching
Hampton Court is by the South-Western Railway, which has a

* For a longer description of Richmond and its Park, the reader may consult
Black's Guide to Surrey.

branch to Hampton Court Bridge. Several trains run to and fro in the course of the day, the time occupied by the journey being about 40 minutes. There are four tolerably good inns at Hampton Court.

Hampton Court Palace is in Middlesex, on the northern bank of the Thames, about twelve miles from Hyde Park Corner. The Palace, which covers eight acres of ground, was founded by Cardinal Wolsey when in the plenitude of his power, and presented by him to Henry VIII., when he saw that the magnificence of the building excited the jealousy of his master. Here Edward VI. was born, and his father married to his sixth wife Catharine Parr. Here Edward VI. resided during part of his short reign, and Queen Mary spent her honeymoon with her Spanish husband. Both Elizabeth and James occasionally resided here, and during the reign of the latter there was held here that conference between the Presbyterians and the State clergy which is noticed as a remarkable event in English church history. James's queen Anne died here; and hither Charles I. and Queen Henrietta retired during the plague of 1625. Here in 1647 the same king was kept in confinement until he made his escape. The Parliament sold the palace, but it afterwards came into the hands of Cromwell, one of whose daughters was married and another one died here. William III. enlarged the palace considerably, and employed Sir Christopher Wren to make the additions. He laid out the park and gardens in the form they retain to this day. His queen was much attached to the place, and here she employed herself and her maids of honour upon needle-work, of which so much was done that it sufficed to fit up one of the rooms. Several succeeding sovereigns resided here, George II. being the last. It is now inhabited by a large number of persons in reduced circumstances, chiefly connected with the aristocracy, to whom the Crown has granted the privilege of having apartments here.

Approaching the palace from the west we pass the low buildings used as barracks by the soldiers stationed here, and passing under an arch, enter a quadrangle, around which are apartments appropriated as previously mentioned. Crossing this we reach an arched passage where are the steps leading to the great hall, and proceeding we enter a second quadrangle known as the Clock Court. On the towers are terra cotta busts of some of the Roman Emperors sent from Rome by Pope Leo X. to Cardinal

Wolsey. The buildings around the next court were erected by Wren as may be seen from the style. The fountain in the middle gives its name to this court, which is surrounded by an arcade below, and by the state apartments above. The way to the chapel is out of the north-west corner of this arcade. The passage on the east side leads into the garden. At a considerable height on the south side of the Fountain Court are some paintings by Laguerre representing the twelve labours of Hercules. The entrance to the *State Apartments* is up the grand staircase, painted by Verrio with allegorical devices intended to be complimentary to William and Mary. Passing through the Guard Chamber, which is ornamented with weapons fancifully arranged on the walls, we arrive at the King's First Presence Chamber, the first of a series of rooms in the south front of the palace looking into the private garden. The pictures hung in the rooms to which we are introducing the reader exceed a thousand, a number far too great to be satisfactorily inspected in a single visit. With the view of aiding the visitor to select those most worthy of notice in so large a collection, where a considerable number are absolutely worthless, we shall give him a few hints in passing along, and must refer him for a full list of them to Mr. Grundy's " Stranger's Guide to Hampton Court, Palace, and Gardens," which may be purchased at the palace for sixpence. Mr. Grundy is the keeper, and his little work contains much information about the objects committed to his care.[*]

First Presence Chamber.
Here are hung the portraits of ladies at the court of William and Mary, painted

---

[*] There were about 200 pictures here before the accession of William IV. Since that time the pictures deposited in Kensington Palace have been brought hither, with many from Windsor and Buckingham Palace, until, as mentioned above, they now amount to more than a thousand. Notwithstanding the complaints that have been made ever since the palace was thrown open to the public as to the utter want of arrangement in the hanging of the pictures, they continue in the same reprehensible disorder. Twenty years ago Mrs. Jameson wrote :—" I do not say that nothing could be worse ; but I do say that even admitting all the difficulty of arranging such a heterogeneous medley of pictures, some of infinite beauty and value, others bad beyond all terms of badness, in rooms not originally adapted for their reception, and where the light is only partially diffused ; admitting all this, and the best intentions on the part of those employed, it is certain that something much better might be done here than has yet been done or apparently thought." Surely it is now time that some better arrangement should now be attempted, looking at the large number of persons who come here in the course of a year (upwards of 200,000), and the wide-spread, rapidly-increasing taste amongst the people for works of art.

by Kneller, known as the Hampton Court Beauties, as well as a portrait of the Queen. William is represented on a white horse, a large tame picture, also by Kneller. Notice No. 30. A portrait by Pordenone. 31. An old woman blowing charcoal, by Holbein. 44. Portrait, by Titian. 45. A portrait, by Giorgione. 46. A man shewing a trick, doubtfully assigned to L. da Vinci. 52, 53, 54. Portraits, by P. Bordone, Tintoretto, and Bassano. 59. The De Bray Family. The carving in wood over the doors and chimney-piece is by G. Gibbons.

Second Presence Chamber.

67. A Sculpture, by L. Bassano. 68. Alessandro dé Medici, by Titian. 69. Italian Knight, by Pordenone. 72. A Sculpture, attributed to Correggio. 79. Artemisia Gentoleschi, by herself. 83, 91. Philip IV. of Spain and his Queen, by Velasquez. 87. Charles I. by Vandyke. 100. Christian IV. of Denmark, by Van Somer. 103. Jacob's Journey, by Bassano. 104, 106. Portraits by Hanneman and Vander Halst.

Audience Chamber.

111. Ignatius Loyola, by Titian. 124. Titian, by himself. 125. Queen of Bohemia, by Honthorst. 137. Death and the Last Judgment (very curious), by Hemskerck. 139. Virgin and Child, by Del Sarto. 141. Spanish Lady, by Del Piombo. 145. Expulsion of Heresy, by Tintoretto.

King's Drawing-Room.

152. Family of Pordenone, by himself. 160. Presentation of Queen Esther, by Tintoretto. 164. The Muses, by Tintoretto. 165. Joseph and Potiphar's Wife, by Gentileschi.

William III.'s Bed-Room

contains Queen Charlotte's state bed; the clock at the head goes twelve months without winding up; the ceiling painted by Verrio. Here are the ladies of Charles II.'s gay court, most of them painted by Lely, and known as the Windsor Beauties; the best of them, No. 170, Lady Byron, was, however, painted by Huysmann. Three of the ladies were ancestresses of three of our Dukes.

King's Dressing-Room.

209. Poultry, by Hondekoeter. The ceiling by Verrio.

King's Writing-Closet.

230. Judith with the head of Holofernes. 239, 240. Still Life, by De Heém 241. Villiers, first Duke of Buckingham, and his family, by Honthorst.

Queen Mary's Closet.

258. Daughter of Herodias, with John the Baptist's head—artist unknown.

The Queen's Gallery,

in the east front, is 172 feet long, and contains several good pictures, but placed in defiance of all chronological or any other order. Some of the portraits are very curious; notice—281. Queen Elizabeth when a Child. 280. The same, when a Young Woman. 299. The same, in a Fancy Dress; and 273. Her last Portrait. 275. Portrait by Durer. 277. Giovanni de Bellini, by himself. 278. A highly interesting portrait of Raphael, by himself. 309. Henry VII.'s Children, by Mabeuse. 310, and 312. King and Queen of Bohemia, by C. Janssen. 313. Henry VIII. when young, by Holbein. 314. The poetical Earl of Surrey, by Holbein. 318. Lord Darnley and his Brother, by De Heere. 322, 326. Holbein, Frobenius, Erasmus

Reskemeer, and Henry VIII., all by Holbein. 329. Will Somers, Henry VIII.'s jester, by Holbein. 330. Francis I. of France, by Holbein. 331. Erasmus, by Holbein. 334. James I., by Van Somer. 336. Holbein's Father and Mother, by Holbein. 345, 346. Portraits of Ladies, by Sir A. More. 346. Laughing Boy, by F. Hals. 381. Sea-piece, by Van der Velde. 391. Infant Christ and St. John, by L. da Vinci. 392. St. Catherine reading, by Correggio. 403. A Sibyl, by Bordone. 410. Lucretia, by Titian. 412. St. Catherine, by Luini. 416. Venetian Gentleman, by Tintoretto. 421. Jewish Rabbi, by Rembrandt. 426. Boar's head, by Snyders. 428. Fruit, and Still Life, by Cuyp. 432. Dutch lady, by Rembrandt. 437. Bo paring Fruit, by Murillo. 438. Venetian Gentleman, by L. Bassano.

The Queen's Bed-Room

contains Queen Anne's state bed, the velvet furniture and hangings of Spitalfields manufacture. Sir James Thornhill, Hogarth's father-in-law, painted the ceiling. 455, 459. James I. and his Queen, by Van Somer. 773. Lady and Gentleman, by Giorgione. 457. Christian, Duke of Brunswick Lunenburg, by Honthorst. 463. Venus and Cupid, drawn by Michael Angelo, painted by Pontormo. 464. Dogs, by Snyders. 466. Virgin and Child, by Giorgione.

The Queen's Drawing-Room

is full of the pictures of West, the favourite painter of George III. His works are little esteemed in these days, but two of his best pictures are here—497. The Death of General Wolfe, considered his *chef d'œuvre* ; and 501. The Departure of Regulus. The view from the middle window of this room is worth notice. The canal, three-quarters of a mile long, and the avenue of lime trees in the Home Park, were formed by William III., and are quite in the Dutch style. Kingston Church is seen down the avenue on the left. The scene reminds us of Pope's couplet,—

" Grove nods at grove, each alley has a brother,
And half the platform just reflects the other."

The Queen's Audience Chamber.

509. The Woman of Samaria, by Palma. 510. Henry VIII., his Queen, Jane Seymour, and his three Children, with Will Somers the jester and his wife, by Holbein. 511. Cupid, by Parmegiano. 514. James I., Whitehall in the background, by Van Somer. The next four are very curious paintings by Holbein. 515. Henry VIII. embarking at Dover. 517. The Battle of Spurs. 520. Meeting of Henry VIII. with Francis I. on the " Field of the Cloth of Gold." 524. Meeting of Henry VIII. and the Emperor Maximilian. 526. The Apostles Peter, James, and John, by Caravaggio.

The Public Dining-Room.

Here are placed the state canopy and bier used for the lying in state of the late Duke of Wellington at Chelsea Hospital. On the walls are some of the prize cartoons exhibited in Westminster Hall in 1845. They were prepared with a view to the decoration of the walls of the new Houses of Parliament.

The Prince of Wales' Presence-Chamber.

543. A Lady's Portrait, by Parmegiano. 554. A Concert, by Giov. Bellini. 560. Ganymede, by Michael Angelo. 577. A Barrack-Room, by C. Troost. 588. Villiers, first Duke of Buckingham, by Janssen. 589. A Foreign Prince, by Mirevelt.

The Prince of Wales' Drawing-Room.

609. Frederick Prince of Wales (son of George II.), with his Wife and Children.

Prince George, afterwards George III., and the Duke of York are inspecting a plan, the others playing; a large picture, by Knapton. 627. Queen Charlotte with the Prince of Wales, afterwards George IV., and the Duke of York when young, by Ramsay.

The Prince of Wales' Bed-Room.

631. Holy Family, by Pordenone. 632. Holy Family, by Giorgione.

We may hurry through the next small rooms (which contain several pictures, but so placed that no opinion can be formed of their merits), and through the *Private Dining-Room*, which contains the state beds of William III. and Mary, and the bed used by George II. when residing here, to the gallery in which are hung the celebrated *Cartoons of Raphael*. The gallery was built by Wren expressly to receive these great works, which are known all over the world by the numerous engravings that have been made from them.* The drawings were made by Raphael in 1513 and 1514 with chalk upon paper (*charta*, whence cartoon), and afterwards coloured in distemper in order that Pope Leo X. might have them copied in tapestry at Arras in Flanders. Two sets were executed, one of which was retained by the Pope, and is still at the Vatican in a dilapidated condition, and the other was presented to Henry VIII., at that time Defender of the Faith. After the death of Charles I., the second set of tapestry was sold to the Spanish ambassador, and went to Spain, where it remained until 1823, when, having been bought by an English gentleman, it was again brought to England. It has since passed through various hands, and is now somewhere in Germany. As to the cartoons before us, seven of the original number (three having been lost or destroyed) were purchased in Flanders on account of Charles I., and added to the royal collection. When that was sold they were bought for £300, by order of Cromwell. George III. removed them to Buckingham House, and afterwards to Windsor. After remaining there about twenty years they were brought back to Hampton Court.

1. The Death of Ananias.
2. Elymas the sorcerer struck with blindness.
3. Peter and John healing the lame man at the Beautiful Gate of the Temple.
4. The Miraculous draught of Fishes.
5. Paul and Barnabus at Lystra.
6. St. Paul preaching at Athens (generally thought the finest of the series).
7. Christ's Charge to Peter.

---

* Photographs of different sizes of these cartoons may now be obtained at the South Kensington Museum for a small sum.

Passing through an ante-room, we arrive at the Portrait Gallery, where are placed the portraits of several worthies of George III.'s reign, as well as some older portraits, amongst which may be noticed—

882. Sir Peter Lely, by himself. 883. A good old portrait of a man with his hand on his breast. 892. Sir Jeffrey Hudson, Queen Henrietta Maria's dwarf, by Mytens. "His adventures would make a romance. He was served up in a pie, shot a man in a duel, was sold as a slave in Barbary, served as a captain of horse in the civil wars, and being imprisoned on account of the Popish plot in 1682, died a prisoner at the age of sixty-three."—*Mrs. Jameson.* 897. Portrait of a gentleman. 902. Portrait of a man with a watch, by Peter van Aelst. 905. A Venetian Gentleman, by Giorgione. 906. Portrait of a man holding a paper. 873-881. The Triumphs of Julius Cæsar, nine water-colour pictures, forming a frieze 81 feet long, painted in distemper on linen by Andrea Mantegna for the Marquis of Mantua in 1476. "Not only his finest work, and in itself a most admirable performance, but interesting as forming an epoch in the history of art, and as being the most important work in the historical style which was produced before the frescoes of Michael Angelo and Raphael."

The Queen's Guard-Chamber.

944. Mrs. Delany, by Opie. This lady's memoirs have only been recently published, although she died in 1788. 947. John Locke the philosopher, by Kneller. 697. Sir Isaac Newton, by Kneller. 959. A wild boar hunt, by Snyders. 964. The Marquis del Gnasto and his page, by Titian. 981. Cleopatra, by Lud. Caracci. 982 Still Life, by Roestraten.

The Ante-Room and Queen's Presence-Chamber

contain some naval pictures, which would be better placed at Greenwich Hospital than here.

Descending the stairs into the quadrangle, we may next proceed to the *Great Hall*, designed by Wolsey, and finished by Henry VIII., when Anne Boleyn was queen. It is in the Gothic style, 106 feet long, 40 wide, and 60 high. The roof is richly carved and decorated with the arms and cognizances of Henry VIII. The oriel window on the south side is eminently beautiful from its proportions and Gothic canopy. It has been filled with stained glass, bearing the king's devices, as well as those of Jane Seymour, and of the several bishoprics held by Wolsey. The other windows of the hall have been filled with modern stained glass, six of which exhibit the armorial pedigrees of the six wives of bluff Hal. Seven other windows contain the heraldic badges of the king. The walls are hung with tapestry, in which are wrought designs by some German or Flemish artist, representing in eight compartments the events connected with the history of Abraham. The tapestry placed near the entrance is of earlier date ; it pictures Justice and Mercy pleading before judges.

The architecture and the decorations of this hall, the mail-clad figures, the arms, the banners, the carvings, the richly-coloured glass, the subdued light, combine to produce a very imposing effect, and admirably realise the grand hall of a royal palace. In the time of Elizabeth and James I. it is said that some of Shakspere's plays were acted here. George I. caused it to be fitted up as a theatre, and Shakspere's drama of Henry VIII. or the Fall of Wolsey, was represented. From the upper end of the hall we pass into the *Withdrawing Room*, which looks extremely bald after the splendours we have been dwelling upon. The tapestry is much faded, and hardly interesting to any but the antiquary. In a recess is placed a recumbent marble sculpture of Venus ; and on the table is a model of an Indian prince's palace designed by an officer of engineers. Over the fire-place is empanelled a likeness of Wolsey, whose portrait, motto, etc., appear in the stained glass of the oriel window.

We now hasten to the *Gardens*, which were laid out by Loudon and Wise, gardeners to William III. A broad walk passes Wren's east front, leading in one direction to the " Flower-pot Gates " in the Kingston Road (which are not opened, as they might properly be, for the entrance of the public), and in the other to the banks of the Thames. Green sward, with beds of flowers and groups of noble trees, extend alongside the walk, and notwithstanding the dead level of the ground, compose a charming scene. The *Private Garden* is entered by a door on the south side of the palace. Here there is an arcade of clipped limes in the olden style ; a conservatory with some large orange trees, and a vinery in which may be seen what is considered the largest vine in Europe. It is more than 110 feet long, and the stem three feet from the ground has a circumference of 30 inches. It is of the black Hamburgh kind, and is very productive, in some years the yield being 2500 bunches. Returning to the broad walk, and passing the palace front and the tennis court, we arrive at a door leading into the Wilderness, planted by William III. with the intention of concealing the irregular aspect of the north side of the palace. Here are shady winding walks, and here is the *Maze*, a green labyrinth which affords much amusement to the young in attempting to discover the right path to the central compartment. This is not far from the Lion Gates in the Kingston Road. If we quit the gardens of the palace by these gates we shall be near the entrance to *Bushey Park*, a flat expanse of ground through which there is a public drive, a mile long, to the Teddington Road. The avenue of horse chestnut trees is striking at any time, but particularly so in June when they are in flower. At the Hampton Court end there is a circular basin of water, and the straight lines of the avenue are here bent into curves concentric with this basin. There are one or two houses in this park retired from the road, one of which was the residence of the late Queen Adelaide.

WINDSOR CASTLE,

The only residence of the English sovereigns worthy of the nation, is situate about 22 miles from London, in the county of Berks, and may be reached either by the Great Western Railway (Paddington Station), diverging from the main line at Slough, or by the Windsor Railway from the Waterloo Station. The Windsor terminus of the former is in George Street, five minutes' walk from the Castle ; the terminus of the latter is in Thames Street, ten minutes' walk from that edifice.

The State Apartments are open gratuitously to the public on Mondays, Tuesdays, Thursdays, and Fridays, on production of the Lord Chamberlain's tickets, which may be obtained in London of P. and D. Colnaghi, 14 Pall Mall East, or Mr. Mitchell, bookseller, 33 Old Bond Street. At either place may be obtained (price one penny) a " Companion through the State Apartments." The tickets are only available for one week from the day they are issued. They are not transferable, and no payment can be demanded for them. From the 1st of April to the end of October the hours of admission are from 11 to 4 ; during the rest of the year, from 11 to 3.

The stately castle crowns the apex of a hill, and is a conspicuous object from a considerable distance. The name of the place is thought to be a corruption of the Saxon appellation *Windleshora*, which signified a winding shore. William the Conqueror, struck with the situation, erected here some buildings which are referred to in Domesday-book. Henry I. and Henry III. both made extensive additions. Edward III. was born here, and after he succeeded to the crown, he built largely, William of Wykeham being his surveyor, and founded the College or Free

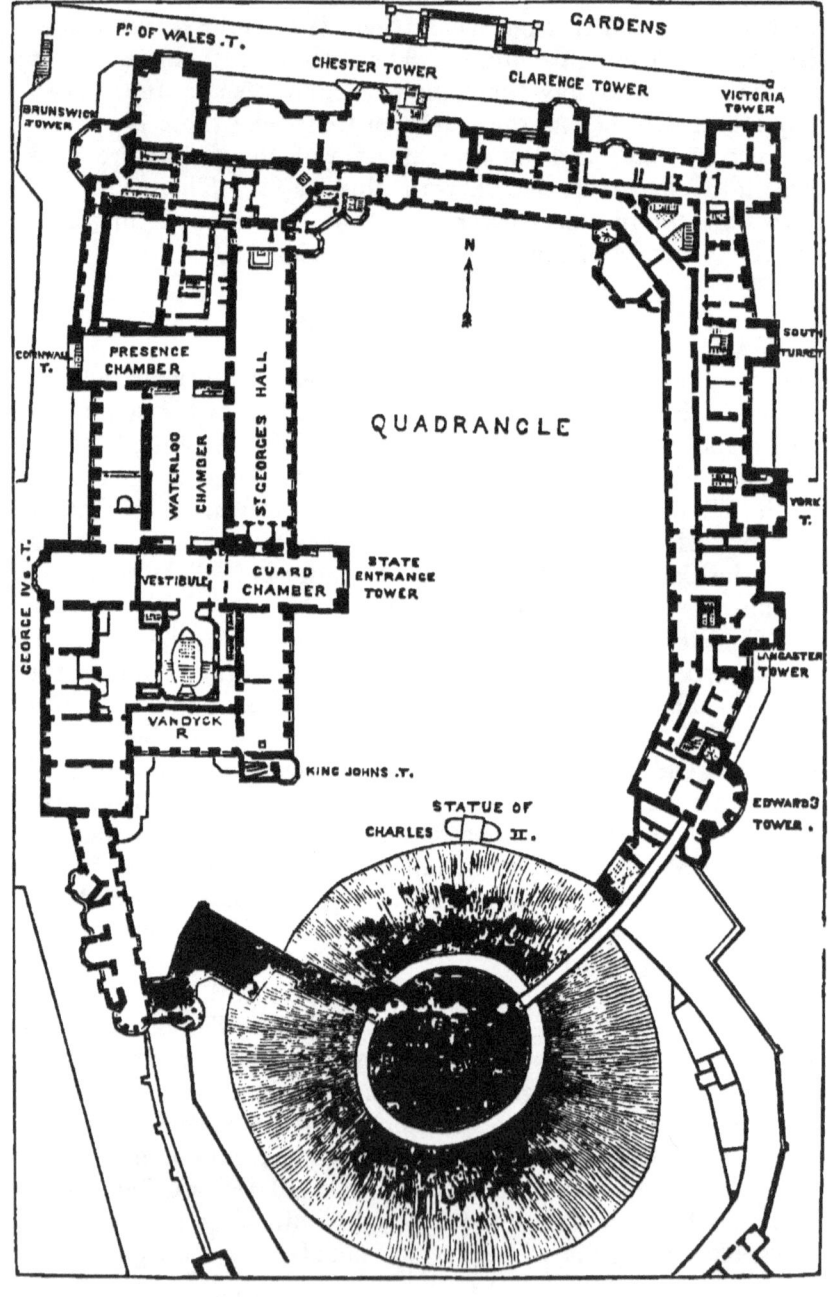

Chapel of St. George.   Here he instituted the order of the garter in 1349.   Geoffrey Chaucer, the greatest of our early poets, was appointed clerk of the works to the chapel in the reign of the second Richard, at a salary of two shillings a day.   The existing collegiate chapel, one of the finest examples of the perpendicular style we possess, was built by Edward IV; the architect being Richard Beauchamp, Bishop of Salisbury, who, on his death, was succeeded by Sir Reginald Bray, the architect of Henry VII.'s Chapel.   That monarch added something to the castle, and part of his structure may be seen near the entrance to the state apartments.   This is still called after him, and the principal room is now used as a library.   Adjoining this is a part added by Queen Elizabeth, who also formed the terraces, one of the most attractive features of the castle.   Cromwell was an occasional resident here, and so was Charles II., under whom Sir C. Wren made many alterations.   What was subsequently done, until George IV.'s time, was in a mean taste, except that his father restored the chapel.   George IV., being desirous of removing the unsightly buildings that formed the palace, prevailed on Parliament in 1824, to grant him £300,000 on account of the works, and Jeffrey Wyatt was the architect employed to construct a new edifice.   The first stone of what is known as George IV.'s Gateway was laid by the king himself, and the architect received the royal permission to change his name to Wyattville.   The king took posession of the private apartments in 1828, but the works continued to be prosecuted after his death, until a total sum of £771,000 had been expended upon them.   New stables, including a riding-house 200 feet long, have been erected during the present reign, on which £70,000 have been laid out.   They are in the immediate neighbourhood of the castle on its south side, but concealed from view by an artificial mound.   To view them, apply for a ticket to the clerk of the stables, and go there between one and half-past two o'clock.

Although by no means beyond the reach of criticism, the general effect of the castle is certainly striking and noble, marked by bold features and well defined masses, over which the round tower grandly presides.   The private Royal Apartments which cannot be seen except during the absence of the Court, and then only by very special permission, are on the east side near the Victoria Tower.   The State Apartments, to which visitors are admitted as before mentioned, are at the west end of the north side; whilst the apartments appropriated to visitors are on the south side. Along this side, next the quadrangle, there is a corridor 15 feet high and as many wide, which is continued on the north side up to the visitors' staircase, near Chester Tower, the whole being 450 feet long. It is richly stored with pictures and other works of art.

The grand entrance to the castle is at George IV.'s Gateway, in the south front, which is opposite the Long Walk, a fine vista of elms three miles in length. The entrance for visitors, however, is through Henry VIII.'s Gateway, and through the lower ward.

THE ROUND TOWER is an enlargement of the ancient Keep, and was used as a prison until 1660. It is not perfectly circular in plan, having a diameter of 102 feet in one direction, and of 93 in another. It has a height of 123 feet above the quadrangle, and the Watch Tower is 25 feet more. It is well worthy of being ascended, by those who have strength to surmount so many steps, as the views are most beautiful. Twelve counties are within the range of vision. In the quadrangle at the base of the tower is a bronze statue of Charles II. Notice the pedestal by Grinling Gibbons.

King John's Tower is on the north side of the Round Tower, and it is under a small Gothic porch adjoining the former, that entrance to the

STATE APARTMENTS

is gained. They consist of ten rooms, and visitors are conducted through them in the order in which they are here mentioned. The pictures best deserving attention are those indicated. In ascending the stairs, notice Lawrence's portrait of Sir Jeffrey Wyattville.

The Queen's Audience Chamber.

The ceiling was painted by Verrio; on the walls are three pieces of Gobelin tapestry, representing the history of Esther. Here are portraits of—4. Mary Queen of Scots, by an unknown artist; 5. Frederick Henry, Prince of Orange; and 6. William II., Prince of Orange, by G. Honthorst, the frames carved by Grinling Gibbons.

The Old Ball Room,

or the *Vandyck Room*, all the pictures being by that artist. Here are portraits of 1. Henry, Count de Berg; 2. Charles I., his Queen, and their two children, Prince Charles and the Princess Mary; 3. the Duchess of Richmond in white satin; 5, 9, 13, 18. Queen Henrietta Maria, several portraits; 6. Venetia, Lady Digby;

7. the second Duke of Buckingham and his brother; 10. Madame de Cantecroy; 11. Children of Charles I.; 12. Three heads of Charles I., painted for the use of Bernini the sculptor, who executed a bust from them; * 14. Lucy, Countess of Carlisle; 15. Sir Kenelm Digby; 17. Vandyck; 19. The three eldest children of Charles I.; 21. Equestrian portrait of Charles I. with his equery.

The Queen's State Drawing Room.

Here are nine indifferent landscapes by Zuccarelli; portraits of the three first Georges, and of Frederick Prince of Wales, father of George III. Passing through the State Ante-Room to the grand staircase, where on the first landing is placed a colossal statue of King George IV., by Chantrey, and proceeding across the grand vestibule, visitors arrive at

The Waterloo Chamber,

a noble room lighted from above, and containing portraits, chiefly by Sir Thomas Lawrence, of the sovereigns and distinguished persons connected with the great events of 1813-15. The two best pictures are the portraits of Pope Pius VII. and Cardinal Gonsalvi; and the worst, that of the Duke of Wellington.

The Presence Chamber,

fitted up in the style of Louis XIV., contains a Malachite vase presented to the Queen by Nicholas, Emperor of Russia; and two granite vases, presented to William IV. by Frederick William III., King of Prussia. Gobelin tapestry, representing the story of Jason and Medea, hangs on the walls.

St. George's Hall,

200 feet long, 34 feet broad, and 32 feet high, contains full length portraits of the English sovereigns, from James I. to George IV., in their robes of state. The ceiling is emblazoned with the arms of the knights of the garter, and at the east end is the throne.

The Guard Chamber

contains some suits of armour, and arms ornamentally arranged. At the south end of the room is a portion of the fore-mast of the Victory, Lord Nelson's flagship at Trafalgar. It has been perforated by a cannon ball, and bears a colossal bust of Nelson, the work of Chantrey. At each side is a brass field-piece taken in the Sikh war in the Punjaub; and close by are two small pieces of brass ordnance, formerly belonging to Tippoo Sahib, and taken at the capture of Seringapatam. Over busts of the first Duke of Marlborough, and the first Duke of Wellington, are hung the last of the banners which the holders of the estates of Blenheim and Strathfieldsaye have annually to present to the sovereign. Over the fireplace is a silver shield, inlaid with gold, presented by Francis I. to Henry VIII., at their interview on the Field of the Cloth of Gold. It is said to have been executed by Benvenuto Cellini from Andrea Mantegna's designs. A chair made of oak taken from the roof of Alloway Kirk, the scene of the spectral dance witnessed by Tam o' Shanter; and a chair made from an elm tree that was standing on the field of Waterloo at the time of the battle, are placed in this room.

---

* " Charles, to late times to be transmitted fair,
  Assigned his figure to Bernini's care;
  And great Nassau to Kneller's hand decreed,
  To fix him graceful on the bounding steed."—POPE.

This bounding steed with Great Nassau upon it, is at Hampton Court, and a wooden affair it is.

The Queen's Presence Chamber,

ceiling painted by Verrio, the walls hung with Gobelin tapestry, representing further portions of Esther's story. Here are three portraits of ladies; one, Charles I.'s youngest child; the other two, princesses of the House of Brunswick. The frames were carved by Gibbons.

The public are now excluded from the rooms called the Queen's Closet, the King's Closet, the King's Council Chamber, and the King's Drawing Room, which contain many excellent paintings.

The *Gardens* at Windsor are scarcely worthy of the palace to which they are attached, but the terraces command beautiful prospects and should be visited. The northern terrace is always open to the public, but access to the eastern terrace can only be obtained after two o'clock on Saturdays and Sundays. At Frogmore, near the residence of the late Duchess of Kent, a mile distant from the castle, are the royal kitchen gardens, which are very well managed, and kept in the highest state of cultivation.

St. George's Chapel may be viewed during the summer months in the interval between the services, which commence at half-past ten in the morning, and at half-past four in the afternoon. One of the sextons is in attendance to take visitors round. This chapel was begun about 1461, but not finished until after the commencement of the sixteenth century. The exquisite beauty of the architecture of the interior, especially the richly-decorated roof, will charm every beholder. West designed the great east window, and a painting of his—the Last Supper—hangs over the altar. The ceremony of installing the Knights of the Garter takes place here, and the banners and escutcheons of existing members of the order will be seen over their carved stalls. Edward IV., who began the present chapel, lies buried beneath the iron tomb executed by Quintin Matsys. The remains of Henry VI. lie under a plain marble in the opposite aisle. Henry VIII. and Charles I. were buried under the choir. Notice the cenotaph of the Princess Charlotte. From the foot of the altar a subterranean passage leads to the tomb-house in which George III., George IV., and William IV., with several other members of the royal family, are interred.

The *Home Park*, containing about 500 acres, lies adjacent to the castle on the east and north sides. It is only connected with Windsor *Great Park* by the Long Walk, a strip of ground planted at each side with a double row of elms. The avenue is continued across the great park to a hill called Snow Hill, which is crowned with a colossal bronze equestrian statue of George III. by Westmacott. The entire avenue is three miles in length. On another hill stands a Gothic building called the Belvidere. Within its area of 1800 acres there is much enchanting scenery in the Great Park, the Windsor Forest, celebrated by Pope and other poets. The walks and drives are numerous. At the south end is a sheet of water called Virginia Water (the largest piece of artificial water in the kingdom), on the banks of which George IV. erected a fishing temple. At the head of the lake is a cascade about 20 feet high, where the water falls into a miniature ravine ; and close by is an obelisk erected by George II., in commemoration of the services of his son William, Duke of Cumberland, the merciless hero of Culloden.

ETON COLLEGE stands on the north bank of the Thames, in the county of Bucks, and in the immediate neighbourhood of Windsor. It was founded by Henry VI. in 1440. It is presided over by a provost, and its revenues are about £7000 a year. The college buildings are chiefly of brick, and consist of two quadrangles. In one are the school and chapel, with lodging for the foundation scholars ; in the other are the provost's house, the apartments of the fellows, and the library. The chapel, 175 feet long, is of stone, and has a handsome exterior. There is a bronze statue of Henry VI. in one of the quadrangles, and another statue of him by Bacon in the chapel. At this famous school, about 600 boys, termed oppidans, are educated in addition to the 70 scholars of the foundation who ought to receive their education gratis. This is a very expensive place, and the education the boys receive has been much complained of. Formal enquiry, so much deprecated in old establishments, has been instituted, and will doubtless lead to the improvement so much desired.

For further descriptions of places in the Neighbourhood of London, see one or other of the Guides to

SURREY	5s.
KENT	3s. 6d.
SUSSEX	2s. 6d.

INDEX.

MEMORANDA

Published by A & C. Black, Edinburgh.

MEMORANDA

MEMORANDA

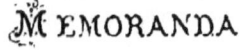

MEMORANDA

MEMORANDA

MEMORANDA

MEMORANDA

MEMORANDA

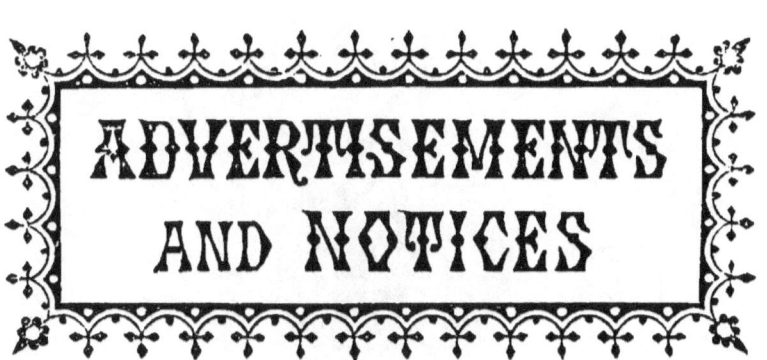

ADVERTISEMENTS AND NOTICES

The Scottish Widows' Fund Life Assurance Society

FUNDS.
£3,720,808.

REVENUE
£438,740.

IS NOW

THE LARGEST MUTUAL LIFE OFFICE IN THE WORLD.

EDINBURGH.
9 *St. Andrew Sq. (Head Office).*

LONDON.
4 *Royal Exchange Buildings.*

The Whole Profits belong to the Members, and are divided among them alone, there being no Shareholders, as in Proprietary Companies, entitled to Dividends, or to participate in the Profits in any other manner.

The Success of the Society.

THERE is no instance in the history of Life Assurance in which progress has been more rapid or success more solid. Established in 1815 without the adventitious aid of Shareholders' capital, when Life Assurance was all but unknown in Scotland, the operations of the Society have attained a magnitude and wide-spread usefulness which the original founders could scarcely have anticipated. The remarkable success which has attended the Society ever since it was founded is exhibited in the following

Table of Statistics of the Progress of the Society.

DATES.	Sums Assured and Vested Bonuses declared.			Sums Assured and Vested Bonuses existing.			Annual Revenue from Premiums and Interest.			Accumulated Fund in possession.		
	£.	s.	d.	£	s.	d.	£	s.	d.	£	s.	d.
1815	1,000	0	0	1,000	0	0	34	12	6	34	12	6
1824	456,259	15	8	373,656	1	8	17,454	0	3	76,509	7	3
1831	1,596,416	7	6	1,332,434	10	6	54,653	7	5	260,046	8	0
1838	4,348,302	0	7	3,557,134	1	10	141,241	14	2	785,272	11	6
1845	8,649,479	11	3	6,798,622	6	3	248,929	0	0	1,701,633	1	6
1852	13,017,619	18	4	9,084,660	17	1	338,362	8	6	2,581,109	5	7
1859	17,273,595	16	2	10,943,853	8	5	412,767	9	2	3,518,230	6	9
1861	18,036,528	17	2	10,894,098	2	0	438,740	13	4	3,720,808	9	5

Moderate Rates of Premium.

The Premiums charged by this Society are generally lower than those charged by the leading Offices of England, Scotland, and Ireland, thus :—

	PREMIUMS CHARGED.				
Average of the Premiums charged by 16 of the oldest established and largest offices in the Three Kingdoms . . .	Age 25.	Age 30.	Age 40.	Age 50.	Age 60.
	£ s. d.	£ s. d.	£ s. d.	£ s. d.	£ s. d.
	2 6 7	2 12 1	3 7 5	4 11 4	6 12 3
Scottish Widows' Fund	2 6 6	2 11 9	3 6 3	4 9 2	6 6 4

The Last Bonus

was ONE OF THE LARGEST ever declared by any INSURANCE COMPANY.

The Sums Assured then added to Policies amounted to

ONE MILLION POUNDS STERLING,

which, according to the duration of the Policies, yielded BONUSES from £1 : 12 : 6 to £3 : 6s. per cent per annum on the original sum assured.

The unusually large Bonuses declared by this Society will be seen from the following

TABLE

SHEWING THE ACCUMULATED AMOUNTS OF POLICIES OF £1000, AND THE TOTAL PER CENTAGES OF BONUS THEREON.

Date of Policy	AMOUNT PAYABLE					Per Centage of Bonus.
	If death occur after payment of the Premium in the following Years					
	1862.	1863.	1864.	1865.	1866.	
	£ s. d.	£ s. d.	£ s. d.	£ s. d.	£ s. d.	
1815	2372 6 11	2409 2 1	2445 17 3	2482 12 5	2519 7 7	152 p. c.
1820	2010 13 1	2041 16 2	2072 19 3	2104 2 4	2135 5 5	114 p. c.
1825	1882 17 3	1912 0 9	1941 4 3	1970 7 9	1999 11 3	100 p. c.
1830	1755 1 2	1782 5 1	1809 9 0	1836 12 11	1863 16 10	86 p. c.
1835	1614 5 2	1639 5 5	1664 5 8	1689 5 11	1714 6 2	71 p. c.
1840	1468 8 2	1491 3 2	1513 18 2	1536 13 2	1559 8 2	56 p. c.
1845	1337 7 1	1358 1 6	1378 15 11	1399 10 4	1420 4 9	42 p. c.
1850	1229 7 4	1248 8 4	1267 9 4	1286 10 4	1305 11 4	31 p. c.
1855	1133 19 3	1151 10 8	1169 2 1	1186 13 6	1204 4 11	20 p. c.

These Bonuses, WHICH IT IS BELIEVED ARE NOT EXCEEDED BY THOSE OF ANY OTHER OFFICE, *have all been declared out of Profits actually realized, and every element of Profit ever possessed by the Society, with vastly increased resources, remains for the increase of present and new members' Policies.*

Days of Grace.

THIRTY DAYS of Grace are allowed for payment of Premiums, but Policies may be revived within THIRTEEN MONTHS of the Premium becoming due.

Lapsed Policies.

When the days of Grace have expired, and the Member does not wish to renew the Policy, a sum equal to the Surrender Value thereof, on the last day of Grace, will be paid to him (see Explanation as to Surrender Values, below), *or a paid-up Policy, free of future Annual Premiums, for a corresponding sum will be issued, as he may select.*

Surrender Values payable on Demand.

Many Offices decline giving any Surrender Value unless the Policy shall have been of a certain number of years' standing, although the premiums paid greatly exceed the risk borne by the Office and the proper expenses of the Assurance. *The practice of the Scottish Widows' Fund is, and always has been, to pay at any time from the day of the issue of a Policy its actual Office value, and even* WHEN THE POLICY LAPSES BY NON-PAYMENT OF THE PREMIUMS *during the thirteen months within which they may be received, an allowance equal to the Full Surrender Value is paid.*

EXAMPLES OF SURRENDER VALUES OF £1000,
Age at entry being 30.

Duration of Policy.	Premiums paid.	Surrender Value.	Per Centage of Surrender Value on Premiums paid.
One Year	£25 17 6	£8 0 10	31 per cent.
Ten Years	258 15 0	160 12 10	62 per cent.
Twenty Years	517 10 0	390 15 11	75 per cent.
Thirty Years	776 5 0	699 10 4	90 per cent.
Forty Years	1035 0 0	1071 19 0	104 per cent.
Forty-five Years	1164 7 6	1435 6 0	123 per cent.

The Tables of Surrender Values of Policies and Bonuses are published in the Prospectus, so that a person, before he makes his proposal to the Scottish Widows' Fund, can see the progressively increasing value of his Assurance (*except future Bonuses, which of course will still further increase the value*) from the beginning to the end of the transaction.

Loans Granted on Security of Policies.

The Policies of this Society, besides bearing a fixed Cash Value from the first, payable on demand, are also available as First-Class Securities, on which advances can be obtained from the Society at any time. Advances of £50 and upwards, to any amount the value of a Policy will admit of, are granted free of expense and without any other Security. The present rate of interest is 4 per cent.

Indisputable Certificates,

constituting Policies unchallengeable Documents upon any ground whatever, are granted, upon application, to Members of five years' standing.
The Laws empower the Directors to refuse or modify the terms of such
Certificates, when the issue of the Certificate would, in their opinion, be
inconsistent with the general interest.

Foreign Residence without extra Premiums.

Foreign Residence is allowed from the issue of a policy in any part
of Europe, in parts of North America, Australia, New Zealand, and
other Colonies, *free of charge;* and the Indisputable Certificate granted
after the first five years, as explained, *cancels all restrictions in the Policy,
and no License or Extra Premium is thereafter required for T* *el or
Residence in any part of the world.*

Payment of Claims.

Claims are paid in full in any part of the United Kingdom, free of
charge, on the simple receipt of the parties entitled.

Value of the Society's Policies.

The moderate rates of Premium charged; the almost unprecedented
largeness of the Bonuses ; the fact that the Policy is practically as con-
vertible as a bank note for its value to the member himself at any time ;
and the absolute security afforded by the unquestionable financial position of the Society for the fulfilment of all its engagements, render Policies of the Scottish Widows' Fund, whether held for family or Business
purposes, instruments of the highest value.

All necessary Information sent Free.

The Prospectus contains Tables, showing—the Premiums charged
for Assurances—the Bonuses declared at each period of Division — The
Surrender Values of Policies—The Cash Values of Bonuses and corresponding Reductions on future Premiums — and the progressive increase
in the Business, Funds, and Revenue, since the Society was founded ;
also detailed explanations and practical examples from all these Tables,
with full explanations of the advantages enjoyed by Policy-holders of
this Society.

HEAD OFFICE,   SAMUEL RALEIGH, *Manager.*
9 St. Andrew Square, Edinburgh.   J. J. P. ANDERSON, *Secretary.*

LONDON : 4 ROYAL EXCHANGE BUILDINGS, E.C.
Hugh M'Kean, Agent.

THE NORTHERN ASSURANCE COMPANY.

ESTABLISHED 1836,

AND INCORPORATED BY SPECIAL ACT OF PARLIAMENT

FOR

FIRE AND LIFE ASSURANCE AT HOME AND ABROAD.

HEAD OFFICE, 3 KING STREET, ABERDEEN.

LONDON,	EDINBURGH,
1 Moorgate Street.	20 St. Andrew Square.
GLASGOW,	DUNDEE,
19 St. Vincent Place.	16 St. Andrew's Place.

LIFE DEPARTMENT.

(REDUCED RATES FOR THE EAST AND WEST INDIES.)

The Directors of this Company beg to announce that they have adopted a new Scale of Rates for the East and West Indies, considerably lower than those charged by this or, they believe, any other Company, but differing from the old system in respect that no reduction takes place on the insured returning to Europe or proceeding to any other part of the world not chargeable with an extra premium.

According to this method, the Assured, instead of being subjected to a heavy Extra Premium during the years of his residence in the Tropics, has the option, by paying a fixed rate, of throwing the Extra over the whole currency of his Assurance.

Detailed Prospectuses and all other information may be obtained at the Head Offices, or numerous Agencies throughout the Kingdom.

WM. CHALMERS, *Manager.*

H. AMBROSE SMITH, *Secretary.*

Office in Edinburgh, 20 St. Andrew Square.

ROBERT CHRISTIE JUN., SECRETARY.

PHŒNIX FIRE ASSURANCE COMPANY,

LOMBARD STREET, AND CHARING CROSS,

LONDON.

ESTABLISHED IN 1782.

INSURANCES against Loss by Fire are effected by the PHŒNIX COMPANY upon every description of Property, in every part of the World, on the most favourable Terms.

The liberality and promptitude of the Phœnix Fire Office in the settlement of claims are well known, and the importance of its relations with the public may be estimated by the fact, that since its establishment it has paid more than eight millions sterling in discharge of claims for losses by Fire.

ALLEN'S PATENT PORTMANTEAUS, AND TRAVELLING BAGS, WITH SQUARE OPENINGS.

Allen's Patent Bag.

Ladies' Wardrobe-Trunks, Dressing-Bags, with Silver fittings.

Despatch-Boxes, Writing, and Dressing-Cases, and 500 other articles for Home or Continental travelling. Illustrated Catalogues by post for two stamps.

J. W. ALLEN, Manufacturer and Patentee, 22 & 31 West Strand, London, W.C.

ANGUS'S TEMPERANCE AND FAMILY HOTELS, 23 New Bridge Street, Blackfriars, London; and at 127 Argyll Street, Glasgow.

VISITORS to London will find that this Hotel is unequalled for situation, the Bed-room accommodation first class, and the Charges Moderate. Private Parlours, Commercial, Coffee, and Smoking Rooms.

N.B.—New Bridge Street is within three minutes' Walk of St. Paul's and the Post Office. Omnibuses to King's Cross every ten minutes.

THE LONDON SEASON.

To all who court the gay and festive scenes the following are indispensable:

ROWLANDS' MACASSAR OIL is a delightfully fragrant and transparent Preparation for the HAIR, and as an invigorator and BEAUTIFIER beyond all precedent.

ROWLANDS' KALYDOR, FOR THE SKIN AND COMPLEXION, is unequalled for the radiant bloom it imparts to the cheek; the softness and delicacy, which it induces to the hands and arms; and for removing cutaneous defects.

ROWLANDS' ODONTO, OR PEARL DENTRIFICE, for Preserving and imparting a Pearl-like whiteness to the Teeth, strengthening the Gums, and for giving a pleasing fragrance to the Breath.

Sold at 20 Hatton Garden, London, and by Chemists and Perfumers.

¸ **ASK FOR "ROWLANDS'" ARTICLES.**

GLASGOW AND THE HIGHLANDS.

Royal Route via Crinan and Caledonian Canals.

The Royal Mail Steamers Iona, Mountaineer, Pioneer, Fairy, Edinburgh Castle, Clydesdale, Clansman, Cygnet, Plover, Dolphin, Mary Jane, and Inverary Castle, sail for the Undernoted Places—Oban, Fort William, Inverness, Tobermory, Portree, Stornoway, Staffa, Glencoe, &c. For full particulars, see Bradshaw's Guide. Sailing Bills, with Maps, and every information, will be sent by post on application to the Proprietors.

DAVID HUTCHESON & Co.,
119 Hope Street.

Glasgow, May 1862.

DORSET, DEVON, AND CORNWALL.

In neat volumes, with Illustrations, Maps, &c.

BLACK'S GUIDES TO DORSET, DEVON, AND CORNWALL.

With New Maps, Plans of Plymouth and Torquay, and Charts of the River Tamar and Dartmoor.

The work may be had, either in one Volume, price 5s., or in Divisions, as follows :—

Dorset	.	1s. 6d.
Devon	.	2s. 6d.
Cornwall	.	2s.

EDINBURGH : ADAM AND CHARLES BLACK.

In One Portable Volume, price 10s. 6d.

BLACK'S PICTURESQUE TOURIST
AND ROAD AND RAILWAY GUIDE THROUGH

England and Wales.

THIRD EDITION, GREATLY ENLARGED AND IMPROVED.

With a General Travelling Map; Charts of Roads, Railroads, and Interesting Localities; Engraved Views of Picturesque Scenery; and a comprehensive General Index, embracing a List of Hotels and Inns.

~~~~~~~~~

EDINBURGH: ADAM AND CHARLES BLACK.

Just published, THE FIFTEENTH EDITION, price 8s. 6d., of

Black's
Picturesque Tourist of Scotland

IN A NEAT PORTABLE VOLUME.

Illustrated by a large and correct Map of Scotland, and upwards of One Hundred other Illustrations, consisting of Maps, Charts, Plans of Towns, and Views of Scenery.

ADAPTED to the requirements of the present day, and containing full information regarding routes, also all the best Hotels, etc.

A few copies have been printed on thin paper for the use of pedestrians.

~~~~~~~~~

EDINBURGH: ADAM AND CHARLES BLACK.

In a Portable Volume, price 5s.,

BLACK'S PICTURESQUE GUIDE TO THE ENGLISH LAKES

INCLUDING

AN ESSAY ON THE GEOLOGY OF THE DISTRICT.

By JOHN PHILLIPS, M.A., F.R.S., F.G.S., Reader in Geology in
the University of Oxford.

ELEVENTH EDITION.

With a Correct Travelling Map ; Twenty-three Views of the Scenery
by T. M. Richardson, jun., Montague Stanley, and Birket Foster ;
Twelve Explanatory OUTLINE VIEWS OF MOUNTAIN GROUPS
by MR. FLINTOFT OF KESWICK ; Six Charts of the more interesting Localities, Itineraries,

AND ALL THE HOTELS.

" Charmingly written ; its intelligence is ample and minute, and its illustrations
are admirable specimens of art. —*Atlas.*

EDINBURGH : ADAM AND CHARLES BLACK.

BLACK'S GUIDES

TO THE PICTURESQUE COUNTIES AND DISTRICTS OF ENGLAND AND WALES.

In Neat Portable Volumes with Maps and Illustrations.

SOUTH OF ENGLAND.		MIDLAND AND NORTHERN COUNTIES, ETC.	
Kent	3s. 6d.	Derbyshire	2s.
Surrey	5s.	Warwickshire	2s.
Sussex	2s. 6d.	Yorkshire	2s.
Hampshire	2s. 6d.	Wales	5s.
Isle of Wight	1s. 6d.	North Wales	3s. 6d.
Dorset	1s. 6d.	Gloucester, Hereford, and	
Devon	2s. 6d.	Monmouth	2s.
Cornwall	2s.	Lake District	5s.

In a neat Pocket Volume, price Five Shillings,

Black's
Picturesque Tourist of Ireland.

A Third and Greatly Improved Edition.

WITH A GENERAL TRAVELLING MAP,

A LARGE CHART OF THE LAKES OF KILLARNEY AND

SURROUNDING COUNTRY, AND PLANS OF THE PRINCIPAL CITIES;

AND CONTAINING ALL THE BEST HOTELS, WITH

THEIR RESPECTIVE CHARGES.

ALSO

Black's Guide to Belfast, 1s. 6d.
Black's Guide to Dublin, 1s. 6d.
Black's Guide to Killarney, 1s. 6d.

Agent for Ireland, W. ROBERTSON.

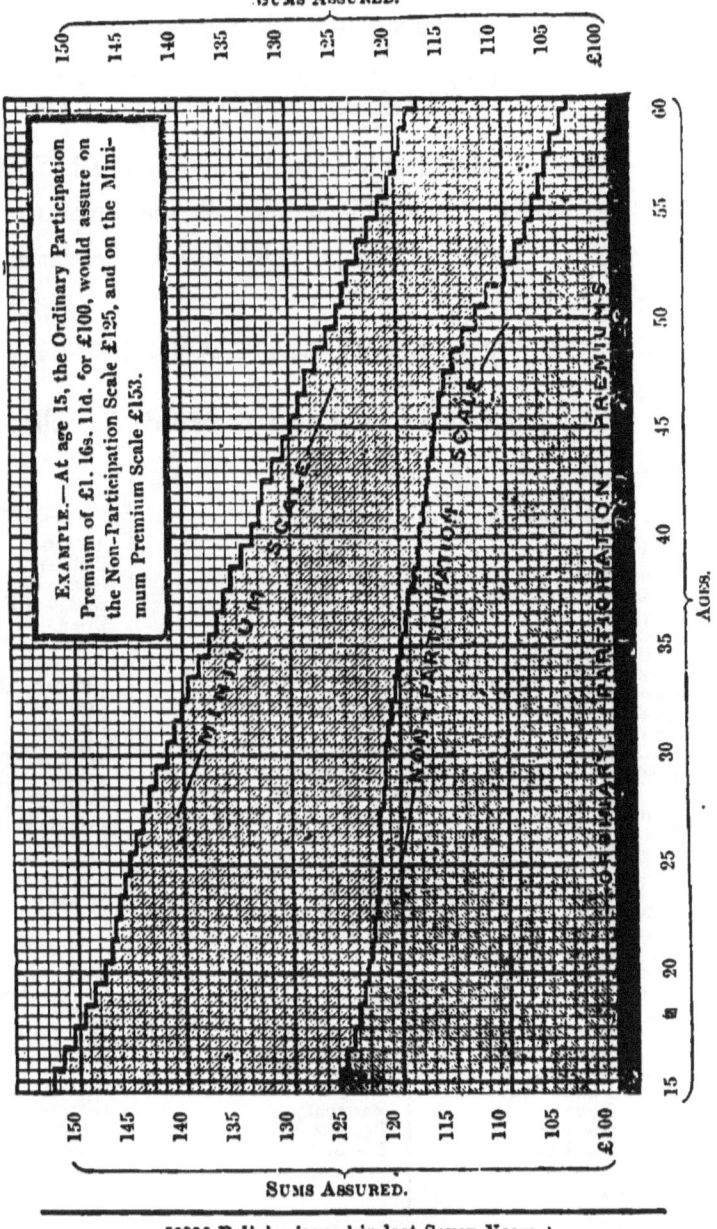

[See Society's special pamphlet as to Minimum Premiums.]

MINIMUM PREMIUMS.

SCOTTISH AMICABLE LIFE ASSURANCE SOCIETY.   ESTABLISHED 1826.

GLASGOW: 29 St. Vincent Place.   LONDON: 1 Threadneedle Street.

Diagram showing the Increased Assurance *at once* obtained under this Society's Minimum Premium System, by application to it of its Ordinary Participation Premium for £100.

SUMS ASSURED.

150 145 140 135 130 125 120 115 110 105 £100

EXAMPLE.—At age 15, the Ordinary Participation Premium of £1. 16s. 11d. for £100, would assure on the Non-Participation Scale £125, and on the Minimum Premium Scale £153.

MINIMUM SCALE

NON-PARTICIPATION SCALE

SCOTTISH AMICABLE LIFE ASSURANCE PREMIUMS.

AGES.

60 55 50 45 40 35 30 25 20 15

SUMS ASSURED.

150 145 140 135 130 125 120 115 110 105 £100

[6230 Policies issued in last Seven Years.]

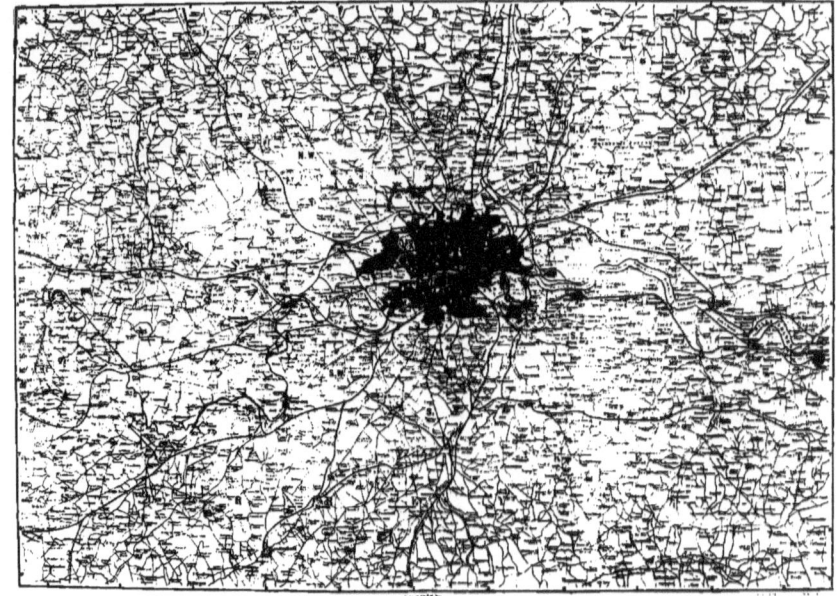